PRAISE FOR K. BROMBERG

"K. Bromberg always delivers intelligently written, emotionally intense, sensual romance . . ."

—USA Today

"K. Bromberg makes you believe in the power of true love."

—#1 New York Times bestselling author Audrey Carlan

"A poignant and hauntingly beautiful story of survival, second chances, and the healing power of love. An absolute must-read."

—New York Times bestselling author Helena Hunting

"A home run! *The Player* is riveting, sexy, and pulsing with energy. And I can't wait for *The Catch*!"

—#1 New York Times bestselling author Lauren Blakely

"An irresistibly hot romance that stays with you long after you finish the book."

—#1 New York Times bestselling author Jennifer L. Armentrout

"Bromberg is a master at turning up the heat!"

—New York Times bestselling author Katy Evans

"Supercharged heat and full of heart. Bromberg aces it from the first page to the last."

—New York Times bestselling author Kylie Scott

"Captivating, emotional, and sizzling hot!"

—New York Times bestselling author S. C. Stephens

REVEAL

REVEAL

WICKED WAYS, BOOK TWO

K. BROMBERG

Montlake
Romance

Published by Montlake Romance, Seattle
www.apub.com

Amazon, the Amazon logo, and Montlake Romance are trademarks of Amazon.com, Inc., or its affiliates.

ISBN-13: 9781542002844
ISBN-10: 1542002842

Cover design by Letitia Hasser

Cover photography by Wander Aguiar Photography

Printed in the United States of America

To Kandace:
Thank you for teaching us to look for rainbows in the storm and for stars in the darkness. You are loved and missed by so many.

You have to keep breaking your heart until it opens.
—Rumi

PROLOGUE
Ryker

Woman, you're beginning to make me want to define things I never imagined before.

My words ghost through my mind right along with the look on Vaughn's face when I said them—cheeks flushed from the sex we'd just enjoyed, lips swollen from my inability to ever get enough of her, and eyes full of the same shitstorm of emotions swirling inside me.

Definitions.

Labels.

Designations.

Whatever you fucking call it, I'd give every last one right now if I could kick all the guests out of the party so I could enjoy Vaughn all over again. But not a quickie against the dresser like we just had . . . no. This time I want to take my time with her. Get drunk on every goddamn inch of her. Lose myself in her—*to her*—in a way I've never allowed myself to before.

I'm a selfish bastard who doesn't want to share.

With a shake of my head and a resignation that I was wrong inviting the Hamptons lookie-loos here, I open my humidor and pull out a carton of Cuban cigars to bring out to the guys.

"You have something I want, Lockhart."

I don't respond. I don't turn his way. I don't ask him what the fuck he's doing here at my party, let alone in the pool house, when I should have figured he'd show. Instead, I close the door on the cabinet, set down the Cubans, and casually push the button on the screen of my cell before placing it facedown on the bar top in front of me.

With a measured sip of my drink, I turn and eye Carter Preston over the rim of my highball glass. "Good to see you too, Senator."

"I figured you wouldn't mind if I stopped by. The whole town's abuzz about Ryker Lockhart and how serious it must be with the *woman* he's brought here for the weekend."

"Since when do you believe bullshit rumors?" I ask, trying to feel him out and his unexpected and *unwelcome* presence.

"Since I've seen the woman here with my own two eyes." He raises his brows and just stares as a slow smirk curls up one side of his mouth. Without asking, he reaches out and takes a cigar from the box, lifting it with a quirk of his brow to ask if he can. Not thrilled with giving him one, I nod and wait for him to lead this conversation. "You haven't returned my calls."

I think of the two voice mails he's left these past few days requesting a private moment and how I blew them off. "As you can see, I've been busy."

"I thought it was all rumors?"

"What did you need, Carter?" I completely disregard his question.

"Like I said, I'm here because you have something I want."

"I'm sorry; my caseload is full," I say and take a seat on the barstool beside me.

"Hmm." He savors the sip he takes and chuckles as if he doesn't believe me. "I'll get what I want, one way or another."

"I'm honored you want me to represent you in your divorce," I say, trying to head this off at the pass, "but it's just not feasible right now. I've got a backlog that—"

"You're really going to pass up having the future vice president of the United States as part of your clientele? You know my name would have new clients—*high-dollar* clients—lighting up that phone of yours."

"Putting the cart before the horse now, are we?"

"The nomination is just a matter of time. I make sure the bills get passed that need to be passed for the party's benefit. I make sure the ones that need to die, die." He shrugs and takes a few steps away. "Who doesn't get off on having that kind of power?"

"Power is often subjective." I have no fucking clue where he's going with this, but screw him and his ego trip.

"Easy to say when it comes from a man who hasn't felt its high." He shakes his head. "I could help you with that, you know. Take you under my wing. Let you help me with a thing or two and really put that law degree of yours to use."

"I'm good, thanks." *Asshole.*

"Come on, Lockhart. Live a little."

"I live plenty."

"There's a lot of money to be made."

"I've got money."

He laughs, his head down, his hands clasped around his glass, and he just stares at it for a beat before looking up at me with a cat-that-ate-the-canary grin that tells me here's his one-two punch. Here's the reason he wanted to see me.

What do you want, Carter?

"Is that why you're not taking me on as a client? Because you've got money already?" He takes a step closer to me. "Or is it because you're representing my wife and now you've got *my* money?" Another smile that holds no amusement. "Two million dollars of it, in fact."

I stumble over how to respond. Over what to say. Over how to justify. *Christ.* Talk about being blindsided. "She came to me before you did."

A tense silence fills the room. Sounds from the poolside activities filter in through the open windows but feel out of place in our silent standoff.

His arms are crossed now. His shoulder is leaning against the wall. His eyes are locked and loaded with an emotion I can't decipher. Fury? Admiration? Disbelief? Nothing about it makes sense to me.

"And yet the check was written and cashed *after* I approached you about representation."

"We were in negotiations."

"I guess so long as one of us gets you." His snort of a chuckle resonates through the space, and the sarcasm in it contradicts his words. "Too bad now I'll have to find another attorney who will rip you to shreds." Satisfaction blankets his expression.

Call it a hunch, call it a gut instinct, but there's something else going on here. Something else I can't put my finger on that has to do with so much more than my representing his wife, Bianca.

"I'm sure we'll be able to figure things out without anyone being ripped to shreds."

His laugh is rich and even, and in a matter of seconds it goes from reverberating off the walls of the small space to silent. "What? No Roxanne?"

His comment about the relationship I had with a married woman is like whiplash to my brain, the implied threat behind it even more so, but I try to hide it with a knowing chuckle. "Roxanne?"

"Ah, come on, Lockhart. Chuck was running his mouth at The Club again. Everyone knows you were fucking her."

Goddamn Chuck.

"That was over before it began."

Carter runs the length of his unlit Cuban cigar beneath his nose and inhales its rich scent. "That's not exactly how the rumor mill is spinning it. She was at your place not too long ago."

"In the lobby, but no farther." *How the hell does he know this?*

"I have eyes everywhere, my friend," he says, answering my unspoken question and loving every moment of my reaction.

"Then your eyes should know she was begging and I was walking the other way." *The questions is, Did his eyes see Vaughn there too? Did they see us go into the bathroom where we argued and then she left alone?*

"Could you imagine if it got out that you were sleeping with your client's wife? Representing a man who thinks you have his best interests in mind when in reality you're betraying his trust? Your word is everything in this business, isn't it?"

There goes the warning shot over the bow. The man is known for toying with his prey before he goes in for the kill.

"Your point, Senator?"

"You want to explain to me why I see a high-dollar madam here? Why I've seen you with her before?"

I fight every immediate reaction I have. The *What the fuck are you talking about?* The *What do you mean there is a high-dollar madam here?* All of them, because he just made the connection that Vee is Vaughn, and what the hell am I supposed to do now? How am I supposed to play this other than to act like it's no big deal when he's staring at me, wanting a reaction?

I refuse to give him the fight he's looking for.

"What's it to you?"

"I believe paying for sex is illegal, Counselor." His scoff fills the small room and drowns out the sounds of my guests outside.

"Says a man who has no problem breaking the law himself," I say to neutralize his thinly veiled threat and to let him know I've heard the rumors about his dealings. About lobbyists and greased palms. About him using an escort service and paying for sex himself.

Something's off, though. He's on edge beneath the designer threads and practiced politician's smile, regardless of how relaxed he pretends to be.

Bianca's words from our conversation earlier this week ghost through my mind. *My husband is struggling right now. It's difficult for a man who's always in control to feel that he's losing it when it comes to me.* I think of her tight smile and the unforgiving look in her eyes. *I will take so much pleasure in being the one to prove to him that he can never have control over me again. Find out whatever you can on him—the women he cheats on me with, the bribes he takes, the hookers he pays—and I want you to use every single one of them to win me more. But be warned, once he knows you're a threat to him and his endgame, he'll do whatever it takes to bury you. Morality isn't exactly his strong suit.*

"Sometimes a man has to do what he has to do." Carter's unabashed shrug is followed by the flash of a smile. "Especially when it comes to getting the upper hand."

"I'm not following you."

"Hasn't your practice had some troubling incidents as of late?" He walks toward the bar and selects a bottle of Jameson off the shelf without asking. The neck clinks as it touches his glass when he helps himself to more. "In addition to Roxanne, of course."

My mind scrambles to figure out what he's referring to but draws a blank.

"Is this you pretending to have some bogus upper hand on me?" I ask through a laugh. I don't care who the fuck he is—vice president or senator or a goddamn errand boy, he's full of crap.

His laugh reverberates around the room. "Nah, we're just two guys shooting the shit here. Sharing stories. Trading favors. Looking out for one another."

That's how he wants to play this? Ask to see me, confront me over Bianca, then Vaughn, threaten me, and now act like we're buddies?

Keep it casual, Ryk. The less you say, the better, until you figure out what it is that he's after. Because he is *after something.*

"Is that so?"

"You tell me. Is it?"

"You said you wanted something from me," I reiterate in this verbal game of cat and mouse, sick of the chase. "Care to tell me what that is so I can get back to my guests?"

"Are you going to answer my question?" he asks with a lift of his chin to the party beyond. "What's *she* doing here?"

"Who?"

It's his turn to respond with a laugh that tells me I know exactly who he's talking about. "The woman who needs to know her threats are empty against my influence." He levels me with a look that only he can. Arrogant. Privileged. Entitled.

He wants Vaughn.

Fucking Vaughn.

"Vaughn." He fights a smile as he studies me for a reaction.

A reaction I refuse to give him.

"Vaughn?"

"Power, Ryker." He takes the cigar cutter off the counter, lops off the end before lighting it, and takes a long draw. His eyes close as he appears to relish the taste, and when he finally exhales, he meets my eyes. "It all comes back to that, now doesn't it?"

"And like I said, power is subjective." *Where the fuck are you going with this, Carter?*

"Are you her keeper? Are you the one pulling her strings?"

"I'm not following you. Wouldn't it be easier if you just came out and asked what you wanted to ask?"

His smile is anything but sincere when he grants it. His eyes hard, his shoulders tense. "The woman has many things I want. *Many.*"

"And?"

"And she should be careful."

"What's that supposed to mean?" *Come on, you son of a bitch. Tell me what it is you want here. Why the threat?* "Why are you telling me any of this?"

"Because it seems she's playing you just as much as she's playing me. Have you wondered what dirt she has on you? Have you figured out how she plans to bring you down should you cross her?"

"I'm not worried about that." I narrow my eyes and wonder what the fuck Vaughn has on him that has him so worried.

"You should be."

I don't say a word but rather run my own cigar under my nose and inhale its scent to buy time and to give him the impression I'm not worried in the least. For all he knows, Vaughn is here on the clock.

"Come on, Lockhart." His chuckle scrapes over my nerves. "Don't tell me I need to school you on how to manage your playthings."

I look at him as the lighter flickers at the end of my cigar, and I suck in quick puffs to light it.

"I wasn't aware I needed to manage them."

"When they could ruin you with their dirt . . . you have no choice. You see, with sex comes a sort of power. With power comes fear. It's so easy to make a woman bend to your will when you have both of those combined—power plus fear."

"Mmm." I don't trust myself to say anything else.

"What I'm getting at is Vaughn needs to be fucked into submission." He takes another long draw on the stogie but keeps his eyes on me, waiting for a reaction. And fuck yes, his words make my fists tense and my blood boil, but I know better than to give him what he wants.

"Every woman does, right?" His head startles, and surprise fills his eyes at my baited lie. "The question is, What would she be submitting to?"

Is this about me? About him exacting some sick revenge because I'm representing his wife? Or is this strictly about Vaughn? About what she has on him? Or is it something else entirely?

And of course the *something else* I fear he wants has me rising from my barstool so I can pour myself another glass. I'm definitely going to need some more alcohol to calm my temper down.

"She has things of mine she needs to give back." His smile is strained, his eyes unforgiving.

"Like what?"

He shrugs. "Let's hope she returns them, or else I'll have to air all her dirty little secrets . . . and there are so many, Ryker, a judge would have a fucking field day. I'm thinking the ladies in lockup would love to sample her sweet pussy." He nudges me. "It is sweet, isn't it, Lockhart?"

"Carter." It's a warning. A caution that my restraint is being tested. A slip in showing him I care for her.

Fuck. Saying that is like throwing chum in the water to a shark.

"What's wrong? You getting feelings for the hired help?" He shakes his head in disgust. "It's wrong of you to let your guard down." He steps in closer to me. "Use the sex. Get the fear. Gain the power. Understood?"

"Mmm." Fuck if I'm walking into a trap willingly.

"So this is the part where you tell me if you're with me or against me."

His words make no sense to me. I'm representing his wife, and yet he's talking to me about wanting to screw another woman.

"How's that?"

"Well, she obviously has things we both want. It would be best if we worked together to get them." He angles his head to the side and stares. "So are you just fucking her, or are you out to make an honest woman of her? One makes you a man; the other makes you a pussy."

"Fuck off." I laugh the words out as my head swims trying to figure out why his words make my stomach churn.

"So I can't trust you, then?" His eyes narrow, his cigar smoke a hazy swirl in front of his face.

They say fight fire with fire. For some reason with the senator I doubt that will play in my favor. I'll fight his fire with gasoline. Add some accelerant, light the match, and see just how big it will explode before it snuffs itself out.

"Think what you will," I say with a nonchalant shrug that could play either way for me before tilting my drink up. The burn of the alcohol doesn't do shit to abate how much I hate this man. I nod and decide to wing it. It's the only chance I have of figuring out what exactly it is he has on her. "I only have Vaughn around because of the sex. Nothing more. Nothing less."

"Well, you've gone to the right place if it's sex. *Lucky bastard,*" Carter says and pulls my attention to his smug smile and bullshit bravado. "Vaughn's a madam and a whore all tied into one neat little bow you get to open up one thigh at a time."

Rage simmers. My fists clench. All I can think about is bashing in that perfectly straight nose of his.

But the challenge in his eyes tells me that's what he wants. The man wants a fight, while I want to nail him to a goddamn wall. First with my fist to his face for being a prick and second in the courtroom if I can get proof that he's willing to cheat—with an escort, no less. The senator who pays for sex. Getting him to admit it outright on my cell phone's recorder will benefit my case, but hell if this isn't fucked up. Throw Vaughn to the wolves—figuratively—to gain an advantage. The only redeeming prospect in this whole conversation is that hopefully he'll spill what he has on her.

He quirks an eyebrow, and a smile plays at the corners of his lips as he weighs the situation.

I do too.

Time to play.

"You can have her if you want her, Preston. Fuck, I'll even pay for your time with her."

Come on, fucker. Take the bait.

I should choke on the lie, but I don't. It comes out smooth and seamless, and for a brief second I wonder what the hell is wrong with me. Vaughn's perfume still lingers on my skin, and yet I have no qualms about saying shit like that?

Maybe I'm not cut out for this kind of thing. A relationship. Love. *Fuck.*

As I struggle with my own desires, I watch the emotions play over his face. Caution. Curiosity. Bravado. They range from wondering whether I'm playing him to being so damn arrogant he actually thinks he has me under his thumb.

"You'd pay for me, Lockhart? Why the generosity all of a sudden?"

"Senator, even I know when it's time to share the wealth. Besides, aren't you the one who has the most to gain here?"

"You let me down, and then you try to soothe me with pussy." Carter's chuckle rumbles through the air. "A man after my own heart."

Stroke a man's ego, offer him easy sex, and he'll believe any fucking thing you say. It's a sad fact that we're such simple creatures.

"I wasn't aware you had one," I say, selling the lie by clinking the edge of my glass against his in a toast.

His smile widens. "What I don't get is how'd you manage to corral her? She needs a real man to put her in her place. Show her who's boss . . . no offense."

"None taken." I speak the words, but every part of me hates myself right now.

Oh shit.

Am I really having this conversation?

Did I really just offer Vaughn to this fucker?

What did I do?

What the fuck am I actually doing?

But when I look up at Carter and see the smug smile on his lips and his posture relaxed, I think he'll actually fall for it. More ammo for me with Bianca . . . and maybe if I play it right, I can find out what the fuck it is he has on Vaughn.

"What'd you do? Fool her into believing that she means more to you than a good lay?"

I think of last night on the kitchen counter—cookie dough and Vaughn—and earlier in the bedroom—pure need and greed—and I hate myself even more for feeding him this bullshit.

I don't trust my own words not to betray me right now, so I just shrug and give an unapologetic smile.

"You're a cruel and brilliant fucking bastard."

"So they say."

He waves his cigar at me. "You better not be playing me, Lockhart."

"Playing you?" *Sell the lie, Lockhart.* "Not you, Preston. You'd see right through it. Everybody else, though? Definitely."

Your justification is bullshit.

"It looks like you might need the shit I dug up on her for yourself. You've played her well enough that I think she's seeing forevers when all you're seeing is what you want between her thighs. She's going to be pissed when you stop calling."

"True. I could definitely use the dirt you have on her. Two people knowing something is always better than just one. That way we'd both be protected." I sit back down and force a laugh to play it all up when I'd rather down another goddamn drink in misery. "Since we're looking out for each other and all."

"And that's why you're offering her to me?"

"Like I said, it's the least I can do, given the circumstances."

"Pass the pussy, please." The senator laughs, and I join in as my stomach churns at the thought of his fucking hands on her. At knowing everything she's been through at the whim of her uncle and how men like them think it's their right to take regardless of consent. "How do you know she'll go along with it?"

"Tell me the time and place, and I'll have her ready and willing for you," I offer, ignoring the senator's question and making his eyes light up. Now it's time to tell him I want the info on Vaughn beforehand. Tit for fucking tat. "But first you'll need to give me—"

"Just make sure she's defiant. I love it when they fight."

"Not going to happen." I hear Vaughn's voice before I see her, and every single part of me dies a miserable and painful death at the sound.

NO!

How much did she hear?

This is bad.

Fuck.

So goddamn bad.

Fuck.

She has to know that I'm lying.

Fuck!

Beside me, Carter turns to face her. He more than likes what he sees—his dick already dipping into her before he's even touched her— and I force my hands to release the fists they've curled into.

"I fucking want her," Preston murmurs beneath his breath so only I can hear it, his fingers fidgeting as if they're itching to touch her.

What the hell am I going to do now? I take a beat as my mind spins and my thoughts tumble out of control.

I fucked up big time. Played the game, and now I'm so fucking far into it, I can't back out. There's nothing I can do but make sure Carter thinks it's true. All of it. That I'd offer her up to him. That I buy his bullshit sex, power, and fear theory. That I need to know what he has on her to save us both from her later.

Sell the goddamn lie, Lockhart.

But at what cost?

I take a sip of my drink and set it down with a clink on the bar top before swiveling on my barstool to face her.

And I know the cost. It's all right there in front of me, and it takes every goddamn thing I have to meet her eyes.

But so is protecting her. So is making sure Carter can never hurt her.

Sell the lie.

Make Carter believe you. Make him think he holds the power. Make him believe you're going to help him get back what's his.

But fuck if it's not going to be the hardest thing I've ever done, as she stands there with hurt, shame, defeat, and defiance written all over every part of her.

Asking forgiveness is my only option now since it's way too fucking late to ask her for her permission to do this.

At least that's what I'll tell myself to get through this. To ignore the tears welling in those aqua eyes and the trembling of her bottom lip.

Sell the fucking lie.

"Vaughn." *Look at me, Vaughn. Look at me and see the truth. That I'm playing him. That I'm . . . fuck, just look at me.* "Perfect timing. Were your ears burning, babe?"

"Make it happen." Another murmur by Preston. I stare at Vaughn but nod ever so slightly to let him know I will.

"Babe?" she says, her voice colder than the goddamn polar ice cap. *"Babe?"*

"Yeah." The word feels like acid on my tongue.

"I'm not yours to share."

"You took the money, so technically, you're mine to do with as I please," I say, more than aware that Carter's paying attention to my every word while each one she hears sounds like a bullet hitting her. *Goddammit, Vaughn. Look at me. See me. I would never . . .* but there's a little quiver of her bottom lip that all but makes me want to throw in the towel on this charade. *But he has something on her.*

Think, Lockhart.

Bring her back.

Let her know.

"It's not like you'd *say no* to me," I say, waiting for her to hear the words, for her to remember our battle of wills when we first started this thing between us, for her to see that I'm trying to tell her this is not what it seems. All the while letting Carter think I'm pulling his put-a-woman-in-her-place bullshit.

"I don't—I can't—how . . ." She fumbles over her words, much like her expression morphs from one emotion to the next.

"Did you really think I had changed this much for you?" I ask as Carter chuckles with a college-frat-boy arrogance that says he's enjoying this. And fuck if I don't die inside a little when the first tear slips down her cheek. I scramble to figure out how to bring her back to the *us* she knows. To realize the *me* she knows would never do this. "Did you really think I want something permanent? Something that can be *defined*? That you were the *exception*?"

There's a glimmer of lucidity in her eyes. For the briefest of seconds, I think she hears me. I think she sees through this bullshit situation and takes it for what it's worth . . . but then she says my name.

"Ryker?" It's a goddamn plea full of hurt and confusion and *you're such a fucking asshole.*

What makes it almost worse is the senator at my side, groaning like my hurting her is making him fucking hard. I force a swallow down my dry throat and know there's no turning back now. I'll sell the damn lie, and then I'll do everything in my power to bury the motherfucker.

"You did, didn't you?" I say and nudge Carter. But this time she doesn't respond. She just stares at me with doe eyes and parted lips as her spine straightens some. "Vaughn?"

"No!" She yells the lone word, but there is so much sewn into her tone that I know she believes all this.

I sold the lie so damn well I hurt the one person I care about the most.

Our eyes lock, and the devastation in hers all but kills me. When she runs out of the pool house, it takes everything I have not to chase after her and explain.

I stand from my stool, my moral compass way off the charts as I realize what I just did to her.

To us.

"I was right." Carter's low rumble of a chuckle fills the room. "The poor thing really thought you loved her," he mocks.

"Mmm."

"C'mon, Lockhart. You've already got the sex and now the power. It's my turn, and fucking hell, I'll create the fear you're too soft to add."

If I clench my glass any tighter, it might break. My cigar is still lit but sits untouched on the edge of the ashtray, its smell suddenly making me want to throw up.

Sell the lie.

"I think I'm going to need that dirt you dug up on her about now. By the way she just bolted out of here, I wouldn't be surprised if she takes out a full-page ad in the *New York Times* telling everyone I pay for sex."

His laugh is longer than it should be, and his sudden lack of a response unnerves me.

"That would damage her ability to make money. She's smarter than that."

"If she's so smart, then what makes you think she'll fall for your fear tactics?"

Carter's expression turns to stone as he takes a step toward me. "She'll fall for it all right," he murmurs with an intensity that bugs the fuck out of me. "I won't give up until I get everything I want from her. The dirt she has on me *and* her fucking pussy as an interest payment for how long I have to wait to get it." He leans in closer, making me more than uncomfortable. "I don't like being played, Lockhart. By anyone." He lifts his eyebrows as if to ask me if I understand his unspoken threat. A moment passes, and then his laugh rings out like the true sociopath he's proving himself to be.

"What?" I ask, confused by his sudden change in demeanor and desperate to chase after Vaughn, apologize to her, and then make it up to her every possible way I can.

"You're so cute how you're worried she's gone for good." He pats me on the shoulder. "Get over it. Man the fuck up. She's the hired help. She'll come back as soon as you snap your fingers. A girl's gotta make a living, after all."

My jaw hurts from clenching my teeth, and I roll my shoulders. "Good to know," I murmur as my eyes drift to the party outside, and I wonder where the fuck she is right now.

"Besides, she needs to come back because there's nothing I love more than sexually harassing the help." He downs the rest of his drink in one swallow. "It's one hell of a party you've got going on here."

"You should go enjoy it." *Get the fuck out.*

"I will." He grins and strolls to the doorway before turning back to face me. "All's fair in paid sex, Lockhart." He shrugs. "Oh, and if you bring up this conversation or my recreational engagement with escorts against me in your settlement requests for Bianca, I'll use Roxanne and every other fucking made-up thing I can against you. While ethics aren't valuable in politics these days, they're still in high demand in the legal world."

Without another word, he turns back around and heads toward the party.

I stare at the empty doorway for a few moments as I fight the urge to run to find Vaughn. That might be a little noticeable, and I'm more than certain Carter is out there watching to see if I do just that.

Jesus Christ, I'm sorry, Vaughn. So fucking sorry.

And then it hits me.

I was so caught up in selling the lie that Carter never told me what it is he has on Vaughn.

Fucking hell.

Please tell me this wasn't all for nothing.

Please tell me I didn't just mess up the best thing I have going for me.

Fuck you, Lockhart.

Fuck. You.

CHAPTER ONE
Vaughn

Bang. Bang. Bang.

I pull Lucy tightly against me and breathe her in, but all I can think about is earlier today.

Bang. Bang. Bang.

Tangled plays on the television, and Rapunzel and Finn own her attention, but mine? Mine is on her.

It's the only place it can be as every emotion ebbs and flows through me.

Drowning me.

Consuming me.

Happily ever afters exist only in the fictional world.

Never in mine.

All I can hear is Ryker's incessant banging on the door at two in the morning. His pleas for me to open up so he can explain. Turning up the music in my earbuds to block him out. Lying in my bed with my pillow over my face, my tears staining the fabric, until he came to the conclusion I wasn't home and finally left about two hours later.

Lucy's giggles pull me back to the present as she looks up at me, her smile wide, her eyes alive, yet I feel broken. That was all I'd ever needed before—*her*—to fix a bad anything. And now it's like her smile is a bandage on a gash that needs stitches.

Ryker made me feel when I'd never felt before. *He made me want to feel.* He made me want to want.

I should have known better.

Last night plays through my mind like snapshots of time.

Leaving the house, the Hamptons, Ryker behind. The world outside the window of my Uber a blurred mess from the tears that filled my eyes and fell like rain the entire way.

The incessant ringing of my cells. First my personal phone, then my Wicked Ways one.

He used me.

The texts that came nonstop until I blocked Ryker's number.

He used me for his own benefit.

The banging on the door.

It's much easier to nurse a heartbreak when you can't hear the person trying to call you, because I don't care what excuse he might have had—there isn't one good enough to justify what he said and did.

If I thought sex could be messy, love is a goddamn disaster. One I was certain I never wanted to be a part of and now know for sure I don't.

I blow out a loud breath, and Lucy shifts to look at me. "Don't be sad that I have to go. We'll see each other in a few days."

Looking into her eyes and hearing her compassion for my misconstrued sadness has more tears threatening. I frame her face between my hands and kiss the tip of her nose. "You're right, but that doesn't mean I don't still want to be with you or that I don't miss you."

"You miss my mama, don't you?"

"I always do."

"It's okay," she says, taking my hand and directing it to lie over my heart with hers atop it. "She's still in here."

"Always." I fight another swell of emotion, realizing how much these past few months have changed the two of us—she has grown so much stronger, and I feel somehow weaker. She hugs me again, and I let her hold on for her as much as for myself. After pressing a kiss to the top of her head, I murmur, "I need to get your stuff. Joey will be here in a minute."

"Do I have to?"

"I know, Lu . . . soon." My promise feels emptier now more than ever, but I give it to her anyway as I rise from the couch to grab her stuff . . . and to give me a moment to put my happy face back on, because as much as I need her here, it's also brutally hard to remain cheerful when all I want to do is succumb to the tears.

I'm in her room when Lucy yells, "Joey's here!"

It's not two seconds before I'm walking out of the room to tell her not to answer the door until I make sure when I hear the squeal of excitement.

My heart drops, because before I even see the person standing in the doorway, I know who Lucy has just let in the house. I know because the sound she made—one of joy and excitement, with a little bit of a crush mixed in—is exactly how I used to feel at the prospect of seeing Ryker.

And then I hear the deep rumble of his voice, and every part of me wants to slide to the floor and cry at the hurt and the shame and the anger I feel over letting myself be duped by this man—at letting myself *love* this man—but I don't. Instead, I steel myself to see him.

I knew he'd be back.

Ryker's not a man who can be ignored or made to wait, so I knew he'd return.

"Auntie, Auntie." Lucy tugs on his hand and pulls him into the house. "Look who came to see us!"

Every muscle in my face has to be told to move to force the smile that attempts to turn up my lips when I look at her. I'm sure the rest of my body language fails at selling the lie.

"Vaughn." Ryker's voice saying my name hurts more than I could have ever imagined.

"Come on, Lucy. You need to get your shoes on because Joey's going to be here any minute," I say and busy myself, moving to the family room where her sneakers were discarded, not daring to look at him myself.

"But, Auntie . . ."

"Vaughn." My name is a plea and one I don't want to heed as I move back across the space that feels so much smaller with him in it.

"C'mon, Lucy Loo. Let's get your shoes on." I drop to my knees before her—his subtle scent of soap and cologne clouding my thoughts, hurting my heart—as her expression falls from excitement to confusion over my actions. "Don't." It's a low growl of warning when his hand closes over my biceps.

"You need to let me explain," Ryker says. Our eyes meet for the briefest of moments, and everything I feel is reflected in his.

And I don't understand. How can he be hurt when he's the one who caused this?

"The lady said not to touch her." It's Joey's voice that speaks through the open doorway, and while I snap my head his way, Ryker is unfazed and remains looking at me.

"Not your business, man," Ryker says, but his hand moves off my arm as he turns to stare Joey down.

"Vaughn? You okay?" Joey asks as his eyes move from Ryker to me to Lucy and back to Ryker.

"I'm—"

"She's fine," Ryker says, cutting me off as Joey takes a step forward. "I suggest you back off."

"You son of a—"

"Hey," I say, stopping Joey and stepping forward to halt the testosterone-laced confrontation that's obviously brewing here, more than a little startled by Joey's temper and protectiveness. And as much as I'd love for him to throw a punch at Ryker for me, it'll do nothing to fix the burning ache in my chest that seeing him has caused.

"Something's obviously wrong, Vaughn. Are you sure—"

"Outside," I say as I push him off the threshold to the front porch, welcoming the fresh air that's not clouded with everything that is Ryker.

Once the door shuts at my back, Joey looks at me with a mix of confusion and concern. "What's going on? Are you all right?"

"I'm fine." I take a deep breath.

"Stop saying you're fine when you're obviously not."

"It was just a fight," I lie, needing him out of here, Ryker out of here. "Just . . . just please don't start anything."

He runs a hand through his sandy-blond hair and blows out a sigh as if he doesn't quite believe me. "I don't like him."

A self-deprecating laugh falls from my mouth. "Right now, I don't like him much either." Tears threaten. "Lucy's ready to go. She just needs to get her shoes on."

"Vaughn." His hand grabs mine as I turn to go back into the house, and the mask I'm trying to hide my emotions behind threatens to crumble. He waits until I face him to speak again. "I . . . you know I'm here for you, right? Not just with Lucy, but . . . we've become friends through all of this, and if you need help, all you have to do is ask."

"I know. Thank you. It'll be—"

"*Fine*. I know," he says.

I give his hand a squeeze and push back open the front door to find Ryker kneeling down and finishing tying Lucy's shoes. "You ready, Lucy?" I ask, ignoring Ryker as he turns my way. "Come and give me a hug. Joey has to get you back. You're having a special movie night tonight." I infuse enthusiasm in my voice to match the smile plastered to my face.

Lucy's arms slide around my waist, and those bright-blue eyes look up to meet mine. "Can Mr. Ryker come to the movie night?"

For some reason, that simple question throws me off and has me stumbling for a response. "Um . . . not tonight, Luce. Mr. Ryker has plans."

Her cheeks turn pink, and she makes kissy-kissy sounds that cause a lump to form in my throat. "Can you make sure he's on my list of people who can come see me?"

"Lucy—"

"Please, Auntie?"

"Yes. Sure." *Anything to get you to leave before I break down.*

"Tell Joey that it's okay for Mr. Ryker to see me," she pleads and squeezes me tighter.

"Lu—"

"I don't have a lot of friends, and he's my friend and makes me happy and—"

"Fine. Yes." I nod and then look up to Joey. "Please add Ryker to her visitors' list."

"Vaughn?" Joey asks, and I can see Ryker physically bristle at him for questioning me.

"I'm serious. Ryker can visit her."

"Sure. Yep." Irritation laces Joey's every syllable. "You ready, Luce? We need to head out."

We say our goodbyes—the awkwardness less so as we all try to shelter her from the obvious fight between Ryker and me.

CHAPTER TWO

Vaughn

The door closes behind them, leaving us bathed in a tense silence. But the minute I hear Joey's car start, I speak.

"It's best if you leave, Ryker."

"I'm not going anywhere until I explain." He reaches out to grab my hand.

"Don't you dare touch me!" I shout at him as I yank my hand away and move to put distance between us. My glare holds his as he opens his mouth and shuts it, most likely trying to decide the best plan of attack. "You don't get to say what you said and then come here and pretend like it never happened."

It's only been a day—the hurt so raw, so real—and when I look at him, I feel like it's my heart beneath his foot where he stands.

"There's an explanation."

"No. There's not." Those three words sound like every emotion I have has been scraped up and used to utter them. "There will never be an explanation good enough to excuse what you said about me. To me. *To him.*" The first tear slips over and slides down my cheek, and I hate my body for betraying me. For showing him that he has in fact hurt me. "Please leave."

"I'm not going anywhere, Vaughn. You're going to listen to me, and you're going to listen to me now."

"There you go again, thinking I care about anything you say when you were offering me up to Carter. You don't own me. You don't have the right to say a goddamn thing to me, and I don't owe you shit that I have to listen."

"You were never supposed to hear any of it." His voice is low, his own emotion raw in the sound of it.

"Am I supposed to apologize for that? The door was open. I simply walked in. It wasn't some planned eavesdropping. Am I supposed to say I'm sorry that I did?" He shakes his head, but I continue before he cuts me off. "I can only imagine what else you would have said if I hadn't interrupted you."

"I was setting him up, Vaughn. I was recording the whole thing on my phone, and—"

"You were what?" I screech, my mind spinning over the fact that somewhere in some digital cloud my name is being linked together as Vee and Vaughn, and there's nothing I can do about it.

"I was doing it to use against him," he says. "To—"

"What about it being used against me?"

"That's not—I wouldn't—c'mon, Vaughn," he struggles to explain. "I already deleted it."

My laugh is low, unforgiving, and automatic, and as feasible as his explanation could be, I reject it immediately. "And that's supposed to make me feel better?" I shake my head in disbelief. "You broke my trust. You outed me. You acted like what we had was all a lie to a person who I despise. You—"

"Fucked up."

"You're goddamn right you did!" I scream at the top of my lungs, and I hate when my voice betrays me by breaking.

"I was . . . there are things I can't explain, Vaughn. Things that would betray my client's confidentiality, but in that moment, I decided to use his obsession with you to my advantage and—"

"His wife is your client?" I ask, knowing it doesn't help one bit if she is or isn't.

Ryker just stares at me. I don't know how I rationalized that the twenty-four hours would make seeing him easier—that my heart would be more hardened, my emotional reaction dulled—but it's just the opposite. I want to hug him and hit him and hold on to him and demand answers, all the while hating myself for wanting any and all of it.

He purses his lips and darts his gaze away before coming back to mine. "It was more than that. It was—"

"Answer the question. Is his wife your client?"

"I can't say any more. Just like you, I have a career to protect. Just like I was trying to protect you."

I emit a laugh laced with the waver of tears, the emotions over-whelming me and drowning out what he's really said.

The woman Ryker took on as a client—the surprise client he said being with me encouraged him to take—is Carter's wife? There's so much irony in the fact that she's the reason he supposedly threw me to the wolf.

"So you can use me, but you can't tell me. Makes perfect sense," I say, sarcasm dripping from my every word.

"Christ. Just listen. Please. He was threatening me. Then you. I was trying to play his game with him to see what it is he wanted. I was—"

"Me! He wanted me!" I scream, my voice breaking right along with my heart. "And if he didn't, now he sure as hell does."

"No, Vaughn. No. You don't—"

"Just stop! Please. Stop." Each word takes more effort than the last.

He takes a step forward, and I take one back as I stare at him and see so many things I love but at the same time feel so many things that I hate.

"This is never going to work," I whisper as if I'm afraid to say it.

"What do you mean? Why can't it? I know I—"

"It won't. Neither of us will ever give up the part of ourselves we need to in order to make this work. We don't trust. We love with conditions even when we think we aren't. We—"

"That's bullshit." He walks a few more feet into the living room, shoves a hand through his disheveled hair, and then exhales a long and frustrated sigh before turning back to look at me.

"No, it's the truth." For the first time since he walked through my door, I acknowledge the tears coursing down my cheeks, but I won't let him see them. I turn my back to him and shove them away.

"He said he had dirt on you, Vaughn."

Everything in me stutters to a halt: my heart, my breath, my thoughts. When I turn to face him, my armor is firmly in place. "Of course he does. With your confirmation, he now knows who I am. *You outed me.*"

I watch my words hit him like a one-two punch. First the denial and then the recognition of what he did when he should have already realized how devastating that part of the conversation alone is for me.

"Vaughn . . ."

"With your offer, he now thinks I'm available to the highest bidder. He can now blackmail me seven ways from Sunday, Ryker, because not once did you deny who I was or defend me or even find a way to stop the conversation. Nope. Not you. Ruse or not, you played right into his hand and used me as a pawn in your high-stakes game." I stiffen my spine. "Just like your mother used you with her husbands."

The muscle in his jaw pulses as he grits his teeth. "It's not—you don't understand. He made the connection on his own. If I'd have argued, it would have made it worse. He'd have gotten off on the fact I was trying to protect you. My lack of reaction was for the best—*Christ.*" He hangs his head, and I hate that the part of me that loves him actually feels bad for him.

And then I get a grip and find my justified anger again. "For the best?" My voice escalates with each word. "For the best for you? Or for the best for me? Because I saw a whole lot of you in there and not the other way around."

"How could you think I'd mean all that shit? How could you think I'd purposely hurt you? After everything we've talked about? After everything we've gone through? How could—"

"Because you said the words to my face without flinching, that's why!" I shout. "For the briefest of moments, I thought maybe there was something going on—that you were playing some kind of game—and all I could do was stare at your side and beg you to make the 'hang loose' sign." I shove my hand out in the sign with my thumb and pinkie sticking out and middle fingers against my palm.

"Vaughn," he groans my name.

"But you didn't. Not a sign, not an anything."

"I'm supposed to remember some silly thing you and Lucy do in the midst of everything that was going on?" He throws his hands out to his sides in frustration. "And I did give you a sign. I was trying to tell you without him knowing. I worked in there about you saying *no*. I brought up our word—*defining*—to try to remind you of what I had said the last time I saw you . . . to let you know—"

"You mean to throw your sarcasm and words that I thought meant something in my face?"

"I tried. Fuck, I tried." He rolls his shoulders as if he has to refocus, and when he looks back at me, I try to ignore the emotion swimming in his eyes. "He's determined to get whatever blackmail material you have on him. He's willing to do whatever it takes to make you return it. What do you have?"

The pictures come to mind. The call logs come second. They're currently in safekeeping, my PI and I still unable to decipher their meaning. We don't totally know why the mix of phone numbers and dates are a threat to the senator—we just know they are.

None of it makes sense, and yet all of it makes sense at the same time.

"So you sold me out to save me?" I laugh, but it doesn't hold an ounce of amusement.

"I tried to act like I was in the same boat as him. Wanting you for sex. Worried about the dirt you had on me. Wanting him to give me what he had on you so we could use it against you if need be."

"And that's supposed to make me feel better?"

"No. Yes. Fuck, Vaughn, at the time I was doing what I thought was best and—"

"And all the while making sure to document that your client's soon to be ex-husband was willing to sleep with an escort to help your case," I impart.

"Fucking hell." He scrubs his hand over his face.

Tears slide down my cheeks as hurt all but radiates in my chest. "Stop trying to turn this on me, Ryker. Stop trying to tell me that you said and did all this for my benefit when you already laid it out that it would benefit your divorce filing."

"You're so fucking stubborn—you're not listening to me!" he shouts.

"You're right! I don't want to listen. I've already heard enough. About how you'd pay my fee for him. How you'd never change for me." And I hate that saying these things out loud with him in front of me makes them a little less believable.

But I know it's so much more than just the words he said—it's the trust I gave him that he betrayed. It's the fact that I told him more about myself than I've ever told anyone. I opened up to him about my fears, my past, my will to never allow anyone to have power over me again . . . and he disregarded every single one of those things in his conversation with Carter.

"Vaughn." His tone begs me to hear him when all I really want to do is just shut him out. "Does any of that sound like something I would say coming on the heels of what we did the night before? Hell, just an hour before?"

"You're the one who said them."

"I did. And then I called and texted and got here as soon as I could to explain everything to you, but you wouldn't listen," he says as I glare at him.

"Please, just go."

"I made a mistake, Vaughn. The bastard threatened you, and the words just came out. All I could think about was finding out what he had on you. All I wanted was to nail his ass to a goddamn wall by using his willingness to sleep with you so I'd have some leverage over him. I knew no one was listening, and—"

"But I was listening! You would've never known if I hadn't walked in. Do you know what you were risking for me? What if someone had put two and two together, and the social worker found out somehow, and Lucy—"

"But it didn't. It didn't!" he shouts back for the first time, and I can tell he's getting frustrated with me. But he has no idea how it feels on my side of this.

My chest burns with hurt. With the urge to give in because I still love him and the need not to for my own pride.

And then the reality hits me.

I'm lying. Even if he had given me the "hang loose" sign, it still wouldn't negate the things he said. The truths he confirmed. The way he made me feel. The information he tried to gain.

Nothing could ever validate or justify or *anything* what he said.

"You disrespected me, Ryker. You used me when you're the one who is supposed to stand up for me. You used me for your own gain—"

"I told you I was trying to—"

"Better whatever situation you have with your client, I know. You've said it enough times." I pause as I swallow over the lump forming in my throat. "For that I can't forgive you."

He opens his mouth and shuts it as his expression falls. "And what about for trying to protect you?" His voice breaks, and I hate that every part of me wants to crumble at the sound.

"The last I checked, destroying someone and protecting someone aren't the same thing." For the first time in this conversation, my voice lacks all emotion, because I see it now. I know it now.

His shoulders visibly sag, and for a beat there's defeat in his posture, but just as quickly as it came, it goes. "So what does that mean?" He strides across the room and puts his hands on my arms, the connection, his nearness, the somberness in his eyes all but breaking me.

And it takes a second for me to find my bearings again. It takes a moment for the hurt to subside long enough so my reason can reign.

I take a step back to create some of the distance that he's clouding. "I'm sorry, Ryker, but Wicked Ways is no longer allowing you to use their services. Your access has been revoked."

"I don't care. I don't want their services. *I just want you.*"

I hiccup over the sob I emit. "I just need—" *To believe you. To trust what you're saying. To know this was real.* "Time." The lump in my throat now almost chokes me. "Can you please just go now? Haven't you caused enough hurt already?"

"Don't throw *this* away. *Us* away."

You already did.

"Please . . ."

My back is to him, my hand on the door. My emotions turbulent. My heart breaking.

"I've fallen in love with you, Vaughn."

And if anything is going to spark the fight back in me, it would be those unexpected words.

"No!" I spin around and stare at him, not caring about the tears suddenly painting my face. "You don't get to say that to me! You don't get to use those words to fix things." I suck in a ragged breath.

"But it's true." He gives me the most nonchalant of shrugs to match his matter-of-fact tone.

I push my fingers against my eyes and shake my head back and forth as I try to reject the words I've never allowed anyone to say to me.

The ones I'd never wanted anyone to say until twenty-four hours ago. The ones that just twisted the knife in my chest and made this whole thing hurt that much more.

Because I love him too.

But not like this.

Not after he used me. Not after he showed me that a woman at his disposal is all he'll ever see. Not after he thought it was okay, regardless of the circumstances.

"Please leave or I'll call the cops. I don't love you in return," I lie.

Emotions play over every muscle in his gorgeous face. Without another word, he turns around and walks out the front door, never seeing my hand in the "hang loose" sign hidden behind my back.

CHAPTER THREE

Ryker

You said you loved her.

I stare at the city streets twenty floors below my penthouse. Taillights brighten and dim, steam rises and dissipates, and people move quickly in and out of my line of sight, but all I see is the turned-off front porch light of her house when I stood on her driveway. How there was a blue hue on the other side of the closed curtains where she probably had those beloved black-and-white movies of hers playing to comfort her. All I can feel is the goddamn panic I felt when I forced myself to drive away after sitting there for an hour after she kicked me out.

You used those damn words out of desperation to salvage your fucking colossal mistake.

When my fist slams through the drywall, I don't feel an ounce of pain. Hell, I didn't even realize I threw it.

All I know is the hole in the wall has nothing on the hole currently eating its way through my fucking chest.

Dignified and always-in-control Ryker Lockhart just punched the wall like a thug.

That's what this woman does to me. She makes me lose all sense of myself, every ounce of reason . . . and fuck if she hasn't made me love every second of it.

Love.

There's that damn word again.

The fucked-up term that people throw around just so they can get back at someone else. The one they wield like a weapon to hold over their lover's head in the future.

It's not real. I think of my mom, of the way she needed the word and then hated the obligations that came with it after it was said. The demands and the conformity and the constant hurt I watched her hide because of that one damn emotion.

Vaughn.

The expressions on her face tonight are snapshots in my mind. Hurt. Shame. Disbelief. Anger. *Love.* One after another.

What's between us can't really be love. That shit doesn't exist. Falling for a woman? *Yes.* Actually loving her? *Not a chance in hell.*

This is not me.

Never has been.

Never will be.

And yet here I am. Fucked and furious and a failure because I screwed up.

Big time.

I wasn't cut out for relationships. For love. For anything that has to do with thinking about someone else before I think of myself. *Doesn't this prove that point?*

Walk away. Do the one thing you know how to do when it comes to a woman—create space and distance to prove to her and yourself that she doesn't matter. That she's disposable. That you are the heartless son of a bitch you know yourself to be.

Walk away.

Fuck you, Lockhart. You're being a coward.

Walk the fuck away.

Easier said than done.

CHAPTER FOUR

Vaughn

The dull throb of the bass echoes around me and irritates me when it shouldn't.

I chose to pick up yet another extra shift. Anything to busy my mind so that I stop thinking about Ryker and what happened last week and what exactly the senator might do with any information he might have on me.

So I opted to lose myself in my job. In the people around me. In the music and dark lights. Too bad I didn't realize all of that was going to amplify my bad mood rather than abate it.

Love. It's everywhere I look tonight. In the familiarity in the simple touch of a man's hand to a woman's lower back as he leans in and whispers in her ear. In the soft smiles and knowing looks across the space between a couple.

All things I miss about being with Ryker. All things I don't want to miss but do.

It's only been a few days. I hope it gets easier. I fear it won't.

"Madam?"

My feet falter in response to the voice at my back. The dark stretch of the hallway, uncharacteristically empty, puts me on edge, as does the lone word the male behind me speaks.

Not here at my work.

Please don't let the senator have ruined that for me too.

I force a swallow down my throat and turn around, expecting to be propositioned for some reason. The man before me is tall, dark, and handsome with a lopsided smirk and an expensive suit.

Handsome? *Yes.* Am I interested? *Not in the least.*

"Yes?"

"Can we get more drinks?" he asks, holding up his empty glass. "We're in the Two Pod."

Not a man propositioning me for my services as a madam.

"Sure. Yes. I'll get your server over there right away," I say, suddenly embarrassed at my assumption.

Just a man being polite.

You need to get a grip, Vaughn.

Stop being so paranoid and get a damn grip.

With a sigh, I go about the rest of my night and try not to mess up any more orders like I'd already done several times up until that point. And I do better. I don't snap at any more customers. I decline the request for my phone number several times, because all I can hear is Ryker saying he's fallen in love with me. All I can focus on is him using those words like a weapon to try to win me back.

"You done for the night?" Ahmed asks as I pull my purse from the locker. I glance his way, and he's tying a clean black apron around his waist.

"Let me guess . . . a drunk woman spilled her drink on you in the hopes that she could pat off the liquid."

"Wouldn't be the first time," he says and flashes a disarming smile. But it's when he takes a step closer that his eyes narrow and his voice lowers. "You okay, Vaughny?"

I force a smile he won't believe. The same one I've been pretending to feel all night long. "I'm good. Just men is all."

"We're sons of bitches, aren't we?" His attempt at humor doesn't win me over. "Seriously, though . . . same guy as before?"

"Mmm."

"A fight?" He reaches out and runs a hand down my arm in sympathy.

"Something like that."

"It sucks to finally allow yourself to need someone and then not have them."

"It does," I murmur.

"Maybe the sun hasn't set yet."

I hate that I smile at his gentle reminder of what he said to me last time he saw me upset over Ryker. How he found me sitting in a Starbucks more than worse for the wear and then gave me his romanticized advice. *Most people look for love in the sunrise, when they don't realize for them it can be found in the sunset.* But I smile at him anyway, knowing it's solely to thank him for being so sweet. Not because I have any desire to be part of Ryker's sunset.

"It'll get better. He'll come to his senses, or else I'll kick his ass to the curb." He presses a brotherly kiss to my cheek. "I've gotta get back to the masses."

"Have fun."

But as I collect my things and start to head home, I find myself thinking about what Ahmed said about needing someone.

My thoughts drift to Samantha and Brian, my sister and Lucy's father. To their codependency that seemed cute at first and then grew to unhealthy proportions. His need for drugs and her need to please him. Then it grew to *their* dependency on the drugs and each other to help score some. Samantha knew Brian was bad for her but kept going back.

Is that what I've done with Ryker? Allowed myself to fall for a man, *to need a man*, who probably isn't the best fit for me? A man who hasn't been in a relationship before. One who coerced me into ours with ultimatums and threats and then used me like he did? A person who I have grown to need despite telling myself after Samantha's suicide that I'd never allow myself to need someone like she did?

"Lot of good that promise did you," I mutter to myself, because hell if I don't need Ryker right now despite everything he did and said.

No.

Not need.

Want.

And this feeling—this needing, wanting, missing Ryker—scares the shit out of me, especially when fate keeps proving time and again that he's bad for me.

The ringing of my cell phone startles me from thoughts I shouldn't be having, because deep down I can already hear myself shutting them out.

"Hello?" Flustered, I answer the phone without thinking.

"Is this Vee?"

The deep tenor of a male voice startles me for the second time tonight, and I realize it's my Wicked Ways cell that I answered.

Heartbreak seems to have messed with all aspects of my life.

"Yes. Sorry. You caught me off guard." I signal a left turn with my blinker and slip into the role I know so well but that now feels like so much more than a lie. "This is Wicked Ways, and I'm Vee. How may I help you?"

The man clears his throat, his discomfort over how to continue the conversation evident. "I—uh . . . I was given your number."

"That's always good to hear. May I ask by who?"

"By a client of yours. Does it matter who?"

"I'm sorry, it does matter. We only take new clients through referral."

"Hmm."

"I assure you, sir, all information is kept completely confidential. Is this your first time calling a service?"

"Yes."

"It's quite common to feel a little anxious over it. I assure you, we'll take good care of you."

He pauses for a beat, combatting his anxiety. "Ryker Lockhart is the name."

My shoulders sag hearing the name, but I shouldn't be surprised considering this is the sixth call I've received like this in the last ten days. A part of me wants to tell the gentleman my client list is full and refer him out to another agency. Ryker's sudden referrals make me feel like this is how he's trying to cement his apology to me.

Doesn't he get that sending me customers doesn't take away from the humiliation and hurt he caused?

"Are you there?" the man on the other end of the line asks.

"Yes. My apologies," I say as I pull into my driveway. "I'm driving and was distracted. I'd love to help you with your needs. Here's how Wicked Ways works . . ." And then I explain the process of becoming a client, the website where he can fill out the beginning paperwork for the vetting process. I then go on to explain how payment is up front and that we provide an escort only for whatever event she's needed for, that companionship is our service, and that anything that happens after that has nothing to do with Wicked Ways.

His chuckle rumbles through the line in response. "Convenient."

"The truth," I correct, toeing that fine line between what could land me in jail and what might save my ass.

"When do I get to see the girls?"

"After you complete the information online."

"Seriously?"

"If someone referred you to us, then I assure you we're worth it." His sigh is drawn out. "Look, I know it's a lengthy process, but I like to keep a certain standard as well as a guarantee of my clients' confidentiality."

"Which I'm sure your clients appreciate."

"Most definitely."

Another nervous clearing of his throat. "Ryker had only positive things to say about you."

"Mmm." It's all I can muster as emotion clogs in my throat. "Please don't hesitate to call with questions."

"I won't."

"Your name so I can look for your information?" I ask, pretty convinced he won't follow through with it, the nerves in his voice more than telling.

"Noah."

"Thanks for calling, Noah. I'll be in touch once you've filled everything out."

When I hang up, I sit in the silence of my car for a bit and fight the sudden swell of sadness that overtakes me. With Ryker near, I felt more invincible than ever before. I knew I could earn money through Wicked Ways, pay off my debt, and then get custody of Lucy. The worry was always there, but the doubt I could pull it off diminished knowing he had my back.

And now? Now . . . I just feel vulnerable. I hate everything about the way it feels. So much so that once again I'm fighting my own resolve against picking up the phone and calling him.

With a resigned sigh, I get out of my car and head up the walk. I see the flowers and chocolates on my porch the minute I turn the corner. A groan falls out of my mouth, and a pang of grief hits me at the same time my cell rings yet again.

But it's not the person I think I was hoping to see on my caller ID. In fact, I don't know who it is at all.

With a sigh and a hunch that it's yet another referral from Ryker, I answer the call. "Wicked Ways, this is Vee. How may I help you?"

"Just how wicked are your ways?"

I jolt at the voice and then curl my lip in disgust. I should have expected he'd call, but with each passing day, I thought less about it happening.

Guess who was just proved wrong?

"What? Cat got your tongue?" He chuckles. "Oh, right. You didn't expect it to be me, did you? Burner cell phones, letting men cheat on their wives for years," he says in an announcer's voice.

"Go to hell." I end the call just as his laughter sounds off.

And then I hate myself for being weak. For not telling him to leave me alone or . . . *Or what, Vaughn? For not telling him you have a damning log of phone calls that makes absolutely zero sense to you? That's great. Threatening him with a paper someone else told you could bring him to his knees even though you don't have a fucking clue what that something is?*

I press my fingers to the bridge of my nose and close my eyes. Sure, I could threaten him with the pictures again, but would that do any good? Underage girls would probably get overlooked by other politicians and be buried by the news cycle within days.

"You don't have a leg to stand on, Vaughn," I murmur to myself as I shake my head, a little dazed and a lot tired, on the front porch and realize I have no position of power when it comes to Carter Preston.

None.

I jump when my cell rings again. The same number. The same asshole.

My same cowardice.

Each ring only adds fuel to the fire of my temper.

My spirits wilt when he's finally pushed to voice mail. Ten seconds pass before his number lights up my screen again like a stalker.

His audacity unnerves me. His refusal to give up even more so.

This is all because of Ryker.

Tears sting hotly with a mixture of anger and hurt as I shove my phone into my bag and stare at the flowers and chocolates in front of me.

Another attempt by Ryker to show me how sorry he is for putting everything I've worked for at risk. *And for breaking my heart.*

The rage I've been waiting to feel finally hits me. The emptiness sparks into a riot of temper as I snatch up the flowers and chocolates and push my way into the house.

I toss my purse on the floor and grab the closest box I can find. It's a file box that's filled with bills, and I dump them on the table without a thought to the disorganization it will cause and begin rushing around my house. Anything and everything that Ryker has ever sent me or Lucy I shove in the box. All the stuffed animals, the chocolates, the deflated balloons—even the flowers.

And only when I shove the lid on it and the wretched sound of the tape gun fills my house as I seal it shut do I allow myself to process everything. Allow myself the huge, heaving sobs I've resisted shedding. Allow myself to admit to the loneliness I feel without Ryker.

Seconds turn to minutes. Minutes turn into an hour. The salt of my tears dries on my cheeks. The hitching of my lungs begins to abate. The fogginess from the hurt begins to settle.

I've finally allowed myself to feel, to grieve, to be sorry for myself, and now I know I can move on. One weak blip on my radar does not define me. No. It makes me stronger.

I keep repeating those words through my shower and bedtime routine. I feel stronger. More resolved. Less wishy-washy. I know what I want, and it's not someone who hurts me like he has. It's not someone who would use me for his own personal gain.

It's only when I close my eyes and attempt to succumb to the exhaustion of the day and the moment that I ask myself the one question I'm choosing to ignore.

If you're done with Ryker, then why in the hell did you keep a few of the cards he's sent you, like letters from a lover you're longing for?

CHAPTER FIVE

Vaughn

"Whewee, girl, you look like hell in a handbasket." Archer waves a hand in front of his face as he crinkles up his nose before waltzing past me and into my house.

At least I have my blinds open today. Sunlight is the first step toward believing everything is going to be all right.

"Gee. Thanks. You're not looking too refreshed yourself," I say as I study him. His hair is matted to his forehead, his clothes may be expensive but look like they've been slept in, and his eyes have a lovely shade of bloodshot to them.

"Maybe not refreshed, but I'm sure as hell revived. I'm going on thirty-six hours without sleep, love. Give a man a break."

"Sounds like you already have." I raise my eyebrows in jest. "He that good?"

"You have no idea," he murmurs with a knowing smile as he walks around my place and judges me without judging. "I'd give you details, but, uh . . . I'm not one to kiss and tell."

My laugh is automatic. "You're such a liar. You're more the take-out-a-front-page-ad type. But please, spare me the details." I follow him as he picks up a picture of Lucy and then sets it down before moving on to the next item and doing the same. "Arch?"

"Hmm?" He doesn't look my way.

"What are you doing here?"

"Just visiting." He sets another tchotchke down.

"You never *just* visit."

"The last time I saw you was too short, and not enough was shared," he says, bringing my thoughts to the Hamptons, where Ryker and I ran into him at the lobster roll place. The pang is still as sharp as ever, thinking of him.

"Hmm." I eye him, crossing my arms over my chest and leaning against the wall, wondering what in the hell he's doing here. A house call from Archer Collins is a rarity these days. "You always seem to be busy nowadays."

"Pft." He waves a hand, always one to play down to me his ridiculously busy party-boy, playboy social life. "You're one to talk. Business good?" He picks up a photo of Lucy.

"Mmm-hmm."

"Lola's interesting."

"Lola?" I ask, and then I remember my most requested girl met him in a club not too long ago.

"Yeah." He looks back toward me and lifts his eyebrows before looking around the room again. "Comes on a little strong, but I can see why men like her . . . if, say, I were into women."

"Archer."

"Yes, dear?"

"You are not one to drop in just to say hi without having a motive or endgame or whatever the hell you want to call it. What gives?"

"Am I interrupting big plans or something?" he asks and then emits a dramatic huff before plopping onto my couch and resting his head against its back.

"Very big plans indeed," I lie, nowhere near in the mood to entertain him while he comes down from whatever his high was last night. Men. Alcohol. Ecstasy. Who knows?

His chuckle rumbles around the room. "Big plans? Like what? Watching paint dry? Paying your bills? Because we both know you're not shaving your legs or pussy for a man."

"How would you know if I'm shaving or not? And why would you even care?" I ask as Archer side-eyes me from the couch. "What?"

"*What?* That's all you're going to say is *what*, Vaughn?"

"I'm not in the mood."

"Good thing. I'm not in the mood either." He winks at me. "But you look like shit—bags under your eyes, way too much of your roots showing, and I bet you a hundred dollars that your lady bits look like a jungle. Add to that the rumors that flew like wildfire around the Hamptons after you left. What's it been? A week?" He lifts his eyebrows.

"More like two."

"Ah, the bags and hairy legs make sense now."

"Rumors?" I ask, ignoring his sarcasm.

"You left the party where you were the main guest. Of course everyone noticed. And then Ryker went looking for you and left abruptly when he couldn't find you." He pats the cushion next to him for me to sit down, but I don't budge. "So I'll ask your same question back at you: What gives?"

"Nothing," I lie. "I'm just not looking for something that serious, and . . . you know me—I'm not good with men."

"And I think you're full of shit. Successful. Handsome. Loaded. Good in bed—or so one can assume," he says when my eyes narrow at him. "Just like me."

"I'm so glad you're modest."

"No one in their right mind would pass up a good catch like Ryker Lockhart, so why are you?"

"I don't need a good catch. I need no one. Nothing."

"Your nose is growing, Pinocchio."

"Do you know him?" I ask rather assertively as I take a few steps toward Archer.

"Of him."

"And?" I prompt.

Archer studies me, those dark eyes seeing so much more than I want him to. "And I think you're nursing a heartbreak. I think you're scared and trying to justify a reason to keep your distance when a part of you is dying inside to figure out why."

I blink away the tears that come, because while I know he's partially right, he also has no idea what Ryker did to me. And I'm almost too ashamed to tell him.

How screwed up is that? Even while hating Ryker, I'm protecting him by not telling others what he did to me.

"Don't cry, love," Archer says as he rises and pulls me into a hug. I accept the comfort and the warmth, all the while realizing how much I miss this feeling. How much I grew accustomed to Ryker's strong arms and instant reassurance whenever I needed it.

He is bad for you, Vaughn. He makes you needy. Remember that.

"Hey?" Archer asks, stepping back and lifting my chin so I'm forced to look into his eyes.

"Hmm?"

"You need to get out."

"I'm fine. I just need some time to sort through shit."

Archer laughs. "Which is code for *I want to hide away in my bubble and be lost to the world.* Well, guess what? As one of your closest friends, I'm not going to allow that."

"I'm fine," I groan.

"Look, I have a thing—"

"Aha! I knew there was a reason you stopped by."

"I need a date for it."

"Then take Mr. Thirty-Six Hours with you."

"Ha. That's funny. His time is already up. Besides," he says and nudges me, "my dad will be there. You know I need to tame the flame when he's around."

47

I roll my eyes and snort, my first smile finally turning up one corner of my mouth. "No way am I going to be used as a pacifier between you and your father. Been there and done that before."

"It's not like that." He waves his hand in indifference. "It's a fund-raiser."

My sigh is exaggerated. The last thing I want to do is get dressed up for something that is fancy and formal, and if Archer is going, then that's exactly what this is. "Arch—"

"Come on." He reaches for my hand and swings it. "It'll be fun. We'll get you out of the house. We'll get those roots done. And we'll raise a shit ton of money for Lucy."

"What?" My head snaps in his direction.

His smile is wide and his expression smug. "Oh, did I forget to tell you? It's for DSAF," he says, so casually referring to the Down Syndrome Advocacy Foundation.

"Dammit, Archer."

"I knew that would get you," Archer says and smacks a loud kiss to the side of my cheek. "So . . . it's a date, then?"

CHAPTER SIX

Ryker

"Bianca . . . I get your frustration, but I can't force your husband's hand."

"Your reputation is at stake here, Mr. Lockhart."

My chuckle is anything but amused at the senator's wife threatening me. "I told you I'd get whatever you needed, but it's going to take time."

And this is why I don't take on women as clients. Because they are irrational and demanding and expect results in a day's time.

"Time?"

"Yes, time." I shift the phone from one ear to the other.

"You said you had audio of your conversation. I'd love to hear it."

I think of the recording on my phone. The conversation I can't even listen to myself.

"It'll never hold up in court," I lie, knowing it could damn well be used as a bargaining chip but not wanting to share it. It implicates Vaughn, even identifies her by name. What the fuck was I thinking? "Besides, he never offers to pay the escort for sex. That's what we need."

"Mmm." It's all she says, and for any guy that's the worst sound in the world. "I'd still like to hear it."

"No."

"No?" She laughs the word out in disbelief. The same disbelief I have over this entire bullshit situation right now.

I think of Carter's threat. Of how badly I want to say fuck it and his threats of outing Roxanne and me. It would make all of this so much easier. Give Bianca what she wants, file the papers for the goddamn divorce, and wash my hands of this dysfunctional couple. I couldn't give a shit less about me, but I know he wouldn't stop at just Rox. Hell no. He's bound and determined to fuck with Vaughn, too, and I can't bring any more on her than I already have.

Regardless of the fact that I've written her off. That I know we were a bad idea from the beginning.

See? That's called growth, Lockhart. The selfish man is still looking out for her, nonetheless.

"No?" she repeats. "I don't think that's the word you were wanting to say. I believe the words should have been *Yes, Bianca. Here's the recording for you to listen to.*"

I scrub a hand over my jaw. "Look, I'm digging. I'm trying to get you info, catch him in a trap, you name it. I attempted to do what you asked. To get your husband to commit to paying for sex . . . but this time around it didn't pan out. I assure you it will."

"How do you know it will?"

"Because I'm damn good at my job, or else you wouldn't have come seeking my representation." I force myself to unclench my fist on the desk. *"Right?"*

Tension fills the silence, followed by another one of her murmured *Mmm*s.

"This type of thing doesn't happen overnight, and it sure as hell doesn't happen when you tell your husband that I'm representing you." I rise from my desk and move about my office to abate my restlessness. "You just made my job ten times harder."

"I thought you said you were damn good at your job, Counselor."

Why do I feel like she's toying with me?

"This is supposed to be a mutually beneficial relationship here. I help you, and you in turn get out of your marriage as painlessly as possible and with you being awarded a majority of your assets."

"At least we can agree on that." She sighs. "Has your private investigator been able to find anything else on him that we can use?"

"If he's doing anything else shady, all I have are rumors. He's smart. There's no trail, no one willing to talk, nothing. Maybe it's just dirty politics that's sparked the gossip."

"And maybe where there's smoke, there's fire."

I nod, more than agreeing with her but keeping the comment to myself. "As I told you last time we spoke and the time before that, I still need your finance and asset breakdown."

"And as I told you, he manages the finances and bank accounts. It's not exactly as easy as you make it out to be."

"It's not as if he doesn't know you're going to file. Would you rather him beat you to the punch?" I ask, trying to figure out where the hesitancy is coming from. Is she getting cold feet? Did she suddenly fall back in love with Carter and now is uncertain if she wants to go through with it?

"It's the nomination, Ryker." There's a softness to her tone that's unexpected. "I may not exactly like him, but I don't want to take that off the table for him if it's in his future."

"If it's in his future or if it's in your future?"

Good ol' Bianca. Proving to me exactly why women and their motives are always in question. Just when I was starting to go soft, she showed me why I shouldn't be.

"That's a shitty accusation to make."

"Why? I need to know where your head is on this. Are we filing if he doesn't get the nomination and holding off if he does? Are you just holding on to see if you get the title and the posh move over to Number One Observatory Circle?" I ask, referring to the vice president's residence. "Is that why you seem to be playing a game with me?"

"I don't play games, Mr. Lockhart."

"Then what the hell is going on here? Am I just wasting my time?" Exasperation comes on the heels of my inability to get a good night's sleep as of late.

"Does it matter? I'm paying you for the time."

"Then I need your assets and finances. Without that, you're making it hard to know what it is we're going after unless you want to split it all fifty-fifty down the middle."

"I'm paying for you to do better than that."

Fuck this.

"Are we good here?" I ask, done with the conversation and whatever game it is she's playing me with that I can't quite put my finger on. I'm not going to force her to talk, and I sure as hell am not going to sit by and take her shit when she won't.

"Yes."

"Great."

I end the call, not caring if I just pissed her off. I can handle a woman who likes to play hardball—shit, look at Vaughn—but there's something here I can't quite place, and I'm hating being on the outside when I shouldn't be.

But fuck, isn't that where I am with Vaughn too? The outside?

It doesn't matter, Lockhart. Not the ache in your chest. Not the sore muscles that you pounded into oblivion at the gym. Not how fucked up your mind is.

None of it does.

This is why you've always used escorts.

But I did.

I used one, and look where that got me.

"Mr. Lockhart?" My intercom buzzes.

"Yes?"

"There's a big box of something that just arrived for you."

"Who's it from?"

"A Vaughn Sanders." She says the name like it's foreign to her, but I know damn well Bella is wondering just what the boss's "lover" has sent him.

"Send it in."

I pretend to be busy when the door opens. "Just put it on the chair. Thanks, Bella." I wait for her to leave before standing and going to it. It's a legal-size file box with my name and business address written in Vaughn's clean penmanship. I grab scissors and cut the tape around the lid to open the box.

The first item I see sitting on the top is a stuffed princess doll I had sent for Lucy.

"You're fucking kidding me," I murmur to my own ego as I shove the lid on and hold back the need to kick the damn box off the chair.

I told myself I didn't need Vaughn. That there's a reason I don't get close to anyone—too complicated, too much drama, too much feeling—but the sight of what I can assume is all of the shit I've sent her being returned only serves to reinforce that assumption.

Anger vibrates through me as I yank the box out of the chair and stand in the middle of my office, uncertain what I want to do with it. One part of me wants to shout for Bella to come and get it the hell out of here, while the other part of me wants to go through it piece by piece.

Fucking sap.

"What's the damn point?" I grumble as I walk over to the corner of my office and shove the box under the credenza. Turning to the city below—the taxicabs and people crowding the sidewalk—I shove my hands in my pockets and just watch the activity but don't really see it.

"Mr. Lockhart?"

"Yes, Bella," I say, shaking myself from my funk and walking over toward my desk and the settlement I need to work on.

"Your mother." I can hear the frustration and timidity in her voice.

"Fuck." I think my groan is quiet enough, but her response tells me it obviously isn't.

"Exactly."

"Send her in."

It takes only seconds before the click of my mother's heels and the resigned sigh that sounds like privilege run amok falls from her mouth and fills my office.

"Darling," she says as she hands me her purse and leans in for an air kiss, "you look troubled."

"Just stress." I give her a tight smile as she studies me and then figure I better remove the scowl or else she'll stay longer to nag the truth out of me. "To what do I owe this pleasure?"

"I was in the city. I had to meet with Baron," she says of her financial advisor, and I immediately wonder if she's having an affair.

"Mother," I warn.

"Relax." She waves a hand my way. "A few months ago I had him buy some stock that was supposed to soar. It didn't."

"That's what you get for listening to the high-society ladies who pretend to know what they're talking about."

"They did know. But some law or something was voted down, which in turn tanked its value."

"How much did you lose?"

"It's my play money, Ryk. Does it matter?" *Spoken like a woman who has never worked a day in her life and whose money was awarded through divorce and despair.* "We're making it up with a sell-off of that stock and a buy-in of another. It's just how the market goes."

"Mmm." The irony isn't lost on me that I just gave my mother the same response that Bianca infuriated me with.

"Then I went for lunch at that new place everyone is talking about"—she points out the window to the east as if I'm supposed to know the restaurant—"and afterward I told my companion I was going to head over here to see my only child."

Companion. Great. That's her warning that we are indeed a go for divorce number four? Five? Who can keep count?

"And is your companion waiting for you?" I ask, trying to feel out what the hell she's doing and at the same time not really caring.

"No, but you can meet him at the function tomorrow if you'd like to."

"He can't escort you when you're still married—wait." I glance over to my calendar on my desk, the blank I'm drawing not good. "What function?"

She laughs as it dawns on me. "You forgot?"

"No. I didn't forget." *Shit.* I have to write a speech. I have to . . . this is fucked. "Are you crazy?"

"Don't change the subject. You forgot about the event, didn't you?"

"I've got a lot on my plate at the moment. Do you want to explain to me how you plan on going with your 'companion' while currently being married?"

"Relax. I'm not going to the event, but he'll be there." She smiles sweetly.

Well, at least there's that.

"Tell me about Vaughn. You'll be taking her as your date, I assume."

Talk about coming out of left field. I glance over to the corner of my office where the box sits. "Never assume when it comes to me. You know better than that."

She gives a dramatic huff. "So she's not going to be your date, then?"

"You won't be there, so I don't see why it matters."

"Oh, you really do like her, don't you?" she asks, making me grit my teeth in reaction. "Tell me all about her." She crosses her arms over her chest, letting me know she wants all the details. Too bad I'm not in the mood to give them.

"She's not from your circles."

"So . . ."

"There's nothing to tell."

Her laugh is disbelieving. "I know you better than that, Ryk. She was lovely when I met her at your party. She's got grit—"

"You don't like grit."

"Personally, no . . . but I think you need it."

"Why's that?" I ask, more to humor her than anything.

She moves toward the windows to admire the view and speaks with her back to me. "Because everything is too damn easy for you. Work. Women. Success."

"You obviously haven't been around lately, have you? Nothing seems easy these days." It's a rare act of contrition for me—letting my mom in to see what is going on in my life—but for some reason, I almost want to right now.

"That bad, huh?" she asks and turns to look at me as I just shrug in response. "Want to talk?"

I opened the door and am now hesitating to walk through it. "I don't know. It doesn't really matter."

Vaughn fills my mind. The hurt in her eyes. The mistrust in her voice. The defeat in her posture.

"What happened?"

"I'm just keeping my distance for a bit."

"Ah."

"What is that supposed to mean?"

"It means you got scared."

"No. That's not it," I refute. "I just . . . it's a long story."

"I have all day." She takes a seat before me and waits for a few minutes, eyes the same color as mine studying me. When I don't speak, she continues without prompting. "Women want to be loved, you know."

Oh, Jesus. Relationship advice from my mother. That's like asking for celibacy tips from a prostitute.

"Thanks, Mom. I got it handled," I lie.

"You're not hearing me, Ryker." She leans forward and squeezes my hand in a motherly way that is so unlike her. "Women like to be loved.

Not fixed. Not coddled. They like to be treated like they can find the stud in the wall but know that they have someone who will patch the hole they make in the drywall without a word if they miss it the first time round."

"Are you feeling okay?" I tease.

"No. Listen. I may be screwed up. I may be addicted to the high of finding love, then run from its fallout. But, darling . . . when you find a woman who lets you patch the drywall over the mistakes she's made . . . you know she's the right one."

"Mom . . ." I groan and think of all the damn drywall patches there must be in her house, then.

"It's a fact."

I just stare at her for a beat until I realize she's dead serious. "Be careful, *Vivian*, this might be the most motherly thing you've ever said to me."

And regardless of everything else she says after that, it's her words about finding studs and holes in drywall that stick in my head as I sit in my office late into the night writing a speech I don't want to write for an event I was supposed to ask Vaughn to be my date for. The city comes to life and then slowly begins to go to bed, and yet it's so much easier to be here at my desk, to be occupied, to be with a drink in hand—than to wander aimlessly around my penthouse. *Alone.*

To be tempted to call her again when I've promised myself I need to step the fuck away for my own sanity.

But that's the tricky part in all of this. The more I see her, the more I lose everything about myself, while not seeing her makes me feel just as fucking crazy. Both are bad. But only one is worth it.

Plain and simple, it's Vaughn.

Doesn't it seem like everything these days comes back to her in one way or another?

Her and the goddamn drywall patches I can't shake from my mind.

CHAPTER SEVEN

Vaughn

This is the last place I want to be right now.

"Smile. This is called socialization, Vaughn. It's good for the mind and spirit."

"So is silence and solitude," I reply between lips forced into a smile as he tightens his fingers on the inside of my arm his is looped through.

"My, my, my," he murmurs beneath his breath as we walk farther into the ballroom. People mill about. Diamonds glisten. The tuxedos have black bow ties. The dresses are designer and glitzy. "There are hunks galore. What a welcome surprise."

"Only you would notice."

"That's such crap. You know you noticed." He nudges my arm. "I'm going to have to fight you for them, Vee."

"All yours. Men are the last thing on my mind."

He laughs and shakes his head before stopping to look at me. "You had a great day with Lucy. You said yourself that you've signed on a shit ton of new clients as of late. What do you have to lose? Besides, there's nothing like a meaningless lay to take your mind off *him*."

Sex has always been that way—meaningless—*until Ryker.*

"Arch . . ." His name drifts off when I catch the sudden startled expression on his face as he looks over my shoulder.

Seriously?

"What ex of yours is here that we're going to have to avoid the rest of the night?" I huff out in irritation, less than thrilled at the prospect of holding myself together while having to deal with Archer's scorned lovers.

"You'll have to excuse me," he says without anything else before striding off in the opposite direction.

I turn around, half expecting to see a man bearing down on me after Archer has left him high and dry.

Who the hell is . . . ? But my thought fades and then stutters—just like my heart does. Because as much as I convinced myself that I was over Ryker Lockhart, the minute I lock eyes with him, that all fades away.

Everything but the hurt.

And the hurt laced with heartache is akin to chocolate laced with arsenic. It tastes so good even when you know it's going to kill you in the end.

Goddammit, Archer. You set me up.

My mind should be telling my feet to move, but it doesn't. Instead, it wants to look longer at the car wreck it's about to be a willing participant in. *Willing?* I think *negligent* seems more apt.

"Vaughn." His voice makes my belly flip and my chest ache, and just being so near what used to be a comfort to me is so very hard.

He steps before me, and the hurt in his gaze that I don't want to acknowledge is present, but just as quickly as I see it, he shoves it down.

Someone passes by and murmurs a greeting to Ryker. He just nods and smiles but never looks their way. For some reason, it makes me so very cognizant of where we are and who could be watching.

With a swallow over the lump in my throat, I finally acknowledge him. "Mr. Lockhart."

Another glance of hurt through his eyes at my complete professionalism. "It's good to see you," he says softly. "You look gorgeous as always."

"It hurts to see you."

"Vaughn." My name again—part plea, part apology, and 100 percent regret. He reaches out to touch me, and I take a step back.

"Not here. Not now."

"Then when?" He asks the loaded question I'm not willing to answer. He keeps his voice low, but his eyes flit around the room to make sure no one is listening.

At least I assume that's what he's doing.

"It's just better this way."

"Better? For whom? You look as miserable as I feel."

"Already lying, I see." He's so handsome, so effortless, it hurts to look at him.

His exasperated sigh is audible. "Anyone who looks your way will see only how stunningly gorgeous you are, but I know the real you. I can tell you're not sleeping well. I can see how you feel about me in your eyes."

"Then stop looking."

"Maybe if you'd stop being so stubborn, we could—"

"We could what? Pick up where we left off? I find that a hard pill to swallow, Mr. Lockhart."

He shakes his head ever so slightly and just stares at me for the longest of moments. Each of us tries to decide what we want out of this conversation and if it's possible to achieve it in the midst of a room full of people.

I don't know the answer to that question. I thought I did . . . but seeing him here, having him near, I hate that my need to forgive him despite the things he did is gaining strength.

"I miss you." His voice almost breaks, and so does my resolve at the sound of it.

"That doesn't fix things."

"Then what does?"

"I don't know." It's the most honest thing I've said, and I wish I knew the answer myself.

"Do you know anything about patching drywall?" he asks, throwing me so off kilter that a surprised laugh falls from my lips.

"What . . . ?" And before I can even ask what he means, the woman who walks up to him and slides a hand around his biceps in a clear stake of ownership has the question dying on my tongue.

And snapping closed the damn lock around my heart.

"Excuse us." She smiles at me briefly before turning her attention solely to Ryker. "You have some people who want to meet you, Ryk."

She's the complete antithesis of me. Tanned skin, jet-black hair in a pixie cut that perfectly accents her cheekbones, and green eyes framed with long lashes. Where I'm average in height, she's almost as tall as Ryker in her heels.

His jaw may clench and his eyes may still burn into mine, but Ryker makes no attempt to tell her he's currently occupied or to shake her hand off him.

"I can see you're busy," I say before turning on my heel and walking in the opposite direction with tears burning in my eyes and his murmured lies repeating in my ears.

My chest burns, and I feel like I stumble aimlessly until I find a set of doors that lead to an outside terrace. It's done in all stone with ivy climbing up the walls and a view of the city beyond, but all I can think of when the fresh air hits my lungs is that I can finally breathe.

With my hands braced on the railing in front of me, I close my eyes for a beat to collect myself.

And of course, when I do and finally look up, Ryker is standing beside me.

"Stop referring clients to me." I say the words in a huff, and they're nowhere near the things I want to say, but they fall out nonetheless.

Good, Vaughn. Fricking perfect.

"Okay." He draws the word out and just stares at me with expectation in his stance and a plethora of emotions in his eyes.

"I don't need your pity, and I sure as hell don't want to owe you anything because you're referring people my way. It might assuage your own guilt for doing what you did to me, but it doesn't fix a single thing on my end."

"I wasn't aware that's what I was doing."

"Pretty damn obvious to me. Fifteen new clients calling out of the blue? All given my number by you? Really?"

"Giving business referrals to clients of mine is just that, a referral. It's part of the reason you took me on in the first place. I won't apologize for that."

"Good." I snap the word out, knowing I'm throwing the whole kitchen sink at him and that I just agreed with him when seconds before I was arguing the opposing side of it.

"Good," he says, and I detest the amusement that laces his voice and ghosts in the curve of his smile.

I hate that I almost smile in response, that he can come out here and think he can charm me with his patience so that I forget what he did and how quickly he found another to take my place.

"You sure move on fast."

He grits his teeth, and I can see him fighting back the urge to shake some sense into me. "She's the president of the charity's daughter."

"Even better."

"And a close family friend."

"Oh, someone of the right social caliber, then. I'm sure you'll be happy." I have so many smart-ass things I could reply with, but I refrain because none of them will do a damn thing to make me feel any better.

"I missed you."

"Couldn't have missed me too much. You didn't chase after me." The last sentence is out before I can catch it, my own mind still hung up on five minutes ago—hell, on what happened in the Hamptons—when he did chase. When he did try to bang down my door only to be ignored. When he did come back to my house after that to speak to me. And of course, he did chase just now when I walked away.

But I don't correct myself. Because even though he came to find me, even though he's standing before me with hurt in his eyes, I'm more hurt. Instead, I just stand there and stare at him with my hands gripping my clutch while his singular look squeezes my heart.

"I didn't chase?" He shakes his head. "Was this a test? Were you trying to see if I'd run after you so you'd believe I cared for you?"

Yes. No. I don't know.

"Because I have chased you, Vaughn. I've chased when I'm a man who never chases, and you know what? Every time I do, you say no in some way or another. Did I fuck up? Yes. So it seems to me it doesn't matter what I say or do. You're going to hold it against me and ruin whatever it was we were working on defining between us."

I've fallen in love with you, Vaughn.

His words from the other night repeat in my head, and I want to shut them out. They run a loop as he stares at me with puppy-dog eyes, and I wonder how the hell I'm supposed to know what to do next. Am I not forgiving him when I should be? Am I being too stubborn, someone others would dub a stupid female, like the ones I sometimes yell at in my old black-and-white movies? Or am I right in my thoughts and deserve more than this? More than him?

"What is it you want from me, Ryker?"

"*You.*"

"You did have me. My heart. My trust. *Me.*" I hold my hands out to my sides. "I think you've had a fair enough chance."

I turn to walk away—back into the party because noise is better—but his hand is on my elbow.

"I already told you what happened. I can explain more if—"

"Empty explanations mean nothing. The damage was done the minute you thought it was okay to do it in the first place."

"Christ, I fucked up." He pounds a fist on the railing.

"Yeah. You used me."

"You're right. I did. I had a split second to make a decision about how to get that bastard to confess what he had on you. The choice was boys-will-be-boys versus making demands I knew he'd balk at. *I chose the first.* It was wrong. I fucked up in the worst imaginable way by doing so. I can't change what I did, and I know I'd do it again in a heartbeat if I knew for a fact I could keep you safe. That I could get him to tell me whatever it is he has on you so you never had to worry about it again. So keep raking me over the fucking coals if it makes you feel better, Vaughn. Keep making me pay whatever price it is you feel I need to pay. Or just keep pushing me away because it's easier to do that than to realize that you and I are fucking incredible together. Your choice."

I stare at him—his words hit to the very core of everything I feel, and yet nowhere in there did he mention how his actions were beneficial to his client. Nowhere in there did he say he put me in more jeopardy than I already was. Nowhere did he explain how offering my body to the senator was going to win him whatever erroneous blackmail items he supposedly had on me.

The words *poor baby* ghost through my mind but don't pass over my lips, because this, him, us, is just all too much. It hurts to look at him. To still want him. To still love him.

To finally want something I can't have.

To maybe believe him.

"Excuse me." I avert my eyes. "Archer must be looking for me."

I escape without saying more, uncertain how I'm supposed to feel and unwilling to forgive.

And with my heart a lot worse for the wear.

CHAPTER EIGHT

Vaughn

"Stop staring at him." The warmth of Archer's voice hits my ears, and I know he's right, but I argue with him anyway.

"I'm not watching anybody."

"Right. Your neck is just permanently angled twenty degrees to the right where one Ryker Lockhart happens to be seated." He takes a sip of the merlot in his hand and emits a low hum in appreciation. "Does he ever *not* look good?"

"You're not helping here," I mutter under my breath as some of the others assigned to our ten-person table glance our way, obviously irritated that we're talking when the emcee is doing her opening spiel.

"Is he good in bed? I bet you he's fabulous. All rough and demanding and . . . *durable*."

"Durable?" I choke out and try not to spray my sip of red wine all over the expensive white linen tablecloth.

"Made you laugh, didn't I?"

I turn to look at him for the first time since the program started and press a soft kiss to his cheek. "Yes, you did. Thank you for being so understanding and supportive and . . . my friend."

"I couldn't let you be the hot mess you were about to become when you came back from the balcony." He pats my leg beneath the table. "I saved you just in the nick of time."

And he did. He whisked me to the hallway, grabbed both of my hands in his, and told me that the best way to show Ryker he doesn't matter is to not give him the time of day.

"Anything that's worth fighting for hurts sometimes, Vaughn."

I narrow my brows. "Who said he's worth fighting for?"

"You don't have to. It's written all over your face."

We're interrupted as the first course is served, and just in time, because I was about to fight Archer to the death to prove there was nothing written on my face.

Then why do I keep looking his way? Why do I keep making mental arguments in my head for when Archer brings the topic back up?

Small talk ensues with those around us who are trying to figure out if Archer and I are a couple or not. But I'd be lying if I said my eyes didn't wander to Ryker's table more often than not.

Not just to stare at Ryker, though, but also to glare daggers at his date.

"Who is she?" I murmur without mentioning who I'm referring to.

"Nobody who matters."

I gotta love a friend who is supportive and catty with me. But when I look from him back over to Ryker, *Nobody* is looking right at me. A smile slides onto her more than full lips, and she arches her brow at me as if she's saying, *Your loss*, before running a hand up his biceps and leaning in to whisper in his ear.

"I need some air," I murmur and scoot back despite Archer's protest that the main course is coming soon.

My heels click down the hallway to the beat of my own chastisements.

This isn't you, Vaughn.

Jealousy does not suit you.

He's bad for you. Stop needing him.

Just as I reach the ladies' lounge area, I yelp as a hand closes around my shoulder and pushes me past it into a small alcove off the hallway.

Ryker's lips are on mine the minute my back hits the wall. I shove against his chest to no avail until he cuffs both my wrists with his hands and just takes everything he wants from me with his lips.

It's bruising and carnal and everything I hate about him and everything I've craved from him, to feel anything other than the pain.

And just as soon as he starts it, he tears his lips from mine.

"You son of a bitch," I sneer at him.

"Never disputed it—"

"You have no right—"

"Yes I do. You're mine, Vaughn. You have been since that first meeting. So you can play this game however the hell you want to play it. You can push me away. You can slap me across the face if you want. You can block my numbers from your cell. But there is nothing—*nothing*—that will make you forget what my kiss tastes like. What my lips feel like. How *I* make you feel. So try if you want . . . but I told you from the get-go, I don't play games, and I won't take no for an answer."

His lips brand mine again with a kiss laced with equal parts lust and spite. This time when the kiss ends, he leans back, and his eyes full of questions lock on mine.

The muscle in his jaw ticks as he waits for me to speak, to tell him I accept his apology and that we can move forward. Call me stupid or obstinate or wishy-washy, but I know my worth, and it's a hell of a lot more than accepting how he treated me.

"So what's it going to be, Vaughn?" He waits for a beat, and he hisses out in frustration when I don't respond at his prompting. When I don't let my body and heart win the war they're fighting against my head. "Goddamn stubborn woman," he mutters before striding off in the same direction he came from.

I lean my head back against the wall in a sad attempt to let my racing pulse decelerate and my mind tell my heart to forget him.

Funny thing is, I'm lying to both of them.

Ryker Lockhart is right. He's not a man who's easily forgotten.

"When I said get laid, I didn't mean by him," Archer mutters beneath his breath when I finally return to my seat.

My cheeks blush automatically. "We didn't. I didn't—I—"

"Well you're all flustered, and he waltzed in here with that alpha-male, take-no-prisoners look on his face, so I just assumed there was some hot bathroom-counter sex going on somewhere in the lobby—"

"No." The single word shuts Archer down, but when I glance toward Ryker's table, he's not there. "He's an asshole."

One whose kiss I can still taste.

"Uh-huh."

"Shh," the lady at the opposite side of the table asserts just as the room erupts in applause. I mouth that I'm sorry and then look back to Archer, who has one eyebrow raised.

"I spent hours last night writing and perfecting a speech about why you should all donate generously to this charity." My head whips to look toward the front of the room when I hear Ryker's voice carrying through the microphone. Smooth as silk but with that little bit of grit that affects me, no matter how hard I try to ignore it. "But being here, walking up to the podium, my words from yesterday don't seem to fit now."

As he stands behind the lectern, his smile is engaging and he commands everyone's presence in the room.

"I didn't know. I promise." Archer reiterates the same thing he's said to me several times tonight, but I no longer think I believe him. It's the millionaires' club up in here, and I'm definitely the penny princess who doesn't belong.

"I had planned to talk about obligation and duty. How those of us who are more fortunate should give more and complain less. Of course, I had some jokes peppered in there to help ease the checkbooks out of your purses and pockets as well . . . but then I realized that my speech doesn't do anything to talk about the incredible people who have been touched by this syndrome in one way or another. So . . ." Ryker takes the speech in his hand and makes a show of tearing it in half, garnering a chuckle from the crowd.

"He looks good in a tux," Archer says, and I just roll my eyes.

"All men look good in one," I argue.

"Nuh-uh." He says something else following that, but my attention is already focused back on Ryker. On his quick wit and easy charm. On the square of his shoulders. On how every part of me remains attuned to him somehow, even when I don't want to be.

"I met a little girl a few weeks back," he begins, and before he says another word, my heart lurches in my throat, because somehow I know where he's going with this. He looks down for a beat as if he's remembering something and chuckles softly. "She'd argue that she's not little, but comparative to my years, we can all agree that eight can be considered *little*. We'll call her Elle. This Elle . . . she has a never-ending smile, a zest for going fast, for accomplishing things others have said she couldn't do. She's funny and intelligent and kind and gives the best hugs out of anyone I've ever met. Many people would look at her and judge her. They'd think her distinct features depict a syndrome that holds her back, when what they really should be doing is seeing those gorgeous bright spots in her eyes. What they would remember about meeting her is how they couldn't help but smile when she laughs and how after seeing her determination, knowing she's capable of anything she puts her mind to."

I hate that my heart swells in my chest, while at the same time I want to get mad at him for loving Lucy. But how can I blame him? How can I use my anger and my hurt and hold it against him for doing good?

"This girl"—he shakes his head—"is incredible. And just as incredible as Elle is the woman who takes care of her. The loving Elle part is something anyone who meets her would do, but the patience and dedication and drive to give her the very best is unmeasured by anything I've ever seen. But this woman . . . she works so hard, she worries too much about where the money to provide Elle with the very best will come from next, and she loves so hard that some nights I know she goes to sleep with tears in her eyes and a heart full of worry."

His words hit my ears and dive into my soul before wrapping their raw and real truth around my heart. I don't want to acknowledge that I've let Ryker see this side of me. That I've lowered my walls for him like I have no one else. That he's seen the ups and the downs, despite how much I've tried to hide them, when it comes to Lucy and has inferred how I feel some nights.

"I know all this because I've seen it all firsthand. It's the thing you pretend you don't see when you're walking down the street with your head down, your latest problem at work occupying your mind, and the next appointment you're already late for hurrying your step. What you're missing seeing is the mom struggling because, at that moment, the city's too loud for her child, or the meltdown going on because someone like Elle wants to ride her bike with the rainbow streamers longer. Ignoring them is easier to do than wondering why she's a little bit different than everyone else."

"He's talking about Lucy, isn't he?" Archer whispers and then squeezes my hand atop the table as the tears well in my eyes.

I don't nod, and I don't respond, because I can't. My eyes are fixed on Ryker, and my heart is trying to start beating again after he cracked and bruised every part of it.

Why do I suddenly want him to put it back together again?

"In the past—before Elle—I would have walked past the family. Maybe the next time I was looking for a place to donate to, I'd remember the mom struggling. I'd think how she might need some help and throw money toward her cause every once in a while. It would allow me to say, *I'm charitable*—to get the tax write-off—but it's not like I really knew anyone who was affected by it." He holds his hand up. "It was Elle's caretaker who called me on the carpet about that. How most of us who can pay five thousand a plate to be here have no problem writing checks, but we never really take the time to see the good our money provides. Now don't get me wrong—I'm asking you to write your checks tonight and transfer your funds. I'd be a horrible keynote speaker if I said otherwise . . . but *Elle changed me*."

He may shrug nonchalantly, but when he looks up from the podium, his eyes lock with mine across the distance. The moment is brief, but his look says so much more than his words. *You changed me too.*

That's what I see in them.

That's what I hear in the words he's not speaking.

If I thought my emotions had been churning nonstop from everything with Ryker, they are like a tsunami crashing through me now.

"Shh. Don't tell anyone else that the hard-ass man I am can also be a little soft too." A muted chuckle filters through the audience. "So please, write your checks. Transfer those funds. But don't forget to learn about the incredible things this organization has done and is doing for those who have Down syndrome and their families supporting them. This charity helps when no one else will. They provide support when others turn their back. They give assistance to those who can't afford the specialists for their children. These kids aren't suffering with this syndrome. They are thriving. They are laughing. They are living and smashing the preconceived notions that people have of them . . . and I, for one, am more than willing to support this organization that is helping them do that."

The room erupts into thunderous applause. People stand unexpectedly as I stay seated, a little stunned and a lot confused.

And then I stand, too, but for completely different reasons than everyone else.

I need to get out of here.

I can't breathe with all of this—all of him—so close and so real and so raw and so overwhelming.

"I have to go," I say to Archer. I'm not even sure if he heard me, but I hurry from the ballroom and the crowd and their praise . . . *and from Ryker.*

His words have touched me in a way I could never have imagined. Words that normally I would be skeptical of. I'd pick them apart and force myself to see that he's just using words—one after another—to trick me into forgiving him and taking him back.

But maybe that's the problem.

Maybe I'm so used to people trying to be something they're not—while I focus so much on trying to uncover the real person beneath the facade—that I've lost faith that some people are just who they seem to be. Good. Sincere. Real. So instead of seeing the truth, I'm busy looking for their deceit, even when it isn't there.

Ryker's changed me, and that's a tough pill to swallow.

He's made me want to see the good in him, even when I've already seen the bad.

And that . . . that's a truth I'm not sure I'm ready for just yet.

I leave the ballroom and head toward Times Square—escaping into the night from Ryker once again, like Cinderella from her prince.

It takes me a few minutes and several blocks to catch my breath and wrap my head around everything.

Me: Thanks for asking me to go tonight, Arch. I had a good time, but I just needed some time and space.

Archer: The girl who wanders to find herself.

Me: You know me better than most.

Archer: Lucky for you, lol. You needed to see him. Your reaction tells me he's definitely worth fighting for. Whatever he did must have been bad. Just remember that it takes a strong person to apologize, but it takes an even stronger person to show forgiveness. Text me when you get home so I know you're safe.

Me: K.

Staring at my phone for a few minutes, I let Archer's words hit me about apologies and forgiveness. And I think of everything Ryker said to me tonight. Everything he said during his speech. The genuine sincerity in it. I can hear it all now, even though at the time he said it I couldn't.

I don't know how much time passes, but I wander the streets like I used to do when I first moved to the city. The only difference is I'm in my heels and evening gown instead of my threadbare hand-me-downs.

Just like back then, I can pretend I have no final destination, that I'm just trying to clear my head and figure out what to do next . . . but deep down I already know.

When I was younger, I was going to head back home and try to help my sister.

This time, though . . . maybe I'm finally going to try to help myself.

CHAPTER NINE

Ryker

"Where the fuck are you, Vaughn?" I mutter from the back seat of the car. The night isn't getting any shorter, and this whiskey I keep refilling my glass with is definitely not making me feel any better.

But the car parked in her driveway sure as fuck isn't hers. Every part of me hopes that it's Archer's, but even I know better than to tell myself that lie. There's no way the privileged party boy drives a grocery getter like that.

Not a one.

So who the fuck is here with her?

"Sir?"

I look into the rearview mirror and meet Al's gaze. "I don't fucking know," I mutter and climb out of the car without another word. Of course my driver thinks I'm fucking crazy. Why shouldn't he? He's been with me for over five years, and not once has he ever seen me sit outside a woman's house and stare like a lovesick asshole without a chance in hell.

The woman is making me crazy.

Absolutely fucking insane.

I don't hesitate, though, when I knock on the door, because deep down I know who is going to answer, and maybe I'm looking for a fight.

She ran out on me. *Again.* She ran out after hearing me say things I never expected to speak but that came out nonetheless. First in the hallway with her and then in my speech.

But when I call I still go straight to voice mail, so I'll assume my number is still blocked on her cell. I'm not spending another goddamn night like this.

I refuse.

The lock jiggles behind the door, and Joey looks startled when he opens it to see me standing there.

"She's not here," he whispers.

"No?"

He lifts his eyebrows as I study the fuck out of him to see if he's lying, and he surprises me when he steps outside and shuts the door behind him. "Lucy's asleep," he explains.

"She's not here?" I ask again.

"Lucy? Yeah, she's here. Didn't I just say she's asleep?"

Sarcastic asshole.

"Don't be a dick."

"She deserves better than you, you know?" He crosses his arms over his chest, and the little *fuck you* smile on his lips has me clenching my fists.

"Are we talking about Lucy here or Vaughn? Because it seems you're trying to be the gatekeeper for both."

"Vaughn deserves better," he repeats.

"You're right. She does," I say, enjoying his little sputter in response. "But it's impossible to fight a battle you never saw coming. Now, you mind telling me where Vaughn is?"

"It's none of your business."

My chuckle carries through the night. "That's where you're wrong, but I'll let it slide." I take a step forward. "She come home after the gala?"

I see the *no* in his eyes before he repeats his line. "Not your business."

"If she had, you wouldn't still be here . . . so I'll take that as my answer." I take a step back.

"Did you ever think maybe she is home and she asked me to stay because she enjoys the company of someone who doesn't treat her like their plaything?"

"So you're dating, then?" I ask to call his bluff. "Isn't that grounds for termination at your job?"

Joey's instant stammering over what to say next is answer enough. She's not home, and he thinks he has the balls to stand up to me, but when the rubber meets the road, he's a pussy.

"Thanks, man." I pat him on the shoulder a little harder than necessary. "I appreciate the help, though."

And when I stride back down the walk toward the car with him staring at my back, I'm not any fucking better off than when I got here.

She's not here.

I am.

Once again, we're in two different places, seemingly wanting two different things.

I'm beginning to think fate has it out for us.

Either that or I'm fighting an uphill battle.

Thank fuck I know a thing or two about fighting.

"Where to?" Al asks when I climb back into the car and slam the door.

"Hell if I know," I mutter and lift the glass to my lips. "Home, I guess."

The night flies by outside. The lights of the city. The red of the stoplights. The darkness as we cross the bridge. The brightness as we enter downtown and then uptown.

Every woman I see out and about, I swear could be Vaughn.

But nothing eases in my chest during the drive.

Not the ache. Not the worry. Not the want.

I blow out a resigned breath when we pull up to the curb of my building. A small part of me hoped she'd be sitting here in the lobby. Nothing. It's empty. My only companion is the hum of the elevator car as I ride to my floor.

The door dings, then slides open.

At the end of the hallway of sorts is someone sitting on the floor with her knees to her chest.

Vaughn.

This time it really is her.

Her thick lashes flutter and look up so that those aqua-colored eyes of hers meet mine across the distance. Emotions war through them—confusion, hurt, forgiveness—each one trying to win its place, and hell if I'm not rooting for forgiveness to win.

Followed a close goddamn second by lust.

I stop in my tracks as she rises to her feet. It takes everything I have to stop when all I want to do is pull her against me and take the rest of what I started earlier tonight.

But she came to me.

She's waiting for me.

While it feels like a victory, I know with Vaughn there's always so much more than meets the eye, so I'll let her take this on her terms.

I'm the one who fucked up.

I'm the one who risked this all.

"Long night, huh?" It's all I say.

CHAPTER TEN
Vaughn

"I keep asking myself how I can be with a man who so blatantly disrespected me. How can I crave your touch? How can I look at you and hate you for what you did and still want you?"

Ryker stands in the hallway to his penthouse—tie loose and draped around his collar, shirt unbuttoned at his neck, cuffs undone—and just stares at me. His eyes are dark and stoic, his lips unmoving as he remains silent.

"Everything you said tonight was perfect, Ryker. Everything. It fit the cause. It will raise money. It . . ." I shrug, unsure how to phrase what it is I want to say.

"I didn't say it to win you back." His voice is full of gravel when he speaks, its deep tone resonating off the walls and echoing throughout me when I don't want it to. "I said it because it was true."

"Why?" It's one word, one question, and it could mean so many things. I'm curious which one thing he'll think it's referring to.

"There's no right answer to that question. I was wrong, Vaughn. The senator wanted to talk, he said he had some dirt on you, and I walked easily into whatever game he was playing. No excuses. No bullshit." He takes a step toward me but doesn't reach out to touch. "I'm a man so used to thinking only about myself. The next client. The next high I can get in court. The next person I can turn to my advantage. It's not a flattering fact, but it's the truth."

"We all have unflattering facts."

"Yeah, but . . ." There's an unexpected uncertainty in Ryker right now. A vulnerability I'm not used to seeing. That softer side he spoke about earlier. "I'm not good at this, Vaughn—the baring my soul shit. It's not me."

"No one asked you to."

His laugh is soft and self-deprecating and punctuated by a subtle shake of his head. "I know you didn't ask me to, but if I don't tell you . . . I risk losing you. The past few weeks have been total shit, so I'd prefer not to repeat it."

I smile. It's slight and soft, but it feels good to know this has affected him too.

He takes another step forward, as if each step of his and my lack of retreating is his way to ask if he can continue.

"You got to me, Vaughn. You got to me when I told myself I didn't believe in relationships or women or the idea of wanting more. We may have fought each other most of the way to this point, but hell if you haven't reached into my chest and grabbed hold of my cold heart."

"It's not that cold." I make the first move and reach out and rest my hand over his heart. He gazes down at it, almost as if he's surprised. When he looks back up, there's a genuine smile on his lips that would melt my own heart if his words tonight and his actions right now hadn't already done just that.

"I'm not going to ask you for your forgiveness again, Vaughn. I'm just hoping in time you'll be able to give it to me and that maybe . . . maybe we can move on from here and see wherever this takes us."

He reaches out and cups the side of my cheek. It takes everything I have not to close my eyes and turn into it. Not to kiss his palm. Not to kiss him.

"You asked how you can want to be with me when I blatantly disrespected you. I did a lot more than just that. I hurt you. I used you. I—"

"You better watch out, Ryker. If you keep pointing out the bad, I might not want to proceed with the good," I tease.

"I don't know the answer to your question. What I do know is that there's something about us that works. It's your stubbornness and my persistence. It's your drive and my determination. It's us both allowing each other to be who we are without shame or trying to change one another. We just work—defined or not."

I give in to the temptation. I shut out the warring thoughts in my mind that I forced myself to leave outside when I walked in here to wait for him. I rise on my tiptoes, lean in, and brush my lips ever so softly against his.

And when I lower myself off my toes, I keep my eyes closed as Ryker presses his lips to my forehead. We just stand here like this outside his front door, my hand still resting atop his heart.

"I was wrong." His lips move against my forehead, the heat of his breath warming my scalp. "There's a reason why I did what I did. It's not a good one. It doesn't validate or justify, and none of these words will take away the hurt I caused. I was—"

I break off his words with another kiss. This time it's more than tender. I slip my tongue between his lips and slide my hands up the side of his neck so I can thread my fingers through his hair, and I just take.

What I want.

What is mine.

What I'm suddenly afraid to lose.

The kiss is loaded with greed and angst and heartbreak and apology.

"Vaughn," he murmurs against my lips as he tries to speak. "I need to explain—"

"Later. You can explain later. Right now, I need you, Ryker," I say and allow myself to give in to everything I've been resisting. *I need you.*

And those three words are almost as powerful as the other three words I feel about him but haven't yet allowed myself to voice. The ones that were front and center and in neon lights when he stepped off the elevator tonight.

I know he can see the tears welling in my eyes when he leans back and frames my face with his hands. The simple gesture makes me feel so protected in that Cinderella princess way, and for the first time, I don't care that it's silly. I've never had this feeling before, so who says I can't enjoy every trite, cliché, ridiculous moment of admitting I'm falling in love?

There's so much apology in his eyes that one doesn't need to be given or accepted right now. I can figure that out later. You can love someone without wholly forgiving them.

"God, I missed you." He groans before kissing me for the first time.

It starts off slow. A touch of our lips. Then another. Each time the kiss a little longer, the need growing a little more urgent, until the dam breaks.

We crash together in a torrent of need right here in the hallway. Our lips and hands and tongues and bodies reconnect as if it's been years since we've been together rather than just weeks. But there's something about Ryker Lockhart that makes me feel like each time is new. Like each time is more special. Like each time is a hint of so much more to come.

My back hits the wall behind me as his body presses against me. Our hands roam over one another, but it's our lips that do the talking with each kiss.

And that's all we do. Kiss. The simplest of intimate actions. But it's his lips that hurt me to begin with, and so I feel like he's trying to show me that they don't always bring pain. No. They can soothe and murmur and caress and cajole and apologize.

Every part of me burns for him. Chills chase over my skin, and the ache is so very sweet at the delta of my thighs.

But every time I try to run my hands along his waistband and cup his cock, he locks his hand around my wrist and prevents me.

"Just this. We need this," he murmurs against my lips and then dives back in to feast on them again.

The transition into the penthouse happens gradually. A step toward the door when we come up for air. His keycode punched in the lock pad as he presses his hand against the small of my back, pulling me into him. The quiet click of the door behind us as we move down the hallway ungracefully but steadily.

The sound of my zipper when he slides it down the seam of my dress and then the swish as the fabric falls to the floor around my feet.

The startled inhale as I undo his shirt buttons and run my palms up the naked planes of his chest. The groan he makes as his head falls back when my hands cup the hardness of his cock.

The dance continues until we're both undressed. We don't take time to look at each other. Our bodies are already known to each other. It's our hearts we're still trying to figure out.

I kneel on the bed, our kisses still as intense but a little slower. A lot softer. Each one telling a chapter in a story instead of a line in a paragraph.

Ryker crawls over me as my hand encircles his dick and guides him to where I want him. With one elbow pressed beside me, he wraps his hand over mine, and we both guide him into me.

It happens so effortless this time—him filling me. The ache turns to pleasure. The burn into desire. Short pants of breath and long slides of skin. Moans of rapture and hitches of breath.

The darkness of the room swallows us and at the same time unites us. The loneliness we felt apart fuels us to want more together.

We make love without words. Because even though I won't accept those three words from him yet, we both know that's exactly what we're doing right now. Loving each other.

We're cementing those emotions that came to light when we were absent from one another's life. With each push in. With every pull out. With the gentle urgency he uses. With our fingers intertwined and resting beside my hip. With the drag of his lips over my collarbone and the grip of my fingers against the skin of his ribcage.

Our bodies work to reach the high. The climax, a slow surge that begins to build within, is undeniable and so very different than I felt previously.

There's emotion pushing it now. There are feelings and commitment and things we've never really expressed but that can be felt in its tides mixed in.

Ryker buries his face against the underside of my neck as his hips begin to thrust faster and my body begins to tense. His breath is hot against my skin. My mewls are loud against the harsh pants of his breath. The slap of our skin is an underlying beat.

And then it hits with white heat and electric pulses and a bliss that warms me from my core out to my fingertips and back again. My head arches against the pillows as my hips buck and my back bows . . . as I beg for everything from him that I never thought possible for myself.

Unable to let go, I wrap my legs around his hips and my arms around his neck as he chases his own, my body his to use.

It's less than a minute before his groan vibrates in the back of his throat. Before his muscles tense and shudder with the adrenaline my own body is slowly falling from. Before his body relaxes and he slowly rolls off me with an audible exhale.

No words are exchanged between us as we stare at the ceiling. The penthouse is so high up that the shadows are stagnant. There are no headlights driving by to light up through the windows. There are no streetlights providing ambient light. Just the moon outside this twentieth-story tower.

Silence smothers the room as our hearts decelerate. His hand slides over mine, and our fingers intertwine much like our bodies just did.

Something has shifted between us.

There's a gravity all of a sudden—a realization that whatever this is between us is so very different than before. Sure, he stated it with so many words when he met me in the hallway, but now? Now it feels real, and there's panic in acknowledging it.

I scoot off the bed without either of us saying a word. The clock on the nightstand reads 11:30 p.m., and I wonder how it can be the same day when everything feels so very different.

It takes me a minute to find my dress on the floor in the darkened room. "Lucy's at home. It was my night. Joey's with her. I need . . ." I slip my dress on as I struggle to explain what sounds so very stupid to me. That I kept my night to have Lucy even though I was going out to the event. That I hired Joey to watch her. That I'm now using her being there as an excuse to leave. "I need to—I just—"

"I understand." His eyes meet mine across the room, but they say the exact opposite of his words.

I don't know what to say to him. I don't know how all the emotion shared between us in the past hour can still feel tinged with an uncertainty, *a hurt*, but it does. I go to leave but find myself turning around to face him. Words and thoughts and emotions bubble up and manifest in the tears welling in my eyes.

He notices but stays where he is—sitting up in his massive bed, the sheet draped over his waist, his hair mussed, his head angled just slightly to the side—and waits for me to lead us.

"Vaughn?"

"I know we just did this"—I point to the bed like a tongue-tied teenager—"but I . . . I need to take this slow. I need to . . ."

"I understand." Two simple words reiterated, but they make a lone tear slip over and slide down my cheek. "Can I walk you out or get my driver to—"

"No. Stay." I shake my head. "Good night."

"Night, Vaughn."

We stare at each other for a few moments as I beg my feet to move, while my heart wants to stay here and my head is uncertain about the limbo I feel.

And when I finally find the courage to leave, I'm not sure if I'm relieved or saddened that he lets me. Maybe we're both finding our footing in this new chapter we've started. Maybe we're afraid to ruin the moment we've shared.

But I leave.

To gain some clarity. To give myself some space to process everything. To make sure I'm ready to accept his love the only way he knows how to give it.

CHAPTER ELEVEN

Vaughn

I had no intention of sleeping with Ryker.

I really didn't.

I had planned to go to his penthouse and explain why I was wronged—*why he had wronged me*—and to explain why we could never be despite how much I quietly wanted him.

But something happened while I waited for him in the hallway.

His words from the gala hit my ears. The between-the-lines things I felt he was really saying to me that no one else would have caught ran loops in my mind.

And so when he stepped off the elevator and I saw him there—broad shoulders, weary and surprised eyes, jaw clenched—the reason I had gone there changed without me ever knowing it.

I wanted to tell him I appreciated his speech at the gala.

Maybe I even wanted to feel him one last time.

But whatever my intention was, it sure as hell wasn't to be leaving after sleeping with him.

It sure as shit wasn't to leave with my heart in my throat, my head more than a mess, and my soul terrified at how much the man can make me feel in all aspects.

But that's what I did.

That's where I'm at.

And still, nothing makes sense. Not our reaction to the sex. Not our need to have time to mull it over. Not my fear about what this means for me and my future.

The sigh I'm about to emit stutters on my lips when the Uber pulls down my street and I see the black limousine parked at the end of my driveway. I hate that I hesitate getting out of the car or that I rationalize its presence.

"Everything okay, ma'am?" my Uber driver asks when I just sit there for a moment.

"Yes. Fine." I smile at him in the rearview mirror before getting out of the car.

I try not to look at the limo as I skirt around it and up my walk, because everything about it scares me. And when its door opens, I know why.

"Vaughn."

His voice.

That voice.

Chills blanket my skin about as quickly as the rage that flows through my veins. He sought me out. He actually got my address and sought me out.

When I turn to face the senator, I startle when I see the man dressed all in black, earpiece in, leaning against the front fender.

He brought his security detail with him? Now my guard is up even further.

The fine line separating Vee and Vaughn is now blurred.

My feet falter. My heart races. I glance around but know that at this time of night no one is likely to be near if I need help.

"I've been looking into you." His deep baritone rumbles through the darkened night.

"Please leave."

"It's not that simple."

"Yes, it is." I grip my keys in my hand and wonder how fast I can slip each one between my fingers to use as a weapon to fend him off if need be.

"I believe you have something that is mine, *Vaughn*." His smile is akin to a great white shark's—deceptive in every way.

"And I asked you to leave." I glance over at the security detail, wondering what it is he knows here and hating that yet another person is aware of my real identity.

"The pictures, please."

"Now why would I do that?"

Carter's chuckle is obnoxious and arrogant, and it stops abruptly. "Because they are my business."

"Just like you being here and me asking you to leave is my business."

He takes a step toward me, and I hide the hitch in my breath. "We both know I like to play dirty . . . maybe it's best not to test just how low I'll go to get what I need . . . that is, unless you like it when I go *down* low." He makes no attempt to hide his blatant stare at the *V* of my thighs as his tongue licks out to wet his bottom lip before he looks back up.

My skin crawls, and my thoughts veer to Ryker and his explanation about what happened in the pool house—how adamant Carter was about having something on me.

"I don't think you're appreciating how much restraint I'm exercising right now," he murmurs.

"Touch me and I'll call the cops." I arch a brow, my words defiant, while my insides are shaking.

"It's a pretty precarious position you're in, Vaughn. Waiting to adopt. In debt up to your ears. Using illegal means to try to pay it off. Nothing with you is what it seems." He leans in and despite my threat twirls a finger around a lock of my hair. His way to show me he's not scared by my warning. When he pulls forcefully on the strands, I have to bite back a yelp. "Can you imagine what would and could happen to you if all of that got out?"

I grit my teeth and steel myself when he leans in, so I can feel his breath feather over my cheek. He stares at me, and I fix my gaze on the tree over his shoulder.

"That would be a shame, wouldn't it? All this work for nothing? All this risk and fear for naught? I'd think long and hard about not doing as I say, or else poor little Lucy might just become a permanent ward of the state."

His words hit me so deep down, I can all but feel it in my bones. But I straighten my shoulders and clear my throat.

"Do you think threatening me is going to prevent me from releasing what I have on you in kind?"

"The pictures?" He laughs. "I'll take my chances."

"You wish I only had the pictures," I counter, hating that he's unfazed by my threat.

He stares at me, debating whether or not I'm bluffing. "You don't have shit on me."

"I'll take my chances, then. It's a hard fall when you're as high as you are." I return the same smug smile he's giving me.

"You're way out of your league. You might want to be careful."

"It's not exactly smart to threaten me." My words hold conviction while I combat the nerves reverberating through me.

"Oh, I don't make threats. That's the best part about being in such a powerful and *high* position. Everyone knows I don't threaten . . . I act. And I have every single resource at my fingertips just waiting for me to use."

"I have resources too. Like people who must hate you so much that they drop information in my lap."

"You're playing with fire, Vee." He tugs on the lock of my hair again and makes a show of breathing in my perfume, followed by a guttural groan. "That's your first mistake."

"So then I should release this *call log* to the public, then?" The question is out, my fear suddenly real enough to mention the one thing I have on him other than the pictures, even though I have zero clue how this list of phone numbers and times is damaging.

But his stuttered reaction—his narrowed eyes, his body tensing so I can step back from him, his head jerking ever so slightly—tells me he's worried. His slip might only be for a second before he recovers, but I still see it. I still know that whatever this list of phone numbers and times and dates is means something to him.

And that in turn makes it more than valuable to me.

"Go right ahead," he says with a shrug, but there's something that darkens in his eyes that completely unnerves me. "I'm a representative of the people. All of my calls are available to the public."

"Good to know, but I don't buy it, Carter." I shake my head with a slight smile on my lips as I try to read his hardened expression through the shadows.

"Feel free to make the mistake and fuck with me."

We stand a foot apart. The chills that chase over my skin have nothing to do with the cool night air and everything to do with the sudden shift from demanding to downright disconcerting.

"Vaughn? Everything okay out there?" Joey calls from the front porch into the darkness, and I all but jump out of my shoes.

"Yes." I clear my throat as my heart races, and I take a step to the left out from behind the corner of the garage where Carter and I are standing. "I'm fine."

Despite the distance, I can see the startle of his head when he notices the silhouette of the limo on the curb. "He's still here?" he asks, confusing me.

"Yes," I answer, not sure what in the hell he's talking about, but the last thing I need is Joey to see Carter and the questions that would follow. "I'll be in in a minute."

Joey takes a step onto the porch and holds a hand over his brow as if it'll allow him to see better in the darkness to where we're standing. I know he can't see much, and for that I'm grateful. "Okay, if you're sure."

"Yes." I'm more curt this time, not wanting him to walk any closer. But as much as I want him to shut the door, being alone with Carter unnerves me. Sure, his security detail is here, but I'm more than certain that my best interests aren't his concern.

Joey stands there a few more seconds in indecision and then goes back inside. Once the door shuts, Carter steps into me. I try to step back, but in the process of trying to get Joey out of here, I unknowingly positioned myself so that the wall is at my back, and I have nowhere to retreat in order to put space between us.

"You are a little whore, aren't you? First Ryker. Now *Joey*. Who else is there, Vee?" I yelp when he steps again so that our chests brush against each other's and the stucco of the wall bites against my back. Despite the chill in the air, there is sweat beading on his temple and a wild excitement in his eyes that alarms me almost as much as his hands sliding up my arms.

"Get your hands off me."

"Why? You want the feel of them on your skin to be left a surprise?" His chuckle is ominous at best and predatory at worst. "Don't worry. I'll ruin you for every single man you fuck after me."

Something has changed in the last few moments from before Joey came outside to after. There has been some kind of shift in Carter. Almost as if he was knocked off stride and has now found his footing.

To say I'm alarmed by it is the understatement of the year.

"Get your hands off me," I grit out again, "or else I'll scream bloody murder."

"Go right ahead," he whispers harshly, almost as if the notion excites him. "Give me a reason to involve Joey and every other goddamn person in this neighborhood. Mr. Nelson across the street owns three handguns. I'm sure he'll come running to your defense. Don't expect

Harvey who lives two houses down to help, though. He left about an hour ago. His wife's out of town. You know what they say about when the cat's away and all."

His words shake me to the core. His facts might be made up—or they very well could be the truth, for all I know—but knowing he's researched my neighbors enough to know their names is more than unsettling.

His attempt to show me he's all-knowing has worked.

"Come on. Give them a reason to call the cops, and then we can each sign statements about the incident. Tell them what you do for a living and you're damned. Lie about it in a sworn statement and same goes. So please"—he rolls his shoulders so that our chests brush together again, and his guttural groan is enough to make my stomach churn— "cause a scene so the police come."

"What do you want?" I ask when I already know the answer.

"Is that a trick question, Vaughny?" He reaches up and tucks a piece of hair behind my ear in an action that's normally intimate but that has the polar opposite effect when done by his hand. "I was coming for the pictures." He laughs and lifts his eyebrows. "But now? Now after you've threatened me? After you've told me no? I think you need to make up for insulting me."

"Go to hell."

"How cute. You actually think you have a say in this." He leans in so that the heat of his breath hits my ear when he murmurs, "Ryker told me you were all mine, and I've never been known not to take what's mine."

I freeze when he runs a finger down my cheek and then squeezes my jaw when he comes to my chin, clearly trying to let me know he is in control. He leans back to meet my eyes as I try to jerk my head from his grip to no avail.

"Leave me al—"

"You owe me an apology." His eyes harden and his grip tightens. "You forget who has the power in this relationship. Who has a nation at his back. Who is more believable. It won't be right now, Vee, as it seems you've already had your fill of men tonight. No. I'll give you a little more time to get used to the idea. I'll let you have a little longer to fantasize about all the things I plan on doing to that tight little body of yours." He emits a groan in the back of his throat that has my stomach churning. "I hear your pussy is worth every goddamn penny."

My free hand is out, and the sound of it slapping against his cheek cracks in the silence of the night. He lets go of my jaw, and in the split second before I yank my hand back, the one clear thought that echoes through my mind is how much I hate Ryker right now.

He did this to me.

He set Carter up to think I'm his.

He jeopardized everything I've ever worked for.

But I don't have more than a few seconds to compute those thoughts, because Carter Preston is glaring at me with murder in his eyes and a hard-on pressing against the zipper of his slacks. His startled look only lasts for seconds before his mask of superiority and arrogant smile slide back over his features.

He scrubs a hand over his jaw and chuckles. "We both know that's not how I like it. I'm the one who causes the pain." The dark undertone to his playful voice is unmistakable. "I suggest you don't do that again, or you'll be very sorry."

"Then I suggest you move your hands off me, or else my knee is going to find its way ramming into your balls," I threaten, the space between us allowing me to think clearly and without the haze of fear.

"Try it and you'll be very sorry. Anything and everything that's connected within a hundred-mile radius of you will be destroyed in the process."

"You son of a bitch."

"Uh-uh-uh, I'd watch what you say to the man who can trump every single one of your cards." He purses his lips as his stare undresses every inch of me. "It's such a turn-on knowing you're going to fight me every goddamn step of the way." He leans in, and as much as I'm repulsed by the fear I have that he's going to try to kiss me, I don't call chicken. I stay perfectly still and don't back down. He stops, his lips an inch from mine, his breath feathering over them. "I get off on that. I'll get off on you. I'll use every inch of you, and then you'll beg me for more. And depending on if you're a good girl or not—if you fulfill the needs I've *already* paid for and then some—I'll decide if I should let good ol' Priscilla know about who exactly Madam Vee is," he says, and panic springs to life. If he's investigated my neighbors, I shouldn't be surprised that he knows who Lucy's social worker is . . . but I am.

"You wouldn't dare—"

"Oh, but I would. And while I'm at it, I might even fill her in on what you did to good ol' Uncle James."

If I had any fight left in me, hearing that name knocks the wind out of my sails and fills me with shock and confusion and disbelief.

"See? I do know everything. I do have eyes everywhere. Give me what I want, Vaughny, or else I'll find a way to get it myself."

He presses a kiss to the corner of my lips that I'm too stunned to reject and turns to walk toward the limo, throwing over his shoulder, "Oh, and if this little conversation gets out to *anyone*? The same threat holds. Good to see you again. It'll be even better next time."

He climbs into his limo without another look my way. The security guard slides behind the wheel, and the limo pulls away.

But I'm the one standing in my front yard staring after red taillights in the distance like I just saw a ghost. I'm the one finally feeling an iota of the fear my sister used to endure. Not only fear of the physicality but more so the uncertainty and constant threat, knowing he could come after me at any moment.

I'm in my late twenties, and I'm petrified. I can't imagine what living with this fear—day in and day out—would have felt like when I was a teenager.

When I was Sam's age.

I stagger in the door, flushed and shaking and needing a drink, and Joey more than senses that something is wrong.

"Vaughn?"

I hold my finger up as I go to the fridge and take out my half-finished bottle of rosé and drink straight from it.

"Vaughn? You're kind of freaking me out," he says, his voice behind me.

I gulp in air once I swallow and shake my head, my hands braced on the counter in front of me. "I'm fine. Just fine." And I'm not sure if I say it more to convince him or myself.

"You really should report him as a stalker," Joey says.

"Who?" I ask, totally distracted as I attempt to calm my nerves.

"Ryker." I jolt when he says the name, grateful my back is still to him. "Who else has been waiting out there for hours for you? He even left and came back in a different car. Does he turn into a pumpkin after—"

"It wasn't—" *him.* But I stop myself from saying it. From telling him differently. First, because I don't want Joey to know anything about the senator being here. Second, *Ryker came here?* He came to my house looking for me earlier while I was at his house waiting for him?

"It wasn't what?" Joey persists as he moves to stand beside me at the counter, turning to rest his hips against it so we're facing each other. "Ryker? Then who was it?"

"No. Yes. Just let it go, Joey." I finally lift my eyes to meet his and force a smile. "Everything is—"

"Don't say fine. Creepy is more like it." Joey chuckles sarcastically, while I just want him to go so I can down the rest of this bottle in peace and then maybe even open another one.

"We needed to air some differences is all," I lie.

"You know if you need to talk about anything . . . I'm here for you."

When Joey puts his hand on mine and gives it a reassuring squeeze, it takes everything I have not to jerk it away in a delayed reaction to Carter doing almost the same thing just moments ago.

"I know." *Please go.* "Thank you." *I just want to be alone.* "It's late. I'm sorry I lost track of time. I didn't mean to keep you so long."

"Totally fine. I was just figuring I'd crash on the couch." He smiles, and there's kindness in his eyes that makes me feel even worse for lying to him. An awkward silence passes between us where I question whether I should offer said couch to him for the night, but I don't because I just want to be alone. Joey rocks on his heels when I don't speak. "So you're good, then?"

"Yes. I'm f—"

"You're fine. So I've heard." There's a smile on his lips but a hint of frustration in his voice that I pretend not to hear.

"Thank you for watching Luce for me," I say to prompt his departure.

We say our goodbyes, and I pay him for his time before heaving a huge sigh of relief once he's out the door.

I'm drawn to Lucy's soft snores. To the need to see the one thing that centers me, because after tonight, I'm not sure what in the hell I'm supposed to feel.

A part of me wants to pick up the phone and call Ryker. Tell him what the senator just did, because I'm scared and unsettled, and Ryker is the only person I've ever known besides Samantha who has seemed to have my back.

The other part of me knows this—the senator being here, his sense of ownership over me—is all because of Ryker and what happened in the pool house.

Ryker is the one who did this to me. I was already a target, but Ryker's actions made me a bull's-eye in Carter Preston's zero-sum game that holds so much collateral damage when it comes to my life that I'm terrified.

Number one being the sleeping little girl whose arms are wrapped around a stuffed animal all while a tiara still sits perfectly straight on her head.

So many things happened tonight—bad, then good, then overwhelming, and then ugly.

What good is blackmail material when the person is undeterred by it? Do I destroy him so that we both go down in flames together?

But was he as unaffected as his words stated? Or was the sudden change in him a tell?

I stare at Lucy with ghosts of my past humming around, trying to make sense of everything Carter said, and one thing stands out more than anything. Ryker is the only person I've ever told about James. *He's it*. And now all of a sudden Carter knows the name and throws him in my face?

Did Ryker tell Carter? Was this another little secret divulged in the Hamptons that Ryker thought would have zero repercussions in his game when in fact it would have momentous ones if it fell into the wrong hands?

A simple phone call would allow me to ask the question and clear up any confusion. I pick up my cell, unblock Ryker's number, and contemplate hitting send.

The problem is, I'm not quite sure I believe the answers I'm already getting about what happened that night, so who says I will believe what Ryker tells me this time?

Another high tonight being with Ryker followed by the ultimate low of right now.

He's not good for you, Vaughn.

He's not good for you, regardless of how he makes your heart feel.

In fact, maybe being with him is even more dangerous because of it.

CHAPTER TWELVE

Ryker

We need to talk at some point. About Saturday night. About us.
About everything.

I stare at the text I sent Vaughn and pinch the bridge of my nose in frustration at her lack of response. She's read it. I know she has. But fuck if she's picking it up to text back.

We're on day two here of radio silence. Two days where I'm left with the memory of how incredible her body felt, how she had that wounded look in her eyes, how it took everything I had to let her walk out, all while feeling how fucking cold her silence is.

"Mr. Lockhart?"

"Mmm?" I don't even look toward the phone on my desk when Bella's voice booms through it, because I'm completely distracted by Vaughn when I should be working.

"There's a Ms. Sanders here to see you."

Now that's a way to get a man's attention.

"Send her in."

I'm already at the door to my office and opening it before I hear the click of Vaughn's heels on the floor.

Office sex.

Maybe that's what she's here for.

But that thought flies painfully from my mind the minute I see her. She looks nervous. Her head may be held high and her shoulders square, but she looks at me only briefly before averting her eyes.

Fuck.

What now?

"Vaughn?"

To what do I owe this surprise?

What the hell is wrong?

God, you're fucking gorgeous.

All three thoughts run through my mind, but none of them are voiced as I step forward and press a kiss to her lips in greeting. I'd lose myself in her right now if I could, but her hands pressing against my chest tell me that sure as hell isn't going to be happening.

"Hi." She offers a tight smile and then skirts around me and into my office.

She's all business. This is not good.

I shut the door behind me and then take a deep breath as I turn around to face her. Her back is to me. She's looking out the windows like I'm prone to do, but hell if I look like her. The pencil skirt is a charcoal gray, and it highlights every damn curve of that body of hers. Ones I've run my hands and mouth over. Ones I'm desperate for again.

Her pale-pink sweater is soft and off the shoulders, and her hair cascades in waves down her back.

I stare at her for a moment longer, partially because I'm enjoying the view and partially because I'm putting off hearing whatever it is that was so important she showed up at my office for.

"Vaughn?" I ask again. My oxfords on the floor moving toward her are the only other sound in my office.

She turns to face me, and her eyes tell me everything I'd feared. "I can't do this again with you."

"Do what again? Talk with me? Be with me? Do what with me?" I demand, my mood going from cautious to defiant in a matter of seconds.

"No matter what seems to happen between us . . ."

"What?" I reach out to touch her and get pissed when she steps away so I can't. "We have a good time? We enjoy each other's company? What the fuck am I missing here, Vaughn?"

"Nothing." She shakes her head, eyes wild with emotion I can't decipher. "We just . . . we're not good for each other."

"That's total bullshit and you know it." But there's something about her—the way she's keeping her distance, the stiffness to her body, her refusal to meet my eyes—that tells me she's goddamn serious. I turn on my heel and walk away from her, hand running through my hair and a disbelieving laugh falling from my mouth. I need alcohol in here. A whole goddamn fifth of it, to be exact. *What the actual fuck?* "Ah, it all makes sense now."

"What does?" At least for once there's confusion in her voice.

"You showing up here at my work." I turn back to face her. "Let me guess, you figured I'd have to be professional and not make a scene when you walked in here and told me we're over."

"We never really were together to begin with."

Every part of my body tenses at her crap answer. "And you're lying through your teeth." I take a step back toward her. "You think I'm not going to cause a scene because this is my office? You think I'm just going to let you walk away without a fucking fight? News flash, Vaughn . . . I fought too damn hard to get you, then to win you back after I fucked up, so no, I refuse to listen to you tell me otherwise. I told you to take whatever time it is you need. Two days isn't nearly enough unless you already knew we were over before you walked out of my place. So tell me you need more time. Tell me you're still confused and angry at me, and I'll believe it. But say we're over again, and I'll let everyone on this floor know what I think—loud and crystal fucking clear."

"Ryker . . . *please* . . . just let me go." But this time when she speaks there is something in her voice that catches my ear. The same thing that has me looking a little bit closer, regardless of how much my chest constricts in doing so, and I notice the tears welling in her eyes and the tremble of her bottom lip.

A chink in her damn armor. She doesn't want to tell me we're over any more than I want to believe her.

"What the fuck is going on here? You're hiding something from me."

"No. I'm not. *This* just can't be." She starts to skirt around me, and it takes everything I have not to reach out and keep her there.

"Don't walk away from me when I'm talking to you!"

"And don't you think for a second you can tell me what to do," she counters, hair flying over her shoulder, jaw clenched.

"I'm not in the mood for your games."

"My games?" she screeches and throws me off guard when I shouldn't be. "My games? You're the one who did this to me. All of it. And you tell me I'm playing games?"

"What the—?" I stop and try to figure out what she's talking about. My hands are on her shoulders, and I'm all but shaking her to force her to look me in the eyes. "Did what to you, Vaughn? What the hell have I done to you besides fuck myself over by falling in love with you?" Words that should be said with kindness come out in a frustrated rage. Truths I don't want to voice, and now I can't take them back.

And she just stands there with her head shaking to reject my words, eyes wide with a hint of fear, and fuck if I don't hate myself right now for everything I feel: rage, desperation, love, desire.

How can you swear you're not cut out for a relationship and love in one breath, then with the next fight so goddamn hard to keep it?

What is this woman doing to me?

I scrub my hands over my face and take a deep breath to calm the fuck down. To force myself to cool my temper so I can keep her here instead of pushing her farther away.

"What is it, baby?" I all but plead with a voice as soft as I can make it. "Tell me why you're walking away when you don't want to." She averts her eyes, confirming there's something more. "I can't help you unless you tell me what happened. I can't understand why the other night meant nothing to you until you do."

Come on. Talk to me.

"Carter paid me a visit after I left your place." Her voice is soft, but her defiance is mounting.

That's definitely not what I expected to come out of her mouth.

"What do you mean, *Carter paid you a visit?*"

"Just what I said."

"Why? For what? That fucking asshole better not have touched you."

"Does it matter if he did?" Her voice rises. "You invited him into my personal life. You gave him everything he needs to destroy me."

"What the hell are you talking about?" My confusion is turning into anger, and it's not her fault, but fuck if I can keep it at bay.

"He threatened my adoption of Lucy. With outing me. You name it."

I stare at her, blinking as her words hit me straight in the solar plexus. "He what?"

"He threatened me. Told me I have to give him what I have on him. My last defense to protect myself . . . and if I don't, he'll ruin me."

"I don't unders—"

"How can you understand? How can you stand there and know what it feels like to be told that it doesn't matter if you do or don't do what he says because you owe your body to him in an apology?" I swear to God, when her voice wavers, I fucking hate myself. "And that's why your apologies mean shit, Ryker. The damage was already done the minute I left the pool house."

"He actually said he was going to cost you the adoption?" I'm trying to wrap my head around this, around the balls that fucker has. I have to focus on one thing at a time, or else the rage over it all will cloud more than my judgment. It will cloud my rationality to the point that my ass will end up in jail.

And that's not the half of what I deserve.

Her eyes well, and she just shakes her head in response.

"Please. Just go step by step through everything."

"He said it would be a shame if Lucy's social worker found out about Wicked Ways. How am I supposed to take it if that's not a threat?"

I try to justify my way out of this. I try to tell myself he could have threatened her even without our meeting because he already wanted her desperately.

But you hung her out there like a carrot for him to chase after.

"Vaughn." Her name is a sigh. An apology. An *I can fix this* when I don't even know where to start. I reach out to hold her hand, and she yanks it back as if my touch will break her.

"Don't."

"This wasn't—I didn't mean—*Fuck*." I pull on the back of my neck. I scramble for explanations—for anything—because what the fuck was he thinking.

"Like I said," she murmurs, "this—*we*—can't be. It's bad all around."

She starts to walk away again, and this time I do grab her arm to prevent her from walking out. "We'll fix this. *I'll* fix this."

"It can't be fixed!" she screams as her body shakes with anger.

"It's a harmless threat. He wouldn't dare follow through with it." I'm looking at her but thinking about murdering him. "Men like him get off on their power. On making women fear them. It's like a goddamn drug to him, so he showed up to your house to lay the groundwork. To make you scared. To make you feel like you have to turn over whatever you have on him so he doesn't have to worry about it coming to light."

"You don't understand, Ryker. He came to my house. *My house!* Him and his security detail and—"

"It's part of his plan. He told me himself that night. Use sex and fear to gain power. Use the power to get what he wants—"

"And yet you still used me when you knew that? When he told you this?" She shakes her head, her mouth lax, her eyes blinking away the tears that I'm now afraid have morphed from tears of hurt to anger.

I want to go to her, pull her against me, use the heat of her skin to reassure myself that I can get us back . . . but for the first time, I'm not so fucking sure, because she's right. He told me that shit, and I still did what I did. I still used the woman I love, even if it was in good faith . . . I still did this to her.

"Yes. I did." There's nothing else I can say. No other apology I can give. I take a step forward, timid when I'm never timid. "There are no words I can voice to take away what I did."

I watch a tear slip over her lashes and slide down her cheek. Just one. A small tell of the hurt that I detonated like a grenade within her.

"He told me he couldn't wait to sleep with me because you told him how good my pussy felt."

Her voice may be soft, but those words are like a cattle prod to my temper.

"I'm going to kill that son of a bitch." My hands fist and teeth grit, and every object on my desk is at risk of being thrown against the wall as I stalk toward it.

All I see is red.

All I feel is rage.

All I know is I hate the fucker more than I ever thought possible, and good thing I'm a lawyer so I know how to post my own damn bail.

"What are you—?" she asks as I grab my wallet off the desk and my jacket. "No!" She emits a sound I want to forever erase from my memory. It's my name, but it's part plea, part terror, part everything bad you can imagine as she runs across the room and holds on to my arms, trying to keep me here.

I could shrug her off in a second without any effort, but there is something about the fear in her voice—about the complete hysteria in it—that stops me.

And when I look at her, when I see the trembling of her chin and the tears welling in her eyes, I know there is so much more going on here than what she said. I know she fears losing Lucy, but this . . . there's even more here she's not telling me.

"Vaughn." I put my hands on both of her shoulders, and I lower my head so that we're eye to eye. "What else did he say to you?"

With each word I can see Vaughn pulling away from me.

"Nothing."

I can handle her attitude. Her sass. But when her voice trembles, it's like something inside me breaks with it.

You did that to her, Ryker.

You used someone you loved like a pawn . . . just like your mom used you.

Jesus fucking Christ.

"Vaughn." I say her name for what feels like the twentieth time in this conversation, but it's the only way I know how to bring her back to me. "What else did that prick say to you?"

"Leave it be, Ryker."

She knows me better than that. "You either tell me what he said, or I go find him right now and ask him myself."

Her eyes flash up to meet mine, and she knows I'm dead serious. She knows I follow through with my threats.

"He told me if anyone found out about our conversation, he'll make good on the threat."

"Sounds like something the bastard would say."

"Don't give him another reason to come after me," she pleads. "You can't confront him. If you did, it would only serve to make him want this more. Knowing he's screwing me over and sticking it to you, the lawyer representing his wife, will only up the ante for him."

She's right, and I hate admitting it.

But there's more to their exchange. I know there is.

I study her and know there's more. She already told me about the conversation, so she's just trying to appease me. Just trying to distract me from whatever else it is that piece of shit threatened her with.

"I won't confront him," I say, the words like broken glass scraping against my throat. "But if I don't, then you have to tell me what else he said to you." The sudden widening of her eyes tells me my hunch is right. Besides the threat of losing Lucy, there's something else there.

She shakes her head as if she's not going to tell me, but words come out. "He knows about my uncle."

If I thought she'd shocked me telling me about Carter showing up to her house, this sure as shit just pulled the rug out from under me. "What do you mean he knows about *your uncle?*"

He told me that night he had dirt on her. I thought he was bluffing—just a big ego trying to play the part. *And this is how you failed her, Lockhart. You used her but never got your end of the bargain. You used her even when you knew about her past. Even when you knew how much it still torments her now.*

"Did you tell him?"

Those four words—the mistrust laced through them—are like a twist of the dagger and knock my thoughts loose in a state of panic.

"Tell him what?"

"You're the only one I've ever told about my uncle. About Sam. *Did you tell him?*" Her voice rises in pitch, distrust in each and every syllable.

"No. That's none of his goddamn business. I wouldn't betray your trust like that."

She gives me a look that says I already have, and fuck if she isn't right.

"You promised you wouldn't confront him."

Like hell I won't.

"How am I supposed to stand by and let this happen to you?" I throw my hands up. "How as a man worth anything am I supposed to not defend you?"

"You've already done enough." And it's those words that quiet and fuel my rage simultaneously.

But not at her. Not at Carter.

Rather, at myself.

"I deserve that."

Her nails score into my skin where she grips my forearms. "There's nothing we can do. He's a senator. He has—"

"I don't fucking care if he's the goddamn pope," I shout, hating that my defiant Vaughn is suddenly lying down on this.

"I can't compete with his power and influence."

"What is it that you have on him, Vaughn? What is it he wants so badly that he'll destroy you for?"

Because it has to be that, right? It has to be her blackmail material he's after. Otherwise, his obsession over sleeping with her would be sick and so very different than his need to use it against her to get what he wants.

"It doesn't matter what I have on him. He could recover from it—others in his shoes have. It was enough to keep him at bay with Lola, but now?" She sighs. "*Now?* The stakes have been upped, and he'd destroy me and everything I care about in the process." She lowers her head and looks at her hands as she moves them off me to clasp them in front of her. Then she nods and begins to leave.

"Don't walk away from me."

She stops, her back to me, her head down. "I'm not walking away, Ryker. I'm just . . . I don't know what I'm doing, but I have to think of me and Lucy first."

I nod, knowing that I have to respect her request and hating it all at the same time.

If I hadn't stepped in, he might have moved on. All this might not be happening.

"Don't make this any harder than it already is, Ryker."

"I'm going to kill him." I've never spoken truer words.

"He'll ruin me." Resignation colors her tone.

"And I'll ruin him." I step up behind her and put my hand on the curve of her hip. Something, anything, to let her know I mean what I'm saying. It's the first time she doesn't pull away from me.

"It wouldn't matter. The damage would already be done. I'd already lose everything that means anything to me." She turns and looks back at me with those eyes I've lost myself in more times than I'll ever admit just as another tear slips down her cheek. "Please, Ryker . . . I appreciate you wanting to wield your sword for me, but it's not going to make this go away."

"Then give him what he wants. Whatever you have on him," I urge.

"And give him complete and total power over the situation? *Over me?*"

She's right in every sense of the word, but all I want is for her to be safe. All I want is for Carter Preston to leave her the fuck alone.

"It's my life you're messing with, Ryker . . . not yours."

"I'll make this right. I'll figure out . . ." *Fuck!* "I'm so sorry, Vaughn."

"I know you are."

And without another word, she walks away.

No. I *let* her walk away, because I feel like a helpless piece of shit who can't seem to do a goddamn thing right.

If I thought I knew rage before, I fucking know it now.

You did this, Ryk. You and your goddamn fucking selfishness. You sicced this pit bull on the woman you love, and now he's salivating over the chance to sink his teeth into her.

And all I have in defense is a shitty garden hose to try to scare him off.

I move from one end of my office to another. The drywall calls on me to punch it, to push a hole through it, but I know it won't do a goddamn thing to fix the situation. To call off the dog.

No. A hole in the wall will be just another reminder of Vaughn.

Of how she needs someone to patch the drywall when I keep punching through it.

CHAPTER THIRTEEN
Vaughn

For the second time in days, I find myself wandering the streets of New York City. I buy a coffee from Starbucks, but it grows cold in my hand without the java ever touching my tongue.

I know this isn't Ryker's fault.

I know that Carter is just finishing what I started when I denied him services, made him pay compensation regardless, and threatened him with blackmail pictures. I'm not naive enough to think we'd end it at that.

But I was naive when it came to thinking that maybe if I didn't poke the sleeping bear, Carter would allow everything between us to grow cold and move on.

And then Ryker went and poked the bear.

I stand in the middle of Times Square. The jumbotrons flash bright colors from their screens. Tourists mill about, their shoulders and backpacks jostling me here and there.

But I've never felt more alone.

This is such a different feeling than when Sam died. With her it was absolute devastation and utter shock. But now? Now I have so many things I never expected right at my fingertips—adopting Lucy, everything with Ryker, the applications I filled out this week to get my teaching credential—and I fear one wrong move could take that all away from me.

My mind keeps circling back to Carter's threat. To his mention of my uncle. And with a clearer head now that I've confronted Ryker, I can focus on why his threat is ringing out of tune to me.

So Carter Preston knows about my uncle . . . *but what about him?* How would Carter outing my sister's abuse hurt me? Privately, it would remind me of the despair and devastation she went through to protect me, but publicly? How could him talking about my creep of an uncle do anything to harm me?

The only way it could is by outing the fact that I'm the owner of Wicked Ways. That I sell sex for a living and take a cut off the top.

So why is Carter using it as a threat? Is there something else missing that I don't remember? It took me over ten years to remember her abuse, so what else is it that I've repressed, if anything?

That's the unknown that's haunting me.

At first it was the fear that my uncle would find me and drag me back—juvenile in thought, but no one can judge a woman who in her adulthood fears the man who haunted her youth and abused her sister—and now it's the fear that there's something else there I don't know.

"What am I doing, Sam?" I mutter, well aware I won't get a second glance in this crowd for talking to myself. "What am I missing?"

My Wicked Ways cell alerts a text, the vibration in my hand informing me. I turn it over to see a text from Ella. Just my bimonthly question. Lol. Are you ready to sell yet?

Ella's been trying to buy me out since the minute I made a name for myself in this business, and I've held off because I need the ongoing income to pay off my debt. For the first time ever, though, I want to text back in all shouty caps YES! YES, I'M READY TO SELL . . . but I feel my client list isn't robust enough to get the offer I need to make it worth selling.

Just one more piece of the life I'm trying to build put on hold.

Just one more dream I have to wait to achieve.

Just one more heartache I have to endure.

CHAPTER FOURTEEN
Ryker

"Is this seat taken?"

"All yours," I murmur just above the bluesy jazz the bar is piping through its speakers. The weeknight crowd is above average in size in this yuppified bar on the East Side.

"You're lucky I was in town," Carter Preston says, and I can see him hold up his fingers in my periphery to flag down the bartender. Once his drink is ordered and his first sip is taken, he leans back in his chair.

I make him wait. Not because I have anything more pertinent to do but more because the fucker makes my skin crawl.

"You going to talk, Lockhart, or am I going to sit here with my dick in my hand and pretend you love me?" He laughs like the self-righteous prick he is, and I'm already annoyed with him.

"A double this time," I tell the bartender when he points to my glass asking if I want a refill. I look at Carter for the first time. "This shit has got to stop."

"Us meeting in private like two lovers? I agree. It has to stop." He smiles like a picture of innocence, and my hand tightens on my glass in reaction.

"Leave Vaughn alone."

Carter takes his time sipping his bourbon, rolls it around on his tongue, and then sets his glass down before leaning back and staring at me. "Ah, so you are falling for the whore. How cute is that? The elusive Ryker Lockhart falling for the indiscriminate Vaughn Sanders." He shakes his head after a beat and laughs. "I knew she couldn't keep a secret. Loose lips in both places, apparently."

I fist my hands and clench my teeth and refuse to take the bait he's throwing out for me. "Just a personal PSA is all." I shrug.

Carter part smiles, part laughs. "She has no idea you're here talking to me, does she? What? Did she threaten to hold out if you did? Such a rebel, Lockhart. Risking the pussy to defend her honor. No worries— your secret is safe with me."

"My secret? Nah, more like I'm trying to make sure both of our asses are protected. She does have shit on you, Carter. I get being a politician and all you're used to people having dirt, but hers . . . ," I say with a lift of my eyebrows that tells him to figure out how bad it is for himself.

"The log she has means shit," he says dismissively. "The pictures will burn themselves out."

The log? Pictures? I slide a look at him over the rim of the glass when I take a drink.

"That's your business. Not mine," I say with a shrug. "If what she has on you is meaningless, then why are you still pursuing her?"

The slight stall of his glass to his lips tells me he's bluffing.

"She must be one magical paid fuck for you to risk losing your career over," Carter murmurs, stare unrelenting, smirk taunting. "Screwing a woman—defending her—when you don't know the truth about her isn't exactly the smartest thing, now is it? You'd think a lawyer such as yourself would be a little more careful with his reputation."

"And you'd think a senator would have stronger morals," I counter with a lift of my brows, but I have no fucking clue what he's talking about other than her owning Wicked Ways.

His laugh carries over the rest of the chatter in the bar, and a few people glance our way. "I see what you did here. Trendy place on the opposite side of town. A little crowded. A spot up front at the bar. Public but private. No one will think twice about the two executives in suits having a tense conversation."

"Stop with the bullshit. The standing in front of her house in the middle of the night. The threats about risking Lucy's adoption. The intimidation. That might work in your fights on the Senate floor, but it doesn't play well here."

"Stop or else what? You're going to make sure my wife takes me to the cleaners? Oh, I'm scared."

"This has nothing to do with your wife."

"You're fucking her too, then?"

"I don't sleep with clients."

"Apparently Vaughn does," he says and then tsks when I shift in my chair, my fist clenched as I bite my tongue. In our last conversation, I basically confirmed that Vaughn is Vee. There's not a chance in hell I'm going to make that mistake again. Stupid, because Carter already knows it, but I've learned my lesson. "It'd be a shame for you to take a swing at me right now. My security detail is a little bored as of late and might be a little too eager to take care of you. Besides, there are too many connections between us right now, so you don't want to risk being noticed."

"It just might be worth it." I meet his glare and lift an eyebrow in a taunt. The tension thickens as I wait for him to make the next move.

It's his call. Ramp this down, or take the hit my fist is begging to throw.

"You know what, Lockhart? I'll tell you the same thing I told your hired help." He shakes his glass so the ice rattles.

"What's that?"

"I'm not the best guy to threaten. While I'm sure your ego is large enough to think that a part of this has to do with me pursuing Vaughn to get back at you for screwing me over with Bianca, you'd be wrong.

While I normally wouldn't put it past me to be that vindictive, don't think so highly of yourself that I care anything about you one way or another. If I want to get back at you, sure, I'd fuck her and take every ounce of pleasure hearing her cry out my name . . . but it's easier than that. All I have to do is let Roxanne talk. Offer to pay my old friend what she'd stand to lose if that divorce settlement of hers is overturned due to her attorney's misconduct. She'd be more than willing to throw you under the bus for that with the whole woman-scorned bit she's playing. A few gossip mills later and your reputation will take a big hit over how you sleep with your clients' wives and then go soft during negotiations against their favor. That would be payment enough."

And Roxanne resurfaces once again . . . *fucking cocksucker*. If he's trying to hit every please-break-my-nose-with-a-punch button, he's more than succeeded. I shift in my seat to abate the urge and take in a deep breath.

Keep your focus, Ryk. While punching the hell out of him will make you feel better, it does nothing to get him to back the fuck off of Vaughn. De-escalate the situation.

"Vaughn's off limits," I grit out. "Not because you want to get back at me, but because she's not someone you want to get tangled with. She goes down, you go down."

"She's going to go down all right, and it's going to be on me." He tilts his glass up and empties its contents with a satisfied sigh. "You see? I don't care if she's with you or not with you or if you've gone soft and now are a pussy. I want her, and I will have her for no other reason than to even a score. Yes. I'm a sick bastard like that. No woman gets the upper hand on me and gets away with it. And I'll fucking get off on every goddamn moment of it."

I try to remain calm and not engage. I'm realizing that the more I react, the more I fight, the more adamant he becomes to have her.

"No man uses fear to corral a woman."

"She's not a woman, Lockhart. She's a whore. And you'll thank me in the future for reminding you of that little fact."

"Half of Washington has dirt on you, Senator. You going to *hate-fuck* all of them as well?"

"If I need to." His smile is cold and calculating and begs me to say more, but I refrain. My body is so taut with anger my muscles ache. "Cat got your tongue?"

"Nope. Just trying to figure out how an asshole like you hasn't been killed by a guy like me yet."

He chuckles and taps his glass against mine. "You go from all but serving up Vaughn's pussy on a platter to me to defending her as if she's your holy grail. What happened to using sex to garner fear and then gain power? Where did that eager little beaver who gobbled up my advice go?" His chuckle rumbles through the bar as I let him ramble to see what else he's going to say to me. And fuck if it isn't one of the hardest things I've ever had to do. "You think there wasn't a reason I didn't tell you what I had on her? You think I haven't been around the block enough times to feel out the fucker who screws me over by taking my wife on as a client and then promises to let me sample his whore? More importantly, I have you admitting on tape that you pay a woman to have sex with you. I have you offering to pay her to have sex with me. Bribing a politician is a serious offense, Ryker. You're a lawyer. You should know that."

"You son of a bitch." It's all I can think to say as my mind tumbles out of control. Over how I walked right into his trap without blinking a fucking eye. I said her name, and it was recorded. Fucking hell. Now one misstep by me won't only screw me but will have enough fallout to devastate Vaughn in more ways than I could ever imagine.

"Don't worry, though. I won't use it against you unless you fuck with me. Unless you intervene between Vaughn and me." He leans in closer so I can smell the alcohol on his breath and the scent of snake oil from his slimy soul. "I play games for a living, Lockhart. You let your guard down and forgot that part. But don't you worry—I'll get what I *need* from you and what I *want* from her, one way or another."

I bite back the rage that consumes me. At him for being a prick and playing the game better than anyone I'd like to admit. At me for walking into a setup I should have seen a fucking mile away. For sitting here like a shell-shocked bastard as he walks away instead of punching his goddamn lights out.

Now what, Ryk?

She came to your office. She finally confessed what happened. And then she begged you not to confront him. Not to push his limits, because who knows how an irrational fuck like him would take it.

And of course she was right.

Nothing's changed now other than that you did exactly what she feared: you stoked the fire, so now it's burning even brighter for the pyromaniac to sit back and play with until everything burns down around us.

CHAPTER FIFTEEN

Ryker

"Stuart." It's how I greet my private investigator when he answers my call.

"Why do I get the feeling this isn't a simple request to see how my day is going?" Stuart asks with a chuckle.

"I want to know every goddamn thing there is to know about Vaughn Sanders." My feet move from one side of my office to the other. They haven't stopped moving, seeing as I keep replaying my meeting with Carter over and over in my mind.

"I thought you told me to hold off on stripping her bare."

"Yes. No. Fuck!" My voice is sharp off the walls as the image his words evoke pisses me off even more. "I didn't. I don't." My own reason wars against my rage. "Just fucking do it."

"You sure?"

I think of the hundreds of reasons why I should back down. The fact that I want Vaughn to tell me her secrets herself. *The need for her to.* To know she values *us* enough to let me in further. The fact that Stuart digging into her past is a violation of her privacy when I've already done enough to hurt her.

And then I think of the one reason to find it all out: so I can help protect her.

"Yes."

"Yes, sir."

"Don't argue with me," I snap.

"No, sir."

"I want to know everything there is about her. Anything that can be used to blackmail her, coerce her, all the way down to the size of her goddamn panties."

Stuart is silent for a beat. "Okay . . ."

"Financials. Past, present." My hand hurts from clenching so hard, but hell if it's not Carter Preston's neck I'm imagining it wrapped around.

"Even the no-go areas you held me back from before?" he asks.

"I need to know about her past," I state, giving him the go-ahead to give me more information about one James Sanders.

The man we found who lives on the outskirts of Greenwich in a house he's upside down in. And besides hoping his dick had rotted off for what he did to Vaughn's sister, I didn't allow myself to know much else.

"So either you want to royally fuck her over, or *she's the one.*"

He could have sucker punched me and I wouldn't have been so surprised by his words. "What the hell are you talking about?" I part laugh, part look around the room like a paranoid mess.

Stuart's chuckle fills the line, and he was just added to my shit list. "I've never seen you like this before. You're passionate about your clients—about getting what you need to win in court . . . but, Ryk, this is a whole next level." I can all but hear him shrug. "That tells me she means something to you. Either you're spooked and need to know her skeletons to make you shit or get off the pot when it comes to taking things further with her in the relationship department . . . or you're not spooked and someone is fucking with her. In that case, have mercy on their souls." His matter-of-fact tone resonates. The words he says with it even more so.

"Maybe the answer is that it's a bit of both." I don't expect to give him an answer. That's not my style. But he's probably the closest thing I have to a friend, and I can't take the words back.

And lucky for him he keeps his mouth shut, because his words reverberate loud and clear and knock loose truths I'm not sure I want to acknowledge. If I do care about Vaughn and she finds out I've ordered this invasion into her privacy, I'm the asshole who's snooping. I'm the jerk who is suddenly a creep and is beyond reason. But if she never finds out because I charge in to save the day on a white horse behind the scenes, then isn't the risk worth it?

I've already done enough to fuck with her. I've already screwed up. It's my job to try to make it right the best I can—and this is the only way I can think to do that. To protect her. To make sure no one else can come after her if Preston sets his bullshit in motion.

"Just get me what I want, Stu."

His laugh fills the line. "Sure thing. But, uh . . . do we need to have a talk about how committing a felony would ruin your law career?"

"I'm well aware."

"Then maybe you should stop thinking about murdering whoever the fuck it is you're thinking about hurting."

"Nah. I'm finding great pleasure in using my imagination."

"I'll get on it."

"Thanks."

When I hang up the phone, my eyes veer to the door Vaughn walked out of the last time I saw her, and my thoughts come back to her as well.

What the hell does Carter Preston have on her?

Revealing who she really is and messing with her livelihood, I get. The fear of social services finding out and her losing the chance to adopt Lucy, I completely understand. But what in the hell is she not telling me about her uncle?

She's a grown woman. He can't intimidate or manipulate her now. I get that the chains of a past like that are strong and the thought of him could be debilitating, but there's something else going on.

Something else that has her spooked.

If only I could get her to talk to me.

If only I could get her to trust me again.

If only I could win her back.

Way to fuck things up, Lockhart.

CHAPTER SIXTEEN

Vaughn

"It was a good night," I agree with Melissa. It's well after two in the morning as our heels click on the concrete floor of the long hallway that leads to Apropos's exit.

Large tips always help to make it a good night.

Hands not grabbing your ass make it even better.

I glance down at my Wicked Ways phone and notice a text from the new client, Noah, and I slow down to read it. I received all the information you sent my way. I'd prefer to meet face-to-face before we proceed. I like to know who I'm doing business with.

With a sigh and a shake of my head, I slip my phone back into my purse. The last thing I want to do right now is don my Madam Vee getup and meet with a client who is already proving to be high maintenance before he even goes on his first date.

"You okay?" Melissa asks with concerned eyes, and I realize I've stopped walking and that she's done the same in turn.

"Yeah. It was just a text. A bill collector," I lie. "It's just been a rough couple of weeks."

"But I thought you had a man now," she says and snaps her fingers in a Z shape.

"Ha. Hence the rough couple of weeks." I laugh, all while hating the notion that she thinks I'd let a man pay my bills for me.

"Does he treat you right?"

I nod. "Yes. Of course. It's just . . . complicated," I murmur and roll my eyes in jest.

"We're talking about a man here, aren't we? They are as complicated as they are simple."

"Very true," I laugh, but the pang hits me just as hard as her words. *I miss him.*

It's been a little over three weeks since the Hamptons. Since I thought the stars were aligning and maybe—just maybe—there might be a little bit of happiness for me. Since the pool house and Carter Preston and the threats that could upend my world.

But I still miss Ryker.

And I'm not sure how I feel about that.

The fresh air hits us when Melissa pushes open the door to the parking lot. She stops momentarily as she steps out into the fluorescent light before humming under her breath. "Mmm-mmm-mmm. I'd take that man even if he had a three-inch dick."

I laugh with her and then realize she's actually talking about someone standing before her. For the briefest of moments I pause, afraid that Carter is waiting outside my work. But then the person speaks.

"Good morning." Ryker's gravelly baritone hits my ears and makes my stomach flutter.

Even after everything—the emotion, the doubt, the heartache—he still makes my stomach flutter.

When I step out from behind Melissa, Ryker's standing there under the streetlight. He's wearing dark jeans and a cream-colored henley with the sleeves pushed halfway up his forearms. He's holding a bunch of white daisies in his hand that look like he picked them in a field, but c'mon, we're in Manhattan, so he must have bought them somewhere.

But it's the shy smile on his lips and the sincerity in his eyes when our gazes meet that causes that flutter to intensify.

I said we couldn't do this. I told myself that the more space I put between us, the easier it would get. I thought I could walk away. But seeing him—wanting him . . . I don't think I'll be able to stick to my own words. Ryker Lockhart is just as potent to me as the drugs that lured my sister.

"Hi." His smile widens as he steps away from the sleek black sports car at his back.

"What are you doing here?" I ask cautiously, looking from him to Melissa and then back.

"You two go and have some fun now," she says, lifting her eyebrows at me and then waving like a teenage girl to Ryker.

"Let me walk you to your car," he says to Melissa, and her reaction—startled head, wide eyes, disbelieving smile—says it all.

"It's just right here." She points to a white crossover a few cars down. "But, uh—thanks."

Ryker nods, and we watch in silence as she climbs into her car, starts it, and then pulls away from the curb.

It's just the two of us now and the rest of the city still awake milling around us.

"Did you have a good shift?" Ryker asks as he takes a step toward me and holds out the flowers as if our last discussion never happened.

Maybe I want to pretend for a little bit that it didn't happen either. Maybe I just want to enjoy the fact that he's standing here waiting for me at two in the morning with flowers and a smile that warms me in ways I'm still not used to.

I'll let myself forget for a bit. I'll probably be mad at myself later for it—for giving in and seeming so wishy-washy—but for now I just want to feel like I did that night in the Hamptons when there was the taste of chocolate chip cookie dough on his lips and the cool chill of the granite sliding beneath my back. Carefree. In love. *Loved.*

"Vaughn?" Ryker's voice pulls me from my thoughts, and I take the flowers from his outstretched hand. Not wanting him to see the flush in my cheeks, I bury my nose in them and breathe in the sweet scent. The flowers are so simple from a man who can afford the world, and I love that they are. "How was your shift?"

"It was long, but good."

"What made it a good night?" He reaches out and tucks a loose strand of hair behind my ear, his fingers lingering on my cheek for a few seconds more. "Good tips?"

"No."

"Good customers?"

"No."

"Then what?" he asks, that smile turning curious and his head angling to the side to emphasize the question.

I give in to the temptation to just accept that he's here and I'm glad that he is.

"You being here."

He stares at me for the briefest of seconds, and this time when he reaches out, he cups both of my cheeks and lowers his lips to brush against mine. Every part of me sags at the tenderness in the simple kiss—so brief, but packed with so much emotion.

"That's a good answer."

I lean back and look at him. The brandy color of his eyes. The mussed hair. The rough cut of his jaw with a day's worth of shadow dusting it. "Why are you here?"

"Because I missed you," he murmurs, and for the first time, I almost feel like we can do this. Like we can face whatever is out there together and make this work.

"So you stayed up late to walk me to my car?"

"If that's what you want me to do, then yes . . . or"—he lifts his chin over his shoulder—"we can go for a drive."

"To where? It's two in the morning." I laugh.

He runs his thumb over my bottom lip. His smile is lopsided and hopeful. "I know I'm supposed to give you space. I know I told you to take your time . . . but dammit, Vaughn, *I missed you* and wanted to see you."

Swoon.

"I missed you too." Our gazes hold, and all I can do is shake my head ever so subtly to tell him I'm not sure what to do but I'm glad he's here right now.

"I think we should go out."

"Right now?" I sputter a laugh.

"We're in the city that never sleeps for a reason." He shrugs like a little boy. "Why not?"

I think of my aching feet and how bone tired I am, but when he smiles, I already know that I'll go.

"I don't think we've ever been on a proper date."

"You're crazy." I laugh and press my lips to his.

"I know."

He starts to head toward his car, his fingers tangled with mine, and when I don't walk with him so that our hands stretch between us, he turns back to stare at me.

"What?" he asks.

I take him in—everything about him—and just smile as I warm from head to toe. "Nothing."

The city may never sleep, but the streets are quieting down as we hum through the concrete jungle in silence. Ryker's fingers are laced in mine, both our hands resting on my thigh as the gentle purr of the Maserati's motor hums around us.

"You know, most dates start before everyone is asleep," I tease as I look down at the bag in my lap. Curiosity has me wondering why he brought me a pair of shoes and a sweatshirt.

"Everything about us is far from normal, so why would we want to ruin it now?" He flashes me a smile before veering to the curb and parking. "Your feet good?"

"I'm beginning to be concerned that you brought me shoes. Please tell me we're not hiking anywhere."

"While I very much like the heels, I thought you might like to get out of them. And hiking? In Manhattan?" He rolls his eyes. "Nah. Maybe a little breaking and entering, though."

"*What?*" I ask as he climbs out of the car and shuts the door with a thud, leaving me to figure out if he's serious or not. When he opens the passenger-side door, I ask, "What do you mean, a little breaking and entering?"

He shuts the door behind me and then steps into me so that my back presses against it.

"Ryker?"

"Shh." He puts a finger to my lips, and I can't help but press a kiss to it. A ghost of a smile paints his lips in reaction as he takes my hands in his and then looks back up. "You and I . . . we're far from typical. We've had a lot of shit happen between us from the get-go. I'll never regret how I pushed you to get us here, but I regret many other things I've done. I put you, this"—he squeezes my hands—"us, in jeopardy, and I was wrong."

"Ryk—"

"Please just let me finish." His eyes are filled with so much honesty that it almost hurts for me to look at them. It's the kind of honesty where you are opening yourself up to getting hurt. The kind where you're stripped bare and completely transparent.

I don't think a man has ever given that much of himself to me before, and I don't know what to say other than, "Mmm-hmm."

"I just wanted a night without distractions. One where it's just you and me and we can pretend like . . . I don't know. Like I haven't fucked up a million times."

"That would be nice."

There's something about him—about this moment—a man who has never come off as uncertain, but now he seems to be completely and utterly on shaky ground. My heart falls, in such a good way.

But just as quickly as I get a glimmer of his uncertainty, his expression changes, and a mischievous smile turns up his lips. "Do you trust me?"

I laugh, his playful question just that, but I don't miss the small pang of hurt that he caused when he breached that trust at the pool house.

I shake it off, shove it down, and smile. "Should that question worry me?"

"C'mon." He tugs on my hand, and I slide a glance his way when he wraps an arm around my shoulder and pulls me close.

Steam sneaks up from the subway grates on the streets, and trash cans are overflowing, but the soft hue of the streetlights above and the comforting noises of a sleepy city surround us.

"Hungry?" he asks when he veers into a hole-in-the-wall pizza place. My hand flies to my stomach as I suddenly realize I am. Within minutes, we are back on the street with a box of pizza and a bag complete with paper plates and napkins.

"Ryker, what are you——?"

"Shh," he says and then presses a chaste kiss to my lips. When he steps back, his laughter rings out as he steers me around a column beneath the darkened shadows of the High Line. Running a little over two miles through the West Side of Manhattan, it's an old train platform that has been repurposed into a park of sorts.

"Here. Hold this." Ryker pushes the pizza my way when we come to what looks like a gate that's been rolled down at one of the entrances. I take it from him as he squats down in the darkness and grabs the lock.

Breaking and entering.

"Ryker?"

"Keep your voice down, will you?"

"What are you doing?"

"You mean what are *we* doing?" I can hear the smile in his tone even though I can't see his face. "*We* are picking a lock."

"Ryker!" My voice is sterner this time, my whisper harsher. "This is illegal. We can't do this."

His laugh is a low chuckle as I hear metal on metal with whatever it is that he's doing. "Stepdad number who-knows-what was a developer who built some of the condos about a quarter mile down the park from here."

"Okay." I stretch the word out as I try to figure out what that has to do with anything.

"After school I'd have to come here and wait for him to finish up before going home. Most times he'd just put me in his car and have the driver take me, since he was too busy to give me the time of day. While I'd wait, some of the construction crew would show me a thing or two." I can hear the reminiscence in his voice. I can also hear the silent animosity over having a father figure who was anything but.

"Did you ever use these skills you learned?"

"I can neither confirm nor deny . . ."

"Ah, the rebellious rich kid who liked walking on the wrong side of the tracks."

"Something like that." There's a clink and then the sudden sound of the metal gate rolling up. Ryker holds his hand out to me. "Come on."

I look over my shoulder and hesitate. "Can't we get in trouble for this?"

Without warning, Ryker tugs on my hand so that I'm flush against him, pizza almost tipping in my other hand just as his mouth meets mine.

Good God, the man can kiss.

It's my only thought as his tongue slips between my lips and reminds me of everything about him that I've missed. The warmth of his body. The taste of his kiss. The scrape of his stubble against my jaw. The hum of vibration deep in his throat.

"Trying not to get in trouble is part of the thrill."

CHAPTER SEVENTEEN
Vaughn

The lights of Hoboken across the Hudson are laid out before us. Ryker and I are sitting on some kind of wooden chaise longue type of chair, the leftover pizza in a box on the chair next to us. Condos tower behind us with most of their lights off, the occupants fast asleep, but there is an occasional bout of laughter or domestic sound here and there.

And of course a siren wails or a horn honks every now and then, making me jump like one just did.

"You really are worried, aren't you?" Ryker asks as his finger draws lazy lines up and down the length of my spine. I'm sitting up while he's lying back, obviously more relaxed at this being-where-we-shouldn't-be type of thing.

"Aren't you worried? You're the one who practices law for a living. What if we're caught? What if they press charges? What if—"

His chuckle rumbles through the silence, and it takes everything I have not to shush him to be quieter. "Relax. I'm not worried about talking an officer or two into letting us off with a warning. Or offering a subtle bribe. Besides, what we're doing is the least of their problems."

"It's ironic that I'm this straitlaced, isn't it?" I laugh. "Most people would think it'd be the other way around—me the rule breaker and you the rule follower."

"Seriously. How did I not know this about you? That you are so scared of getting in trouble."

I glance back at him and give a resigned shrug. "Because if I get in trouble, the fallout can have dire consequences."

"We'll be fine. I promise you. But I have a feeling this need to follow rules and this fear of getting in trouble started way before now."

"You don't get it because you're you."

"What?" he says through a laugh. "That makes no sense."

"Of course it doesn't . . . but just like you breaking in here—how you don't worry because you know a cop would see your expensive clothes and might know of you or your reputation and let you off with a warning—they'd never do that to me. People see me—a woman in the skimpy outfit at work or the person who runs Wicked Ways—and . . . and they assume what they want about me. Nothing I say or do can change their opinions."

He leans forward and presses a kiss to the back of my neck, his lips moving against my skin when he speaks. "Fuck their opinions. I'm glad I get to see the woman no one else gets to see." He pulls me back so his arm is around my shoulder and my head rests on his chest. He murmurs against my scalp, "Relax, Vaughn. We're going to be just fine."

His words soak in, and I know he means right now in our trespassing and also in the greater scheme of things.

I hope he's right.

We sit in comfortable silence for a bit with the sounds of crickets and the trees rustling in the light breeze coming in off the river. This feels so normal. So right. It makes me afraid to leave this platform, because I don't want that to change.

"When you were little, what did you want to be when you grew up?"

His question startles me and then makes me smile as the faint memories of my mom ghost through my mind. "A mom."

"A mom?"

"Mmm. I wanted to be just like my mom. She was my world."

"What was she like?"

"Vibrant. Fun. She always made you feel like you were the most special person in the room so that when she turned to pay attention to someone else, you were almost jealous over it."

"Is it hard to remember her?" Another kiss to my head. A hand running up and down my arm.

"Yes. It's been so long that I'm not sure if what I remember are truly memories or just ones I pieced together from pictures and created myself. But I remember her voice clear as day. How she used to sing silly songs to us when we were tucked in her bed. Her family was super formal, and then there was her—this wildflower among all the perfectly pruned roses."

"I bet they hated that."

"Probably." I smile at the memories that hit me, one after another, and am grateful that he allows me the silence to just close my eyes and think of her. "What about you? Tell me about your parents."

"Nothing much to tell other than what you already know."

"Where is your dad? What does he do?"

"He's down in Palm Beach, Florida. He's an angel investor in companies." He sighs. "I don't know—we're not really that close. After my mom took him to the proverbial cleaners in their divorce, he bailed. I spent vacations and summers with him . . . and whenever my mom deemed that she needed less responsibility, I guess."

"That must have been hard."

"It's all I've ever known. Him gone and her falling in love, then out of love, and then the drama of a divorce. The *woe is me* as she collects another hefty check in her divorce settlement, only for her to do it all over again."

"Were any of your stepdads nice to you?"

"They all were nice to me. More tolerant than nice, really," he says, so matter-of-fact, and my heart breaks for the little boy who I can imagine was always trying to fit in an ever-changing landscape. "But they were moguls in their own minds. One owned some restaurants, one was a developer, like I said. One was a capital investor, and one was connected to the Vanderbilts somehow. None of them had time for a son."

"I'm sorry."

"Don't be. I figured shit out after a while. I knew when to be absent, how to play the part for dinner parties, and how to be used as a pawn when my mother needed something."

"That's so wrong." And the opinion he had of women when we first met makes so much sense now.

"It is what it is. Now"—he pulls me in tighter against him—"can we get off this topic? I didn't take you on a romantic date on the Hudson to talk about my boring childhood."

But it was anything but boring. Sad and lonely, I'm sure, but not boring.

"What do you want to talk about?"

"Anything."

"When I was little, the town we lived in used to have this wish lantern festival," I say, pulling the memory out of the blue.

"Wish lantern?"

"They're the paper lanterns like—" *Like the ones in the movie* Tangled. But I don't finish the thought because there is no way he's watched *Tangled* before. "Like the ones you light, and then after the hot air fills them, they float into the sky."

"Yeah, I know what you're talking about."

"Anyways, we used to have this festival, and people would write their wishes on them or their worries, and the theory was that once they floated into the sky, their wish would be granted or their worry would be taken away."

"That's a cool concept."

"Mmm-hmm."

"What made you think about that right now?" he asks.

"I don't know. I was looking at the Hudson, and it reminded me of watching the lanterns fly high above the Atlantic after they were lit and let go."

"If you could have one of each right now, what would they be?"

"They don't come true if you tell anyone," I lie.

"Nice try, Sanders. If you're writing the words on the lantern, then everyone can see your wish and your worry anyway."

"You're a pain, you know that?"

"The best kind of pain," he jokes and presses a kiss to my temple. "Your wish and your worry?"

So many flit through my mind that I am too cowardly to give voice to. Getting my teaching credential. Starting a charity for kids with Downs. But I know none of those will ever be able to happen if I don't take care of a few things first.

"My wish would be to finally adopt Lucy. My worry? I have too many worries to pick just one." Another lie, but the last person I want to bring up tonight is the senator and wishing that he'd leave me alone and be out of my life. "What about yours?"

"My wish would be for you to stop holding back from me. And my worry . . . my worry would be that the senator doesn't stop obsessing over you."

Silence hangs heavy between us, and I don't speak, afraid to ruin what's left of our date.

But it's not lost on me that both his wish and his worry have to do with me.

◆　◆　◆

"You sure it's okay for you to stay here?" Ryker asks as he unclasps his watch from his wrist and sets it on the dresser.

"If you're asking if I need to call home to ask my parents if it's okay if I spend the night at a boy's house, I'm pretty sure the answer is yes." I bat my eyelashes and offer him a coy smile.

He lifts his eyebrows and grants me a smile. "Where were girls like you when I was a teenager with an empty house for weeks on end?" he teases.

"I shudder to think of the trouble you got yourself into."

"You have no idea," he says with a shake of his head and a knowing chuckle. I picture him as a teenager. No doubt handsome, definitely privileged, and most likely lonely. He probably lost himself in girls and sports and pushed everyone away or held them way too close.

I watch the man he is now from my seat on the edge of his massive bed as he pulls the henley over his head and tosses it into the hamper. His broad shoulders and the defined muscles of his back are on display. His trim waist leads down to his very fine ass, perfectly framed by the denim covering it.

He's gorgeous in so many ways it hurts to think about it.

"At some point, we need to talk about the senator, Vaughn." He turns to look at me again, the playful smile from moments ago replaced with a measured intensity.

"No."

"We do. We need to figure out how to deal with him so you can stop worrying."

"Please, not now." I force a smile to my lips despite the anxiety the mention of Carter Preston brings to me. "Please don't ruin the night . . . morning . . . whatever this was."

"It's a date."

"Yes. Our date. Everything about it was perfect. I just . . ." I look out the window as I try to find the words to explain what I need to say, suddenly shy from his unwavering attention. "I just need to be Vaughn right now. The sad little girl and confused twentysomething like I was before I had to be Vee. I need you to like Vaughn, to be okay with her and everything that comes with her . . . because that's who I really am."

"Hey." I don't turn to look his way as he steps beside me. "Vaughn?" The dip of the bed. The feel of his finger moving my chin so I'm forced to meet his gaze. "While ball-busting Vee intrigues the hell out of me, it's you I always see, Vaughn. *Just you.*"

He leans in and kisses me. The reassurance I find in this most intimate of acts is almost unnerving. The need to want him to give me the assurance even more so. My hands slide up the firm planes of his chest, then up over his shoulders before sliding down his back and then dipping below his waistband.

"Uh-uh," he warns with a chuckle as his hands lock over my wrists and prevent me from grabbing what is within inches of my reach before he abruptly stands from the bed.

My lips still tingling from his kiss, I look at him like he's crazy. "What do you mean, *uh-uh*?" I ask. "I thought you were thrilled that my parents were out of town so you could lure me to your house with promises of a big party. And then I'd pretend to be shocked when I arrived to find no party, just an empty house with you drenched in cologne asking me if I wanted to see your big, cozy bed."

"Jesus," he says through a laugh. "I'd love to see what else that imagination of yours thinks up"—he adjusts his grip on my wrists when I try to show him—"but not right now."

Something I'm not quite used to hits harshly: rejection.

My face must show it because his smile widens and he shakes his head ever so slightly as he meets my eyes. "In case you haven't noticed, I'm trying to take things slow with you."

"What?" I all but laugh the word out.

"The first time we met face-to-face, it ended with my fingers slick in your pussy." He quirks a brow as his smile turns suggestive. "And while I'm all for that—man, am I all for that—I think we started off on the wrong foot. We started off expecting sex and then nothing more."

"And now you're expecting . . . ?"

I can see him mentally chastising himself for turning down sex. It's in the way he shifts to readjust his raging hard-on. In the way he takes in a deep breath and looks away from me for a moment to see if he can keep his restraint intact.

When he looks back, the gold in his eyes burns with a desire he's trying to deny and that I'm all for igniting. "And now I want to do this right."

And if there was one thing he could have said to surprise me and knock the defiance to prove him wrong out of me, it was that.

"Right?" My heart constricts in my chest.

"Yes. *Right.*" He struggles with words, with the intensity of the conversation that I'm sure neither of us expected, but the tension in my hands to resist his grip eases. "I've messed a lot of things up, and I think you've had a lot of things messed up for you in your life. You, Vaughn Sanders, deserve to have something done right for you."

"Oh." It's all I can say, because everything about this late-night, early-morning date has been unexpected, just like my feelings for him have been.

"So are you going to let me do this for you? Because I've gotta admit, it's proving a hell of a lot harder to keep my hands off you than I thought it would be."

Thud. My heart can't fall many more times for him, or else it's going to end up battered and bruised from being offered.

This man. What in the hell is he doing to me?

I look up at him through my lashes, a coy smile on my lips, because even though I'm not going to fight him, I sure as hell am not going to make this easy on him. "So what's this called on our scale of right?"

"Our scale of right?"

"Yes. Is this considered our first date?" I lick my bottom lip and watch him take notice.

"If that's what you want to call it."

"Does that mean I'm going to get a first good night kiss?"

"I wouldn't want to deprive you of that, now would I?" A shy smile lights up his face.

"But I'm in your bed. Most first good night kisses do not happen anywhere near your date's bed."

"You suck at pretending, Vaughn." He laughs, but then before I can prepare myself, he has me lifted over his shoulder, ass stuck in the air.

"What are you doing? Stop! Put me down!"

But he doesn't stop. He walks through his penthouse, and only when he opens the front door and shuts it at his back does he let me slowly slide down the front of him. When his face comes into view, one eyebrow is quirked up. "Is this front door good enough for you?"

"Yeah, but it's kind of odd that it's your front door when it should be mine—" My mock complaint is cut off when Ryker places his lips on mine to shut me up.

The kiss smothers our laughter, along with erasing any other thoughts of being difficult from my mind. It's like a sweet seduction. It starts off soft and slow and then builds with an unfettered desire that's almost palpable.

My hands roam up the firmness of his chest to thread through the hair at the base of his neck, while one of his cups my breast and the other presses against my lower back. There isn't an inch of space between our bodies.

I can't help the groan that emits from the back of my throat, but the minute he swallows its sound he steps back and breaks the kiss. I'm left breathless, my body on fire and desperate for more of his touch, as he stalks into his place without a word.

My smile is almost as automatic as my desperation for him. The man is struggling to keep his word. I have to admire him, but oh this is going to be so much fun.

"That sure was one incredible good night kiss," I say as I enter the penthouse, shutting the door before following him down the hallway toward his bedroom. "I'd love to see what you do for an encore."

His strained laugh is his only response as he walks into his closet, where I can see him brace his hands against the island in there. His head is hung forward, his smile disbelieving, and he shakes his head as if he's trying to come to terms with the fact that he's really doing this. That he's really denying himself sex.

The minute he seems to rein it in, he shoves his jeans off and throws them somewhere I can't see in the depths of the closet.

I slide the sweatshirt he loaned me off and then make quick work of undoing the bustier of my uniform. "Hey, Ryker?" I ask innocently.

"Hmm?" He walks to the doorway, his impressive cock pressed against his boxer-briefs, which only serves to make that deep-seated ache I have for him burn that much brighter.

His eyes meet mine momentarily before scraping down to my bare chest and over to the bustier that I let drop unceremoniously onto the floor without looking. I make a show of giving his body the same once-over he's just given mine—him in his underwear and me in my skirt, stockings, and nothing else.

"Impressive." I lift my brows.

"That's the least of things I could use to impress you," he says, followed by a groan as I reach my hands to the back of my skirt so that the distinct sound of the zipper fills the room.

"I could take care of that for you, you know," I say, pointing in the general vicinity of his pelvis.

"Pajamas. You need pajamas right now." He's flustered, and it's adorable.

"Oopsie." I let my skirt fall to the ground around my ankles, so now all he's greeted with are nylons and lacy boy panties beneath. "I didn't bring any."

He struggles—the clench of his jaw, the flexing of his fists, the twitch of his cock. "I've got the perfect thing for you," he says and disappears into his closet, leaving the sexual tension in the room so thick I can almost feel it. He reappears in seconds and throws something at me from the other side of the room.

"What?" I laugh as I catch it. Then groan when I open it up. "No way. Uh-uh. I am not wearing this." The T-shirt has **RED SOX** emblazoned across the front of it, and I can't help but laugh thinking of our non-Wicked-Ways-sanctioned date. The Yankees game. His rooting for the Sox while I jeered at him for going against my Yankees. Taking the subway across town to his place. Sleeping together for the first time.

He flashes me a megawatt grin. "I think it'll look nice on you."

"Over my dead body."

He levels me with a look. "While I more than enjoy that body of yours, you need to cover your tits up if I'm going to be anywhere in your vicinity."

I look down as I cup both of my breasts, shirt falling to the floor, and run my thumb and forefinger over my nipples. "They are nice breasts, though, aren't they?"

His eyes darken with desire. "Put it on, Vaughn."

"I will not. I refuse to sleep with the enemy." I pout, then close my eyes and let my head fall back in mock rapture as I gently pinch my nipples once again.

"You already have." His voice is strained.

"I thought this was our first date, though," I say coyly as I fight my smile.

"I'm warning you."

"Does this bug you?" This time I let an exaggerated moan fall from my lips.

"Vaughn."

And before I even have time to squeal, Ryker has snatched the shirt up off the floor and tackles me on the bed in one continuous swoop.

I squeal in shock and then protest when his fingers find my rib cage so they can dance with tickles up and down their line.

"I'm not putting it on!" I say through the laughter.

"Yes, you are."

He straddles me so that he sits on my pelvis, his knees squeezing me in place as he tries to shove the shirt over my head. The motion has the thick hardness of his cock pressing against the underside of my breasts.

He pauses for the briefest of moments as its tip slips just between my cleavage when he tries once again to pull the shirt over my head. This time I push my arms together so my breasts squeeze against him.

"Stop," he part groans, part laughs, with eyes that totally beg me not to listen.

"Or what?" I'm winded and can't stop laughing.

"You're making this harder than it needs to be."

I still and lift an eyebrow and wink. "It's much better when it's hard." I squeeze my arms together again.

"Vaughn." This time my name sounds like a swear word.

"Oopsie."

After a playful struggle where more tickling is involved, he manages to grab my arms and pin them to either side of my head.

"How are you going to get the shirt over my head now? Huh?" I ask.

He realizes his mistake and that his hands are full, so he tries another tactic. "I have Red Sox sweatpants and a sweatshirt somewhere I can force you into if need be. Hell, I'd welcome another barrier between me and your skin, so I suggest you stop struggling and put the shirt on." He smiles smugly at me, and I do the only thing I can do—laugh.

And God, does it feel good to laugh with him. Over something stupid and silly and without a care in the world other than how I'm going to make him put his hands on me, all the while swooning over the reasons behind why he doesn't want to.

This time when he tries to pull the shirt over my head, I let him.

"*Why?* Why are you torturing us?" I ask as I obediently let him put my arms through the sleeves.

He leans over and presses the softest of kisses to my lips. "Because *you* matter." Another kiss of lips. "Because *this* matters." And one more to top it off. "Because tonight was *perfect.*"

Every single sarcastic comeback I can think of dies on my lips as I run a hand over his jawline and lift my head up so I can find his lips just one more time.

The kiss is a languorous one. Soft and slow and detailed in its attention. When it ends—when we're both equal parts sexually frustrated but intimately sated—Ryker rolls off me, pulling me with him, and just holds on tight.

"Well . . . ," I say to add some kind of levity to the torrent of emotion this whole evening has brought to me, but it ends up sounding like drugged satisfaction. "For a man who doesn't want anything else from me—"

"Oh, I want all right." He chuckles and presses a kiss to the crown of my head.

"You sure are holding on like you're afraid I'm going to bolt."

"Maybe that's because every time you've been in my bed before, you've left."

"Maybe I'm afraid your mom and dad will come home, and when they tell my parents what happened, I'll be sent off to reform school for sleeping in a bed with a boy."

"It wouldn't matter. We'd still figure out a way to see each other." He tightens his arm around me and lowers his voice. "We've managed to find our way back to each other so far." He nuzzles his nose against the back of my neck. "I want you to be here when I wake up, Vaughn."

I love you, Ryker Lockhart.

I don't voice the words, but every single part of me feels them as the sky outside turns that dull gray that happens in the hours before the sun begins to brighten the sky.

While I don't say the words, as I fall asleep cocooned in his arms and with the steady rise and fall of his chest beneath my cheek, every part of my being feels them.

If I thought him making me *need* him was bad, now he's made me *want* him too.

CHAPTER EIGHTEEN
Vaughn

What was that?

I jolt awake in my bed. Lungs heaving. Mind fuzzy. Adrenaline coursing.

Samantha. Where's Samantha?

Patting the bed beside me as if I've missed her when through the moonlit room I can clearly see she's not there.

My throat is dry, and for some reason my hands tremble with fear.

Toot. Toot.

I jump at the sound and emit a startled yelp.

The train. It's just the train is all. A nightmare and the whistle have me freaking out.

But the thump outside my closed door only adds to it.

That and the cry I give when Samantha flings it open and turns on the light.

"Let's go." Her voice is on the edge of hysteria yet has a calm urgency to it as I blink to let my eyes adjust to the light. She's already halfway across our room to the closet before I can really see.

"What do you mean—"

"C'mon, Vaughn. You need to get up right now. We're leaving." She yanks open a dresser drawer and takes the first things she comes to—a faded pair of jeans and then a T-shirt—and throws them at me.

"Sam. What's wrong? What's going on?"

"You need to trust me." She drops a bag on the carpet with a thud and then proceeds to go to the back of our closet so I can't see her.

Pushing myself off the bed with my clothes clutched in one hand, worry begins to course through me. "Sam? Are you okay? What's—"

"Get dressed!" she yells at me without any care that she'll wake up Uncle James. But it's when she all but runs out of the closet and I see her face that I freeze.

Her complexion is pale, her eyes are wide with worry, and everything about her seems to be on edge and rushed.

"Sam?" I ask, much calmer now even though my pulse is racing and unease is tickling at the base of my neck. Tears I don't understand well in my eyes.

"Here." She pushes a suitcase at me, refusing to meet my eyes or answer my questions. "Grab whatever you want to take with you."

"For how long?"

"Forever."

My hands still, and my suitcase falls on its side at her words. "What do you mean?"

"We're leaving, Vaughn. This town. This house. Him. We're leaving." Our eyes lock for the first time since she stormed in here.

I find it hard to swallow as fear of the unknown future stretches out before us at the same time hope tries to bubble its way up in the crevices the fear of living in this house has created within me. And even though I know this is a good thing—us leaving—it's still terrifying.

"Yes, Vaughn. Everything I told you we were going to do—leave here, make a life for ourselves—we're going to do it right now. So I need you to pack, okay?" Without waiting for me to comply, she begins shoving her *own clothes from her dresser into her suitcase in one big scoop of items after another.*

Stunned, a little off kilter, and still watching her, I kneel down to open my suitcase, but my hand hits something odd. When I look down, a gasp falls from my lips as I stare at the bag she'd dropped on the floor with a thud after she came in here.

It's jewelry. Lots of jewelry—it's my uncle's Rolexes and diamond cuff links and rings, when he never wears rings—and cash. A thick stack of bills folded inside his money clip. I stare at the pile, my fingers coiling back as if the items in the bag that I now notice is a pillowcase will burn them.

"It's our payoff." She keeps her head down as she flits around the room and slides a bin out from beneath the bed to grab her vast collection of journals where they're hidden beneath the winter clothes we've stored them in.

"I don't under—"

"Pack. Please, pack," she urges. "All of that is what Uncle James is giving us if we leave and never come back."

"But . . ." The word dies on my lips as our gazes hold, and the look in hers tells me not to question. Not to ask. And to believe her lie that we're not stealing these items so we have something to pawn and live off.

Holy shit. This is real.

I just nod but don't move, frozen by the change swirling through the room like a hurricane.

"We have to go, Vaughn."

I look at her, my eyes blinking, as I try to process everything and the urgency with which she's requiring me to do it.

And then I see it.

The blood. Little specks on her shirt. On her cheek.

"Sam. Your shirt. There's blood. Are you okay? What did he do to you? Are you hurt? Did he hurt you?" Tears flood my eyes as my own hysteria amps up with each and every syllable.

She looks down at her shirt and blinks slowly as time feels like it passes in slow motion. In automatic reflex, she closes one hand around the key on the chain around her neck as she stares at the little dots of blood speckled on it.

When she looks back at me this time, there is more determination than ever before in her expression. In her eyes. In everything about her.

"Yes. He did. *He hurt me again, and it's the last time I'll ever allow him to. That's why we're leaving.*" *She steps forward and grabs both of my cheeks in her hands and looks into my eyes.* "I know this is scary, Vee. I know it's the middle of the night and I'm worrying you, but Uncle James is, uh . . . passed out on his bed, and this is our chance to leave and never look back. We'll get a place of our own. We'll never have to see him again. I'll take care of you. I promise you, I'll take care of you."

I nod. It's all I can do as I imagine a life where my sister doesn't have to tiptoe into our room late at night, scrub herself raw in the shower, and then climb into bed, where she lies to me and tells me she's okay.

I'll do anything she wants me to so long as she never has to do that again.

"Okay. I'll pack."

Toot. Toot.

Another train this time. Maybe we'll be on the next one.

Toot. Toot.

I startle awake and bolt to an upright seated position in bed. It takes a moment for me to make out my surroundings—with my breath labored and my heart racing.

Ryker's.

I'm at Ryker's place.

Not the mansion in Greenwich.

"Hey, you okay?" Ryker's sleep-drugged voice rasps through the silence, and his hand rubs lazily up and down the line of my back.

"Yes. Yeah."

"Bad dream?" he asks.

"Yeah."

"C'mere." He hooks an arm around my waist and pulls me against him. My immediate reaction is to fight against him for some reason, to keep some distance and gain some space to allow my mind to settle at the memory and the little details of that night I haven't thought of in years.

But I don't.

I lie back down and allow Ryker to wrap his arms around me so that the heat of his body seeps into the chill of mine.

"You sure you're okay?"

"Mmm-hmm." I don't trust myself to speak.

"I'll make your bad dreams go away, Vaughn," he murmurs and presses a kiss against the crown of my head. "All of them. You don't need to worry anymore. I've got you now."

And with my hand pressed against his heart and his chin resting atop my head, I revel in this foreign feeling as his breath slowly evens out with sleep.

In the comfort.

In the feeling of being safe.

In the notion that I'm not alone.

How could I have wanted to fight this feeling? How could I have thought all this time that being alone was better for me?

Sure, we're not perfect . . . but this—Ryker and his arms around me, helping to chase away the demons of my past—is something I can't describe.

And almost as much as it scares me . . . it also feels so very therapeutic.

It makes me realize that this feeling might just make everything worth it.

I've got you now.

Every last thing.

CHAPTER NINETEEN
Ryker

The Red Sox T-shirt is bunched around her waist, and she's sprawled diagonally across my bed. The sheets are twisted around her legs, when thirty minutes ago those long temptations were tangled around mine as we slept.

I let her sleep. As much as I want to wake her up, I let her sleep. My mind ghosts over her bad dream last night. The trembling of her hand against my chest. The racing of her pulse at her temple beneath my lips.

And I wonder what it was she dreamed about.

She shifts, her shirt lifting a little higher, the curve of her thigh revealed a bit more, and I find it impossible to take my eyes off her.

What is it about this woman that makes me fight to *not* have sex with her?

Am I fucking crazy to turn those legs and that ass and that goddamn vise-grip pussy down like I did last night?

I button up the rest of my dress shirt as I watch her. The light hair fanned on the dark sheets. The dark lashes on the pale skin of her cheeks. The pink lips that would make any man beg for mercy. I want her in the best way. In the worst way. Hell, *in any way.*

I'm crazy all right, but now it seems I'm crazy for her.

How'd that fucking happen? When did I become a man who wines and dines without expecting a thing in return?

My phone vibrates on the dresser next to me. A reminder of my court date in two hours and another about my meeting with Stuart at three.

He'd better have something for me. Her stockings at my feet catch my eye, and then the bustier a few feet beyond that. I smile. Her blatant defiance shouldn't cause that reaction from me, but it does.

She shifts on the bed, and a soft sound of contentment sighs from her lips—the same one she gives when I push into her during sex—as she snuggles back into the comforter.

What if Stuart has dug up information on her that you're not prepared to hear? What are you going to do with it then?

Is it going to change how you feel about her, Ryk?

How bad would it have to be to make that happen?

Fuck.

I blow out a sigh, and even though I know I need to head into the office, my feet move toward her. To the one person I keep being drawn to over and over despite telling myself that it's too much work, too much hassle, too much feeling.

I rest my hip on the side of the bed and press a kiss to her temple.

"Please tell me you're not dressed yet," she murmurs but doesn't open her eyes. Instead, she turns toward me and buries her face between the outside of my thigh and the mattress. The heat of her breath warms my slacks. The scent of her shampoo is faint but there. "It's too early."

"Mmm." The drapes are drawn to mute the light, so I get why she thinks that. "Not early, no."

"What time—"

"Shh." I cut her off and link my fingers with hers. "I have to get to court."

"Noooo. Don't go."

Goddamn it. The temptation to call the judge and postpone—give some bullshit reason that won't hold—so that I can slide back into the bed beside her has never been more appealing.

"I have to go." It pains me to say those four words.

"Aren't you tired?"

Exhausted. "That's what espresso's for. Stay here and get some sleep. Just lock the door on the way out, and don't drink all my parents' alcohol so I get in trouble when they get home."

I can feel her lips spread into a smile against my leg. "Promise. But only if I can keep a Yankees shirt here to sleep in."

That ridiculously simple statement made in that sleep-drugged rasp of hers just made me way too fucking happy.

Yeah, I definitely need help.

She takes our linked hands and pulls them so she can press a kiss against mine. "Promise?" she prompts.

"Promise." I run my other hand over her hair. "I left a new toothbrush on the counter for you and one of my shirts for you to wear if you want."

"Efficient," she murmurs as her breathing begins to even out again.

"Always." Another kiss to her cheek. "Thanks for not running away this time."

"Mmm."

It's the only sound she makes as she slips back to sleep. I don't move, though. Like a fucking sap I sit and watch her. The rise and fall of her chest. The curve of her body beneath the oversize shirt. And for a moment I'm more than tempted to break every ounce of resolve I held on to last night. I'm more than certain that burying myself to the hilt in her right now would trump the high I expect to claim in court later when I walk away with the settlement in my client's favor.

Get up, Lockhart.

You'll have more time for this—for her.

You definitely will.

I head to the door but look back one more time at her and shake my head.

She's here, in my bed, and she didn't run.

Maybe we're getting somewhere.

And just maybe if I get used to saying those three words in my head enough, one day I'll be able to say them out loud again when they really matter.

CHAPTER TWENTY

Vaughn

"What do you mean, I can't see her today?"

I stare at the counselor manning the front desk. She pushes her glasses up her nose and glances back down at the computer screen in front of her. "It says right here that Lucy isn't able to leave the premises this week."

"I don't—what in the—" I take a deep breath and look at her name tag. "Rachel. Thank you, but there's been some kind of mis-understanding. I have a regularly scheduled time that I get with my niece. Every week. The same days. The same time. There has to be a misunderstanding."

"I'm sorry, Ms. Sanders, but when I pull up her name here, it states there is a hold on her file at this time."

Panic bubbles up, hysteria close behind it, and my thoughts strug-gle to connect. *Did they rule that Brian gets custody? Is she being taken from me?*

"Joey. Is Joey working today? He can vouch for me."

"Joey is working today, but there is no one able to override the mandate."

"Can I talk to him, please?" I ask, knowing full well I could text him myself, but I don't want to get him in trouble.

"I'm sorry, but—"

"Rachel. *Please.* I just—Lucy gets frantic when her schedule changes. I can tell Joey what he needs to do to calm her."

She sighs, and I can tell she's completely uncomfortable, but thankfully she picks up the phone. "Can Joey come to the front for a moment? I have a question for him."

"Thank you," I tell her as I take a step away from the desk and stand close to the door that I typically walk through without any hassle.

Each second that passes has my thoughts spinning out of control and my anxiety flying through the roof.

When Joey enters the lobby, he tenses the minute he sees me. "Let's go outside for a second," he says in a lowered voice and places his hand on the small of my back to direct me out the door.

"What in the hell is going on?" I ask the minute we're out of earshot from anyone.

"Vaughn." I hate the sound of my own name right now.

"I'm freaking out here, Joey. Why are they not letting me see her? This is my normal time. It's not like anything has changed."

"Everything is fine," he soothes in a voice that all but tells me to calm the hell down. "I'm not sure what's going on. It's the first I've heard of it."

"Is this normal? Have you seen this happen before?"

His pause before he responds makes me even more nervous. "It happens occasionally. When there is a contentious custody battle or a counselor feels the child could be in danger."

"What did Brian do to her?" Rage courses through me at even the hint of a thought.

"Nothing. Nothing happened to her." He holds up his hands to get me to stop jumping to conclusions. "Sometimes orders come down for the child to remain on site."

"Why?" I laugh, the nerves getting the best of me. "It's not like they think I'm going to kidnap her or anything." And then the minute the words are out of my mouth, I realize that's what they think. "Wait. Do they—"

Joey sees it on my face and immediately jumps to react. "No. That's not it. It's just—I'll get answers for you. I'm not supposed to, but I'll see what I can find out."

"Thank you. I just—I—"

"I know."

I drop my head and draw in a big breath to try to steady my shaky nerves before looking back up at him. "Can I at least see her so she knows I didn't forget her?"

His shoulders sag. "I'm sorry. I could get fired for allowing it."

Christ. Tears burn in my eyes, and my stomach churns as much for me missing her as for her thinking I don't want to see her. "She's been through so much, Joey. Some days she still thinks her mom just up and left her instead of died. I can't have her thinking that I did too."

"I'll smooth it over."

"But she has her calendar and she counts the days. She knows this is Tuesday. She knows I take her."

"Vaughn. The facility has been more lenient with you seeing her and taking her for overnight stays than they are with most others."

I stare at him, feeling completely helpless and hating every damn second of it. "I don't understand." My voice breaks, and I press my fingers to my eyes to prevent the tears from spilling over.

I say I don't understand.

But I'm fearing I actually do.

◆ ◆ ◆

"Ms. Sanders? What are you doing here?" Priscilla looks tepid as she peeks her head out of the door that separates the offices from the general public and sees me.

I know damn well that the receptionist told her why I'm here, so I'm not buying her *I'm innocent* look.

"Can we talk somewhere?"

Priscilla's head startles. "About?"

"I think this conversation is best suited to privacy," I explain, "considering I went to see Lucy and was told your office gave them mandates saying that I couldn't."

She exhales. "The conference room, then."

I follow behind her as we walk through the cubicles. Heads pop up over the edges like meerkats to see who Priscilla is guiding through their inner sanctum of red tape and bureaucracy.

The conference room is crammed with a scarred wood table top and eight chairs around a six-chair table. She motions for me to sit and then takes a seat directly across from me, making a show of scooting her chair in and squaring her papers up before clasping her hands over the top of them.

"I was expecting a phone call from you, but isn't this a nice surprise. *In person.*" Her smile is tight, and her eyes behind her glasses look two different sizes, normal size above the frame and rather large through the lens.

"Why is no one allowed to visit Lucy?" I cut to the chase.

"It's in her best interests." Her voice may be monotone, but her words are like nails on a chalkboard to my ears.

"How so?"

"It's evident there are some . . . *issues* with both of the candidates for her guardianship."

"Issues?"

She offers a judgmental smile, and I find it hard to swallow all of a sudden. "Sometimes during our lengthy process, things come up that have to be investigated further."

"Like how Brian showed up to my house and was high as a kite, offering for me to buy his daughter a few weeks back? Like you actually tested him and it turned up positive? Those kinds of things?"

"I'm sorry, I'm not at liberty to discuss Lucy's welfare or potential issues at this time."

"Considering I'm a candidate, shouldn't I be in the know on what's going on?"

"As I said, some things aren't up for discussion. I can't override orders from the bosses." Her mouth straightens into a line, and her eyebrows lift as if to ask if we're done here.

What does she know? What the hell happened? What the hell is going on here?

And then in the midst of panic, it hits me: *Carter Preston.*

His warning. His threat.

Oh my God.

Did he do something? I clasp my hands together to prevent the rage I suddenly feel from shining through.

"Priscilla." I pause and force myself to contain my emotions. It's been a long few weeks—hell, it's been a long damn year—and before I ruin all chances of being awarded custody, I take a deep breath. "I'm not quite sure what is going on here, but I know it's not normal. You have a little girl dying to be loved and put in a home where she can be loved unconditionally. Whatever it is that you seem to think you have against me, I assure you it can be explained." I hold her gaze and tamp down my anger, forcing my hands to relax instead of fist.

Time stretches, and defeat hits me harder than ever before.

"Running a brothel out of your house now, are you?"

Every single ounce of blood drains from my body in an instant. "Excuse me?" I sputter out the words, the room suddenly sweltering, my head dizzy.

She lifts an eyebrow. "Four men in one night, Ms. Sanders? Is this a suitable environment for a young, impressionable girl with special needs?"

I must blink a hundred times as I try to process what it is that she's saying. "I'm—I'm sorry. I don't think I understand what you're talking about?"

My heartbeat rages in my ears. My breath hurts to draw it in.

"Well, let's see. It's been reported that you went to a charity event with one gentleman. Then you have a male babysitter who didn't leave your house until the wee hours of the morning. Two different cars sat in front of your house at different times, stayed there for a while, and then parted ways." She leans back in her chair and crosses her arms over her chest. "A revolving door? Is this really a suitable environment for Lucy?"

Each word she utters makes my jaw want to drop a little farther open, and when she's finished, my laugh rings out loud and clear in the stuffy conference room. I can hear the hysteria in it bouncing back to me; I just hope she doesn't hear it too.

"This is absolutely ludicrous."

"Is it?"

"I'm sorry, but were you having me followed?"

"A concerned citizen took it upon themselves to call this suspicious activity in."

"A concerned citizen?" Another disbelieving laugh falls from my lips. "At two in the morning a concerned citizen just happened to be watching my house. One who somehow knew my personal business and that I was in the process of trying to adopt my niece?" With each word my voice rises, and my mind zeroes in on the only person who could have done this.

"Perhaps."

"And what? You just believe a random stranger who happened to see something and read into it?"

"I haven't heard you deny it."

"Are you actually accusing me of being a madam?" I shriek, the irony so lost in my rage of emotion that I don't even notice. Because even though that's my job, I never really think of myself that way. "Are you kidding me?"

I shove my chair back and begin to pace whatever part of the room that I can.

"Ms. Sanders. Now, I assure you my comment was in gest, but it does lead one to question what was going on at your—"

"Nothing! Nothing was going on. My friend—*who's gay*—invited me to a charity event for the Down Syndrome Advocacy Foundation. His name is Archer Collins. Feel free to look him up and accuse him of buying sex in my house. He'll sue you faster than you can look up his net worth, and you'll be laughed out of your job. The man I'm dating stopped by for a bit to wait for me afterward, but I wasn't home. His name is Ryker Lockhart. I'm sure you can Google him and see he's not exactly a man who has to pay for sex. Lawyers aren't in the habit of breaking the law. My babysitter is just that—a babysitter. He stayed late and left when I got home. And . . . the last person?" I scramble for an answer that stays as far away from the senator as possible but won't make her worried for Lucy. "He was a coworker from Apropos—you know, the club where I work. A group of people were going out partying—hence the limo, to avoid drinking and driving—and they stopped by to see if I wanted to go with them. Are you happy now? No sex. No drugs. But sometimes there's a little bit of rock and roll."

My hands are pressed against the table, my body leaning forward so she has no choice but to see the gravity and anger heavy in my expression.

"Thank you for the explanation"—she clears her throat—"but I can't exactly take your words at face value."

You're a miserable human being, I want to scream at her, so frustrated with the unwavering stick up her ass.

"And why would you decide to attend an event on the one night you have Lucy stay over if being with her is so important to you?" she asks.

"Because life happens is why," I say. "Because I can't exactly change the night of a charity function that in fact benefits her in some way. We spent the entire day together, hours on end. Painting and bike riding and therapy and snuggle time. I left for the function about an hour before her bedtime, and I left her with someone she knows and I trust. Feel free to come at me about being irresponsible, but I assure you not having that night with her would have been even more so, because she needs predictability. A missed or moved day throws her off for some time. You know, kind of like me not getting to see her today will."

She purses her lips and squares her papers again, even though they are still perfectly aligned. Anything to abate the unease my explanations are bringing her.

"Did you ever think that it could possibly be Brian who reported this anonymously? He's the only person who has anything to gain by trying to paint me in a bad light. Hell, he was probably lighting up down the block, half-high, while he was being a Peeping Tom."

I walk back to the conference table and grab my purse so aggressively she jumps with a yelp.

"The next time I go to see Lucy, this better be cleared up so that I'm not given any trouble. My file better not have a hint of any of this in there either. Remember that man I'm dating? I wasn't lying when I said he's a lawyer. Try to taint my image in this adoption process to prevent me from getting Lucy, and I'll be certain to have it cost you your job."

Without another word or waiting for her to close her mouth, I stalk out of the conference room with my body shaking from anger and tears of fury burning my eyes.

And when I push open the doors to the outside and the fresh air hits my face, I keep walking. Down the street, block after block, and only when my lungs feel like they are burning can I actually breathe again.

I take huge gulping gasps of air and wonder if I just fucked things up for myself or improved them.

My anger is focused on everything and everyone.

At Carter Preston, because who knows if he had anything to do with this interesting scenario, and even if he didn't, I still hate him anyway. And if he did have something to do with it, then I could be caught in the lie I just told, saying he was a coworker.

At Brian, because he would have the most to gain out of all this. But if it was him, what a dumb move on his part, because couldn't I just do the same thing to him in the hopes that I'd catch him using and report him for that?

At Joey, because he's the only person who really saw all these people at my house. Was he questioned about the two people vying to be Lucy's guardians? And if so, did he say something that made Priscilla question everything? Or is he at risk of getting in trouble at his job because he was babysitting for me when he probably isn't supposed to be?

At Ryker, because I keep trying to forgive and forget, but each time I feel like I might be able to get to that point, something that is a ripple effect from that night comes up and slaps me in the face.

And more than anything, I'm furious at myself.

Sure, I entered into this with the endgame—adopting Lucy—in mind, but what in the hell was I doing thinking I could run an escort business and not get caught? What was I doing in there threatening Priscilla's job by siccing Ryker on her, let alone telling her that a man like him would never pay for sex?

Lies.

Everything is lies, and I feel like I've spun so many of them that I can't keep straight who I've told what to.

At some point these lies will intersect like the crosshairs on a target. All I can hope is that I'm not standing there when they do.

CHAPTER TWENTY-ONE

Ryker

"Are you having an affair?"

Bianca Preston makes a sound on the other end of the line that leads me to think she's offended. "If I were, I'd be in a lot better mood, now wouldn't I? I'm thinking I should be offended my attorney asked me that question."

"And I'm just wondering why you were in such a rush to hire me on retainer, but there's not an ounce of urgency to file and serve your husband with divorce papers."

I purse my lips and lean back in my chair, my cell at my ear, Bianca's even breathing filling the silence on the other end of the line.

"It's complicated," she finally says.

"Divorce typically is."

"What's the rush? Aren't you getting paid for your time?" she asks, and I want to laugh.

"It's hard to bill hours, Bianca, when we're not doing anything but trying to dig up dirt on Carter."

"At least you get to bill for that." She speaks to me like I should be lucky she's giving me the time of day, and fuck if it doesn't irk the hell out of me. "And what have you found? Anything?"

I think of Stuart's frustration. The wild-goose chases he's been on to come up with only rumors and hints of impropriety on Carter's end but nothing concrete.

Nothing but the pictures of him with girls who seem to be under-age. The same pictures no doubt Vaughn has and that Carter knows she has.

"Just the pictures I told you about."

"Mmm," she says and falls silent, as one would expect when you find out your husband prefers teenagers over you. "That's it?"

"So far." I start to ask the question, stop, and then figure fuck it. "How exactly does he think he's going to be nominated for vice president and make it through the entire vetting process without any of that coming out?"

The question has nagged at me.

"Perhaps it's happened only during the last term."

Why is she defending him instead of raging about him?

"He just happened to develop an appetite for underage girls now?"

"It's possible."

"And what? He thinks he's Teflon and no one is going to dig up this dirt when we were able to in a matter of days?"

"He can be very persuasive and convincing."

"Either that or he's planning on paying off a whole lot of people," I throw out there and am met with radio silence.

"You'd be amazed at the things money can buy," she says, and I roll my shoulders in frustration.

I'm not a peon. She knows who I am and no doubt has researched my net worth, so I grit my teeth at her little holier-than-thou dig at me.

"The American people won't buy it. Are you just going to stand by and let him ruin your reputation too in the process?"

"I'd rather not discuss this right now. It's too painful." She says the words, but it's not pain lacing her voice. Rather, it's irritation at me for asking the glaringly obvious question.

"Okay." I sigh into the line to let her know my own frustration. "Any luck on the assets and accounts?" I ask.

"I'm working on it."

I lean back in my chair and rest my feet on the desk, crossing them at the ankles. The night is coming on—the city's lights sparkling to life—and I try to figure out what is going on here, because she's been working on it for some time now.

"I'm on your side here, Bianca. If there's something I need to know, it's important that you tell me."

"Nothing that matters in the divorce."

"Got it." But I don't get it. Far from it.

"Mr. Lockhart. You know what I need. I'm paying you more than adequately for your services."

"As you sought me out."

"Are you still the best there is?" she asks, her voice hinting at irritation.

"Yes."

"Then I made the right decision. Don't make me doubt it again."

When the connection ends, I pull my cell from my ear and stare at it like an idiot, more confused about the conversation than when I started.

Is the woman transferring offshore bank accounts into an alias or something to cheat Carter out of them? Is that why it's taking so goddamn long getting me her assets and financials? Something is going on, but fuck if I know what that something is.

Warm definitely isn't a term one would use to describe Bianca. Not in the least.

"You ready for me?" Stuart asks as he comes in carrying a file box that has me raising an eyebrow.

I glance at my watch to check the time. "Yeah. I've got to head out in an hour or two, but we can go through what you've brought me."

It takes Stu a minute to stack piles on my desk in order of client and file. We wade through whether we can use the information or not, if the facts can hold up in negotiations, and if we'd rather hold it close to our vest for a bit longer to see how everything pans out during mediation.

We also discuss the information he's gathered on the clients I'm representing so there are no surprises from opposing counsel.

"We good?" I ask.

"Got a bit more for you on your other interest," he says, referring to my request for him to dig deeper on Vaughn and her past.

"Is that so?" I ask, feeling like an asshole for uncovering everything about her layer by layer without her knowledge, but I know I'm only doing it because I'm trying to protect her from Carter.

"Her last name is technically not Sanders."

I do a double take when I look at him, a little put off, a lot confused, and try not to be pissed that I didn't know this. "Continue."

"Her father's name was Henson, but she wasn't given his last name."

"True, but Vaughn told me her mom's family didn't accept him. I bet you money her mom talked him into using the family surname with some excuse about inheritance simply because she was too chickenshit to go against her parents."

"It happens."

"More than you think." I scrub a hand over my jaw. "So then what's the last name on her birth certificate?"

"Dillinger." It takes a second for the name to hit my ears and recognition to fire. *The Dillingers of Greenwich.* Stuart sees the minute it does and nods. "Yes, she's one of *those* Dillingers."

"Well, shit." I rise from my desk and walk to the windows as I wrap my mind around all this. The small world we live in. This unexpected connection Vaughn and I somehow unknowingly share. And the quiet fury that rages beneath my more than calm demeanor . . . but Stuart knows I'm trying to rein it in. He knows better than to talk right now.

"So her last name is Dillinger?"

"Up until she was seven years old it was. Then her mother filed for a legal name change to Sanders. I'm assuming there were reasons for her to give her children the maiden name of their maternal great-great-grandmother, but none that I could find."

I slide my hands into my pockets, and I continue to stare out the window but never really focus on a single detail.

I think of my college roommate, Chance Dillinger, and the stories he'd tell me of his cold family steeped in generations of tradition. The old-school rules they adhered to that weren't allowed to bend to modern ways. Marriage only to those with a specific bloodline. The requirement for the males of the family to be sent to boarding school and away from their mothers so they'd never get soft. Soft men don't become captains of industry.

How convenient that they send all the boys of the family away so all the little girls are left as perfect prey for their perverted uncle. My stomach churns.

"It's a good name. Sanders," I finally say. "A hell of a lot better than Dillinger."

"Mmm." It's all he says in response, and I can hear him shuffling through papers. "The interesting thing is I messed up first go 'round. She has two uncles named James. Both brilliant in their own right. One named Dillinger. Another named Sanders."

"And you thought the Sanders one was—"

"—the one you were looking for. Yes."

"It makes sense why there was nothing there," I finish for him, referring to why we couldn't find anything nefarious on the James Sanders we'd found . . . but then again, there aren't often neon signs pointing to child predators. "Anything on James Dillinger?"

Stuart's silence weighs down the room until I turn around to face him. His look says everything.

"What?" I ask.

"Things don't exactly add up."

I walk toward the desk, take a seat in my chair, and study the papers he's laid out on it. I shuffle through them, each one confusing me more than the last.

"I don't understand." I pick up the two arrest warrants—Vaughn's name is front and center on the first, Samantha's on the second one—almost as if I don't believe what I'm seeing.

"James Dillinger is a paraplegic." Stuart's eyes meet mine.

"And?"

"And those papers"—he points to the arrest warrant naming one Samantha Dillinger for attempted murder—"state that she's the one who pulled the trigger."

"The fucker deserved it." It's my automatic response, my moral compassion for a man who preyed on young girls less than nil.

"Not going to argue with you there . . . but your girl here is in some serious trouble."

I stare at the warrant. At the charge of accessory to attempted murder. At the name "Vaughn Dillinger" on it. And while none of it makes any sort of sense to me, I know it would be perfect for a man like Carter Preston to see. To threaten with. To hold over Vaughn's head to try to coerce her—to blackmail her—into doing exactly what he wanted.

"How come it names her as Vaughn Dillinger and not Vaughn Sanders?" I ask. "Same goes for Samantha?"

"Maybe the Dillingers rejected how her mother changed her name? Maybe they felt slighted and wanted to claim her back?"

"Or maybe they didn't want her caught?" I propose.

"Meaning?"

"Meaning if she legally goes by Vaughn Sanders, then file the warrant under Vaughn Sanders and it's easier for the law to search for her and find her. File the warrant under a name she doesn't legally hold and . . ."

"And it's a window dressing for everyone to think you're prosecuting."

I twist my lips and lower myself to my seat and try to imagine myself in Vaughn and Samantha's shoes. Scared, motherless, abused. The need to survive, to thrive, and Samantha's need to protect her sister from that monster at any cost.

Good for you, Samantha. I never met you, but I admire you more now than ever. Protect what's yours at all costs.

Just like I will.

With a purse of my lips, I toss the copies of the warrants onto the table, lean back in my chair, and meet Stuart's eyes.

"Something doesn't make sense here."

"You feel it too?" he asks as he mimics my posture and sits back in his chair.

"You have an extremely wealthy family. One many know and who have a shit ton of power and influence. One of their prized sons is a fucking pedophile. Maybe they know it, maybe they don't. But they keep it on the down low if they do, because why risk the scandal that would tarnish their family name, right?" I rise from my seat, my need to work through my thoughts while on my feet as inherent in me as my need for air.

"But then their prized son ends up getting shot."

"Maybe it's in his niece's room in the middle of the night. How would one explain why he was there and why she shot him? Then maybe said niece and sister leave and never come back." I twist my lips, my eyes veering to the corner of my office in thought. They land on the box Vaughn sent me. It's still sitting under my credenza, still opened but its contents not fully gone through.

Still reminding me of the hurt I caused her.

"And maybe one niece knows what happened and the other one doesn't."

"That's a lot of maybes," I say with a laugh, but fuck if it doesn't make perfect sense.

"It is . . . but if you're a wealthy family trying to hide a secret . . ." His words lead into my thoughts.

"So what are you saying? That there are accusations made of attempted murder against two young teenagers. A robbery gone wrong is what those statements make it sound like. Like they were ungrateful orphans the Dillingers took in. They took care of them, but they were so messed up by the death of their mother that nothing—not even the love and money the Dillingers lavished upon them—could fix them."

"Are you thinking they pressed charges on principle only?"

"I'm saying money can buy you a shitload of things, including pressing charges and an arrest warrant that never got followed through on." I turn to look at him. His elbow is on the chair, and he's running a finger over his jawline in thought as he stares at me. "Think of it this way—you're a PI who dug this all up quicker than shit, and yet a police force pushed and pressured by an extremely influential family wasn't able to find two inexperienced teenagers? I find that hard to fucking believe, don't you, Stu?"

"I think if I were in the Dillingers' shoes and I knew exactly what was going down with Uncle Creep-Fest, I'd probably turn a blind eye too. I'd level those charges against the sisters to help protect my bullshit family reputation. I'd hope it would be a deterrent for them to come anywhere near the town of Greenwich—let alone Connecticut—because the farther away they are, the less chance they have of coming back as grown adults."

"And the accusations made by grown adults hold so much more weight than those asserted by grieving kids." I shake my head. *Shit.*

"You about summed it up with that one word."

With my fingers fiddling with a pen, I hang my head and stare at my tie as I contemplate the believability of our theory. But I know it's more than believable. I know that two grown men who have never even talked about this just both came to the same conclusion. That says a whole hell of a lot.

"A safeguard to protect your dirty family secret," I murmur.

"I find it rather odd that when you search the *Greenwich Gazette* there isn't one story about James Dillinger and his run-in with thieves. Not a single mention. His interviews mention his paralysis, how it doesn't hold him back from creating his brilliant economic theories, but nothing about the tragedy that took his mobility or the person responsible for it. That's more than odd."

"Small towns. Big money. Bigger family name. Deal with the paralysis without any fanfare, press the charges so you can keep up the front, but with all that clout, tell the police department not to pursue the assailants. They were just confused kids still grieving the loss of their mother. We'll forgive them. Blah, blah, blah."

Is this Vaughn's secret? Does she know about this, or did Samantha keep yet another thing from her sister? Did Samantha turn to the drugs to ease the pain of the abuse and to deal with the guilt of actually hurting a human being in order to save another?

With my head leaned back and eyes closed, I run through the scenario piece by piece, motive by motive, appreciating the moment Stuart gives me to deal with my thoughts.

I can hear his movements about my office: his shoes on the floor, the snap open of the cupboard, the glasses clinking, and the sound of the bottle being set down on top of the credenza.

"Thanks," I murmur as I take the whiskey from him, mind still mulling over all of these *maybes*.

"Are you going to tell her?" he asks and takes a seat again.

"No."

"No?" He sounds as surprised as I was by the word when it came out of my mouth.

I fall quiet again, the repercussions of telling her and not telling her a never-ending loop through my mind.

Does she know about her uncle? Was she there when Samantha pulled the trigger in self-defense? Is that why she's so scared of Carter outing her publicly? Or did she leave in the middle of the night at her sister's insistence without a clue as to what had happened? And if that is the case, then what exactly has her so spooked by Carter's reference to her uncle?

"No," I reiterate, the irony not lost on me that I've hung up on Vaughn in the past for saying the same word.

"*No* about knowing about this," he says and waves to the papers all over the desk, "or *no* to telling her that you personally know the Dillingers?"

"Not sure, but what I do know is that I'm going to pay the motherfucker a visit myself."

"You think that's smart?"

"No. It's going to take every ounce of restraint I have to not wrap my hands around his throat and finish the job Samantha started . . . but going there is something I need to do." To protect Vaughn. To nullify anything Carter thinks he has over her. To feel like I can do something right as a man to help the woman I love.

"You need any backup, I'll be glad to tag along."

"Nah." I shake my head. "I've got this."

"And then what?"

"Well, I'm going to pay him a visit, threaten him within an inch of his goddamn life to drop the charges and to never come near Vaughn again. Then I'll finally use the open invitation I get every year and show up at the Sunday family dinner of my old college roommate, Chance Dillinger. I'll sit right across from his old, poor, paralyzed uncle named James and make sure he understands that I mean business. And if he doesn't, then I'll be sure to let his whole goddamn family—as well as most newspapers in the country—know about what exactly happened."

"You're a bastard, you know that?" Stuart asks with a chuckle that says he'd love to watch every minute of my confrontation.

"Not going to apologize for it either." I flash a smile his way that I'm sure is loaded with deviance.

"Everything else you needed is right here on your desk," he says, followed by the plop of a stack of papers.

"Thanks. I'll give it a look later." I take a long sip from my glass.

"Give me a heads-up when you decide to go."

I laugh. "Why, so you can be ready to post my bail just in case?"

"Something like that." He meets my gaze. "You good?"

"Yeah. Thanks for"—I wave a hand through the air—"everything."

"Night, Lockhart."

"Night."

When the door shuts behind him, I shift in my seat so I can get a better look at my desk. The papers are still there, still inked with her name, and a silent rage runs through me. The same one that started when Vaughn came into my life and I knew there was very little I could do to protect her.

But I can do this.

I know the right thing to do is to tell Vaughn I know the truth about her past. The best for us as a couple is to confess that I snooped in order to protect her. Sure she'd be mad, but at least it would be me telling her. At least it would be me showing her I learned from my last mistake at the pool house when I tried to find out information to protect her better.

I sigh into my glass and drink the rest of the whiskey as I contemplate what to do next. Regardless of the decision, I know one thing is for certain: I'm going to protect what's mine *at all costs.*

CHAPTER TWENTY-TWO

Vaughn

"Can I see you tonight?"

My smile is automatic at the sound of his voice. My desire to be in Ryker's arms or even sitting silently beside him is so intense that I just close my eyes and fight back the tears that burn there from sheer exhaustion.

"As much as I want to, I can't." I hate myself for even uttering the words.

"Why not?"

"I'm having trouble with a girl." I flip the page on my pad of paper and glance down at the notes there. The complaints from a client about her unprofessionalism. How rude she was to him. And then below that is a note to call my new client Noah back—*yet again*—his nerves getting the best of him that he's going to get caught.

"You are?"

"Yep." The word comes out in a sigh.

"What's wrong with your girl?"

"It's a long story."

"It's good that it's a long story. I like listening to your voice."

And those simple words, ones that tell me I have someone in my life who cares about me, are so hard to accept, all the while so very incredible.

"She had dinner with someone last night and proceeded to insult him after getting drunk."

"But you have a three-drink maximum," he states. Leave it to the lawyer to have read my entire contract, even the small print.

"I do, yes."

"How exactly did she insult him?"

"Let's just say there was some laughter and then some mention of a minimal number of inches."

"Ouch!" He hisses the word as he bites back a chuckle. "I'm assuming we're talking about—"

"Yes. We're talking about those inches. Or lack thereof."

"Poor bastard."

"True. But now I get to deal with the fallout."

"I'm sorry. So I can't see you, then?" His voice deepens when he asks, and I'm so tempted to call in sick to work but know that I can't. I'm about to make a big payment on my debt and need to have the hours on my timecard in case Priscilla questions it. I'm already pushing the envelope with her thinking I make tips that large, so remaining on the down low is paramount.

"First my shift at Apropos and then dealing with my girl. I have no idea when I'll be done or if I'll be anything close to coherent with how tired I already am."

"Mmm." I can all but hear his disappointment in his murmur.

I'd rather be with you too. But I don't say the words. I don't let him know how much I want to see him.

"So what you're saying is that I need to rent out a pod at Apropos to see my girl, then?"

"Don't be silly. Save your money." But a smile spreads on my lips at the thought.

"I could do a whole lot of fun things to you in that pod. Just you and me and the loud music and your short skirt."

"Is that so?" I shift in my chair to abate the need he stoked last week with his kissing but no touching that he hasn't fulfilled yet. "Too bad they don't have a lock on the door."

"The risk of getting caught is part of the thrill."

"The risk of getting caught and fired is more of a cold shower in my book," I respond.

"So all those men in the club get to see you tonight and I don't? Can I admit I hate that about your jobs? The men who look at you and want you and see everything you're not."

"That means you're the one who looks at me and sees everything I am."

"True . . . but I still don't like it."

"A jealous Ryker isn't one I've seen before."

"Baby, I'm jealous of any man who gets to be with you when I don't."

"You're being ridiculous." And I love it. The way it makes me feel. The burn it leaves in my chest. The butterflies it prompts in my belly.

"Have you heard from Priscilla?"

"I have. Yes. I'm sorry, I thought I texted you that I had."

"You're just too busy for me anymore." The playful tone in his voice makes me want to be sitting across the table from him, watching his smile spread across his lips and light up his eyes.

"Too many men, too little time."

"Better not be." He laughs. "What did good ol' prissy Priscilla say? I take it everything is cleared up and you'll be able to see Lucy soon?"

"Yes."

"Did she say anything else?"

"Not really. She wasn't exactly warm, so I'm sure I didn't do myself any favors in the likability department, but—"

"I'm surprised she had the gall to call you. I'd figure her for the passive-aggressive, nonconfrontational email type," he says with irritation lacing his voice. I may have gone to him crying and looking for someone to comfort me, but I was surprised how angry he was on my behalf. "You should have let me make some phone calls, Vaughn."

"For what? So she can think that I need someone else to step in and fight my battles for me?"

I can picture the look on his face right now. The same one he gave me when I told him I could handle this myself. That it was handled. And that I was just waiting to see what she was going to do about it.

"It's okay to ask for help," he murmurs.

"Just like it's okay to be self-sufficient."

"Screw her," he mutters.

"I need her, though."

"And I need you."

"Ah, nice segue."

"You noticed?"

"Pretty hard not to."

"So tonight? Can I see you?" he asks again.

"I told you—I have work."

"After, then?"

"I told you"—I laugh—"I have to meet a potential client, and you have an early court date tomorrow."

"Are you telling me *no*, Vaughn?" he teases and reminds me of how stubborn he can be.

"I'm telling you I have to go now," I say and hang up with a smile on my lips.

My cell rings again instantly. I laugh when I see Ryker's name again.

"This is Vee. Can I help you?" I answer like I always do my Wicked Ways number.

"Yes, I'm having trouble with one of your girls, and I'd like to file a report."

"*A report?* Is that so?" I ask, my heart beating faster at the sound of his voice, even though I just heard it.

"Mmm-hmm. She's gorgeous and stubborn and works too damn much, but I admire her for it more than she'll ever know."

"Well, I'm sure she'd be flattered to hear that, but it can't make the girl she has to deal with, the day job she has to attend, or the nervous Nellie client she has to meet with—any of those three things—go away. It's an awful lot to pack into one night and then have enough energy to give you the proper attention you deserve."

"Something's standing at attention all right," he jokes, and before I say anything, he continues. "I hate that she has to work a day job. A night job. A job that doesn't suit her."

"I'm sure she does, too, because she'd rather be with you."

"And I hate that she has to meet with random men at all hours of the night. It's not safe."

"I'm at the club. It's safer than most places."

"But meeting the man after . . . I don't like that in the least."

"Becoming overprotective, are we?" I ask, all the while secretly loving that someone is. That someone cares. "Besides, you know this person because you referred him to her back in the days when you were trying to apologize by referral."

"Can't blame a man for trying."

"I'm not." I lean back in my chair and close my eyes. "But like I said, you referred him my way, so I'm pretty sure he's safe."

"Who is it?" he asks.

"You know I can't answer that," I say with a sigh.

"Why are you meeting him so late? What time do you get off?"

"He's nervous and doesn't want anyone to see us together. He's afraid I'm an undercover cop, I think."

"The irony."

"I know, right?"

Silence falls for a beat before he carries on. "I still don't like it that you have to meet with men on your own."

"I can take care of myself just fine." I say the words but realize now that he's in my life, I hate these meetings with clients more and more with each passing day. The thrill is gone. The risk I'm taking with each and every one is more and more evident.

"Maybe I want to take care of you instead."

I let the silence float on the line as his words take root and then cause a panic to settle in. The fear of needing him—of wanting to need him—is so new and foreign that it causes my palms to sweat and words to falter.

"Let me pick you up after work and bring you home," he finally says to break the silence that's not hard to miss.

"I'll text you during my shift. I'm not sure what time I'll be off. There's a huge private party tonight that might run long. If it's not too late, then we'll figure it out."

"Don't blow me off, Vaughn."

"Good night, Ryker."

And when I end the call, I sit and stare out the window of my office for a minute, my ears hearing the neighborhood boys playing their usual game of baseball but not really listening to them. My attention is pulled to the picture of Samantha and me on the bookshelf to my left. It's crooked in its spot; I must have knocked it askew when I came in last night to shuffle through my desk for my paperwork. I reach out and straighten it, the ache in my chest over missing her still as prevalent as the day I found out she was gone.

I wonder what the sober her would say about all of this. Wicked Ways. Ryker Lockhart. The senator. Would she be proud of me for fighting so hard to keep the only piece of her I have left—Lucy? Would she like Ryker, or would she tell me to walk away without looking back?

With a shake of my head to clear the questions I'll never get answers to, I glance at my stack of college applications on the opposite corner of my desk.

Hairs on the back of my neck stand at attention when I see Birmingham University's application on top when I swear Stony Brook was there last night.

I glance around my office in an unexpected panic, suddenly creeped out that someone has been here snooping through my things. The crooked photo, the reshuffled college applications to get my teaching credential—what else is off other than just the general feeling that is disturbing me?

I wouldn't put it past Carter to break into my house to try to find the call log.

"You're losing your mind, Vaughn," I mutter into the empty room, convincing myself that I was so tired last night when I was working that I easily could have moved the stuff.

I probably switched the order when I was double-checking all the information I entered on the applications to make sure I didn't make any errors.

College. A teaching degree.

I shake my head. The possibility is a little more real now that I'm about to submit my applications. I wonder what a normal life would be like for me? What does that feel like? What is it like to be safe and cared for by someone other than my mom and Samantha?

Maybe I want to take care of you instead.

It's Ryker's words again in my head. It's the tone in which he said it that wraps around my heart—sincere, caring, proud.

This is real, Vaughn. Men like Ryker don't say shit like that unless they mean it.

He's already gotten the sex, so there's no need to make promises and say words he doesn't mean to get you into bed when you're already there willingly.

The big question is, Why is this notion causing me such panic? Didn't I already know there's so much more between us? Isn't this why I was so upset about the Hamptons and everything after? Or was I just waiting for it to fall to shit? And when it didn't, I was subconsciously thinking I'd self-sabotage it so it wouldn't work.

Because I don't deserve this. A man who wants to take care of me. Not that I'd let him—not in a million years, because that would mean my independence would be tied to reins—but because this is so different and new, and it scares the shit out of me.

But sometimes good things come by conquering your fears.

CHAPTER TWENTY-THREE

Ryker

The club is loud and crowded and the last fucking place I want to be right now after my phone call with Chance. The Dillinger family is at a wedding overseas and won't be back for the next ten days.

I should go to the gym and work off this rage I feel. At Vaughn's uncle. At Carter Preston. At the life Vaughn had to live and the secrets she's had to keep.

So many things still run through my head from my meeting with Stuart. So many what-ifs. So many need-to-knows.

I should go and punch the heavy bag and spar until my arms and legs turn to Jell-O, but hell if I can stay away from the one person who owns my mind tonight: Vaughn.

But when it comes down to it, none of it fucking matters other than . . . I miss her.

"Hey, man," I say to the bartender when I walk up. He's tall, with darker skin and a smile that I'm sure earns him legs propped on his shoulders more often than not.

He lifts his chin to me. "What'll you have?"

I peer at the bottles on the wall behind him. "Gin and tonic. And Vaughn Sanders."

"I can help you with the first. Not my place to help you with the second." He gives a laugh, but his eyes fire off a warning that I kind of fucking like, kind of fucking hate. She's mine to look after, not his.

"Good answer."

He slides a drink across the bar top to me. "You the prick who keeps hurting her?"

I stare at him as the couple beside us turn their attention our way. The music is loud, but our voices are louder.

"Guilty as charged."

He eyes me a bit closer, takes in my watch and the quality of my shirt, before pursing his lips and nodding as if he now believes me.

"You here to cause trouble?"

"Nope. Just here to see her. It's been a long week, a lot of hours, and"—I shrug—"she's who I want to end my night with."

He licks his bottom lip and holds up a finger when a waitress calls his name. I glance her way, and it's the woman who walked out with Vaughn the other night.

"Hey. Hi," she says when she sees me. "What are you doing here? Oh. Vaughn. Right. Sorry. I'm lame," she says in a breathless and broken sentence as her cheeks flush some.

"You know him, Mel?" the bartender asks.

She nods. "Yeah, he belongs to Vaughn."

The phrase makes me smile against the rim of my glass as I take a sip and meet the eyes of the bartender. I raise my eyebrows as if to say, *See?*

"She's up in Pod Two. There's a private party up there. If you catch her now, you might get a second with her away from customers." He points to the stairs at the left of the bar.

"Thanks, man."

I head up the stairs at a jog, following the signs for each pod until I come to two. When I walk in, the beat of the song has slowed down some, and the lights darken to go with it.

And there she is.

Fuck.

I take in the thigh-high stockings with the seam up the back and the band of lace at the top that hits just below the hem of her skirt, the sky-high black heels, and her hair piled on top of her head with a few pieces falling down onto her bare shoulders.

How is it possible to miss someone as if you've never had her before, and yet you already know exactly how she tastes and what the curve of her neck smells like?

She laughs at something one of the four men in front of her says, and fuck if I don't roll my shoulders at the sight.

All of them want her.

I can see them vying for her attention. I know they're already imagining what she'd be like in bed.

Fucking pricks.

She says something and they all laugh, one of them saying loudly, "Come back soon, sweetheart."

Asshole.

"Vaughn." I bark her name out across the space, and her head whips my way. Her smile is automatic, but her eyes are confused as she walks toward me. All the men at her back size me up.

"What are you—"

And I don't care that she's at work or that I'm a man who doesn't fucking beg, because the minute she's within range, my lips are on hers.

She's startled at first. Then resists momentarily as she remembers where she is and what she's supposed to be doing. But I slip my tongue between her lips and take just a sliver of what I want from her. A tiny sliver at that.

And just when I think she's going to give in and let me pull the clip from her hair so I can fist my hand in it and take even more, her palms are pressing against my chest until they break our kiss.

Her breath is ragged, her lips parted, her eyes firing with anger. "What are you doing?"

"Letting everyone know you're mine."

She lifts her chin ever so slightly, almost as if to say she isn't . . . and that lights my temper.

Especially when she drags me from the pod. She doesn't even touch me either, but the look she levels me with has me following without a word.

And I'm not sure what pisses me off more—the fact she fought my kiss in front of those assholes or that I'm following her without a word.

She stalks her ass down the hallway, and the minute we turn into the next pod that's empty, her hands are fisted in my shirt, and her lips crash into mine the same time as my back hits the wall.

Her kiss is anger and hunger and irrationality and desperation all combined into one addictive action that drags me under and grabs hold of every ounce of my testosterone.

The heat of her body. The possession of her kiss. The ownership in her touch.

I'm not a man to follow a woman's lead, but hell, if this is where it ends, I just might follow a bit more often.

And just as thoughts of sliding my fingers up the hem of that skirt to dip inside her wetness begin to own my mind, she pushes against me and tears her mouth from mine.

"Don't you ever walk into my work and do that to me again."

Her lips crash back against mine.

"You don't own me, Lockhart."

A duel between our tongues.

"They wanted you," I manage as I grab her ass and squeeze, prompting her to lift her face up so she's forced to meet my gaze. Her lids are heavy with arousal, her lips swollen, her eyes filled with violent desire.

"A lot of men want me." The dig of her fingernails. "Just like a lot of women want you."

She sucks on my tongue, and it causes every goddamn part of me to stand at attention.

"I don't like it."

A nip of my lip that has me swearing at the sting.

"Tough."

"You're mine," I say and pull her into me so I can grind against her.

"I'm no one's."

"Like hell you aren't, and now they know it."

And this time . . . this time, I take charge.

I'm being completely irrational. She's at work, and I'm dying to fuck her . . . but hell if I care.

Some things can't wait.

Some things are a necessity. Like air and water and food and *Vaughn*.

She wants a fight?

I'll give her a goddamn fight.

But not with words. No. Those are weapons and something I probably can't win with when it comes to her.

But this? I can win with this.

I push her backward so she's against the far wall of the pod. Away from the door. More in the dark. When her back hits the wall, when my lips find hers again, when our bodies are pressed against one another's, I push that hem up to do what I've wanted and dive my fingers between her thighs.

I swallow her gasp.

And then her moan.

As my fingers find her wetness and her heat and tuck inside her without any warning.

Good. God. What am I doing to myself?

"Fuck," I groan as I force myself to stop, to voluntarily lose this fight.

"Cancel with your client tonight," I tell her, my fingers still buried in her, my hand still wet, my cock still hard as a rock.

Only so I can win it later.

"No." It's part growl. Part moan. Both pure sex.

"What was that?" I ask as I chuckle against her lips and curl my fingers against the parts of her begging to be rubbed and fucked.

Her legs tense, her fingers tighten on my shoulders, her breath hitches. A simple "Ohhh" falls from her lips, its heat hitting my ear.

I still again. "Cancel your meeting." I nip her earlobe and circle my fingers against the rough patch inside her. "And we're going to finish what we started here."

"Ryker." My name breathless has never sounded better.

"Cancel." A rub of my thumb over her clit so that she bucks her hips into my hand.

"Yes." Another rub. "Damn it, yes."

"I'll be waiting."

And without another word, I remove my fingers from her and walk toward the stairs.

Hell if that's not the hardest thing I've ever done before. Leaving her wet and wanting while I'm hard and needing.

And need her I do. To abate my anger. To take a hit of the drug she's become. To forget the bullshit.

To be mine.

CHAPTER
TWENTY-FOUR
Vaughn

I've thought about Ryker all shift.

How could I not?

Christ, he worked me up—in anger and arousal, so that the scent of sex is so strong I can smell it on my skin—and then left me high and dry and wanting.

But the thrill of anticipation trumps everything as I walk down the exit of Apropos.

The town car startles me at first. My thoughts veer to the senator, and fear has me thinking it's him. But when Ryker opens the door and steps from it, I swear that every part of me clenches—chest, lungs, thighs, knees—at the sight of him.

He's standing at the dimly lit curb, making it hard to read his expression. But his eyes—his eyes I can see. They glint through the darkness and are just as telling as the tension in his posture.

A small thrill reverberates through me with every step I take. This whole liking sex thing is still new to me, and yet each and every time we're together, Ryker shows me a different side of him. Of it. And of us.

I stop when I reach him where he's standing with his hand on the roof of the car. We share a look—one that is riddled with so much tension—before he glances toward the inside of the limo, telling me to get in without words.

And I do just that: slide into the limo with a glance back toward Ahmed—who's watching us like a big brother on his little sister's first date—and nod.

Ryker is beside me in an instant, the town car on the move as if the driver already knows our destination despite the privacy shield never being lowered, but he doesn't say a word to me. He doesn't even offer a glance my way. He just sits with his fingers tapping on his knee while his other hand runs over his jaw as the lights from the city around us glitter and glow.

"Is something wrong?"

He chuckles, but it's strained. "Everything is wrong." He lifts a glass to his lips and then looks at the ice in it rather than looking at me.

"What do you mean, everything is wrong?"

Where is the man from earlier? The one who waltzed in and has had me strung so tight, one touch and I'm going to snap?

He shakes his head and looks out the window. "I tried to work. I tried to figure shit out. I tried to do a million goddamn things, and fuck if it doesn't help one iota."

He's not making sense. "What is it you need help with?"

"It's nothing you can fix."

"Ryker? Did something happen?" I reach for his hand, and he moves it the minute we touch.

"Yeah," he chuckles. *"You."*

"Me?" I laugh and turn so that my knee is angled against the back of the seat, my other on the floor. It's the first time he looks my way, down to the darkness between my thighs where my skirt has risen up with the motion, before finally meeting my eyes. "What the hell have I done to you?"

The muscle in his jaw pulses, and his hand flexes on his leg. "You've made me want you like I can't fucking live if I don't have you."

And before his last word is finished, his lips are on mine in a kiss that bruises my mouth as much as his love has marked my heart. Unrelenting, unforgiving, and irrevocable.

"Fucking hell, woman," he murmurs between licks and nips and kisses. "The shit you do to me isn't legal."

I chuckle with pride and then gasp when he lowers himself to his knees and buries his face in the *V* of my thighs. He makes a show of inhaling my panties, and I know damn well how wet I was when he left me earlier. The scent of my arousal is on them. From then. From now.

"Ryk," I moan when his tongue licks a line up the seam of my panties to press against my clit in a pleasurable pressure.

"You." He grabs both of my thighs and pulls me down some so I can spread my legs farther apart. "Fucking irresistible." A flick of his tongue. "Your scent." An audible inhale. "How wet you are." The hook of his fingers to pull my panties to the side. "Christ." His moan as his fingers dip into me. "Your taste." The heat of his mouth as the barrier is gone and his mouth closes over me. "Goddammit, Vaughn."

My hands grip in his hair. My hips buck up. My teeth bite into my bottom lip as Ryker takes his time showing me just what it's like to be pleasured properly.

I lose all sense of my surroundings. The driver up front who can no doubt hear my moans. The people in the cars beyond the tinted windows. The honk of horns from the cars around us.

I lose sense of everything except for the man between my thighs.

When I finally come, when my heart is racing and muscles are tensing and body is awash with so much pleasure that speaking or thinking isn't an option, Ryker sits back on his knees and watches me. My arousal on his chin glistens from the lights of the passing cars.

But it's his eyes as I come undone that hold my attention. His fingers are still sliding in and out of me, but it's his expression, the lust mixed with desperation and paired with love etched in the lines of his face that owns every part of me when I crash over the edge.

"So beautiful," he murmurs when he leans forward and kisses me as my body still pulses from pleasure.

And when he slips into me, the tires of the car still moving, I can't help thinking I don't want it ever to stop.

It's just him and me together in here.

A world where no one can touch us.

It's just us.

Two people who can't seem to stop fighting their way toward each other despite everything trying to hold them back.

CHAPTER
TWENTY-FIVE
Vaughn

"Hey there, pretty girl, are you all set?"

Lucy's smile widens, but then without warning her bottom lip trembles. The sight of it kills me. I lower myself to my knees and run my hand over her hair. "What is it, Lu? What's wrong?"

"You didn't come last week." She fights the tears that well in her eyes and refuses to look at me.

"Oh, Lu. I tried. I was here, but there was something going on, and they wouldn't let anyone go on outside visits."

"But you promised. Every Tuesday was our day."

"I know." My voice breaks right along with my heart. "But it's a new week, and while Tuesday is our day, we never just have Tuesday." I try to sell her on why she shouldn't be disappointed when I know it won't work. "I always see you more than that. In sleepovers at the house. In dates to the park. You're my Lucy-Loo. I need you more than just on Tuesdays."

I pull her into a hug, hold her tightly against me, and squeeze my eyes, praying this won't happen again.

"Promise?" Her voice is muffled against my shoulder.

"I promise. You know I'd rather be with you than anyone else in the world. And even when I'm not with you in person, I'm still here in your heart."

"But that's where my mommy is, and I never get to see her anymore."

I take a deep, fortifying breath and kiss the tear tracks on her cheeks as I try to hold my own back. "I know, sweetie. I know." I hug her one more time and then put her hand in mine. "You ready to go have some fun?"

She nods, but I stare at her with a funny face until I get a smile.

"Yes?" I ask.

She nods more emphatically. "Yes."

"Good, because we have two Tuesdays' worth of fun to make up for."

"Like?"

"Like pizza and . . . I don't know, but it will be fun!"

"Pizza?"

"Yep. Pizza. Does that sound good?"

Her squeal of delight is probably the best thing I've heard all day. "There's my girl," I say and head to the front desk to sign her out. She chatters away—music to my ears—as we head out into the sunshine toward the parking lot.

"Hey. Wait up!"

I turn to see Joey jogging after us, out of breath and with a jacket under his arm. It's the first I've seen or talked to him since the last time I was here when he told me I couldn't take Lucy. He never called with the more information he said he'd find out. All I have in my head as I look at him and force a smile is that for the first time, I'm not sure if I trust him.

Was he the one who spoke to Priscilla? Was he the one who told her about the various men I had at the house—all innocent but portrayed to be anything but?

"Joey. Hi." I stop, and Lucy's hand tightens in mine, her instinct the same as mine. *Don't take her away from me.*

He stops and looks at me for a beat, head angled to the side, confusion etching the lines of his face. "You're going just like that?"

"Like what?" I look down at my clothes, wondering what in the hell he's talking about. Did I get something on them?

"No." He laughs and waves a hand at my shirt as if it's fine. "I meant, you're just going to leave? It's the second Tuesday of the month. Pizza night."

And for the briefest second, I look at him like he's crazy. Like I'd really invite him with us for pizza on the second Tuesday like I usually do after all the weirdness that happened here. "Oh. I'm sorry. You wanted to—"

"Go. I *always* go."

"I—uh—" I look over to where we're parked and then back at him. "Not today. We're not going to do pizza today." The words tumble out of my mouth, and I mentally cringe, hoping that Lucy doesn't say differently.

"You're not?"

"We're not?"

Both Lucy and Joey speak at the same time.

"It's—I—there was a change of plans."

"Mr. Ryker!" Lucy yells, surprising both of us when she runs into Ryker's arms as he approaches. My heart warms seeing her reaction to him and even more so when he gets down on his haunches and straightens the crown on her head after telling her she looks just like a princess but even prettier.

Ryker stands with Lucy's hand in his and nods. "Joe."

I glance toward Joey. His expression is guarded, and yet I notice the brief lift of his eyebrows and subsequent clench of his jaw when Ryker addresses him.

"Joey," he corrects.

Ryker returns the same insincere smile that Joey gave him before glancing to me and then back to Joey. "Was there a problem? I saw you running out after Vaughn and Lucy, and I wanted to make sure everything was okay, *Joe*."

Ah, jealous Ryker is in full effect.

"Yes, everything is fine. I was just . . ."

"Sometimes Joey goes with us for pizza on the second Tuesday of the month because he gets off early. It's just something we've always done," I say, ignoring the lift of Ryker's eyebrows.

"Yeah. That." Joey shifts on his feet, clearly not comfortable. "We do."

"How sweet." Ryker's tone is anything but genuine, and I shake my head at him. "I'm sorry for the confusion today, but we have plans already."

"Fine. Yeah. Sure." Joey shakes his head and licks his lips, and for the briefest of moments I feel bad for him. For forgetting to tell him there was a change of plans from our usual. But then I think of Priscilla and last week and know that I really don't owe anything to him.

Especially if he's spying on me for social services.

"Maybe next time, then," Ryker says before leaning over and saying something to Lucy that has her giggling like crazy. The deep kind of belly laugh you hear every once in a while and that makes you stop just to enjoy the sound.

"Yeah. Next time." There's defeat in Joey's tone, and now I feel like shit.

"She's spending the night tonight," I explain even though I don't have to, as Ryker begins walking hand in hand with Lucy to the car. I know I don't have any obligation to say anything, but it's my way of trying to feel less guilty. If I'm not coming back here like I usually would, the break in routine explains to him how I forgot it's pizza Tuesday. "I was able to get approval to have her stay tonight to make up for not getting to see her last week."

"Great. Good." He glances over my shoulder to Ryker. "Have fun."

"You sure you don't mind?"

"Not at all. I just didn't know you were still with him is all. After the other night when he was at your house . . . never mind."

I roll my shoulders at the mention and hate that it only serves to prove he was one of the only people who knew. I look out to the cars in the parking lot, debating whether I should just ask flat out if he said anything or not.

"Is everything all right?" he asks, bringing my attention back to him.

"Everything is fine."

"You sure? I didn't hear from you at all the past week."

I narrow my eyes at him. Did he forget what was happening? "That's because I wasn't allowed to see her. Remember?"

"You could have called, though. I would have picked up." He looks back again to the facility, his hands fidgeting with the jacket in them. "Everything's all better now?"

"Appears to be. I'm getting to see her, aren't I?" Something is off here.

"Yeah. I'm sorry. It's just been a long week."

"For you and me both." I pause as he looks back to the office yet again. "Is everything okay with you?"

"Fine." He takes a step backward. "I need to get back inside."

CHAPTER TWENTY-SIX

Vaughn

"Keep your eyes closed," Ryker instructs as Lucy and I walk over uneven ground.

"This is ridiculous," I mumble as Lucy giggles, and then I remind myself to see this through the eyes of a curious eight-year-old instead of a woman who isn't too fond of surprises.

"It really is hard for you to let someone else be in control, isn't it?" Ryker's voice heats up my ear. "Relax, Sanders."

"You're right." He is right. But having to cover my eyes with my hands while being led through wherever he's leading us is downright ridiculous.

"Can we write that down? That I'm right?" His laugh rumbles over my skin as Lucy keens in excitement beside us.

"Funny."

"Where are we?" I ask as the sound of people laughing in the distance can be heard. Horns honking. Birds chirping.

"I asked you to trust me," he warns.

And I take heed of the warning, all the while trying not to be a little miffed that he took complete control of my first day with Lucy in a while.

"I had things planned out perfectly fine," I say, knowing I sound like a brat, but the unknown is unnerving me.

"Up these steps here."

"Because that's easy to do when you're blindfolded." Another grumble from me.

"It's like we're on a secret treasure hunt, Auntie Vaughn," Lucy says, the excitement in her voice snapping me out of my grumpiness.

"Right, Lucy? Just like that one princess movie," Ryker says and chuckles because I know damn well he has no idea what he's talking about.

"Smooth, Lockhart."

"I try. A few more steps, ladies."

"'Kay," Lucy says.

The sounds all around us are so familiar, recognizable, and yet so generic that I have absolutely no clue where we are.

"Stop here," he says and holds our arms in place. "Are you ready, Lucy?"

"Yes, yes, yes," she squeals.

"I figured since you were a princess, I needed to arrange a date fit for royalty."

Her giggle fills the air as she all but vibrates in anticipation beside me. "Can I look?"

"Yes."

And if I thought her squeal was loud, then I don't even know what to say about the sound she emits when she sees the scene set before us. We are on the terrace of the Belvedere Castle in Central Park. The whole thing has been transformed.

There is a canopy draped in some kind of sparkly fabric that sits over a table complete with candles and fake gold goblets and covered in all kinds of arts and crafts. Standing beside the table are two women who are wearing royal garb, and their smiles are as wide as Lucy's.

"What?" she exclaims as she looks at Ryker and me with wide eyes and a disbelieving smile, all but bouncing out of her shoes.

"Well, if you're a real princess, then you need to do real princess things. These two ladies-in-waiting are here to transform you into the princessiest princess of all time. And after you have your makeover and complete your majestic art, then we'll have a feast fit for royalty out here."

"You mean this is all for me?" The way Lucy looks at Ryker has chills chasing over my skin, and it has nothing to do with the air chilling with the setting sun.

Ryker nods as tears well in both Lucy's and my eyes but for completely different reasons. "You're a princess, aren't you?"

She nods fiercely.

"Then go get ready!"

She jumps up and down and all but runs toward the two women standing there waiting to pamper her.

I don't have words—*none*—as I look around the space. Fairy lights have been hung between flags and crests. There is a sunbed behind us draped in elaborate fabric with tables on either side. A bottle of wine and a charcuterie board sit on one of them.

"Ryker." My voice sounds as awed as I feel. "What did you—? We can't accept this."

He runs a hand down the small of my back. "Who said I did this for you?"

When I turn to look at him, he just lifts an eyebrow and gives me a shy smile that all but warms all of me in every way possible.

And of course, I feel like an ass. Not only for doubting that he'd know what Lucy would like but for thinking he hijacked my time with her to do something for himself . . . or whatever my excuse was going to be.

Because this . . . this is insane.

"You rented out a castle for her."

"Technically, just the terrace. They don't allow people to rent inside the actual castle." His laugh rumbles against my lips as he presses them to mine.

"You're crazy."

"Perhaps."

"This is too much."

"She deserves this."

"But . . ."

"Don't try to figure it out. Just let her enjoy it."

And she's doing just that—enjoying it. Lucy is talking animatedly, her hands flying to her slack jaw every few seconds as she takes it all in—the rack of princess dresses I can now see, the vanity loaded with makeup and hair supplies, the snacks stacked on platters.

"But . . . why?"

When I turn to look at him, he angles his head to the side, and I try to rationalize the man before me. The one who says he's heartless and unfeeling but loves me with a violent desire I can't explain. And *love* he does.

I may have told him he can't say it to me. I may have not allowed myself to say it to him either. But we both feel it. There's no denying that.

And in turn, he loves Lucy.

Ryker frames both of my cheeks with his hands and leans down so that his lips are a whisper away from mine. "Because I can."

My mind reaches back to our first conversations. To his question asking me what would impress me. To my answer: *the unexpected.*

How is it he keeps giving me *the unexpected* time and again?

"She's on cloud nine. I'm never going to be able to bring her down to earth." I rest my head on Ryker's shoulder where we're sitting together on the sunbed. Wine has been drunk. The charcuterie board has been devoured. The fabric draped on the canopy above us gives us a small bit of privacy.

I know how Lucy feels, because I feel the same way. The fact that he did this for her—for me—shouldn't surprise me when it's at the hand of a man who continually does just that—surprise me.

"That's not necessarily a bad thing."

"Hmm." It's all I say, but I fear bringing her back to the clinical facility after she's been made to feel like one in a million here. "Thank you for this." I motion to everything around us.

"You can stop saying that," he murmurs and takes a sip of wine. "I have to say it's been quite the experience."

My own laughter rings out, and Lucy looks our way and waves ecstatically. "If Lucy would have had her way, you would be wearing sparkly lipstick right now." My smile widens as I picture Ryker sitting at the small vanity as Lucy demands to give her own princess makeover to the two of us.

"There's only one place I allow lipstick on me, and your shade of red would look lovely in a ring around it right now," he murmurs against my ear, causing me to snuggle in against him. My head on his shoulder, my hand on his chest, my body wanting him . . . but then again, when does it not want him?

"Watch me!" Lucy says to us as she follows the ladies to the middle of the terrace. She has a new princess dress on, her hair is done and adorned with a tiara, and the ladies are demonstrating some kind of "royal dance" they are going to teach her the steps to.

"She's nervous," I murmur.

"How do you know? She looks happy to me."

"She keeps reaching for her necklace." We both watch her as she reaches up several times over a short period to grab the key on the chain around her neck. "That's her tell."

"What's with the necklace?" he asks after she does it again.

"It was Sam's. She used to wear it all the time when we were teenagers. I forgot about it, but after she died, I found it in some of her stuff. Lucy thinks it's the key to her mom's heart. It's her way of coping, of thinking she has her mom near."

"What does the key belong to?"

"My sister used to tell everyone it was the key to her secrets." I laugh and hear her voice saying it to friends. "It was really the key to our old house. The last one we lived in with our mom before she died. That's all."

"I like her story better," Ryker murmurs, pulling me back into memories of another place and time.

Of laughter before the darkness. Of the bed we shared together and the late-night giggles we'd try to hide. Of innocence shattered and a past I don't want to think about.

"Come back to me, Vaughn."

"Sorry," I say and lift our joined hands to my lips and kiss his, more than grateful I'm with a man who can read me so well.

"Don't be."

Lucy's giggle carries over the distance, and I study Ryker out of the corner of my eye as he watches her. His smile is soft, his eyes kind, his body relaxed.

"You're good at this, you know."

"At what?" He looks over to me and then back to Lucy.

"The dad thing. Have you ever thought about having kids?" I say the words and then realize what they sound like. And of course he responds at the same time I realize my gaffe.

"Are you offering?" His laugh rings out.

"No. That's not what I meant. I just meant . . . you're good with kids. Surprisingly good—"

"Kids I can handle. They're a lot like men. You give them the shiny things that make the most noise and they're satisfied. Now women, on the other hand . . . I fail at understanding."

"So you want kids, then?"

He purses his lips and angles his head to the side in the way he does when he really ponders something. "I've never really thought about it. That sounds stupid, but I haven't. My stance on relationships was that they were temporary at best."

"That's promising," I tease with a nudge.

"Yeah, but . . . when you don't have something, don't grow up with a set ideal, the thought of living it is scary."

"Isn't that the truth," I murmur.

"You can talk about it with me, you know."

"What do you mean?" I ask the question, although I already know the answer.

"Connecticut. Samantha. Your uncle. I promise you I have a good record keeping secrets." He squeezes my hand. "At least my clients think so."

"Thank you," I say softly. "There's nothing more to tell."

"I know, but . . . I'm here." He pulls me in tighter against him.

I look up at him and press my lips against his. It's a soft kiss but one packed with so much emotion that it's hard to open my eyes when the moment ends.

So I don't. I just rest my forehead against his and breathe him in, surrounded by a silence sprinkled with Lucy's laughter and the distant sounds of the city.

"You're wrong, by the way," I whisper against his lips.

"About?"

"You understand women better than you think."

Another brush of lips.

"No. I understand you." A rub of his nose against mine. "You changed things, Vaughn. You changed them in ways I never saw coming."

Those words are like the soft sigh my soul has needed after so many years of holding my breath.

My mind wanders to places I rarely let it go. To futures and possibilities. One that has Ryker in it. I've been living in the next moment—one bill after another. I've been living for Lucy, with her as the endgame in mind.

But what if I wish for more?

What if I wish for one that has happily ever afters fit for the princess dancing in front of us?

CHAPTER
TWENTY-SEVEN
Vaughn

"At some point we need to talk about Carter," Ryker says when he puts the car in park in my driveway.

"Please don't ruin tonight," I say.

"But that's what you've said the last three times I've brought him up."

"I know. It's just . . ." I lean my head back on the seat rest and close my eyes. Lucy's sound asleep in the back seat, and maybe I don't want to ruin a perfect evening talking about him. And maybe if I pretend he never happened, then he'll never follow through.

"You're naive if you think he's just going to go away," he warns as if he's read my mind.

"Ryker—"

"Just hear me out—"

"Please."

"I'm not going to ruin tonight, but . . . he needs to be dealt with." His hand twitches on the gearshift as he reins in his temper.

"It's not that easy."

"Yes, it is. You have dirt on him. He knows it. You two are playing a game of chicken that neither of you are going to swerve on. Vaughn, men like him . . . you don't want to mess with men like him. They're cowards who ruin you out of spite. They'll ruin you simply because they like to watch you cower in fear. They get off on it."

"Then there's nothing I can do if it's out of spite. I don't give in, he'll ruin me. I do give in, he'll still ruin me to prove he can. When a person's endgame is to fuck me over in every way possible, it seems so much easier to stick my head in the sand and pretend he doesn't exist. When I do, he leaves me alone." I unbuckle my seat belt and move to get out of the car.

"What does he have on you, Vaughn?"

I try not to be pissed off the minute I meet his eyes and see the doubt woven into them. "Nothing that I don't know of."

"What about your uncle? You said he mentioned your uncle."

"Hell if I know. I left with Sam and never looked back. *Ever.* I've had my private investigator that I use for Wicked Ways check to see if he's alive or dead. It's a shame he's still alive, but I'm not going to apologize or be sorry about whatever karma-induced accident left him paralyzed. That's about all I care to know. That family doesn't deserve an extra second of my time. Not one. So what does the senator know about my uncle? Beats the hell out of me. But if Carter's a man who gets off on fear like you say he does, then just bringing up my uncle has me scared when most days I can rationalize that he can no longer touch me."

"What do you mean, 'most days'?" he asks.

"Most days I know I'm out of his reach, but sometimes when you're rich and want something bad enough, you have everything at your disposal to get it. Let's just hope Sam and I were blips on his radar who he thinks fell off the face of the earth." I push the handle to open the door and climb out.

"Vaughn." He exits the car and looks at me over its roof. "I didn't mean to upset you."

"Then why even bring it up?"

"You can stick your head in the sand all you want, but it'll just make you more vulnerable because you won't be able to see it coming. Carter's not going to go away. Not until he gets everything he wants from you—your body, what you have on him, everything."

"Then I guess you should have never offered me in the first place," I whisper harshly, well aware that Lucy is sleeping a few feet from me. I push off from the car and take a few steps to get some distance from him and the ever-present reminder that is beginning to ruin this perfect night.

But I force myself to calm down and turn around and face him. I hang my head for a beat before I meet his eyes. "I'm sorry. That was uncalled for."

"I deserve it."

"Yeah, you do—"

"I exacerbated the situation. The one you refuse to let me apologize for . . . so we keep going on, and this huge fucking elephant in the room rears its ugly head every time we get two steps forward only to pull us ten steps back."

"I promised myself I was going to forgive and try to forget . . ." I look down at my hands twisting together and know he's right about all this, but at the same time I would prefer to live in the fairytale land we just left at Belvedere Castle.

"We're both works in progress."

I smile softly. "Definitely works in progress."

"Again, I'm sorry. He had his eyes set on you, Vaughn, and . . . and when he said he had dirt on you, I played his game. Fuck, did I play it." He runs a hand through his hair in frustration and walks to the end of the driveway and then back.

"And now we know what he thought he had," I say, thinking about my uncle and what it is that Carter was using his name for other than to try to scare me. To let me know he could hold the same kind of fear and power over me.

"If there's anything else, Vaughn—anything at all about your uncle that you're hiding—you need to tell me."

I stare at him and just shake my head. "This is never going to go away, is it?"

"It will. I'll make sure of it."

"At what cost, though?" I ask, my voice breaking in ways I don't want it to.

"I don't know," he murmurs as he pulls me against him and wraps his arms around me. And it feels so good, to be here, to feel safe, when I'm sure the sense of security is just as false as me pretending Carter is going to go away. "I just don't know."

"Maybe I should just hand over what I have on him. Losing all of this isn't worth it," I say with my cheek resting on his chest and his lips pressing a kiss to the crown of my head. Lucy. Him. My freedom if Carter calls the authorities. The three things that matter the most to me.

"What do you have on him, Vaughn?" he asks for a second time.

I tense at the question, at him asking to know the secrets I keep from everyone to protect myself. My safekeeping. At the last piece of myself that I haven't given him yet—my confidentiality. "Pictures of Carter. . . let's just say with his pants down."

His pause in response tells me he knows just how big of a deal my answering him was.

"The underage girls." My head whips up at his comment, and he simply nods. "His wife is my client. I've investigated him as well."

"Oh." But for some reason I feel a little more at ease divulging the information now, because I hadn't thought about it that way.

"What else do you have? There has to be more."

"Some kind of phone records."

"And he knows you have these?" he asks, leaning back so he can see my eyes when I nod.

"Yes."

"He knows specifically what they are?"

I shrug. "I just told him I had a call log. He acted like it wasn't a big deal and said his calls were public record, but . . ."

"But what?"

"I don't know. They mean something to him."

"What are they of?" he asks. "What—"

"I don't exactly know." I shake my head and feel stupid that I don't have an answer. "They were emailed to my investigator anonymously. The IP address and fake email address were traced back to a terminal at a public library. The email just said that this paper was extremely important if someone connected the right dots. It was signed, *A Concerned Citizen*."

Ryker angles his head to the side and narrows his eyes in thought. I wait for him to ask for more—to see the call log—and I struggle between giving myself completely to him or drawing a line in the sand I can't let him cross.

"And they're in safekeeping?"

I nod, almost breathing a sigh of relief when he doesn't ask.

"What a clusterfuck," he mutters with a shake of his head. "I need to think about this. About all of it. We'll figure it out. I'll help you figure it out."

"Ryker . . . you don't need to get involved. The last thing you need—"

"It's you. I'm already involved." He leans forward and brushes a tender kiss to my lips that feels so resolute, almost as if he, too, is wishing away the situation.

There's a subtlety to him right now—a softness—that I've never seen before. It's in the way he stares at me across the distance, brandy-colored eyes looking at me from under thick lashes while Lucy sleeps soundly in the back seat of some ridiculously expensive sports car. A car that most men would freak out over because the glitter in her hair might get on its precious leather. And the whole of the moment—of him—is enough for me to realize that he knows he screwed up.

We all do.

If Lucy could comprehend things like I do, when she's older would she judge me for the mistakes I'm making now? For running Wicked Ways, even though in the end the risks are all for her?

How can I not forgive him?

How can I not love him?

I don't think that's possible.

"Let's get her royal highness inside," he says, holding on to me a little longer before heading back to pick up a dead-to-the-world princess snoring in his glitter-laced back seat.

CHAPTER TWENTY-EIGHT

Ryker

"She still asleep?" I ask as Vaughn shuts the door to Lucy's room.

"Out like a light."

She stares at me, arms crossed over her chest and exhaustion written all over her body, but the softest of smiles is on her lips. For a brief second her question from earlier comes back to me: *Have you ever thought about having kids?*

This is what it would look like.

Her tired after a long day. Me staring at her, thinking how gorgeous she looks just like this: hair messy, lipstick long gone, a million pieces of dusted-off glitter dancing on her skin.

This is what it would feel like times a million. *I bet.*

Me wanting to pull her on my lap, nuzzle my nose under her neck, and think about sinking into her body to release the frustrations of my own long day.

And then I realize that I'm saying *with her. With Vaughn.*

My body tenses. *Slow the fuck down, Lockhart. You played princess for Lucy. You did it because you felt bad for being the catalyst that is causing Vaughn's world to spin out of control. You did it because it was the right thing to do, and hell if getting a killer blow job out of it in gratitude didn't cross your mind in the process.*

Panic hits me.

The kind that makes your thoughts misfire, and you question every-thing about yourself, because this isn't you. These thoughts aren't yours.

"Hey." Her hand slides over my neck, fingernails scratching gently, as I sit on her couch. My eyes close at the sensation, at the desire to just be here with her with no expectations, with no demands.

I love her.

The word hits my ears, and I jolt up out of my seat as if it's the first time I ever thought them when it came to Vaughn.

I have said them, though. In a rush to win her back after doing something awful, I said them. Words I thought I knew the meaning of but realize now I didn't have a goddamn clue.

I told her I loved her before to try to win her back. That's what you're supposed to say, right? But it was only panic then, only words said through the haze of lust and the supposition of need.

But now, after we've been through all this drama, all this conflict, I'm still here when normally I would have hit the road. I'm still here because she's taught me things about myself that I never knew—that I'm good with kids, that there is something to be said about sleeping with someone without having sex, that forgiveness is more powerful than anything—but most of all she taught me that I *am* capable of love.

I love her.

I repeat the three words in my head and know that for the first time in my life, I truly understand their meaning and the power they hold. They're not to be feared or taken lightly. They're not to be wielded like a sword.

They're to be *meant*. To be spoken at the right moment. To be used sparingly.

I love Vaughn.

My chest constricts, and my entire body heats as her eyes flash to me while I stand like a deer in headlights in the middle of her living room.

"You okay?" She takes a step toward me, concern loaded in her tone. "You look like you just saw a ghost."

"Yes. Fine." *What are you going to do, Lockhart?* "I . . . uh . . . forgot something in my car." I throw my thumb over my shoulder to sell the lie.

"Okay." She says the word, but I just stand there without moving. "Are you going to get it?"

"Yeah. Sure. I'll just"—*move your feet, Ryk*—"be right back."

"'Kay." Her smile lights up her eyes. "I'll pour the wine."

Her smile lights up her eyes?

You have it fucking bad, Lockhart.

Pathetic and bad.

I open the door, distracted in more ways than I ever thought possible, shut it behind me, and then stumble to a stop.

He's medium height, lanky, without an ounce of muscle on him. His hair is an oily brown, his fingers stained with what looks like grease under his nails, and his clothes look out of place on him. Expensive threads on a sketchy man.

His eyes widen and his head startles when our eyes meet. I'm on edge immediately.

"Can I help you?"

He takes in my dress shirt unbuttoned, my cuffs rolled up, and zeroes in on the watch on my wrist. His gaze stays there for a beat before he shifts on his feet and jerks his arms oddly.

"I should've known."

"Excuse me?"

My first thought: the fucker is a client who somehow found out Vaughn and Vee are the same person.

My second thought: the asshole is her private investigator, the man who should have known about her uncle and warned her about the warrant out for her arrest but didn't.

The third? A homeless man looking for some blow? A man lost? Nah. Neither. Not quite sure yet, but every damn part of me hates him already.

His laugh rings out into the quiet suburbia night. "You the sugar daddy Vaughny's using now?" He lifts his chin toward my Maserati parked in the driveway before his eyes glance to my watch again. "Sell your soul for some of her pussy now?"

My body tenses. My fists clench. My personal demand to shut my mouth falls on my own deaf ears. "Get the fuck out of here."

His laugh rumbles on the verge of hysteria. He seems crazy, but there's an awareness in his eyes that tells me to use caution.

"The price just went up."

"Price?"

"For Lucy."

"Brian, I presume." My voice is unaffected despite the sudden rage and need to protect that owns me. Does he know Lucy's inside? Is that why he's here?

"Ah, rich *and* smart." His smile widens, exposing stained but perfectly straight teeth.

"I suggest you turn your ass around and never set foot here again."

"Or else what?" He throws his hands up. "You gonna sic the Big Bad Wolf on me?" He laughs. "That's got nothing on the hell I've gone through. Losing my wife. My daughter." Not a single word holds an ounce of sincerity in it.

"You don't give a rat's ass about Lucy, and you sure as hell didn't give one about Samantha either."

"Is Vaughny telling lies again?" He tsks and makes the shame motion—his index finger running over the length of his other index finger. "She has a bad habit of that, you know. Twisting the truth to fit whatever it is she wants at any given moment. I'd question everything she tells you. Sam was always warning me about that."

"All you care about is where your next high is coming from."

The grin he flashes sends chills down my spine. "Don't be so sure about that, Daddy Warbucks, because I definitely care about how much you're going to pay me."

"Fuck you."

"Oh? You think you're not going to write a check out to me?"

"For what?" I ask, although my stomach is already churning, because I know what he's going to say.

"To pay me off so I don't steal the adoption right out from underneath that cunt of a sister-in-law of mine's nose."

Each word he speaks ignites a fire in me like I've never known before. My body vibrates from the physical restraint to not swing my fist before he says another word.

"No one's paying you a dime, you worthless piece of shit." I take a step closer to him, shoulders squared, fists clenched. "You think *this* is going to win you favor in the whole process? Selling your daughter to pay for your habit? Huh? You might think you can get away with saying it to Vaughn. That people won't believe her. But I'm a lawyer. I know a lot of people who can make your life fucking miserable."

He claps his hands slowly, his expression one of complete indifference. "Congratulations. I'm so impressed. You must be really smart to screw people out of money for a living."

"I said it before, and I'll say it again. Get the fuck out of here."

"Or what?"

It's my turn to laugh, loud and disbelieving, as I imagine breaking the fucker in two. My hands itch to. "Take your pick. Broken nose. Hospital bed—"

"She really has you whipped, doesn't she?"

"Last warning."

"Tell me," he says as he sniffs loudly and completely disregards my comment. "I always wondered something about Vaughny."

"Your choice."

"Is her pussy as tight as she is uptight?"

In my mind my fist is plowing into his face. One punch after another until my knuckles are bruised and his face is bloody. In my imagination this all takes place, and there isn't a single repercussion to beating the shit out of this loser.

But I've let my reactions govern too much when it comes to Vaughn. When it comes to fucking things up for her.

And it takes every ounce of restraint I have to not throw the punch.

Every.

Ounce.

My muscles ache from being so tense.

"So it *is* that good, huh?" It's not his words but rather the way he looks at Vaughn as she opens the door and gasps at the sight of him.

"Get the fuck out of here," I grit out, every single vestige of control I have snapping in my words. I take an aggressive step toward him, and the fucker jerks to step back and trips, plowing face-first into the concrete retaining wall of her raised flower bed.

He yelps as I watch him flounder on the ground, and I feel nothing at the sight of the blood where the brick has cut his cheekbone.

"Vaughny," he says when his eyes finally focus on her standing beside me, and the hairs stand up on the back of my neck from the way he undresses her with his eyes, like he's imagining violating her every way he can. "You didn't tell me you had a man."

"Leave, asshole." My fist clenches, and I push her behind me so he can't look at her.

In his delayed reaction, he finally reaches up to feel his cheek. When he looks at the blood on his fingers, a slow, taunting grin slides onto his lips.

"You can thank your sugar daddy," he says to her as he hunches over and pushes himself up, his laugh sounding so odd right now. "Just think what the cops are going to say when I head there looking like this, pointing the finger your way."

"Go right ahead," I grit out, my body vibrating with adrenaline. "I didn't touch you."

His laugh echoes through the empty night. "They're not going to know any different."

"Try it." I take a step forward, and he stumbles back, that sick smile still on his lips.

"I'll sue you for everything you're worth, lawyer boy."

"Be my guest."

"You don't get it, do you?" He angles his head to the side, suddenly serious in a way that fucks with my head.

"Get what?"

"Who's smart now? The lawyer . . . or simple me who just wrote his own ticket?" He runs a hand down his cheek and smears the blood over his skin. "Pay, or I go to the police."

"Go to hell." It's all I can think to say as I push his words away, not wanting to acknowledge every fucking ounce of truth they might hold. "They won't believe you."

He pretends to hold a phone up to his ear. "Yes. Hello, Mr. Police. Vaughny is shacking up with an out-of-control psycho. A man who punched me right in front of my own daughter." Vaughn and I both whip our heads to the doorway, expecting to see Lucy standing there, but find it empty.

"Leave, or I'll call them myself." I take a step toward him.

"Please, Brian. Just go," Vaughn pleads, and the broken sound in her voice—the fear woven into its tone—fucking kills me.

"Congrats, Richie Rich. You just cost her the only thing she cares about. It's not you. It's Lucy. Good luck ever getting the adoption now."

Brian holds his hand up and rubs the tips of his fingers together as if he's rubbing money and lifts his eyebrows.

I might not have touched him once, but the blood on his cheek and the contentious custody battle between these two make his threat very real.

It's only after I watch him walk across the street, get in his car, and drive off that I finally breathe. When I turn around, Vaughn is gone.

"Vaughn?" I ask when I enter the house, but I stop when I see her.

She's pacing the room, her face a mask of fury as she moves. All that contradicts the anger emanating from her are the tear streaks on her cheeks.

"Nothing is going to happen. He doesn't have the balls to go to the cops. As much as I had visions of knocking him out, I didn't. That would have invited the problem. But that?" I hook a thumb toward the door. "That's nothing we can't explain. It's our word—sensible, responsible citizens—against his."

"You don't know him." It's the first time she's looked my way—albeit briefly—since I walked in the door.

"I consider myself lucky, then."

"This isn't a joke, Ryker. This is . . . this is . . ." Her hiccupped sob throws me.

I move to stand in her line of pacing so she's forced to stop and look at me. When she does, I pull her in against me and hold her tight. "It's not a joke. I know that. But I also know we did nothing wrong." I press a kiss to the top of her head and just breathe her in. Her fear. Her uncertainty. Her desperation to take care of Lucy.

All of it.

And I know I love her even more because of it.

There are those words again. That thought again.

"I've got you, Vaughn," I murmur against the crown of her head. "I've got you."

CHAPTER
TWENTY-NINE
Vaughn

I toy with the card on the flowers that were delivered an hour ago.

Sorry for what happened. I'll make this right by you.

The flowers are vibrant, while I still feel washed out from the gamut of emotions that have owned me over the past few days.

Hell, who am I kidding? The past few weeks.

The bright side? Ryker just might be right. Brian is too much of a wimp to go to the cops and make a false report.

The call I waited for all day never came. The one from Priscilla asking me what happened to Brian and then having to disprove her crazy accusations.

It didn't come the next day either.

Maybe Brian didn't go to the police after all.

I bury my nose in the flowers again, draw in their perfumed scent, and sigh in relief for what feels like the first time since Brian left here with his threats.

I jump when my cell rings. My pulse calms when I see it's one of my girls. "Hey, Ivy. Everything okay?"

"Always." Her throaty laugh fills the line.

"What's up?"

"Couple things. Does the name Carter Preston ring a bell with you?" I sigh at her mention of his name. "Ha. Your sigh says it all."

"It's a long story, but yes, I know the senator. He's someone I choose to steer clear of. Why?"

"Guy's got a real hard-on for you."

I snort because I don't trust myself to speak in response. "What do you mean?"

"I was at an event. Lots of bigwigs. Lots of money. Lots of politicians. There was an ol' boys' conversation. Services like ours came up. The senator asked if I knew any good ones—kind of a lead-in, since later my date told me he'd already told Carter the company I work for. I wasn't aware there was any history between you, or I wouldn't have said anything to him about Wicked Ways."

"What'd he say?" I ask.

"Just that you're not what you seem. That you sleep with clients and steal them from your girls." She's guarded when she speaks, and I can tell she's trying to feel me out from my answer alone.

"So in other words, he's trying to cause trouble for me. Trying to rile up my troops with lies and turn them against me?"

Christ. I roll my shoulders and have to tell myself to relax the clench of my jaw.

"Either that or he's forcing your hand to confront him. Some men get off on the power play of shit like this."

"Lucky me," I murmur, but I know she's right. He's playing a game right now. One I can't afford to engage in—*or lose.*

"Sorry to be the one to tell you, but I thought you should know."

Silence hangs on the line, and then I realize I never officially answered the question for her.

"I met with a client to discuss a replacement girl for him when the one he chose couldn't meet his needs. The client and I hit it off. We've gone on a few dates. I can see how it could be perceived as stealing clients from my girls without all the facts," I lie, omitting the money he transferred to my account in the early days. "But it wasn't anything like that."

"Thank you for telling me," she says, and I can only hope she believes me. Otherwise, the shitstorm that Carter is trying to stir up will be working.

"Anytime. What else? You said there were a few things."

"I have a nervous Nellie," she says, our term for a client who keeps scheduling and then canceling. "He wants to talk to you."

"Name?"

"Noah B."

"Shit," I groan. "That's my fault. I had to cancel our meeting the other night at the last minute."

The other night? That was over a week ago. And of course my mind veers back to the town car ride. To Ryker's mouth between my thighs and the magic of his tongue. To the emotion in his eyes as he looked up at me, face framed by my thighs.

I think of Noah's voice mail that I forgot to respond to because I was preoccupied with everything else.

You're dropping balls left and right here, Vaughn.

"I'll handle it. I'll call him the minute we hang up."

The quickest way for a girl to turn on you is if you mess with her ability to make money. My lack of response to Noah did just that.

"Thanks, Vee. He's willing to pay. He just needs to show up."

"I hear you. Like I said, I'll get on it right now."

I end the call and click on my computer to get his contact information. In less than a few minutes, I have a meeting set up with Noah and have offered numerous reassurances to him.

The rest of the day flies by, and as I do my weekly check-ins with my girls, I'm not surprised to find a few of them have heard the same gist from either the senator himself or another girl asking about it.

My first line of defense is to give the same explanation I gave to Ivy.

My second is to worry how Carter was able to get in touch with so many of my girls. *One is too many.*

The safety net I thought I'd built around this business seems not to be as secure as I once thought it was. Either that or he's digging through my electronic footprint somehow so that he knows how to contact them.

All of it is troubling.

Then I think of my day planner on my desk. Of my thoughts a few weeks before that someone had been going through my office.

You're drawing conclusions out of fear, Vaughn. Get a grip.

With my head in my hands and a deep sigh, I look up when I get a new email.

"It's almost as if she knew," I murmur to myself when I look at the message I just received from Ella. Yet another check-in to see if I'm ready and willing to discuss selling my book of business to her.

I stare at the screen until my eyes blur. Tell her yes. Tell her no. Financial security versus insecurity. Keeping myself vulnerable to the illegalities of this business versus stepping away from the constant worry of being caught.

I sigh with a shake of my head. The offer to sell is so tempting, but the price she'd pay for my book of clients isn't nearly enough to cover my outlying debts. The plan was to sell in a year's time. To build and bolster and grow my reputation so this is all worth more.

If I sell now, I won't completely pay off my debts. Will paying off a large chunk be enough for Priscilla? Because the tips at Apropos simply aren't enough to live off while repaying the remaining balances.

But selling it would make you safer. It would give you a chance to have a future where you're not constantly looking over your shoulder.

For the first time since she began contacting me, I reply back with a message other than no.

Hi Ella,

Thank you for your message and persistence. I think I'm closer to talking than I've ever been. I need to figure out a few details and have a bit of time to wrap my head around it all, though. I'll be in touch in the next few weeks to set up a meeting with you.

Thank you.
Vee

I stare at my response for the longest time and then hit send before I lose the courage.

CHAPTER THIRTY
Ryker

I eye the man who walks into my office. His eyes never stop glancing around—judging, measuring, assessing—until they land on me.

"Can I help you, Officer?" I ask.

He's in plain clothes. Light hair. Dark eyes. And he more than takes his time responding.

"You having a good day?"

What the fuck do you want?

Instead of asking the question I really want to, I smile. "Your badge, please?" He looks surprised when I hold out my hand to see it. "You've been sitting down in my lobby for the past day or so. You know my name—it only seems fair that I know yours."

He fights the twitch of a smile at being made and reaches in his pocket for his badge. I look at it for a beat: Dan Brower, detective with the NYPD.

Detective.

I hand it back to him, but not before I try to memorize his badge number.

"I can write down the number so you don't forget it," he says, that twitch turning into an I-know-your-type smile.

"No need," I bluff. "And your recorder?" I motion to his pocket. "Is that on too?"

"No." He pulls his phone from his pocket and levels me with a stare that's less than amicable. "Thanks for reminding me, though."

"Just want to make sure you get this all down the first time, seeing as I'm certain both you and I are busy and have better things to do than talk about whatever it is you're here to talk about."

"How generous of you." Sarcasm of a seasoned detective edges his tone.

"You set?" I ask like an overeager schoolboy.

"Yes."

"What can I do for you, Detective Brower?"

"We had a complaint filed by—"

"Oh, you forgot to say who I was. You know, for your records. You might want to say who it is you're speaking to."

He clenches his jaw. "Yes. This is Detective Brower speaking with one Mr. Ryker Lockhart in regards to case number"—he looks at something on his notepad—"4657894."

"Great. Thanks. You can ask your question now." I motion to the list of things on his pad.

He eyes me again, frustration in his expression and defensiveness in his posture. "Can you let me run this now? You good with that?"

"Sure. Shall we?"

"As I was saying. We had a complaint filed by one Brian Vaden."

I nod. "And you're following up on it why? Run out of beat cops today?"

"As I said, Mr. Vaden filed a complaint."

"Through your office? Through social services? Where did he go exactly to file the complaint?"

"You're being difficult, Mr. Lockhart, and I haven't even asked my question yet."

"Not difficult. Just trying to get the lay of the land to figure out why a detective is wasting his time coming to my office to ask about a man he probably never even spoke to personally."

I can play cat and mouse all day, fucker. Bring it on. I need this. Someone to play this game with.

"Brian Vaden," he says. "Do you know him?"

"Briefly."

"Care to expand?"

"Was this a *high* Brian or a *sober* Brian?" I ask, laying the groundwork.

"Excuse me?" He picks up a paperweight on my desk without asking and measures its weight in his hand before looking back at me.

"Was he sober, or was he high?"

"That question leads me to believe that you know him."

"And your response leads me to believe I was right—you've never met him face-to-face. You've never seen him twitching from his need for more blow or smack or whatever the fuck it is he's always high on."

"I'm not quite sure what this has to do with anything."

"It has to do with everything." I smile broadly.

"Again, I'll ask you to expand if you so desire."

"Well, a high Brian will come and lie to you about how I threatened his life and then punched him for nothing more than showing up at my girlfriend's doorstep close to midnight. How we chatted about the nice weather we're having, and then when he told me he loved the Yankees, I chose to punch him, since I'm a die-hard Red Sox fan."

"So you did punch him?"

"A sober Brian," I continue without missing a beat, "would inform you how he showed up to my girlfriend's house in an attempt to extort money from her. And then when he found me there instead, after assessing the watch on my wrist, tried to extort even more money from me. How he asked me to pay an exorbitant amount for him not to protest the adoption of his daughter to his sister-in-law, a.k.a. *my* girlfriend.

He'd tell you he's just looking for some more cash to fund that nasty habit he has that makes him unfit to parent said daughter as well. He'd tell you that as much as I would have loved to plow my fist into his nose, I didn't. Instead, after he made a more than vulgar comment about my girlfriend that had me fearing for her safety, I took a step toward him, and he promptly turned to run like a chicken. How he tripped over his own feet and fell face-first into the little retaining wall she has around a raised flower bed." I shove my hands in my pockets and lean back against the desk behind me and shrug. "He might even tell you that if you head over to her house, you'll probably see a small spot of his blood on the edge of said wall where his cheek cut open when he hit it. I can guess which person you talked to, though."

"Who's that?" he leads me when he has no clue I'm pulling him by the reins exactly where I want him to go.

"I don't think sober Brian has seen the light of day for some time now. Maybe he cleans it up when he has an appointment with social services, but he's at the point where he needs drugs just to maintain his normal. But no, sober Brian hasn't been around for some time. Not since way before his girlfriend committed suicide because the drugs he continually fed her were too much for her to break the chains from so she could be a good mother. On a scale of one to being a stellar individual, I think you can see where he stands."

"I didn't ask any of that, Mr. Lockhart."

"Just doing my civil service, Detective, and giving you the whole picture. Sometimes it's important to get a feel for the person who filed the complaint before you go out and question the person he's pointing the finger at."

That and saying it places all the shit he's done on a permanent record. Something I can corroborate in court if need be. Documentation a judge won't be able to overlook if it comes down to a custody battle between Vaughn and Brian over Lucy after social services decides who should be her legal guardian.

"Let's get back on task here."

"Oh, I'm sorry. It's a habit of mine to paint a picture in opening arguments."

The detective shifts on his feet. I'm driving him crazy. Good. That was my plan.

He glances back down to his notepad to remember where we were before I distracted him. "So your story is that he cut his face when he fell and hit a wall?"

Wide, blinking eyes. Slowly shaking head. "Yes, but you don't have to take my word for it. I'm sure he gets beat up regularly. You hang with a nasty crowd, you run the risk of getting the shit beat out of you when you don't pay up. At least that's what I've seen time and again in my line of work."

He eyes me, and I don't give a flying fuck if he believes me or not. "You're a divorce lawyer, correct?"

I nod and point to my business card on the desk with a cheesy grin.

"Don't think you see many beat-up druggies from missed supplier payments in your line of work, now do you?"

I chuckle and cross my arms over my chest, never breaking eye contact. "It's amazing the things people will do when money is on the line and love has been broken."

He twists his lips as we just stare at each other in the silence of my office. A challenge is given. An acknowledgment that I am enjoying talking in circles.

"Is there anything else you'd like to add?" he asks.

"You tell me."

"Mr. Lockhart, I don't play games."

"Believe me, neither do I."

"Then we're done here?" he asks.

"You're the one who came to me. Did you get what you needed, Detective?"

"You live in New York long, Mr. Lockhart?"

His question does what it's intended to do—throwing me momentarily. "You already know the answer to that question." I change my tone from amused to cut-the-bullshit. "Now why would you ask something like that?"

"Ever heard of the High Line?"

My smile is automatic. Is he really going to nail me for trespassing right now?

"Of course I have. I'm a New Yorker through and through," I say.

"Except for that Red Sox part."

"Except for that." I laugh.

And when he leaves, I sit back in my chair and run the conversation over in my head.

Again and again.

If anything, I've started the ball rolling to try to lay the groundwork of just who Brian Vaden is. It's not solving all Vaughn's problems, but it's a start.

Carter is still an unknown, as is how to fix his fascination with Vaughn. She's at least told me what she has on him, but fuck if I have any clue what a call log would be about.

I can at least be thankful that he's been on a congressional envoy overseas for the past few weeks. His radio silence has been needed.

But it won't last.

Then there are the Dillingers. Seven days and counting until I stand face-to-face with the pedophile James. I'll let him know exactly how he will be contacting the prosecuting attorney in Greenwich and telling him how he wants Vaughn's warrant recalled. And I might have a whole lot of fun letting him know the leverage I have over him if he ever so much as breathes in Vaughn's direction again.

With the warrant gone, Carter's main threat will be nonexistent.

But then I'll have to explain to Vaughn that I invaded her privacy and why.

When I told her I wanted to take care of her, I meant it.

Now there's just one more thing I need to do.

I look down at the printout in my hands. At the balances lining the right side of the spreadsheet.

Fuck it.

I push the number on my phone. He picks up on the third ring.

"What's up?"

"Pull the trigger, Stu."

"I thought you said you weren't touching that part of her life. That it was off limits."

"Yeah, well, I changed my mind."

CHAPTER THIRTY-ONE

Vaughn

I watch the news halfheartedly. The only reason it caught my attention was the mention of Carter Preston's name. Is it sad that I sigh in relief when they mention his name in connection with meetings top congressional persons are having in Europe on a two-week tour?

Will I ever know what it's like not to have to look over my shoulder at every turn? Will I be able to get my teaching credential without anything from my past rearing its ugly head and ruining any background check that might take place? I press my fingers to my temples and close my eyes, the latest round of bill paying just the icing on the cake to a rather shitty week.

When my phone rings, I half expect it to be Priscilla on the other end of the line but am surprised to see Ryker's name.

Every part of me sags in elation at the sight of it.

"Hello?"

"Hi." His voice. *Sigh*. "It's okay for you to pick up the phone and call me sometimes, you know." His chuckle rumbles through the line.

"I know."

"Do you?" His tone is playful.

"I do."

"Good, because I was worried you were over there sitting behind your desk convincing yourself of every reason we shouldn't be together instead of every reason that we should be. I vote for the glass-half-full approach."

"I prefer it half-empty."

And isn't that the two of us in a nutshell? My whole life I've been left hoping for more while dealing with less. And then there's Ryker, who has had access to everything, and yet he allows himself only so little.

"You need to change your outlook."

"I do?"

"Mmm. Like one where you look up and see me standing in your doorway because I missed you and wanted to see you," he says, and I immediately turn around to look at my front door, half expecting him to be there and being slightly disappointed when he's not.

"You're not standing here, though."

"You haven't invited me to be."

I laugh. "You've never been one to wait for an invitation."

"Now. Tomorrow. I need to see you," he says, and the raw emotion in his voice hits me deep in my core.

"Seeing you scares me." My unexpected confession takes me by surprise.

"What?" His voice is part amused, part leery, while I fill the line with nervous laughter.

"Everything has been calm. Quiet. Uneventful. I bet you a hundred bucks that if we see each other, the crazy will somehow reveal itself once again."

"Stop thinking that way."

"You know I'm right. Brian. Carter. A meteor strike. Who knows?"

It's his turn to chuckle now as he realizes I'm right. "True enough."

I pick at my nail polish as I weigh what to say next. "Yes. But . . ."

"Outside influences shouldn't matter."

"It seems these days everything matters." I sigh.

"Just let us be us, Vee. We'll figure the rest out."

"Easy for you to say."

"It's the truth," he says matter-of-factly.

"How do you know this, though?"

"Because I'm fucking miserable sitting here not knowing when I get to see you next. Because you and I are better when we're together, even if a meteor might strike. Because why would we let us be anything else?"

"A work in progress," I say to cut him off.

"Exactly." His laugh makes me smile. "So do I get to see you again?"

"Yes."

"When?"

I hesitate to answer, even though every part of me is screaming *yes*. What I'm fighting against I'm not quite sure.

My battle against needing someone? My fear that he's bad for me and therefore I don't need him? Or is it my fear that he just might be that fairytale ending that Lucy always watches? The one that's never happily ever after until you turn to the very last page?

Maybe I'm just trying to see what chapter we're on so I know how much more there is to our story until we can turn to that ride-off-into-the-sunset page.

"When?" I finally respond.

"Yes, when?"

"The next few days."

"Should I pick you—"

"I'll come to you." I draw in a shaky breath, suddenly nervous. "Good night, Ryker."

"Good night."

And when I end the call and hold my cell to my chest, the smile on my lips just might reflect a glass half-full.

CHAPTER THIRTY-TWO

Vaughn

"Aren't you a sight for sore eyes." Exhaustion etches the lines of his face, but his expression is one of pure surprise when he sees me standing out front of his office building.

"Truth be told, I was debating whether to come in and see you."

"*Yes.* The answer is *always* yes." He says the words but doesn't make a move toward me.

We stand and stare at each other like two awkward teenagers for a few moments as the world buzzes on around us. People are leaving for a night out after work. Some are rushing home.

But it's just Ryker in his sleek suit, a little rumpled, a lot sexy, and me in my exercise clothes with a bag under my arm that holds my uniform for work.

"You're leaving early today." I take a step closer, knowing he typically leaves the office long after rush hour, and reach out to run a hand down his cheek. "You look exhausted."

When I go to pull my hand away, he reaches out and keeps it where it is with his hand over mine before turning his face toward it and kissing my palm. It's such an unexpected action that it takes me a moment to process his public display of affection.

"It's been a *long* week," he murmurs into my hand before bringing it down to link his fingers with mine.

"Everything okay?"

I can see him mentally run through all the things that have gone wrong for him this week, although he doesn't verbalize anything.

And sadly, by my own fault, I see him differently for the first time. How selfish have I been to always need him and not realize he just might need me too? That he has rough days and difficult clients to deal with? That maybe just as he brings me comfort, I bring him the same?

Why have I been so blind to this? So selfish? Always retreating into myself when trouble strikes instead of turning to him?

He just nods at my question and grants me a shy smile. "Everything is much better now."

My heart swells in my chest, and a tentative, shy smile that matches his spreads on my lips. I haven't seen him since the Brian incident—what felt like weeks ago when it's been only days. Just seeing him does something to me—calms me, in a way that still surprises me.

"Going somewhere?"

"No," he says without hesitation. "You?"

I lift my bag as if he has X-ray vision and can see my uniform in it. "I have to work later."

"Where?"

"The club. Eight to closing."

He nods solemnly, and I'm not sure how to read it as another bout of silence stretches between us.

"Is everything okay?" He asks the same question I did him, his eyes darkening, and it's then I realize he's afraid something has gone on with Lucy. With the Brian situation.

"Nothing I can't handle," I lie, wondering about the odd questions Priscilla asked me when she called today, wanting to leave the outside noise aside for now.

He gives a measured nod. "Did you need something?"

You. Always you.

"No. I was just . . . yes."

"Yes?" he asks, a ghost of a smile on his lips.

"Yes." I look down at our linked fingers and then back up at him. *"You."*

He squeezes my fingers, his smile widening and a swell of emotion flooding into his eyes. He could make a big deal about my admission, but he knows me well enough to understand how hard that was for me to say. What a big step that was for me to make.

How big a step that was for *us*.

"Have dinner with me, then? Not at a restaurant, just at my place. Something simple. Just us so we can talk, sit in silence, whatever it is you want . . . then I'll drive you to work."

I shake my head no. "I'd like that."

His smile widens. "I'm not sure if that's a yes or a no, but I'm taking it."

The ride to his place is silent. Our fingers are tangled together on the seat between us, and other than that sole connection, we don't touch or speak as his driver navigates the short distance to his place. He fires off a text here and there as I stare out the windows and ask myself how we always come back to this.

To him and me trying to reconnect after some kind of chaos rains down on us.

The doorman greets us when we arrive, and the take-out food I didn't even realize Ryker was ordering via text is waiting for us when we reach his front door.

"There's nothing much to eat in my place right now. I've been working a lot of late nights. This was just easier," he explains, almost as if he's nervous as he moves into the kitchen while I shut the door behind us.

I follow him through the unique mixture of modern and old-world style. The glass walls of windows framed by the dark woods and rich colors that make the room still feel cozy. He puts the food on the kitchen counter as he slips out of his jacket and begins to loosen his tie. I step up and for some reason want to do it for him.

Maybe just so I can share this with him—normalcy, something everyday when we always seem to steal bits and pieces on borrowed time that ends up being given back when the time expires.

His hands still as I take over. Slipping the tie off from around his neck. Unbuttoning the first and second buttons on his shirt. Removing the cuff links from his sleeves.

It's only when I finish that I look up and hold his gaze.

"Thank you." My voice is so soft, I almost can't hear my own words.

"For?"

"Not punching him. For always standing up for me. For always trying to protect me."

He nods very subtly, but his eyes fire in surprise at my words. "Mmm?"

"I've been walking on eggshells for so long, Ryker, fearful of every little thing that might hinder me in getting Lucy, that I stopped standing up for myself."

"You can't ever stop standing up for yourself, Vaughn."

I nod, but tears fill my eyes, and he steps into me and pulls me against him. It's the one spot lately where I feel like I can truly relax. Where I can close my eyes and feel like the outside world fades away, just like it did when I saw him today outside his office.

He presses a kiss to the crown of my head and just holds me like that for some time.

"Priscilla finally called me today." It's the first time I've mentioned it, the first moment I've thought to since we had dinner with small talk about our weeks leading the conversation.

"And?"

His phone alerts a text.

"Do you need to get that?" I ask.

"Nope." A run of his hand up and down my arm. "What did she have to say?" There's caution in his voice.

"She said a detective had a very interesting conversation with you."

"That's all she said?"

"Mmm-hmm," I lie.

His chuckle rumbles through his chest into mine from where I'm sitting against him. "*Interesting* is the word she used?"

"I believe so." I look up at him, but he keeps his focus on the city lights beyond. "What made it so *interesting*?"

"Nothing, really." He chuckles again, and the sound tells me there was so much more to the conversation than *nothing, really*. His text alerts again, but he doesn't even look toward the counter where it sits and carries on.

"Ryker?" *What did the detective say? Do you need to get your text? What are we doing here?* All three mix in the sound of his name.

"I toyed with him a bit and then made sure that all of Brian's background was discussed . . . so that it now becomes part of a permanent record child protective services won't be allowed to ignore. Or a judge, for that matter." I can hear the pride in his voice. "Now, I know she had to have said more than that. What else did she say, Vaughn?"

"Nothing, really." I repeat his phrase, silently surprised that he'd think to do any of that, while not wanting to ruin the evening by rehashing the rest of our conversation. How she asked for my version of events between Ryker and Brian. Her questions about how I intend to care for Lucy when I work nights, to which my reply was "The same way parents take care of their kids who work during the day." Then I went on to outline my plans for school once my debt is paid off, which was met with skeptical silence.

"Now that we're both telling each other half truths, I have a real one to tell you."

"Oh?"

"I lied to you."

My body should tense at his confession, my anger should fire, but it doesn't. Instead, I sit right where I am in the crook of his arm—where we're resting against the back of his couch, our feet propped up on a coffee table that I'm sure is way too expensive to have feet on—and just keep my eyes closed.

"About?"

"After Carter went to your house and you begged me not to confront him . . . I did it anyway."

I don't speak, because I know there's more and because I'm not exactly sure how I feel about this. He groans in frustration when his text notification rings out again. I go to stand and get it for him, but he just holds me in place.

"No. Leave it," he says and presses a kiss to my temple. "I started all of this with Carter, and I knew I needed to be the one to end it."

"And?" His heavy sigh answers the question I'm afraid to ask. That despite confronting him, Carter didn't budge on whatever his stance is besides just being a dick.

"I should have told you about it when we talked about him the other night after Belvedere Castle, but I didn't." He shrugs and clears his throat. "I realize if I tell you I did it in your best interests—to try to stop the blackmail threat—that it doesn't matter, because it sounds like a broken record to you. And rightfully so." He laces his fingers with mine. "You're a bigger person than he'll ever be, Vaughn, and it pisses me off to no end. What I did. What he thinks he can do. The fact that he won't even meet somewhere in the middle."

"Thank you for trying," I murmur.

His body jolts. "You're not mad?"

"I should be. I should tell you it's my life and who the hell are you to think you can interfere without my consent. I should be mad at myself for being too blasé when your actions have risked so much for me . . . but I'm so sick of being mad, Ryker. I'm so tired of worrying and wondering and *missing you*."

"Vaughn—"

"You want to be with me even with my flaws and all the crazy outside factors that keep affecting us. You still want to fight for me. You still want to stand up for me. Yes, I should be mad at you, but I'm so tired of being mad that sometimes I just want to *be* with you."

"Just like you don't deserve any of this bullshit going on, I don't deserve you."

"I guess that's why we're works in progress," I murmur, a soft smile on my lips for the first time.

"You know, if I could take all of this away for you, I would."

I nod but don't speak, because I don't want any conditions on our unspoken love. I don't want there to be strings that make me obligated to repay or regret the things he's tried to do for me.

But that's what love is, Vaughn. Protecting what's yours. Loving without fault. Celebrating the flaws. That is love. I can all but hear my mom's voice. It's so crystal clear—*so her*—that my breath catches.

"Thank you."

I love being with you.

I love being just like this with you—relaxed, without expectations, without pretenses.

I love you.

I wait for the panic to come, and it doesn't.

"You owe me a hundred bucks, you know," he murmurs with a laugh, the heat of his breath warming the crown of my head, as his bet on the phone comes full circle.

"I do?"

"Yep. Here we are. Together and perfectly fine. No crazy revealed. No chaos ensued. You bet me a hundred bucks last night that this wasn't possible."

"Then I guess that means we just have to stay in this little bubble surrounding your tower over the city and never leave."

"You might get bored with me."

"I've got some time yet."

I turn and tilt my face up to his. He looks as tired as I feel. His lips meet mine in a tender kiss before I snuggle up against him even closer.

His phone alerts again.

"I think you need to get that. Someone really wants to get ahold of you."

"It's just Leo."

"Who's Leo?"

"My friend I stood up tonight."

"Ryk—"

I try to move to look at him, but he just holds me in place. "Shh. No. I'd rather spend the night with you than him any day of the week."

My struggle subsides as my heart melts. This man of epic screwups, a hard-ass with a soft heart, a knight in training . . . owns my heart. *How did I ever think I could fight this?*

I hold on to him a little tighter. I sink into him a little farther and just relish the moment. The feel of him. The no longer feeling so alone because of him. My flaws that he embraces without question. My chaos he defends without reason. The friends he stands up just so he can spend a few hours with the woman who continually pushes him away.

And when his soft snores fill the room around us, I slide my cell phone off the armrest and do something I have never done in all of my time being employed at Apropos.

I call in sick to work.

Being with him tonight is more important than any paycheck I'll ever receive.

CHAPTER THIRTY-THREE

Vaughn

"See you tonight after work?"

"You're getting greedy with my time, Lockhart." The reprimand is countered by the grin on my lips.

"And the problem with that is what?" His voice rasps over the line and puts my anticipation into high gear like it seems to do every time we talk to each other.

"Goodbye." I end the call as he's still talking and then hit send on my email, confirming with Noah our meeting tonight after I get off work.

My cell rings again, and I laugh when I see Ryker's name on the screen. "What?" I answer with a laugh.

"Hanging up on me is akin to saying no to me."

"It is, is it?"

"Yep. I'm going to hold out on you if you hang—"

I end the call and laugh out loud when it rings back instantly.

"You're relentless, you know that?" I say breathlessly.

"I am. You'd be wise to remember that."

The smile on my face falls at the sound of Carter Preston's voice. I was so lost in our playful banter that I picked up, assuming we were continuing it.

And then I realize why I thought it was Ryker—this is my personal cell phone.

"How'd you get this number?" I demand, glancing at the screen and another new phone number he's calling from.

"A man like me can get a lot of answers to a lot of things with a simple snap of his fingers."

"Then I'll block you."

"No you won't." Arrogance edges his tone and has me gritting my teeth.

"Watch me—"

"I wouldn't do that if I were you. You hang up on me before I end this call and there will be hell to pay." He singsongs out the words like some nursery rhyme. "Umpf." He groans the sound out. "Then again, I sure have imagined what it would be like making you pay."

My finger hovers over the end call button, but a part of me fears the repercussions while the other part hates giving him any kind of upper hand.

"What do you want?"

"That Lucy sure does need you, doesn't she? So many strings I could pull to cause that whole world of yours to come tumbling down."

My hands fist and teeth grind. "What do you want?" I ask again.

"You know what I want." He lowers his voice, and the suggestion woven into every single syllable makes my skin crawl. "How long are you going to make me wait?"

Forever.

"I told you, there is nothing about me that is for sale."

"Everything has a price."

"You're right. Those photos will go for a large sum to the right buyer. How old was the girl sucking your dick? Seventeen? Sixteen?"

"Don't fuck with me, Vaughn."

"No problem there." Sarcasm rings through every part of my tone.

"There's something about women like you that make me so fucking hard. Ripe for the picking and ready to be put perfectly in their place. *Beneath me.*"

"Is there a purpose to this call other than to listen to you want things you'll never get? Because frankly, it's getting old," I say, refusing to let him know he gets to me every time. "I already have the paperwork filled out for a restraining order against you. All I have to do is file it." The lie comes out of nowhere.

He laughs in response. "All I have to do is pick up the phone and your whole word comes apart. I think your fallout is ten times worse."

"Apparently you're used to picking up your phone and making calls," I say, assuming the call log I still can't make heads or tails of shows his calls, even though none of the numbers match up to ones he's dialed me from.

"You've got a mouth on you. I can't wait to put it to good use." Chills blanket my skin at the calm and cool way he makes the state-ment. "I'm back from my trip."

"Good for you. I'm sure your wife is happy to see you."

Another low and unforgiving chuckle rumbles through the line. "Ask your boyfriend about how that's going. I'm sure he'd be happy to fill you in."

"So that's what this is all about? He's representing your wife, so you think you get dibs on me?" I rise from my seat and move through my house, suddenly on edge. This conversation is as unexpected as his comment.

"No. That's not what this is about. This is about how you have things I want."

"So what? I hand them over and we're even? I find it hard to believe you'd let me go at that."

"You'd be correct."

I shake my head and squeeze my eyes shut as I try to make sense of him. "So what are my options?"

"Hand over the pictures. The call log. The ten grand I paid Lola. And one night with you so I can collect my interest."

"You're dreaming."

"That's the American way."

"I can't do the first two. I'm not the one who's holding the items. The ten grand was for services you screwed up. And you can forget about a night with me—"

"*You. You. You.* Did anyone tell you the first line in business is *the customer is always right?*"

"You're no longer my client," I state, trying to keep this away from him talking about me personally.

"He came to me, you know," Carter says, his tone devious, his intent to cause problems more than clear. "You told Ryker not to, and he came at me anyway. It was a pathetic attempt to call me off, when he's the one who gave me the okay in the first place. That alone will make it that much sweeter when I fuck him over."

"I'll be sure to let him know that. We're meeting up for dinner after my interview with the *Washington Post* tomorrow," I bluff.

"And I'll be sure to call Chief Okawa down in Greenwich and tell him I happen to know where Vaughn Dillinger is."

My bluff is immediately forgotten as my heart stumbles in my chest, but only because it stops beating momentarily. *"What?"* That's not what I meant to say, but it comes out anyway. "You fucking—"

"Now you're getting the hang of it. Fucking is indeed on the menu." He laughs. "And I know you think you have shit on me, sweet Vaughn. I know you think you can play this game as deftly as me . . . but you can't. Not a single thing will matter once I make that call."

I don't speak. Can't. My stomach churns, and my heart is lodged so far into my throat that it's all but suffocating me. I hate that my skin becomes coated with sweat at the mere mention of Greenwich.

"What do you want?" I ask for what feels like the millionth time.

"Call whoever you need to call to get my stuff. I'll be requiring an NDA to be signed by the person doing the safekeeping. You'll sign it, too, of course . . . and if you don't, we both know how hard it would be for Lucy to lose who she considers her mother now. Jail is an awfully scary place for a pretty little thing like you."

Go to hell.

"So I turn it over and then what?"

"We'll see what kind of mood I'm in. How long you make me wait."

"What?" He's making no sense. "I'll be giving you what you want."

"Wants change." He laughs. "Oh, I'll reiterate the same thing I said before, but maybe this time you'll actually listen. It's best Ryker knows nothing about this little conversation. He seems to have a hero complex—how cute, trying to save the whore—but if he interferes again, I make the call. No warnings. No questions asked. I'll call Priscilla in that little cubby where she sits in the back corner with her fake plants hanging from the ceiling. I'll let her know where your money to pay down your debt really comes from. And of course, I'll make sure Ryker goes down with you. The little audio recording I have of him doesn't exactly paint him in the best light. Why do you think he's been so obedient? He's just as scared as you are."

Without another word, he ends the call, and I'm left staring at the television. *Splendor in the Grass* is on, but I don't remember a single scene.

And for the first time since the Hamptons, I understand Ryker. Why he did what he did. His need to protect me when someone threatened me. My need to pick up the phone and call Carter back to find out what he has on Ryker so I can try to help fix it owns my thoughts.

My urge to call Ryker and ask him myself.

But Carter's threat was loud and clear, and the stakes are so much higher this time around. His mention of the detective's name. His threat against Ryker. His admission that my handing over my blackmail material might not appease him.

All I can focus on is that I have no way out of this. Who knew coming to Lola's rescue months ago would cause this domino effect in my life?

His threats about Greenwich unnerve me. How he connected me to the Dillinger name. But it's the unknown that worries me even more. It's not like Samantha was exactly forthcoming with me about what happened that last night.

But I remember the snippets from my dream the other night. The bag of jewelry and cash that she said was his payoff. The speckles of blood on her shirt that she later told me was from a nosebleed she'd gotten after he'd slapped her while in a drunken state.

And then I remember the details that have always been there. Stealing away in the dead of night to the Greyhound station and the promise she forced me to make: to never look back at Greenwich or *him*. That if I searched anywhere for him on technology, he'd find us.

Are the Dillingers looking for us now? Did Samantha lie to me? Did she steal the valuables, and the police have been looking for us since that night?

Or is it something more nefarious than that?

A chill chases down my spine, and all the while I know damn well that whatever Samantha did that night, she *had* to. Knowing what I know now, *she had to.*

Is that what Carter Preston is alluding to?

But if that's the case—if we're technically fugitives—then why haven't the authorities found us? It's not like we've been in hiding.

I sigh and just sit in the silence as I try to rationalize my way through each and every scenario.

The tears fall without me ever realizing it. Salt on my lips, wetness on my eyelashes, fear in my heart.

It takes everything I have not to call Ryker. Carter's threat is more real to me now than it has ever been. I pick up the phone and begin to dial him more times than I care to count during the hour I sit numb to everything.

It takes even more to get ready for work, one methodical step at a time.

And even more so, it takes everything I have not to want to pick up and leave without a trace.

But there's Lucy.

And Ryker.

The only two people I have ever loved in my life besides my mom and Samantha.

The only two people I've ever needed and allowed to need me in return.

I can't leave them.

CHAPTER THIRTY-FOUR

Vaughn

I put the finishing touches on my makeup and wig. It's weird to don these clothes, this personality, when it feels like I've become such a different person over the past few months.

Madam Vee feels like a ruse more than ever before. Sure, the money is coming in faster now, but it's like I'm selling my soul for it.

That's not a good place to be.

Add to that Carter tonight. His ultimatums owned my thoughts during my entire shift. Ahmed even noticed something was off, and I let him assume I'd had a tiff with Ryker.

And when I stare in the mirror of the hotel room I rented after work to make my transformation to Vee, I see everything I hope my potential client, Noah, doesn't. Uncertainty instead of resolve. Fear where there should be strength. A lack of identity when I should own the red lipstick and perfectly stylish ensemble, complete with sky-high heels.

My phone alerts a text, and I force myself to ignore it. I can't talk to Ryker right now. I need to get through this appointment—the man I've blown off more times than is professional—and then I can break down.

And then I can be weak.

And then I can ask Ryker what I should do.

"Get it together, Vaughn," I mutter to myself as I check for lipstick on my teeth before lifting my head high and walking from the room.

The lobby bar isn't crowded, but it's New York City at ten o'clock on a Thursday night, so it isn't exactly dead either. I'm not immune to the glances that shift my way, the nudges between men as they debate whether to approach me or not, but I make sure to stare at them with my resting bitch face to let them know I'm nowhere near interested.

A man slides next to me at the bar on my left. A few moments later another on my right. I catch the eye of the man to my right and offer a smile. His hair is reddish brown, his freckles prevalent.

"A gin and tonic, please. Bombay Sapphire," the man to my left says, pulling my attention to the phrase we'd agreed upon over the phone. The one that lets me know he is the man I am supposed to be meeting.

"Noah?" My voice is throaty, my smile warm as I turn to face him. He has dark hair with a subtle wave to it and killer gray eyes highlighted by his light-brown skin tone.

His eyes flicker to the other patrons of the bar, and his fingers fidget on the glass that is pushed in front of him before he finally turns to face me. "Vee?"

"Mmm." I in turn take my own sweep of the bar crowd, looking for anyone who gives me bad vibes, fooling myself into believing that I'd know a cop or a setup if I saw one. "Would you like to head somewhere a little more private to discuss what needs to be discussed?"

He takes a sip of his drink and nods slowly. "Yes, I would." He slides two twenties across the bar to pay our tab without ever asking the total. "There's a sitting area in the lobby, just to the other side of the elevator banks. It's private. We can talk there."

I lick my lips and nod. I'd prefer to stay where we are, but he's explained to me how crowds unnerve him, so I oblige.

We move from our spot at the bar, and Noah places his hand on the inside of my elbow as if we're a couple and he's escorting me on our date. Nothing out of the ordinary. Laughter echoes across the lobby and accompanies the click of my heels on the tiles.

Just as we pass the bank of elevators, I'm more than startled when he tightens his grip on the inside of my arm at the same time as someone takes my other one. It's the freckled man from the bar.

I try to jerk my elbows away as fear and panic and confusion course through me. "What—"

"FBI," Noah says beneath his breath, flashing a gold badge he holds in the palm of his hand. "I suggest you don't fight us." I stiffen my arms as my mind tries to catch up with how this is happening. With how I've let this happen.

"This is a mistake—"

"All we want to do is talk," the freckled one says as they both steer me toward the elevators.

They push the button to summon the elevator. One of them nods at a couple who glance our way. Another pulls out his phone as if he's reading messages.

But me? I stand between them with my pulse pounding so loudly in my ears that I don't think I could hear a thing if they said it. My legs feel like they are going to give out—my knees act as if I have no tendons holding the joints together.

My chest hurts in the elevator. My hands tremble. My breath is shallow and doesn't draw in enough oxygen to give my body what it needs. My head swims to the point I feel like I'm going to faint.

"Steady there, Vaughn," Noah murmurs as we exit the car, and the sound of my name on his lips—the fact that he knows who I really am—makes my breath catch. "Here we are."

Within seconds, Noah and Freckles have me in a hotel room much like the one I rented for myself to get ready in. "Would you like something to drink?" Freckles asks as he motions for me to take a seat on the couch.

"No. I'll stand," I murmur, my feet needing to move.

"I suggest you sit," Noah says as he takes a seat in the chair across from where I slowly sink down. In fact, there are two chairs—one for each of them—set up opposite the couch.

They had this all planned out.

Something about that has tears springing to my eyes, and I fight them back. "What's going on?" I ask, knowing that I can't play innocent when Noah's been to the client access portal on my website, but I try anyway.

"I'm Special Agent Noah Barnes, and this is Special Agent Abel Grossman," Noah says as Abel tips his head in acknowledgment, "and you're in some serious trouble."

"But you said you were a referral. You said—"

"I lied." There isn't an ounce of remorse in his tone.

The tears I fought well up and spill over now. But as soon as the first two fall, I shove them away and straighten my shoulders. "I'd like to call my lawyer, please."

"It's probably best if we don't involve anyone else yet," Abel says as he moves about the room.

"I don't care—I want my lawyer," I assert.

Noah chuckles as I feel a rivulet of sweat streak down the line of my spine. "Solicitation, moving money offshore—"

"I don't have the slightest clue how to move money offshore!" I all but shout.

"You seem to be getting your money from somewhere, then, because we know Apropos doesn't pay you enough to make the big payments you're making against your debts."

"I don't have—I'm not—"

He whistles a long, low note. "Those all hold pretty tough penalties."

"Jail time," Abel interjects. "Lots of jail time. In fact, Lucy wouldn't even get to see you anymore. Time would pass, and her memory of you would fade, and eventually she'd think of you like her mother—a ghost she can't quite remember but can't quite forget either."

The claws of panic close around my throat as my synapses fire again at the mention of Lucy. At the fact that they know enough about me they can even say her name.

I struggle to breathe. To not throw up. And then I realize they want something from me. What? I have no idea, but this is too coordinated, and they were too patient when I canceled time and again on Noah, for this to be an ordinary bust.

"Wicked Ways only sells time, companionship," I say, repeating my company line. "Anything that happens after the money is exchanged isn't—"

"Save me from your bullshit lines," Abel says and laughs. "Ain't no one got time for your lies."

"I want my lawy—"

"Who's your lawyer?" Noah asks.

"Ryker Lockhart," I say as calmly as possible.

Abel's laugh rings out and startles me. "Not a chance in hell."

"What do you mean?" *What's wrong with Ryker?* "I want my lawyer."

"Not one who has ties to this case you don't," he says.

I stare at him, eyes narrowed, pulse pounding. "What do you mean, ties to the case?"

Abel looks at Noah and says, "To think we could tie this up with a pretty little bow all at one time." Noah laughs.

"What does this have to do with Ryker?" I ask again, every one of my senses in overdrive.

"We'll get to that," Noah says, and the sound of his Sprite can cracking open as he lifts the tab fills the room. He takes a sip and then sets it down before squaring up his papers on the table. When his theatrics are done, he leans back and stares at me much the same way Abel is.

"What do you want?" My voice is barely a whisper as chills blanket my skin, fear of what their answer is going to be the realest thing I've ever faced.

"See, Abel? I told you she was intelligent. She'd figure out she can help herself while helping us," good-cop Noah says as he smiles over to bad-cop Abel.

"We'll see just how much she wants to help before I make a decision on that," he replies and leans against the wall, folding his arms over his chest.

"So is it Lucy that matters the most here?"

I shake my head. "I don't understand—"

"Well, when we called good ol' Priscilla to report a hotbed of activity at your house, you jumped right into action."

"That was you?" I say the words as if I have a hard time believing them, and yet I'm here, right? That's hard enough for me to believe too. "You were watching me?"

"FBI." Abel holds up his badge. "We watch everything."

"I don't—"

"You see, Vaughn, we were rather impressed with you and your ability to hold things close to the vest."

"Excuse me?" I ask as confusion ratchets to an all-time high.

"Lucy is one thing. You sprang into immediate action. But then there's Carter. He isn't exactly the subtlest of men, is he?" Noah asks.

"I'm not following."

"All it would take is one anonymous call to highlight those pictures you have of *your friend* there."

"Carter Preston is *not* my friend," I assert.

"Oh, we more than know that." Abel's smile is tight and knowing and makes all the blood drain from my face, the other part of his statement hitting my ears and registering.

"You've been listening to my phone calls?" I ask, each word louder than the last.

"It's easy to get a warrant for things like a wiretap when you have a madam catering to a dirty senator," Abel says, his stare unwavering, his smile chilling. "You can imagine the leads we can chase there. Each one of your clients getting calls by the feds, one by one, until your reputation is ruined . . ."

The panic humming through my veins jumps to new heights as I think of all the phone calls I've made. To my clients. To Archer. To Ryker. The ones I've received from Carter, like tonight's, for instance.

The mention of Greenwich.

"Wait—"

"*Yes*"—Noah smiles—"all of them."

I press my fingers to my eyes for a moment as I try to gather myself and think five steps ahead to know where this is going. To figure out what they want. To . . . fuck if I know.

"Is this about the underage girls, then? I have no problem giving you the pictures so you can pursue that avenue and charge him." My words come out in a rush, my desperation to find an out in this situation all-consuming. Then it dawns on me. "You knew about the pictures, about the underage girls, and you did nothing? Isn't your job to protect and serve?"

"Our endgame is much bigger," Abel states without any emotion, and I hate him on the spot.

"You let young women be manipulated by him and—"

"Yes." No apology. No anything. "Much the same way we knew about your operation and did nothing about it."

I open my mouth to say something—anything—and then shut it without speaking a word.

"The senator," Noah continues. "Why didn't you release the photos when he was obviously threatening you?"

"You've seen how these stories end, right? The senator has a few months where he hides his head from the world, and then all is forgotten. But the woman? She's ruined. Her name a joke. Her life in shambles. Her reputation the constant butt of jokes."

"So you have blackmail information, but you refuse to use it?" Noah asks with an astounded shake of his head.

"I have it on all of my clients, but it has to be played very carefully or else it can backfire. The threat of it is typically enough to keep my clients in line."

"But Carter isn't your typical client? Is that your reasoning? Why you didn't do anything more than just threaten?"

"Because I'm scared of him." My voice wavers, and I don't think I realized until now just how fearful I am of Carter and what he could do to my life.

"Understood," Noah says. "Can I speak with you a moment in the other room?" he asks Abel.

"One moment," Abel says to me with a smile. "No phone calls or texts, please. We'd know."

I can hear the low murmur of their voices as they step into the other room, door open. Their discussion is heated for a moment while my head spins and my ears strain to try to catch what's going on.

And then it hits me. Maybe it's because I don't have the two of them staring at me. Maybe it's because I have a chance to breathe. Regardless, the gravity of everything about this situation blindsides me.

Oh my God.

This is really happening.

The FBI.

All of it.

And just as I sink into the reality of all this, the two men walk back into the room, Noah scratching his head, Abel resuming his bodyguard stance against the wall.

"Change of plans," Noah says.

"There were plans?" I ask, and Abel nods. "Care to expand?" I laugh nervously as they both fix their unrelenting stares on me.

"We planned on waiting until he made his move on you . . . then we'd make ours on him. We'd push and pressure and use you as leverage," Noah explains.

"But I don't understand. It would be simple solicitation. Sleeping with underage girls is a way stronger case."

"Yeah, but if we add aggravated assault—"

"You already have that in my proof. The pictures of him and a minor," I interject, and Abel clenches his jaw in reaction.

"Do you care to let us run this discussion, Ms. Sanders, or should we just press those charges now?"

I stare at Abel and his threat and dutifully fold my hands in my lap to hide their trembling. "Sorry, but I'm not following what . . . oh." It's all I can say as my thoughts fall in line. "You were going to *use me*. You were going to wait for him to hurt me and then swoop in and use that against him as leverage for whatever it is you want from him." I blink as I try to comprehend that they would really do that.

They don't waver in the least at my accusations. Instead, Noah takes a sip of his Sprite, his eyes on mine.

"You've told the senator you have something else on him, and yet you've never quite elaborated what it is." Abel lifts his eyebrows, neither confirming nor denying my accusation, and that in itself sends chills down my spine.

"Wait a minute. After you got what you wanted from Carter, what was going to happen to me?" My voice is barely a whisper.

"You were collateral damage," Abel says, eyes boring into mine as he lifts his eyebrows. "We were using you, and if the Southern District of New York wanted to press charges against a madam who became known in the midst of our process or from the fallout"—he shrugs—"then so be it."

My ears ring. Collateral damage? Press charges?

Am I going to lose everything I've worked for? Everything I took all these risks for? The irony isn't lost on me—that I started Wicked Ways as a means to save Lucy, and it just might be the reason I lose her.

The panic attack hits me full on without holding any punches. Assuming it is one thing. Living with the hint of its fear for so long has almost dulled the thought, made it blend into the background, but now—now that I'm sitting here with two federal agents, now that I've heard the actual words spoken out loud from an FBI agent—this is a whole dose of reality I can't fathom.

Noah is up in an instant, his hand on my shoulder as he urges me to breathe slowly. As he tells me to calm down while I want to scream at him that there's no way I can be calm.

Abel pushes a bottle of water across the coffee table, and Noah picks it up and hands it to me.

A few minutes pass before I feel like I can continue.

"You good?" Noah asks, and I do the only thing I can. I nod.

"As I asked before, what else do you have on the senator?"

I force myself to keep my voice steady in the two seconds I have to respond to his question before he knows I'm lying. "Nothing."

"Nothing?"

"I was bluffing him," I reassert, and for some reason I stand my ground, uncertain why it is I feel the need to keep the call log I have a secret, but in that split second, I do. The only time I mentioned it as a log to Carter was when we were face-to-face in my driveway, not on my phone, so they couldn't have heard what was going on. "He didn't seem fazed by the photos, so I needed something else to hold over his head since the damage he could inflict on me was much greater."

They both eye me, and I lift my eyebrows and stare back so they buy my lie.

You are lying to the FBI, Vaughn. You have something more on him. Are you out of your goddamn mind?

"Like ruin your life."

My eyes snap over to Abel, his threat more than loud and clear.

"So if I was bait in a plan that you're no longer going to implement . . . why am I here, then?"

Abel grins, but there is zero humor in it. "Plan B."

"Plan B? What's plan B?" I ask.

"Instead of waiting for him to come to you . . . we're going to push the envelope, and you're going to tell him you're ready to sleep with him."

I measure my reaction, but I'm more than certain they can see the disgust and rejection in my expression.

"And then what? There's no way in hell I'm sleeping with him, let alone allowing him to touch me." I push up out of my seat and start to move about the room. This is all way too real, way too raw, and I know that I'm in a shitload of trouble. "I'm not a prostitute."

Abel lifts a single eyebrow, and I glare at him.

"No one is asking you to sleep with him," Noah says.

"Just make sure you get what we need before that part of the program arrives."

I whip my head over to Abel at his comment, and right now I hate him with every part of my being.

"What exactly is it that you want from him? Don't you think that would be pertinent for me to know?" Tears of frustration well, and again Abel points for me to sit down. I hate that I have to obey, but I do.

"The senator is selling votes."

And with those five words, I know that I won't be able to walk away from this hotel suite unscathed. I know what they are looking into. I know who they are looking at. It's not like they are going to dust their hands of me.

I take a deep breath. "Selling votes? Isn't that normal in Washington?" I ask naively. "Lobbyists gift things to senators to persuade their votes?"

"This makes it so much easier that you're educated on the topic," Noah says and leans back in his chair. "But this goes a little bit further than that."

"As in?" I push.

The two of them look at each other as if they are in silent agreement to proceed, and then Abel answers. "There was a large vote a few months back on a bill that dealt with stem cell treatment. It was expected to pass. A yes would push the bill through and allow the research and development of a certain technology by a company called Tecolote R&D."

I'm more than aware that both men are watching my every reaction to see if there is any flicker of recognition on my part—there is none.

"And not passing the bill would tank the company, I presume? The stocks that were suddenly soaring would plummet? I feel like I've heard this story before," I say sarcastically, wanting them to know I may run an escort service, but I'm far from ignorant of current events. "So what happened? Did the bill not pass? Did someone know this ahead of time and sell their shares on insider information and save themselves from losing their asses?" I look back and forth between the two of them. "Is that what this is all about? Did Carter participate in insider trading?"

"Told you she was smart," Noah says to Abel, almost as if they have a bet going, before turning back to me. "We looked at that because it would fit the bill, but no, there was no insider trading."

"Then what?" I ask in exasperation.

"The bill's approval hinged on one vote."

"Let me guess—Carter's?"

"Yes," Abel says. "And surprisingly, his yes became a no because he suddenly found his pro-life, stem-cells-are-humans belief when his entire political career he's voted a different way."

"I'm not following," I state as my mind swims.

"We believe that Carter was paid the sum of two million dollars from a rival of Tecolote's to tank the bill," Noah says, connecting all the dots for me.

"Who is their rival?" I ask.

"Alpha Pharmaceuticals." Again, both men study me for any kind of reaction, but I have none.

"But why would this Alpha company do that?"

"Because a bill and grant given to Tecolote would put Alpha out of business when they've created a new way to manipulate stem cells. Alpha had one more month until their trials were complete, and then they could push their own bill through Congress. They've spent a ton of money on this, and if Tecolote's bill passed, it would all be thrown to waste."

"But two million dollars is a ton of money," I say.

"It's a drop in the bucket in DC. Besides, two mil is pocket change to a company that stands to gain hundreds of millions."

I stare at my water bottle, at the condensation ring forming on the table around its base, and try to process everything and understand it fully.

"So Carter took a bribe. Isn't that enough to pull him in for questioning?"

"If only it were that easy," Noah says. "We can't originate where the money came from in Carter's account, just that it showed up there a week before the vote. And then it left his account a few days after that."

"Can't you just ask him where it came from?" I ask.

"No. That's not how this works. We don't exactly have probable cause to be rooting through his bank accounts."

"Then how do you know he did it?"

"Because another vote was bought that we caught. Small-time stuff. The senator wasn't as crafty with their paper and wire trails on that one," Noah explains.

"Can't you get him on that incident?" I ask.

"Sure, but we'd rather get him on this one," Noah says.

I draw in a deep breath and try to digest all I've heard. "Okay . . . so you think he took a bribe to throw a vote. You can't pin it on him. I get all of that, but what does it have to do with me?"

"Everything." Abel grins. "You couldn't have played into our hands any better than you did to Carter. That bluff of yours is more than brilliant for what we have in mind."

"You're going to tell him you'll give him everything he asked for during your conversation tonight. The pictures. The signed NDA. The ten-thousand-dollar refund. You'll explain that you've seen the error of your ways and know the only fair way to settle this is to just get it over with," Noah says. "Then when you meet with him, you're going to let him know about your second piece of nonexistent blackmail. You're going to question him on it. Push his buttons. And get him to tell the truth."

I laugh out loud—part nerves, part incredulity. "You actually think he's going to confess that he took a bribe? To me, of all people?"

"Yes." Abel smiles.

"But—"

"There's something about the way he is when he's with you."

"When he's *with* me?" I ask, my skin crawling at the thought of them watching from afar somewhere. How they could see us interact but not hear a word. How they might assume what they want through the silence.

For some reason, that seems like more of an invasion of privacy than the phone tap.

"Your driveway. How he watched you in the lobby of the Four Seasons when you met with one of your girls the other night. How he—"

"No more!" I hold my hand up to stop him, because his words just sucked all the oxygen out of the room for me. I struggle to breathe as I think of them surveilling him. Me. Us.

As I think of Carter watching me when I didn't know it.

What other places has he sat and spied on me from afar?

"Did you think we pulled you in here on phone calls alone?" Abel asks with condescension in his tone.

I meet his eyes and pull myself together as best I can while my thoughts swirl and my world spins counterclockwise. I glare at Abel and his arrogance and then look back at Noah with a lift of my eyebrows, silently asking him to continue since I can't seem to find my voice.

"When Carter interacts with you, it's almost as if he has to one-up you. Always prove he's better and in control, and what better way for him to show he's smart and conniving than to brag about it."

"That's a stretch, Noah."

"Well, you better get flexible," Abel says and leans forward, "or we'll proceed with processing you down at the station."

Asshole.

"So I do this, I get him to admit to it, and then what? What happens to me? Am I just collateral damage again? You use me and then throw me to the wolves?"

"It's not like that," Noah soothes.

"It's exactly like that." I throw my hands out and stand to pace the room again. "I'm your bait and then your chum to feed to the press when they need something to sink their shark teeth into."

"It's not like you have a choice in the matter," Abel says, and I swear he takes pleasure in rubbing my nose in it.

I close my eyes and hate that one tear escapes. That I give them a show of weakness. That I have my hands cuffed in a way I never expected.

"Look, Vaughn, all we need is proof," Noah says after shooting his partner a look. "We have nothing to tie Carter to Alpha Pharmaceuticals. No phone calls. No emails. No anything."

"Except for his sudden change of heart in the vote and a mysterious two million dollars in his account," I say.

"Exactly."

"And the check for two million that he wrote out," Abel says.

"What?" I ask, at the same time realizing that he'd originally said the cash moved in and out of Carter's account. I just assumed it went into another one of his accounts. "Who'd he write the check to? Is it someone who helped him throw the vote?"

"You tell us." I meet Abel's stare when he speaks, sarcasm dripping from his tone.

"There is one connection between the head of Alpha Pharm and Carter Preston," Noah says.

"Who?"

The look they exchange has hairs standing up on the back of my neck.

"Ryker Lockhart."

I can't hide my reaction this time as I sputter in response. "What?" I all but laugh in disbelief.

"A two-million-dollar check was written to one Ryker Lockhart a day before the vote was defeated," Abel says.

I study him, I hear what he's saying, but I don't believe it. "You're saying you think Ryker was a part of this? That's comical."

"Ah, she's blinded by love. How cute." Able nudges Noah.

"Ryker hates Carter Preston." I spit the words out, but I hate that doubts seep and creep into my mind. The you-owe-me's of the pool house conversation rule my mind.

"Can't hate him too much if he's paying him that kind of cash," Abel says, hitting his stride, his disgust so palpable the room is weighed down with it.

"I'm serious. I know him. It—it was a retainer. Has to be," I say, each word escalating in pitch. "Ryker is representing Carter's wife. She's filing for divorce. That has to be where the check came—"

"A two-million-dollar retainer? A woman who hires a lawyer but never actually files papers? Paid to a man who represented the CEO of Alpha Pharm during his own divorce, no less? Sounds like the Prestons have Ryker sitting on the money for a bit before taking it back . . . less some fake billable hours that Ryker charges them, of course. I mean, he deserves a fee, after all, since he is taking on some of the risk and all but cleaning, laundering—whatever you want to call it—their money until any heat they feel subsides."

"He's rich. He doesn't need to risk something like this for money," I say, trying to explain it to myself more than anyone.

"*Powerful men like to play God.* They get drunk off the feeling of it. You know that more than anyone, Vaughn."

I'm numb. My mind is a mess, my heart even more so.

"Yes, Vaughn, you just might have been used here. Two men who like to play games. Two men who pretend to be at odds to make sure they are not connected in any way possible. Two men—"

"You're lying." I grit the words out as the fear he's right when I know he's not takes root. "That's not the man Ryker is."

"No, you're right. It's not. He just offers his girlfriend up for no reason other than to pay back a debt."

"I've heard enough." I rip my purse off the counter when I don't even remember setting it down.

Abel's laugh rings out the loudest. "Like we care. Remember, *Vee,* we have all of your phone calls. We have everything on you. *Everything.*"

My body vibrates with fury and shame and embarrassment like I've never felt before. I fight back the sobs from manifesting, but my shoulders heave like I'm already crying.

I jump when Noah's arm rests on my shoulders, and as much as I should buck it off me, I need to know what it is he wants to say.

"We know this is a lot to take in . . . but like we said, we wouldn't have picked you if we didn't trust that you could pull this off."

Lies. All fucking lies, I want to scream at him. *You're blackmailing me.*

All the while tearing my world apart.

I don't trust myself to speak, so I nod.

"You do this, we don't prosecute you. Simple as that," Noah explains.

"And if I don't?" I fear to ask.

"Let's just say this would make a great episode for *Law and Order*, ripped straight from the headlines," Abel jokes.

"We'll be in touch in the next few days," Noah says with a glare directed at his partner. "We'll get everything set up, and—"

"And we suggest you don't speak a word of this to anyone. *And I mean anyone.* Or the problems you're facing right now will be minor in comparison," Abel says, unable to resist one last threat. "We've put a lot of man hours into this investigation, and if you tell anyone and screw it up, it won't be just the two of us you're screwing over—"

"But the whole bureau as well," Noah finishes for him.

I nod again, the tears burning.

"We know where to reach you," Abel says. "You're free to go . . . for now."

And with that, I walk out the door and leave the life-altering change that room and those men just caused for me.

The elevator ride down feels like it lasts hours.

The walk through the lobby feels like it's miles.

But I put one foot in front of the other, never more sure of two things. First, I'm sick of men feeling like they have power over me and asserting it. My uncle James, my brother-in-law Brian, Carter Preston, Ryker in the beginning . . . and now the FBI.

Second, this is my worst nightmare all wrapped up into one ball of barbed wire. No matter what I say or do, I'm bound to be cut and injured.

Nothing is safe right now.

Least of all me.

CHAPTER THIRTY-FIVE

Vaughn

I wander the streets of New York.

My wig still on. My heels still high. My outfit still impeccable. But everything about me an absolute disaster.

Time passes in corners turned, in blocks counted, in neighborhoods walked through.

At some point I hear my phone ringing.

I don't know how many times Ryker calls before I answer it, more than aware that my every word is being listened to. My every verb scrutinized. My every noun analyzed.

"Hey." *Fake it till you make it.*

"Vaughn? Is everything okay?" Concern edges Ryker's voice, and I shove away the hot tears the sound causes with the back of my hand.

"Fine. Yes. I'm fine." I take a left on the corner of Eldridge and Grand. Another walk to nowhere.

His silence causes me to stop. "You're walking."

"No," I lie. "I'm out front. I had to get something out of the mailbox."

"You didn't call me."

"For what?" I'm having a hard time focusing on anything, let alone Ryker. Everything hurts—my head, my heart, my body—exhaustion and fear taking their toll.

"You were going to come over after work. I was going to send a car. We'd have a late dinner. Vaughn?"

"Yes. Sorry. I'm—uh, I'm just not feeling well. The new client bought oysters. I think I ate a bad one."

"I'll come over."

"No." I say it more forcefully than I should. "My head's fuzzy, and my stomach is upset, and I just want to lie on the bathroom floor and sleep."

"Vaughn, let me take care of you."

"No. I don't want you—I don't want to get you sick," I correct myself.

"You said it was an oyster. If it's food poisoning, I won't get sick."

"It could be the stomach flu too. It's going around the staff at the club."

"Vaughn." My name says he doesn't believe a word I'm saying.

"I have to go. I'm going to throw up," I lie and end the call.

And then I stand with my back against some building, my face lifted up to the moonless night, with tears coursing down my cheeks.

"I'm sorry," I whisper into the night.

But I'm not sure what exactly for or who the apology is meant for.

Lucy.

Samantha.

Ryker.

Me.

CHAPTER THIRTY-SIX

Ryker

"That's the best butterfly of all butterflies I've ever seen drawn before," I say about the asymmetrical multicolored butterfly on the construction paper in front of me.

"Auntie likes when I draw pictures of myself," Lucy says, her smile wide, her eyes so alive and full of life. "She says I capture my spirit, whatever that means." She rolls her eyes and then bats her lashes as well as any teenage girl can.

"It means when you look at the photo, it makes you feel just as good as being with you and hearing your laugh does."

"So pretty good then, right?" She fills in some more purple on the wings. "That's who I am, Lucy-Loo, the feel-good girl."

I throw back my head and laugh and draw the looks of others in the art room of the facility. With a smile their way, I study my surroundings. Light-blue walls are coated in layers of art—some scribbles, others exceptional—with the large windows letting light into the room. If you look closer, you can see the wear and tear—scuffed baseboards, cracked chairs, uneven tables—but the staff's smiles are all bright and their voices cheerful.

Still . . . this is no place for any of these kids.

My chest constricts at the thought. My home wasn't one full of cuddles and kisses—unless we're talking about my nanny—but this isn't a home. This is a facility where people are paid to take care of and love children.

"Mr. Ryker?"

"Hmm?" I turn my attention back to the reason I'm here. Bright-blue eyes, a crooked princess crown, and a barely there temporary tattoo on the inside of her wrist from our royal festival over two weeks ago.

"Why do you look so sad all of a sudden?"

My smile is instantaneous. "No reason," I lie.

"You can't fool me." She reaches out and pats my hand, so very wise beyond her years. "I get sad sometimes too."

"You do?"

"Mmm-hmm." She sniffs, and it breaks my heart. "When I miss my mommy. When I miss my auntie. When I want to sleep in the princess bed and wake up to chocolate chip pancakes that Auntie Vee makes. When I can't watch one of my movies because it's lights-out time." She twists her mouth to combat the quivering of her bottom lip.

"What about your dad? Do you miss your dad?" I can't help myself from asking something I have no business knowing.

She shrugs and averts her eyes. "Sometimes."

"What's wrong?"

"There's always lots of people in his house. Lots of loud music and noise and them acting like I do when I have way too much sugar and Auntie has to tell me no more. It hurts my eyes and ears so much that sometimes I just put a pillow over my head and sit in the bedroom with the door shut."

Jesus Christ. And the system can't see this? A goddamn drug den is no place to raise a little girl. Not Lucy. Not anyone.

I grit my teeth and force my voice to remain calm and even despite the anger that roils around inside me. "I think that's a good plan. To stay in your room. Maybe even draw more pictures. Adults who have too much sugar are not a good thing."

"Mmm." She adds antennae on her butterfly, and I draw a yellow sun in the corner. "What do you do when you're sad, Mr. Ryker?"

"Me?" I set the yellow crayon down and pick up an orange one to add rays to the sun. "Sometimes I go for a run or I work longer."

"You don't see Auntie Vee? She always makes me feel better when I'm sad."

"She does, does she?" I ask to avoid answering the question, because right now she's part of the reason I'm sad.

She canceled last night without warning.

She isn't answering her phone at all.

I thought we'd turned a corner when she admitted she needed me . . . now I'm not so sure.

Hell, she isn't even answering her door today, for that matter. At least she croaked out that she was sick as a dog from behind it or else I would have been breaking down the damn thing to make sure she was all right.

"Yes. She always makes me feel better. You should try it. All you have to do is tell her you're sad."

"Thank you." For some reason I have a hard time getting those two words out. Emotion I don't want to acknowledge clogs my throat.

"Either that or I can let you borrow my special necklace. Sometimes when I rub it, it makes me feel better."

"Your special necklace? Does it have magical powers?" I ask, full well knowing I had planned on asking her about it.

"Just love." She shrugs, her smile widening as she pulls a chain out from under the neck of her T-shirt. It's the key she wears—a simple silver beaded chain with a tarnished key hanging from it. She surprises me when she takes it off over her head and holds it out to me.

"That's beautiful. I can see the love on it." I smile, expecting her to put it back on, but she just pushes it toward me.

"You take it."

"Me?" I startle out a laugh. "I can't take that."

"You can borrow it. When you're not sad anymore, then you can give it back to me."

I can't explain the burning in my eyes caused by the sweet gesture of this incredible little girl.

"I can borrow it?" I ask. "You sure?"

She eyes me briefly. "If you're a friend of Auntie Vee's, then I know you'll take care of it and won't lose it."

"I won't lose it." I rub the key between my finger and thumb before looking back up to meet her gaze. "You're sure?"

"I'm sure." She adds eyelashes to the butterfly's eyelids and then sits back with a smile. "It's all done now. What do you think?"

I take a few moments to study it. "It's perfect."

She angles her head to the side. "Yeah. I think so too."

"Should we hang it on the wall and then go have our picnic?"

"Picnic?" Her body begins to vibrate in excitement. "You're taking me on a picnic?" Tears well in her eyes, and I can't put words to what the sight of them does to me.

"Technically, we have to do it on the grounds here because I don't have permission to take you off-site, but I saw a super cool spot in the shade under a tree."

"By the fairy garden? That's the best place ever." She's already standing, already tugging on my arm in that direction.

"We have to hang your picture first."

"No, I want you to keep it."

"Oh. Okay. Sure."

She tugs on my arm again. "This will be my first date, you know," she states matter-of-factly as we head toward where the counselors let me stash the lunch I'd thought to bring.

"Friend date," I correct.

"Yes. Sure. Friend date. Now you need to go and pick me some flowers. That's what all the princes do these days."

It's hard to leave when my time is up and Lucy's daily classes resume. My fingers worry over the key I have in my pocket as I head to my car.

The necklace. Is that why I came here today? Simply to get a closer look at it for my own purposes? Or was it because I wanted to see Lucy and in turn remind myself why Vaughn is fighting so damn hard?

As if I needed a reminder.

Maybe it was because she blew me off again today, and deep down, the man who never cares or panics when it comes to women kind of is.

She's pulling away from me bit by bit.

I try to shake the thought from my mind but can't. Scenes from my childhood replay in my head—the parts where my mom gets what she wants from a man and then ultimately decides she's done with him.

The underlying reason I have always represented men before—because they don't stand a goddamn chance once a woman turns cold or bored.

But relationships can work, can't they? I thought that was what Vaughn had shown me. I thought that was what I was starting to believe. That if you fight hard enough, listen silently, and put in the effort, they could work.

Then why is Vaughn going radio silent all of a sudden?

Is she tired of me already? Has she played her side of the game—made me chase after her, fight for her, reeled me in, and now that she's accomplished it, she's done with me?

Is that what this is?

The thought eats at my mind. I can't shake it. I should know better when I call Bella and have her cancel my afternoon meetings.

But I don't acknowledge it until I pull into Vaughn's driveway for the second time in one day.

My knock sounds heavy, but so is my goddamn heart. I'm almost desperate to prove to myself that she still cares. That this isn't over.

It can't be.

"Vaughn. It's me."

Silence.

Pound. Pound. Pound.

"Open up. Please. I'm worried about you."

The thoughts that have been swirling around in my head spin out of control with a clarity that was previously clouded by my insecurities. She canceled with me after meeting a potential client. She won't show me her face today.

Did her new client rough her up? Did he hurt her?

Pound. Pound. Pound.

"C'mon, Vaughn. Just show me you're okay."

Carter Preston. He's back in town. That fucker better not have touched her.

Pound. Pound. Pound.

"I'm not going away until I get to see you."

For some reason, I know she's on the other side of the door.

I lower my voice and force myself to be calm. "I just want to know that you're okay. I'll leave once I do." I rest my forehead against the door. "You can't want people to care about you, then expect them to turn it off when it suits you."

"I'm fine." Her voice sounds anything but fine. My pulse leaps at the sound of it.

"Let me see you, please?" My hand fists on the door. "I'm having all these visions in my head that your client beat you up or worse, and it's driving me crazy. I can't get them out of my mind until I see you."

"It's okay. I'm fine."

"Please."

I hear the deadbolt click, and I step back. Vaughn's standing there, eyes puffy, hair a mess—the worst I've ever seen her but so goddamn beautiful compared to the horrid images in my mind of her bruised and battered.

"Baby, what's wrong?" My hands are framing her face immediately, because there's *sick* and then there's *swollen from crying*.

And she's swollen from crying.

"I'm fine. I thought it was food poisoning, but it's an allergic reaction. I think. My eyes keep watering and swelling and—"

"Shh. Shh. Shh." I pull her against me and almost sag with relief when she not only lets me but slides her arms around me and clings tightly. This—her in my arms—is a million times better than listening to her lie to me or letting my imagination about her being bored with me take hold.

Because something is wrong.

Majorly wrong.

But there's nothing I can do to get it out of her, and holding her like this—her letting me pull her against me—if this is all I can get, then I'll take it. Anything she needs right now is hers.

Her body shudders as she cries. I can feel the heat of her tears against my chest. The desperation in the grasp of her hands. The defeat in the sag of her posture.

"What's wrong?" I murmur against the crown of her head, the subtle scent of her shampoo filling my nose.

She just shakes her head and hiccups another sob. My hand smooths down the back of her hair, and the other pulls her against me, the only way I know how to comfort the unknown.

"Vaughn?"

She doesn't respond.

"I don't know what's wrong, baby, but we'll get through it. You're not alone anymore. You've got me."

She nods for the first time.

I don't know how long we stand there on her porch with my arms wrapped around her and her face buried in the underside of my neck, but eventually she steps back. Those aqua eyes of hers are red rimmed and filled with so much confusion, and I hate that there's not a single goddamn thing I can do to help her since she won't tell me what's wrong.

"I'm here, Vaughn. Use me if you need to. Let me help you."

She just shakes her head as if she doesn't trust herself to speak.

"Please."

This time she nods and whispers, "Thank you."

The door clicks shut, and the deadbolt turns in, all without my ever having stepped foot inside her house.

I don't know how long I stand there and stare at her door, but I do.

My need to fix and know and take care of her is stronger than my will to leave her to suffer silently through whatever it is that's troubling her.

Losing Lucy. Something with Brian. Fucking Carter Preston. An issue at Apropos or with Wicked Ways. Maybe all the talk about her uncle has thrown her for a loop.

I wish I knew the answer.

Fuck, how I wish I knew.

CHAPTER THIRTY-SEVEN

Vaughn

I know Ryker doesn't leave for a long time. He stands at the door and then sits in his car in the driveway for even longer.

That in itself tests every ounce of strength I have not to fling the door back open and tell him everything.

But I can't.

I can be weak with Ryker. I can let down my guard. I can be the woman no one else gets to see because he makes me feel secure enough when we're together.

And how he just reacted? Coming here because he was worried and then silent when he knew something was wrong. Comforting when I'm more than certain he wanted to shake answers out of me. It was everything I needed him to be and then some.

There's no way Ryker is a part of this payoff with Carter.

No damn way.

A man capable of being that devious wouldn't have come to my door twice in one day to make sure I'm okay simply because I said I wasn't feeling well. A man that full of deceit would be glad I was out of the way so he could carry on scheming and fucking me over.

I've spent my whole life being screwed over by men or watching those I love be screwed over. I've spent so much time forcing myself to go at it alone because I thought I was better off for it.

And now, just as I've finally found a man I love and trust—because we've worked through our issues, regardless of how unconventional those issues may be—I'm left with the rest of my life beginning to fall down around me. I have Carter after me. I have the FBI threatening me and telling me Ryker isn't trustworthy. I have Brian telling lies to try to extort money.

At some point, I have to shut the white noise out. I have to trust my own instincts. I have to allow myself to rely on others. I have to believe in myself and have conviction in my own opinions.

I have to realize that no matter how damn hard the fight might be—how much it might scare me—it's time to fight it with both fists and everything I've got.

If I don't, I just might lose everything, and that's not an option.

Leaning my head back, I close my eyes and see the concerned look in Ryker's eyes before he left, and deep down, I know the truth. Ryker might be a bastard in court, he might be a hard-ass who demands without reason, but at his core, he's a man who lives his life by the law. He doesn't need money. He doesn't need the thrill of defying the rules.

He had nothing to do with this.

The question is, Was it just Carter, or is his wife in on it too? Did she hire Ryker as a front, a place to hide the money? And if so, how would she ever expect to get it back?

I give a deep sigh and settle back into the silence of my house, which is full of unanswered questions these days.

With another good cry under my belt, I know exactly what I need to do.

The lie I told the agents—that my second piece of blackmail was simply a bluff—just might be my bargaining chip.

It might be the only thing I have going for me. It's one way I'm choosing to fight.

There is clutter all over my kitchen table.

Papers I've printed. Documents I'll use as proof. The highlights and circles a road map of truths. The missing link they needed that I never even knew I had.

Then there's the legalese I tried to understand. Things that Ryker would have been able to explain in seconds, but I couldn't ask him. Questions my private investigator could clear up for me, but my trust factor in general isn't exactly high right now.

Maybe I wasn't crazy thinking stuff was moved in my office. Maybe Noah and Abel slipped in here to investigate themselves. It's not exactly legal, but I have a feeling Abel doesn't play by the rules most days.

"Come on, Vaughn . . . *think*."

I shuffle through the papers again. The same ones I've read and reread so many times that I can't see straight.

With my hands on my hips, I nod.

I can do this.

I can make demands myself.

And I can dangle the goddamn carrot to make them agree.

My shower is long and hot, and when I step from it, I know more than anything that I can do this.

I pick up the phone and dial Noah.

He answers on the first ring.

"I'd like to talk." It's all I say.

"Meet us at Central Park. I'll text you the location. See you there in an hour."

I take a breath to steady myself. "Yes."

And then I make my second call.

CHAPTER THIRTY-EIGHT

Vaughn

"I want immunity," I state as I look from Abel to Noah and back and revel in the surprised looks on their faces.

"And just where do you get off thinking you get any say in this?" Abel says.

"I will do this—invite Carter Preston with the promise of sex and then ask him whatever it is you want asked with whatever fake black-mail you have—and for that I want immunity from any prosecution. I also want a formal recommendation to social services without specifics that I am the better candidate to adopt my niece, Lucy. Either that or arrest my brother-in-law for drug possession with intent to distribute, but I believe that is way below your pay grade."

"Anything else, madam?" Abel asks with a smarmy smirk and a disbelieving laugh that tells me I'm reaching for the moon with my demands.

I twist my lips and take a deep breath as I run through everything I've told myself I want. "Yes, I want Carter charged in connection with underage sex, and if he's not, I just might release the information myself that the FBI chose to pass up." That gets their attention, all right. "I also want a restraining and gag order on Carter Preston and his wife, Bianca Preston, from being able to come near me or speak about me publicly in any way."

Noah chortles and blows out a sigh. "And why should we agree to any of that? It should be you thanking us for letting you work off your bad deeds."

My smile is tight, my voice condescending. "Because while my good deeds will be fresh in your and the FBI's mind now, who knows down the road what they will or won't be. I want it in writing so no one can *accidentally* forget in the future."

"I have to give it to you, Vaughn. You've got some serious balls telling us how this is supposed to play out," Abel says.

"I'm aware." Another sweet smile is followed by my comment. "But you *need* me."

Abel shakes his head and winds up to go off on me, but it's Noah who's taking in my smile and demeanor and holds his finger up for his partner to be quiet.

"What is it?" Noah asks.

"Get my demands for me in writing, and I'll give you the one thing you don't have." Both men whip their heads up from where they are taking notes on their pads. "The proof that shows Carter Preston was in communication with Alpha Pharmaceuticals."

CHAPTER THIRTY-NINE
Ryker

"You okay?" my mother asks as she looks at me from across the table.

Sterling silver scrapes on fine china, and aged whiskey is poured into Waterford crystal.

"Fine." I survey the room but don't find the one person I'm searching for. And it's not like she'd be here anyway, but fuck if I'm not looking for Vaughn in every woman whose back is to me.

"With that dreadful Roxanne out of the picture, I figured you'd be somewhat happier."

I all but choke on the sip of water I just took. "Roxanne? Out of the way? What are you talking about?"

My mother waves a hand at me as if it's no big deal. "Women talk, Ryker. *That woman* especially."

"What about her?" I say in a long, drawn-out sigh, not even bothering to hide the affair from my mother.

"Well, it seems she's finally moved on to some other man who'll buy into her dramatics."

Now that? That gets my attention. "What do you mean?"

"Do you remember Baron's old friend Pierre? She's dating his nephew now and making sure everyone knows it."

Good fucking riddance. "Where do you hear this shit?"

"All women have their ways, dear."

"Apparently."

We fall into a lull as the waiter comes and goes, and my thoughts veer toward the women currently fucking with my life.

"You're still not talking," my mother says.

"I never talk much."

"It's not that. What is it that's bothering you?" she persists.

"I told you. There's nothing."

She narrows her eyes and studies me, her hands stilling on her silverware. "Are there holes in the drywall, Ryker?"

"A shit ton," I say without thinking, my mind preoccupied and already out of this stuffy restaurant I don't even want to be at.

"What happened?" she asks.

"Fuck if I know." The four words come out in a sigh. The same four words I've been saying a lot of late.

"Your mouth is very unrefined at the moment," she scolds.

"Yeah, well, it matches my mood." I toy with my knife for a moment, trying to think about anything other than Vaughn and the goddamn hole she poked through my heart with her tears and puffy eyes and complete misery she wouldn't explain to me yesterday. "Tell me something."

"Yes, darling?"

"Did you ever hire a divorce attorney, pay him a retainer, but never actually file the papers?" I ask.

Her laugh is low and telling. "Considering you've been my lawyer for two of them—"

"Before me. Your first two marriages. Did you?"

She purses her lips, and then a soft smile spreads on them. "Not that I can remember. If you hire an attorney, you're pretty serious. Most of the time, people file, and once it becomes real is when they decide they want to talk to their spouse, and sometimes they work it out. Why?"

"Nothing really. It's just that I have a client I can't figure out is all. She's connected to my life in certain ways, and . . . I don't know. The longer I work with her, the more I question her reasons for contacting me."

I can't put my fucking finger on it. Any of it. Vaughn. Bianca. And only one of them I really want to.

"Her?" she asks in surprise.

"Yes. A woman."

Her eyes narrow, and a slight smile paints her lips. "You'll figure it out, dear. You always do." She pats my hand, and I order another drink.

◆ ◆ ◆

"Hey, you okay?" I ask, Vaughn more than surprising me when she answers the phone.

"Mmm. Yeah. Getting there." She sounds sleepy, like I want to curl up behind her and pull her against me.

"Want to talk about it?"

"Yes . . . but not yet."

"If you're looking for some grand gesture to make you feel better— me holding a radio outside your bedroom window—I'm afraid boom boxes are dead, and Bluetooth speakers don't exactly have the same effect."

Where the hell did that come from, Lockhart?

But it earns a laugh from her, and God, does it do things to my insides I'd rather not admit.

"Have you ever done something you know is wrong, but you do it anyway because it's the right thing?" she asks and totally throws me for a loop.

What is she getting at?

"I think everyone has at some point in their life, don't you?"

"Hmm."

"Hmm?" I ask. "Does this have anything to do with the other day?"

She doesn't answer.

"Vaughn?"

"If you made a mistake, I'd forgive you, you know. Just like I'd hope you'd forgive me."

"You're not making any sense. Are you sure you're okay?" In my mind I'm already halfway across the bridge to her house.

"Yes. I'm fine." Her breath hitches. "I've had a glass or two or three of wine. I miss you, Ryker."

"I miss you too. When can I see—"

But I don't get to finish my sentence because she ends the call.

She might have just told me she misses me, but hell if it doesn't feel like that was a goodbye.

CHAPTER FORTY
Vaughn

The pounding on the door startles me awake.

The family room is pitch black, and for a moment I sit there thinking I've just had a nightmare.

Then it starts again.

Instinct has me moving toward the peephole, fearful it's the police—that something has happened to Lucy—when it should have me pretending I'm not home and dialing 9-1-1.

And I'm not sure if it's the remnants of the bottle of wine still in my system, but when I see Ryker standing on my porch in the middle of the night—or is it early morning?—I open the door without question.

His fist is midknock when I pull it open. There's anger etched in the lines of his face, and concern owns every muscle in his expression as we stand a few feet apart.

Without speaking a single word, Ryker frames both sides of my face and brings his lips to mine. The kiss starts out slow—a silent show of desperation—and has us both moving into the house, the door being kicked shut behind us.

It's heaven and hell at my fingertips. It's certainty and doubt in my touch.

It's him.

It's Ryker.

And I need him more than I've ever needed him before.

We undress between kisses. Shirts and shoes and pants. The darkness of the night hiding the things we're still keeping from each other. Secrets that are tearing me apart. A love I'm afraid to profess in case my world comes tumbling down around me.

He moves from memory down the hallway and lays me on the bed, his mouth between my thighs before I have a chance to protest. Before I can stop him from making me even more vulnerable than I already feel.

His fingertips part me, and his tongue makes its slow descent to dip inside me before sliding back up and circling around my clit.

The groan he emits into the room is like his fingertips dancing over my most intimate of flesh—all-consuming and everywhere at once.

There is no urgency. No rush to get me off. Just a slow dance of his mouth and the soft slide of his tongue as he worships me in a way no one ever has.

And when the warm wave of bliss hits me with its pulsing vibrations, I allow myself to fall prey to him once more. I let him have one more piece of me I'll never be able to get back.

He rises to his knees and presses a row of kisses up my thigh to my navel. He rests his forehead there as his fingers reach out to find mine.

"I love you, Vaughn." His words float out into the room and make every part of me he didn't just warm with his tongue light on fire.

"Ryk—"

"No. I love you, and I'm sick of pretending that I don't because you're not ready to hear it. I love you, Vaughn Sanders, and I don't know what the hell is going on right now, but I know whenever it's done and over with, I'll still love you."

We stay like that for a few moments, entangled in every way imaginable. When he slips into me like a soft sigh moments later, tears course down my cheeks and fall to the pillow beneath my head.

I love you too, Ryker.

I'm just so afraid I'm going to lose you.

Everything I've loved before I've lost.

But I close my eyes and force myself to live in the moment. To feel his sweet push in and soft grind on the way out. To memorize his hiss of pleasure. To revel in the way he touches me—as if he can't get enough of me and how he never wants to.

And when he leaves the house under the same cover of night he came to me in, he doesn't ask any questions, and he doesn't beg me to explain the tears he kissed from my cheeks as he brought us pleasure. He just kisses me tenderly one last time and trusts that I'll tell him the truth when the time is right.

Yes.

I love you, Ryker Lockhart.
More than you'll ever know.

CHAPTER
FORTY-ONE
Ryker

"I have to admit, this is a first if I've ever had one before." I shake my head and stare at the speaker on my desk phone as if Bianca can see me through it.

Obviously she can't, but it doesn't stop me from doing it.

"You didn't deliver on what you promised," she accuses.

"I didn't deliver?" My voice starts to rise in pitch. "How about you didn't hold up your end of the bargain? How about every question I asked you to answer took weeks to get a half-assed response?" My temper simmers to boiling at her accusations. "How about it feels like you hired me to represent you as some kind of fucked-up challenge to your husband? You never had any intention of actually filing for divorce. You just wanted to make sure to put him in his place by letting him know you could. By waltzing in here with some outrageous check as if it were some kind of challenge to see if I would throw it in his face."

"You're fired, Mr. Lockhart." Her voice is cold and unfeeling, just like she is.

"Good. I'll gladly cease representation. I refuse to be a pawn in your dysfunctional relationship."

She chuckles for some reason. "You already were."

"Good. Great. Go play your fucked-up games with some other firm. I won't be manipulated."

"I'll expect my retainer returned less the small amount of billable hours, which are yours, of course. *Promptly.*"

I'm dumbfounded as she sits on the other end of the connection with her demands and bitchiness.

"Fine," I finally answer.

The dial tone meets my ears.

I lean back in my chair, put my feet up on the desk, and steeple my fingers in front of me as I think.

What the fuck was that?

Definitely a first.

One I don't want to repeat.

So this is what it feels like to be fired.

CHAPTER
FORTY-TWO
Vaughn

"Not very smart, Vaughn."

I startle when I see Abel and Noah at my front door. They push their way past me without asking and shut the door behind them.

"What do you mean?" My voice jitters in a way I've never heard it before—pure fear. Especially when I see the handcuffs hanging from Abel's belt loop.

He didn't have those last time.

Why does he have them now?

Do they think I'm bluffing on having proof? Are they not going to grant me immunity?

They both stare at me as I shake my head and tears well in my eyes.

"So you give us ultimatums. Then you call Ryker. His car arrives shortly thereafter and remains parked here for three hours in the dead of night and you think we won't notice?"

"I didn't care if you noticed," I say with a partial laugh to hide my nerves. "Isn't a girl allowed to see her boyfriend for some much-needed sex?"

I hope my truth will shock them some. Will make them realize I'm not playing the games they seem to think I am. And the surprised expressions my statement causes tells me I might just have succeeded.

"Sex?" Abel asks.

"Yes. A booty call," I say and hate that it cheapens everything about what Ryker and I shared, but I also refuse to tell them that. "I wasn't aware I couldn't see him."

"The tough-girl act doesn't fool us, Vaughn," Noah says.

"Or shock us," Abel interjects. "You'd be surprised the things people lie about to try to throw us off track."

"Why would I do that? Throw you off track."

"Ah, is that your precursor to get out of explaining your big buyout? Let me guess—you're going to refuse to cooperate with us now?" Abel accuses. "You can handle us all on your own, you can afford some big hotshot attorney who can explain it all away and—"

His words make no sense. I admitted to seeing Ryker. I'm not lying. So what is the big deal here?

"I have no idea what you're talking about."

Abel crosses his arms over his chest and assumes his pose of intimidation against the wall. "So what, you were just stringing us along until you could see who the highest bidder was?"

"You." I point a finger at Abel. "You need to stop with the cryptic bullshit and just come out and say it. I haven't slept well in the past few days, so I'm having a helluva time following whatever else it is you're accusing me of."

"You want me to spell it out? How about this: you ask for immunity, and while you wait for us to get the paperwork drawn up, you try to get the best of both worlds. How much did you let Ryker buy you with, huh? Did you think we'd sign the paperwork with you before we noticed?"

"Paperwork? Buy me out?" I feel like I'm not an active participant in this conversation, because I have no idea what in the hell is going on. "I don't—"

"This." Abel slaps down a stack of papers onto my table. "Your immunity deal."

"Oh." I startle at the sound but then narrow my eyes in confusion when another stack lands with a thud beside it.

"And this."

I look between the two stacks, too far away to read any writing, too close to ignore that whatever they say determines my fate.

"What are those?" I point to the second stack, my voice cautious, my hope on edge.

"You tell me." Abel points for me to approach and pushes the stack closer.

I look at the top one. The company is familiar, the printed form akin to a type of statement I see every month. My name is at the top, but the balance at the bottom shows a big fat zero.

I glance up at both of them in utter shock and then absolute fear before rifling through the rest of them. "This can't be." My eyes jockey between them as I see that each of my monthly statements show a zero balance due.

Every single one of them.

Almost $300,000 worth of expenses I incurred for my uninsured sister has been wiped clean.

"I don't understand." My voice is hollow, my eyes disbelieving.

"Looks to me like you just wished it all away, and poof, the magic money fairy paid every last cent of it. And let me guess . . . he wanted something in return for doing it that cost a lot more than a midnight booty call."

Goddamn it, Ryker.

Tears threaten, and I shake my head as if I can reject what I'm seeing with my own eyes. The mix of emotions is so strong and powerful that I'm not sure which one to focus on.

Anger at him for thinking I needed him to do this.

Fear because even though I know they are wrong in thinking Ryker bought me off, I can see how this all looks in their eyes, and it doesn't play in my favor.

Why would he do this?

Maybe I want to take care of you instead.

Every part of me riles against this, against his generosity, with an unrivaled fierceness.

I can take care of myself. I got myself into this mess. I can get myself out of it. I don't need some knight to come in and save the day.

The other part of me has tears in her eyes from a relief I never thought I'd get the chance to know.

But he can't do this. I won't let him.

It's just money to him. Play money.

Powerful men like to play God.

Abel's words come back to me as I lift my eyes to his and shake my head.

I run to my computer and frantically punch in websites of my big creditors. Are the agents tricking me? Are they going to tell me there is no immunity, make me sign their stupid papers, and bind me to them by telling me lies?

But the lies are true. Each website. Each balance. *All zeros.*

Every single one of them.

How do I protect Ryker right now from their assumptions? How do I protect myself? How do neither of us become collateral damage in the agents' pursuit of Carter Preston?

"That two-million-dollar *retainer* sure is going a long way," Abel says.

"I had nothing to do with this. I didn't know. I didn't want this. I . . ."

And then the tears come because Ryker might have just risked everything for me. His good deed—a deed I am so angry at him over because I don't need a savior, I just need him—paints a different picture depending on what angle you're observing it from.

And the FBI is definitely looking at it differently than I am.

"It's not a bribe." I shake my head over and over. It's the only thing I can do. "I didn't know. I . . . this is a total surprise."

"If it's not a bribe," Noah says and pushes the first stack of paperwork across the table, where he's remained seated, "then you'll have no problem signing this right now. *As is.*"

Feeling like I'm walking through a fog, I rise from my seat and move slowly to the table. All I want to do right now is rush to Ryker's house and chew him out. Tell him without spelling it out what he almost just risked for me. Kiss him and hug him and hit him and yell at him for paying off my bills, all the while swearing that I will pay him back.

Every single penny.

How does one read all this while being stared down by special agents? If I hesitate in any way, they'll think I'm lying. If I don't, I'm an idiot who trusts way too much.

"Is it all in there?" My voice is barely audible.

"Yes." Noah nods.

"Immunity. Cleared of wrongdoing. Letter of recommendation for Lucy. Charges for the underage girls? Restraining and gag orders from the Prestons?"

"Technically, we can't promise what the senator will or will not be charged with. That's not something we can guarantee. We can only deal with what we *won't* be charging you with," Noah explains. "But I'd find the agency hard pressed not to file charges against him once those photos got out somehow."

I nod, hearing what he's saying but hating that there's nothing concrete.

"And what about solicitation? He won't be charged with it, right? Because if he's charged with it, then my name will be in there somewhere."

"We can't make that promise either, about what he will or will not be charged with," Abel reiterates.

My head flies up to Abel when he speaks.

"No deal," I say.

"Told you this was all bullshit," Abel says in disgust.

"You add solicitation, then my name will be publicized. It won't matter if I have immunity or not—my name will be out. Ruined. Slung through the mud so that every reporter from here to kingdom come will dig into my past, uncover ghosts I'd rather remain buried. It won't matter what's true or not—they'll report it all as fact." My breath hitches, and my fists clench. "My chances to adopt Lucy will be taken away. I did all of this for that. All this risk. All this bullshit. All this . . . everything," I yell, tears on my cheeks and fury in my voice, "I did for that little girl."

I push away from the table and walk to the window. To the view of the boys playing their daily game of baseball. To the *here, batter batter* I can all but hear through the closed window when I see their lips move. My shoulders shake; my chest burns.

This was all for nothing.

All of it.

I'm going to lose her anyway.

"If you charge him with solicitation, the deal is off the table." I turn to look at both of them.

"Do you have the proof?" Noah asks, and I nod. "Here? In the house?"

"Does the solicitation charge still stand?" I ask.

Noah looks at Abel, and I can't decipher what the look says. "Answer the question," Abel demands.

"You answer the question," I repeat.

"You're maddening," Abel says in a huff, but that term almost makes me smile as Ryker's voice saying it ghosts through my ears.

"So I've been told."

"Christ," Abel mutters and grabs the paperwork from the table. I move forward to watch him take a pen and X out a paragraph of the document. He initials the change and hands the pen to Noah, who does the same, before holding the pen out to me.

With my eyes locked on his, I take the pen, scan the paragraph that has been crossed out, and initial beside theirs and add a date beside it.

From there I proceed to take a seat and go word for word through the deal. I skip the standard boilerplate and focus on the specifics, despite their grumbling that it's all there.

When I'm satisfied, I take a deep breath and throw up a silent prayer that I'm doing the right thing here, that I'm not missing some huge loophole that's going to land me in jail, and sign my name.

I slide it back across the table with shaky hands.

"Now it's your turn," Abel says with an edge of impatience and a lift of his eyebrows.

I walk to my office, grab my own stack of papers from the top drawer of my desk, and return to the two agents sitting at my kitchen table.

"That's the proof?" Abel asks with skepticism.

"Yes." I push the call log across the table. The one I was originally given without any of my notes on it.

"What's this?" He dismisses it immediately.

"It's a call log."

"No shit, Sherlock. Do you care to expand here?"

"That log was given to me some time ago. I didn't know what it was, what secrets it held . . . just that it pertained to Carter Preston and that he'd be in a world of hurt if this fell into the right hands."

"So you lied to us then about having something else on him?" Abel questions.

"Do you want me to continue, or do you want to argue semantics?" I defer, hoping he'll let that tiny detail go.

"Where did you get it from?" Noah asks, and I breathe a cautious sigh of relief.

"A generic email account sent from an IP address located at a New York public library. I can get my PI to turn over to you the details of it, as I'm sure your reach is much farther than ours was."

Noah and Abel exchange a glance and look back down at the log. "I don't understand—"

I cut Noah's words off when I slide across the table a different version of the same call log. This time it's covered with my notes.

I find immense pleasure in watching their eyes widen as it dawns on them just what this is . . . and intense satisfaction knowing I'll be the one who put Carter Preston in his rightful place: behind bars.

"So this is—how did—I don't have . . ."

I step around the side of the table. "I researched when the vote was. I noticed all these calls going back and forth took place in the weeks leading up to it followed by a flurry the day of."

"Okay . . . ," Noah says.

"That number right there is the CEO of Alpha Pharm." I point to one and then to the second. "His private encrypted cell phone, actually. He might have used the services of a rival escort service before. I made a couple of calls, had to make a few promises, but this here is his number. There's proof in that stack over there"—I point to a pile of papers— "that ties this cell phone number to his credit card."

"That's fine and all, but none of these are Carter Preston's number," Abel says, pointing to the other cell numbers on the sheet.

"Yes, actually, they are. At least they're the one he uses from his burner phones to call and schedule dates with a certain escort service." I meet both of their eyes. "I can trace these numbers to calls placed on my cell phones. Ones you probably recorded him using since you were tracking our calls. And if that's not good enough, I have a few voice mails with his voice on two of those numbers."

"Son of a bitch," Noah mutters.

"A goddamn burner," Abel says.

"It's smart. He's a senator who doesn't want escorts or . . . I guess bribes able to be connected to his name."

Noah runs his finger under every call as if he's remembering some invisible timeline to compare them against.

"Where did you get this?" Abel demands. "How did someone know to email it to you?"

I shrug. "I don't know. That's the only question I can't answer. Maybe because my PI was asking questions about him? I don't know."

"Almost too convenient," Noah says to Abel with a snort.

"That's what I thought . . . but it is Washington, and I'm sure Carter has burned a lot of bridges. Another woman scorned, perhaps? The ex-wife of Alpha Pharm's CEO? Maybe it's her way of getting back at her husband? Or maybe even someone who works at the cell phone company whose family member will be affected by the veto of this bill? I don't have answers for you. I just know I've had this, and it took me some time to connect the dots."

"This is enough to nail him right now. There are still a lot of questions that need to be answered, but we finally have something connecting the two men. We pull up a warrant, we—"

Noah holds his hand up to stop Abel and slides a look my way as if to say, *Not in front of the non–special agent people.* "We need to get our ducks in a row first. He's slipped through our fingers before," he says, his words surprising me. "I don't want to let it happen again."

"It seems to me you won't need me to confront him," I say, more than relieved at the thought.

Noah looks at Abel and heads toward the front door, his cell already in his hand. "I'll find a judge who'll sign this warrant and—" The front door shuts behind him, and I am left to look at Abel with raised eyebrows.

"We'll leave the confrontation on the table. We need to see what happens first. Judges are fickle creatures sometimes."

So are agents, it seems.

I nod, all the while biting my tongue to keep from pointing out that Ryker's phone numbers can't be found anywhere on that month-long call log. It's nowhere.

But I don't.

And just as if fate is giving me a different way to prove his innocence and eradicate all doubt I should feel guilty for even thinking, I point to the stack of papers. "Let me see those again."

The smirk on Abel's face says so much more than any words can. He's a hunter, and his prey is so close within reach he can smell him.

But I'm about to remove one less person for him to go after.

I thumb through the papers again. I look past the sticker shock of the cover sheets that show the return address, my name, the balance due . . . and look at the pages after. The payments applied. The interest charged.

"There," I all but shout when I see the date of the balance payoff.

"What?" He fights the smile on his lips, his tone feigning innocence.

"You knew all along, didn't you? You knew these balances were settled before you guys even approached me. That Ryker didn't pay me off to keep me quiet." I sit down in the chair. "Son of a bitch!"

His laugh rings out through the house. I wasn't sure he was even capable of having one. "We all have to play games sometimes to get what we want."

I stare at him, blinking, slack-jawed. "So he's in the clear?"

Abel twists his lips as he weighs how much to tell me. "Not exactly. But that's a start."

Two hours later—after we've gone through everything I have, including my own phone records showing calls from that same number of Carter's, saved voice mails recorded from one of his burner cell numbers—I'm finally all alone in my house.

By then, the desire I have to chew Ryker out has dissipated.

It's still there all right . . . but it's being stifled by some major exhaustion and the elation that I just might have gotten myself out of being bait for the FBI to use to lure Carter Preston.

I refuse to be collateral damage.

CHAPTER FORTY-THREE

Ryker

"Where are you?" I jolt at the sound of her voice. Guilt springs up at being here without her knowing.

"I'm out of town. A quick business trip. Why? Are you okay? Do you—"

"We need to talk when you get back." The high of hearing her voice crashes down when she says the words every man dreads being told.

Especially after the odd week between us that sewed doubts into every part of me, no matter how hard I wanted to grab her shoulders, shake her, and beg her to tell me what was wrong so I could fix it.

Or at least try to.

But the one thing I know for certain is that she's not bored with me. That she hasn't written me off. I felt the exact opposite from her the other night when I told her I loved her. I know she feels the same way, even though she never uttered the words.

And while that might seem simple to most, that's huge to me.

"Okay. What about?" I ask, trying to keep my thoughts and voice upbeat.

Her lack of an answer—rather just a sound—only adds more uncertainty to whatever's going on with her.

"You're okay, though, right?"

"You paid off my debts." The sudden chill to her voice makes me smile. Now this? Her anger and defiance and independence? This I can handle. This I was expecting at some point.

I had it all planned out, what I was going to say when she realized it. Reasons and explanations and how now she's free and clear with nothing standing in her way to keep Priscilla from giving her Lucy.

I wanted to take care of you.

I wanted to help fix the screwups I seem to keep making that continually put your getting Lucy at risk.

I wanted to see your face without the lines of stress etched into it, without the fear in your eyes, without the constant pressure to right your sister's wrongs.

But I know better than to say any of those things. I know better than to assert the *you're vulnerable* bullshit she'll buck back against.

Instead, I take the path of least resistance.

"I did? Hmm. I guess I must have had my accountant pay the wrong bills."

"Ryker, this isn't funny. It's crap. I can't accept this. I can't—"

"It's not like you can tell them you made an oops! Guess it will have to stay as is."

"You looked into me. You snooped through my finances to know where my debt lay. You invaded my privacy—"

"You're right. I did. I'm sorry." Well, shit, that was easier to admit than I thought it would be. But now it's the silence that follows as she digests what I did that unnerves me.

"I'm not okay with that."

"Understandably," I say. "When I get back to town, I'll open all of my finances for you to look at if that makes you feel better. That way we're both on the same page."

"Ryker . . . that's not what I'm asking. That's not—I am not a *kept* woman. I will not be a *kept* woman." I can hear the fury in her voice, and my smile widens.

There's a bit more of my girl back.

"I'd like to see anyone try." I laugh. "We both know *kept* isn't a word anyone would ever use to describe you."

"I—you can't—this isn't—you don't understand what this looks like—" She huffs in frustration. It takes a lot to make Vaughn Sanders speechless, and I've succeeded.

"What does this look like?" I ask.

"I can't accept this." But this time instead of defiance and anger in her voice, there's a waver and then a break on the last word. Then a sniffle.

"Vaughn? What's wrong?"

"It's just too much. This is all too much." I can't tell if she's crying, and I'm pretty sure if she is, she'll just deny it if I ask.

"I just wanted to give you something no one has ever given you before."

"Money?" The word is two drawn-out syllables.

"Yes, but it's so much more than that. It's me telling you I believe in you. It's me telling you that you're worth it. It's me wanting you to know that I think you're going to be an incredible mother to Lucy. It's me wanting you to look in the mirror every day and instead of trying to figure out if you're Vee or Vaughn or a server at Apropos or a madam, you know that you're *you*—a little bit of all those people mixed together to make up one incredible woman." Her hiccupped sob fills the line. "Oh baby, please don't cry."

"I don't deserve this."

"But you do. I'm sick of watching you work yourself to death. Sick of seeing you worry over what will come of it. Wonder what it will be like after you get it all paid off. Well, now it's *the after*. Now it's your turn to do and be and live for yourself."

"Ryker."

"There's nothing to say."

"I'll pay you back."

"I won't accept it."

"I'll find a way."

"I want—*no, need*—you to know something. I pulled the trigger on this way before whatever happened the past week or two happened." *Spit it out, Lockhart.* "Yes, I was worried that you were going to break up with me, but I don't want you to think that I did this to buy you into staying."

There's silence on the line, and I immediately feel like a dumbass for making the comment.

"You have no idea how much I needed to hear that." She laughs. "Did you hear that, everyone?" she shouts out and laughs again. "He did it a while ago."

"Um . . . am I missing something?" I ask, thoroughly confused.

"Nothing and everything." A giggle that sounds part hysterical. "Ryker Lockhart?"

"Yes?"

"I love you." Her voice is barely a whisper, but those three words hit me as if they were spoken through a megaphone. Loud. Unapologetic. Genuine.

And after the events, her actions, and everything that I don't understand, I sure as hell didn't expect to hear that.

I clear my throat. It's all I can do, because it feels like something is stuck there momentarily. "Vaughn." Her name is a murmur on my lips. "You surprise me at every turn. Please don't ever change that."

"I promise. And I didn't tell you that because you paid off my bills, because I have every intention of paying you back."

"If you believing that is the only way you'll accept the funds, then yeah, sure. Whatever you say, dear." I laugh, and fuck if it doesn't feel like a huge weight has been lifted off my shoulders I didn't even know was there.

"Don't mock me, Lockhart."

"Yes, *madam*."

"Ah, so very clever."

"I try." I glance up to the house in front of me. "Was this what you wanted to talk to me about when I get home?"

"Yes and no. There's just . . . we'll talk when you get here."

"Sounds good."

"Oh, hey. Tell me something," she says.

"What?"

"Are you still representing Carter Preston's wife?"

Her question completely throws me for reasons she couldn't even know.

I think of the drama this week at work. Bianca revoking my representation in the oddest conversation ever.

"No. I'm no longer representing her. Why?"

"No reason." Her tone is indifferent when mine is anything but.

"Why did you ask? Is Carter causing problems for you? I can cancel this meeting and be back—"

"Carter's always causing problems," she says with a laugh. "It would be stupid for you to jump to my rescue every time he did."

"Is he bugging you? I can have Stuart—"

"I'm fine, Ryker. Better now that I talked to you. I promise."

"You sure you're okay?"

"Goodbye," she sings the word out.

And just like that, the woman who has had every part of my life in an uproar over the past week ends the call as easily as she owns my heart.

She loves me.

Whew.

I shake my head and smile, then pick my phone back up and dial.

"What's up, boss? Need something?"

"Keep an eye out for Vaughn, will you?" I ask Stuart, her comment about Carter sticking in my head.

"Will do. My load is light. You want me following her or just checking in?" he asks.

"Whatever you think is best. He's been too quiet for my liking."

And she loves me. I have to protect her at all costs.

"Ten-four."

He ends the call, and I'm left looking at the one thing left I have to do.

CHAPTER
FORTY-FOUR
Ryker

James Dillinger's house stands before me.

It's quite the spread. There's no masking the Dillinger money when it comes to this structure. And inside is even more impressive than the outside when the hired help lets me in and has me wait in the formidable foyer.

"Is he expecting you?" the woman dressed all in black asks.

"No. Just a quick visit, really. I was in the area waiting to catch up with his nephew, Chance, and thought I'd stop by to let him know about a little shared connection I discovered."

"Oh, how sweet of you. He doesn't get many visitors these days who aren't here to try to pick that brilliant mind of his, so I'm sure he'll be thrilled to see someone and not feel obligated to discuss complex dynamic systems or capital theory."

"Hmm," I murmur, not caring in the least. The fucker doesn't deserve any visitors.

I look around the place as I wait. It's stuffy and stately, and I have a hard time picturing Vaughn and Samantha here as young girls. There's no way this cold place could have given them an ounce of the warmth children need. Not at all.

The help comes back out with a warm smile. "He'll meet you in the library, Mr. Lockhart. Right this way."

She leads me into a room lined with walls filled with all the literary greats. It smells like leather and wood and paper and is rather impressive, but I wonder if it's all for show. Not a single thing in the room looks as if it's been touched in years.

"Can I get you anything?" she asks. "Water, soda, wine?"

"I won't be staying long. Thank you, though."

"Just let me know if you change your mind." She heads to the doorway. "He'll be right in."

Alone, I move toward the rows and rows of books. Each literary work looks like it's an original, with spines bound in leather and creased from being used at some point.

I hear him when he enters the room. The hum of his motorized wheelchair. The rasp of his breath. The stop and start of the joystick controlling his movements. But I don't turn around. I let him sit in his feeble state and wonder what this strange man is doing in his house. I let his curiosity build.

"Those are all first-print publications," he finally says. His voice has a hint of New England with the lilt of aristocracy.

"I noticed." I run my hands along them, knowing if these truly are his prized possessions, he's cringing at the oil from my hands running across them. I keep touching them on purpose.

"Dickens. Austen. Brontë. Twain." He moves his chair closer.

"I was expecting to find something more along the lines of *I Know Why the Caged Bird Sings* or *Lolita*," I say, referring to books that deal with child molestation. "Those are more up your alley, aren't they?"

I turn to face him. To see the weak man with pale skin and dark hair shorn short. He's dressed in expensive clothing—a sweater over a collared shirt, slacks, and shoes that cost more than most people make in a month. His eyebrows are raised, his lips twisted as he studies me the same way I am him.

I hate him instantly.

Our eyes lock, and I swear to all things, my flesh crawls. Chills run over my skin and tighten my scalp.

"So Beatrice told me that you said we have some kind of connection besides both knowing Chance?" he asks as if I never made the comment about the books.

"Yes. It's quite funny how it came about, actually." I move now, around the massive couch, so I'm able to rest my ass on its arm and sit directly in front of him.

If he moves his chair, he'll show me he's uncomfortable. If he stays where he is, he has no choice but to see the vitriol in my eyes.

"Funny? How so?"

Absently, I pull Lucy's, formerly Samantha's, necklace with the key on it from my pocket. I don't look at it, I don't even acknowledge that I'm doing the action, but James sure as hell does. He tries not to look but can't resist. And then looks again, eyes widening, mouth falling lax. The swallow he's trying to work down his throat seems like it's a battle.

"What did you say your name was again?"

"I didn't." My smile is wide and unforgiving. When I hold out my hand, I make a show of transferring the necklace from my right to my left hand to free it up. "Ryker Lockhart. Nice to meet you, *James.*"

We shake hands the best he can with his atrophied muscles, and then I resume my spot on the arm of the chair.

"And the connection?" he prompts.

"You know, I was surprised when I looked you up to find a man of such stature. The John Bates Clark Medal for economics? Your family must be so proud." I clasp my hands in my lap, the worn key resting against the dark fabric of my slacks.

"My family is very accomplished. It's one of many medals that gets lost in the accolades in our lineage."

"Don't play it down, James. You should be proud of it, just as they should be proud of you." I smile. "I mean, it's not the Nobel Prize, but it's pretty damn close. They should be as proud of you as a family can be of a man who preys on and rapes children."

"What?" He chokes on the word. Then sputters to connect thoughts for a few seconds. I enjoy the show—his face turning red, his eyes widening, his lack of coherency.

"You heard me just fine. You might be paralyzed—we'll get to that in a moment—but you're not deaf."

"Beatrice!" he shouts as he moves his chair back.

I step toward him, my foot going behind the wheel to stop his progress, and then lean down to his face. He smells of cigar smoke and Old Spice and urine. "I wouldn't do that if I were you," I whisper the warning. "We wouldn't want your secret to get out. The only award for a child rapist is one you can get behind bars." I move my foot from behind his wheel and look him in the eye without flinching. "Do I make myself clear?"

He nods, his head moving up and down slightly, his body trembling, his eyes wide and wild.

"What do you want?" he asks in a strained voice.

"A villa on Lake Como. World peace. Fuckers like you to die a slow, painful death." I shrug callously. "But beggars can't be choosers. We all can't get what we want."

"Why are you here?"

"So a rich, *brilliant*"—I roll my eyes—"man like you gets custody of your sister's two girls. Most people would try to give them the best life possible. They'd love them and nurture them. They'd treat them as their own. But you're not most people, are you, James? No. You figure it's the perfect way to feed that urge you have. The one that only sick fucks have whose dicks need to be cut off for even thinking such thoughts let alone acting on them."

"I never—"

"Save it for your family who will buy your bullshit. Not me. Uh-uh. What I don't understand is this . . . if Samantha really shot you like you told the police she did, then why did you never pursue it? Why did you not take all this money you spend buying books you'll never read and get vengeance on the person who turned you into a bag of useless bones? A single shot to the spine? Isn't that where Sam shot you? Oh, yes. *I forgot*. That's what the police report says, but the medical records show that the shot was more aimed at your pelvis. Can't imagine why you wouldn't want those details out there."

I chuckle and shake my head. My own restlessness breathing the same air as this piece of shit is more than I can stand.

"You don't know what you're talking about. You're lying—"

"Took you a minute to find your backbone to stand up for yourself, but I guess Samantha took care of that when she shot you after you raped her one too many times. Huh?"

"Beatrice!" he shouts again, and within seconds I have the doors shut to the library.

I'm nowhere near finished with him yet.

"I want you out of my house, right now. I'll call the cops. I'll—"

"Please do. We can square up this matter right now and get their files updated with what really should be in there." I point to the phone on the desk. "Should I dial for you?"

"Whatever Samantha told you is a lie."

"It is?" I hold the chain up so the key swings back and forth. "Remember this? She used to wear it all the time."

He shrugs as best as he can. "So?"

"This right here is the key." I laugh. "Get it? *The key?* The one that holds all the evidence to prove she wasn't lying."

"And I'm supposed to believe you?"

"Believe me. Don't believe me. I couldn't care less. The documents don't lie." But I do. Hell, I'm lying through my teeth. At least being a lawyer pays off at some point. "Journals that document your threats to her. Calendars with each and every time you touched her notated. It's like a road map to your sick and twisted abuse."

"I didn't touch her."

"You say the words, but the look on your face, the sheer terror that I'm going to let the world know that the brilliant mind is also a sick fuck? That paints a whole different story."

His face grows paler, if that's possible. "What do you want?"

"I want you to admit you did it."

"No."

"*No*, you won't admit it, or *no*, you didn't do it?" I press. "Just a few simple words and I'll leave." My smile is less than sincere.

"Why are you here?"

"I just told you."

"You want something else, though. I'm not naive enough to believe there isn't more to it."

"See? They were right. You do have a brilliant mind. That Uncle James is a smart one." I squat down so I'm at his eye level. "Here's what I want. I want you to drop any and all charges against Samantha and Vaughn Sanders."

"I can't—"

"*Oh, but you can.* I'm a lawyer. I know how these things work." I lift my eyebrows. "So here's what you're going to do. You're going to call the prosecuting attorney who got the warrant issued way back when and tell him you want a motion brought before the issuing judge to get it dropped."

"That's not how it works."

My laugh holds everything but humor as it ricochets off the walls. "I'm more than aware how the process works, but there's no way in hell I'm making Samantha or Vaughn surrender themselves to the court to ask the judge to release the warrant." I rise to my feet and cross my arms over my chest, my physical threat undeniable. "So figure it out. It seems you've paid off enough people in Greenwich that greasing a few more palms won't turn heads."

"Just like that?" he asks. "You think they're not going to question why?"

"Obviously you're skilled at telling lies and keeping up false pretenses, so I'm sure you can think of something to explain why you've had a change of heart. Why you previously thought it was your nieces who assaulted you but now know differently. You were shot in the spine, so how could you have seen who the assailant was?" I wink. "See, this is where your lies catch up with you and make it easier for me."

"They'll see through that." His voice is a rasped wheeze at this point.

"Like I said, you've paid them enough to keep quiet so far, so I'm sure shelling out some more cash really won't be that taxing for you."

"What's this to you?" he asks.

I take a moment, draw in a deep breath, and nod. "Because you've hurt Sam and Vaughn enough for a lifetime. You've scarred them so deeply that no matter how many calluses have grown over the scars, they still turn to blisters with the simplest mention of your name. I'm sure it gives you great pleasure—that hearing you've fucked them up for life gets you off—but I'm here to put an end to it. Right here. Right now."

"Leave it to Sam to find a vigilante to protect her," he sneers, and I don't correct him.

"What's it to you?" I shout, and I'm in his face in a split second. I'm more than aware of how helpless he feels right now. Me, big and strong and threatening—and him, paralyzed, weak, and defenseless. "You wouldn't want them now. They're too old, right? It's only the underage ones who can get you hard." I keep my face within inches of his and just stare. "You disgust me."

"Fuck you." It's the first sign of a temper, and I welcome the resistance.

"You gonna give me a fight, Dillinger? Huh? You going to come out swinging so I have no choice but to turn all this evidence over to, say, the *New York Times*? What's the saying? No press is bad press? Or even better, did you ever take them into New York? Please tell me yes, and then I can turn you over to the FBI for crossing state lines. I'd love to see you try to bribe a federal agent."

"You're crazy if you—"

"What's it going to be, James? Are you going to do what the fuck I asked? Get the charges dropped. Admit to me that you're a sick fuck who abused Samantha. And never—ever—speak of them again. Not to newspapers or police or so much as your own goddamn conscience. But then again, we both know you don't have one."

"Who the fuck do you think you are? I don't take orders from anyone, let alone—"

"Tick. Tock." I hold the necklace up, the key swinging, and take measured steps toward the telephone on the desk.

"Jesus Christ."

"Not even he can save you," I grit out, looking at this pussy of a man unwilling to fess up to his sins. "Make the call."

It takes ten minutes for James to get the prosecuting attorney on the line, explain that after all this time he thinks he may have been wrong in pointing the finger at his nieces, and that he needs to know how to go about getting the warrants withdrawn.

"I don't understand, Mr. Dillinger," the prosecutor says through the phone's speaker. "This has been one of those cases that has haunted Greenwich forever. Why do you suddenly think differently? Are you under duress? Is someone forcing you to—"

"No. No duress," he stutters as he glares at me. "Just getting older and want to clean my conscience. I'd hate for them to be arrested some-day should they come back home when they never committed the crime in the first place."

The prosecutor emits a loud sigh. "The warrants for theft still hold, though, right?"

I shake my head.

"No. No charges."

"You sure? Ten thousand dollars' worth of jewelry and cash is an awful lot."

"It is, and if we ever find the person who broke into the house and shot me, I won't hesitate to go after them to the full extent of the law."

The lies roll off his tongue, and I just shake my head in disgust. Is this what Vaughn thought Carter Preston was referring to when he brought up James Dillinger? That she'd be arrested for theft?

"Only if you're sure."

"I'm sure," James says.

"Okay, I'll file to get an appearance before Judge Benedict as soon as possible. He'll want to have the ladies appear in court—"

"That can't happen. I don't even know where they are." James glares at me, and I love that he hates everything about this. Serves him right.

"Then—"

"I hear you want the state's attorney appointment. I can make that happen if you get this taken care of for me." Silence sits on the line for a bit. The prosecutor clears his throat. "Did I not make good on my promises before when this first happened?"

"Yes." His voice is soft, cautious.

"Then why do you doubt me now?" James asks, and I hate knowing this asshole is so good at manipulating people.

"I'll get the record set straight," he finally agrees.

"Thanks. And I'll start making those phone calls on your behalf."

I hang up the phone and then shift my hip on the edge of the desk, a condescending smile on my lips. "That wasn't too hard, now was it?"

"Fuck you."

"Just a few more things and I'll be out of your hair, and in turn you'll stay out of jail."

"What more do you want from me?" he asks, visibly tired.

"I don't want you to ever search out Sam or Vaughn. If I so much as hear that you're even asking about them, the contents of that locker are turned over to the authorities."

"Yeah, yeah. You're blowing hot air now."

My temper snaps. The temper I swore I'd keep in check is obliter-ated as my hands fit perfectly on either side of his neck and squeeze with enough pressure to put the fear of God into him. "At least I have a breath I can blow."

"Fuck you," he forces out with what little oxygen he has left.

"For a man as intelligent as you, your vocabulary is seriously lim-ited. Now tell me the last thing I want to hear. Admit to me you did it. Admit you got your sick rocks off by molesting your niece."

"No."

I squeeze a little harder, his labored breathing becoming a wheeze. "No?"

His face starts to turn red, his fingers trying to claw my hands from his neck. My own conscience questions what I'm doing, but all I can think of is sweet Lucy without a mom. All I can hear is the hurt in Vaughn's voice when she so much as mentions her childhood here in this mausoleum.

"Still a no?" I ask, worried he's not going to care how far I take this high-stakes game of chicken.

"Yes. *God.* Fuck. *Yes.* I did it. I fucking did it. Are you happy?" Spittle flies off his lips and hits my cheek.

"Did what?" I demand.

"Had sex with Samantha."

I release my hold on him and wipe the spittle off with the back of my hand. It takes all I have to look at him, my stomach churning, my heart hurting.

"You sick fucking bastard." Fury riots through every single part of me as I look at the wasted man. "I would add that if you so much as go *near* another little girl, the same goes with the contents of this locker. I'll turn everything over to the police." I run my eyes up and down the sorry sight of him. "But I guess Samantha made sure that wouldn't hap-pen again with where she aimed, now didn't she?"

He grits his teeth as my smile widens.

"If you ever come near me again . . . ," he says, his face a mask of fury.

"You'll what?" I laugh. "It'll be because you broke your word, and I'll be at your sentencing in court. You're a pathetic piece of shit. May you rot in hell."

I head toward the library door, and once I have it open, I turn back to face him one last time. "For your information, Samantha didn't tell me a thing. I never had the pleasure of meeting her. You sealed her fate the minute you chose to violate her. You sealed your own as well." I remove my cell phone from my pocket so he can see that the record button on the screen has been engaged. "You go back on your word to me, I have your confession right here."

Without another word, I move to the foyer, where Beatrice is heading toward me.

"Leaving so soon?" she asks cheerfully.

"Yes. Poor James isn't looking too well. You might want to check on him."

Just as I pass through the gates and take a breath of non-creepified air, my cell rings. I chuckle when I look at the screen and wonder just how fast good ol' James rallied up the Dillinger family.

"Chance. Brother. Are your senses on high alert? I step foot in Greenwich, and it's like you know I'm in your town."

"I know, and it's about damn fucking time. You didn't call. You didn't write." He laughs.

"Yeah. I wasn't sure how long my business was going to last."

"You done now? Can we have drinks? Dinner with my fam? What?"

I think of the woman I have at home. The woman who is a complicated mess of gorgeous chaos, feisty innocence, and flawed perfection. She's the one I'd much rather be with right now.

I look back at the house behind me and hope to never see it again.

Fuck that. I will see it. In fact, I'm going to buy the place when the old buzzard dies, and then I'll burn it to the ground.

For Samantha.

For Vaughn.

For Lucy.

Demolishing to ashes a past that never should have been would be worth every goddamn penny.

"Thanks for the offer, Chance, but I have a sour taste in my mouth after my meeting."

"One of those fuckers you'd like to wrap your hands around their neck to shut them up?" He laughs.

"Exactly. One of those."

"So that's it? In. Out. Done?"

"I'm sorry, but yes, that's it."

"Just like the college days. Nothing changes," he jokes.

Interestingly enough, everything has, though. My thoughts flash to Vaughn and the long drive home. To how I can't wait to see her and look in her eyes knowing I've taken one more step so that she never has to worry about that prick again . . . even though I'm not even sure I'll tell her.

Now Carter's threat holds no weight.

"Hey, Lockhart? You still there?"

"Yeah. Sorry. I was just staring at a piece of real estate I have my eye on."

"Here?"

"Mmm. Yes."

"Lots of gorgeous places to buy."

"Not this one. I'll raze it to the ground."

"Really? Here in Greenwich?" His shock would be even greater if he knew what I was looking at.

"Yep. Here in Greenwich."

"So you'll be back, then?"

"Someday, yes."

CHAPTER
FORTY-FIVE
Vaughn

"So that's it?" Ella asks me, her grin beaming, her enthusiasm borderline annoying.

"I guess so."

Shouldn't I feel excited? I made this—Wicked Ways—into something that someone else wants. Something they are paying handsomely for. Shouldn't I be proud of that?

I am.

I'm just exhausted in ways that no one can ever understand. There will be no more looking over my shoulder constantly. No more fear I'll mix up who I am with the wrong person. No more hiding the money and trying not to trigger interest by the police despite all the precautions.

But it's also a little bittersweet. Despite all the cons, there was something about being Madam Vee, something about running the business, that was empowering.

I smile at Ella. "If all goes as planned, it will be official by the end of next week. Upon your wire, I will transfer my book of business and everything else with it to you."

"That's great," Ella says. "And the legal paperwork?"

I think of Ryker and the shock that's going to be on his face when I ask him if he can help me write up the contract selling my assets to her. I don't know why the thought fills me with even more pride.

"I'll get the paperwork drawn up. You can have your lawyer look at it beforehand."

"Perfect."

"I think it would be smart to hold a joint conference call with all my ladies. That way they can see that I support you and your success, and so they don't have to worry about how things might adjust as ownership changes."

"I think that's a great idea. Thank you. I'll look at my calendar when I get back to my office and let you know some dates that work for me."

"Sounds good."

She reaches across the table and shakes my hand. "Do you mind me asking . . . why sell now when you're just starting to make a notable name for yourself?"

"Sometimes you just know when to quit." I stand from the table. "And it's time to quit."

I think of my immunity deal. How I'm walking away, hopefully unscathed. How you can only tempt fate—and the law—so many times before you end up being caught.

"I admire you for walking away."

With one more smile and a bittersweet tug on my heart, I exit the bar.

Ironically, it's the same one I met Ryker in that first night. I think of the nerves I felt, of the anger I held, and of the fear I had upstairs in the hotel room.

So much has changed since that night in so many ways. All for the better. All for the future.

It feels so strange to walk across the hotel lobby. To feel relief and not have the weight of the world resting on my shoulders.

Sure, Ryker paying off my bills will put me in a better standing with social services. Add to that the letter the FBI said they'd be providing today on my behalf. Adopting Lucy is far from a done deal, but for the first time since I started this process, I feel like I might just be seeing the light of day.

Now to head home and wait for Ryker to tell me he's back in town so we can celebrate all these things. And maybe I'll be able to do a little explaining about what was going on that he didn't know about.

That's assuming I get the all clear from Special Agent Noah that everything I provided them with panned out.

Desperate to get out of this costume and wig for what might be the last time, I enter the elevator to head to my room, where my Vaughn clothes are.

Even now, even with immunity, I still feel the need to be cautious doing the change-in-the-hotel-room thing.

Old habits die hard, I guess.

Trying to be as inconspicuous as possible, I keep my head down in the elevator and scan through the emails on my phone. Emails on an account I'll no longer have to care about.

People exit floor by floor, ding after ding.

"I can't remember the last time I saw you dressed like this, Vee. It's truly stunning."

I jump when Carter's voice hits my ears and more so when his hand slides into the crook of my arm. I immediately try to yank it away, but his grip holds firm.

"Uh-uh-uh. Not so fast. You and I have a few things we need to discuss."

The elevator car is empty. The panic coursing through me is almost debilitating.

"Go to hell."

His chuckle is low and unforgiving, and I yelp out as he tightens his grip hard enough to leave bruises. "Don't cause a scene, and I'll play nice."

He pushes me off the car when the door opens and steers me to my room. "Key," he demands.

I stare at him and don't obey.

I yelp as I'm slammed up against the hotel room's door, my arm twisted against my back, my face pressed to the cool wood. My vision goes white for a beat from the pain as the heat of his breath hits my ear.

"Pretty please, Vaughn. Be difficult. Give me a reason to punish you more than I already want to. Your cry is my aphrodisiac." He slides a hand over my ass, and I try to buck him off me, but he yanks my arm farther up my back in response. "The fucking key, Vaughn."

My purse is ripped off my neck, the thin strap snapping without much force. His body is pressed against mine, but he manages to open the door with his free hand. I fall forward as it gives, and I land on my hands and knees on the floor.

I scramble up immediately but not before the door is slammed shut. "I warned you, Vaughn. I have eyes everywhere in this town. *I know everything.* I have a snitch in the courthouse. Immunity in exchange for goods on me? Really? You sold me out to the fucking feds? And I thought we were so much closer than that."

My back is against the wall farthest from him. The moment is so very similar to the first time I faced him down in a hotel room, but this time the stakes seem so much higher. So much more damaging.

My eyes scan every damn thing in the room around us to see what I can use as a weapon.

"I wouldn't even attempt it," he warns as I see the phone on the nightstand, the lamp I could swing, anything and everything.

"What do you want?" My voice betrays me. Fear woven into false strength.

"Oh, you know what I want. We both know that. I'm over playing the games. You tried to hurt me today. Now it's my turn to hurt you. And apparently time is of the essence, since someone will be knocking down my door to serve warrants soon."

He smacks his hands and rubs them together before starting to undo his belt as he moves toward me.

CHAPTER FORTY-SIX

Ryker

"Where are you?" Stuart's voice comes through the speaker on my car.

"Stuck in this goddamn traffic. The Midtown nightmare on this goddamn island." I slam on my horn, frustrated with my lack of movement and tired of driving. "It's like the universe is—"

"The Chatwal. Now."

And there's something about his tone that doesn't have me bristling at being ordered around and silences me immediately.

"Stuart?" So much is loaded in his name, but *I already know.*

Vaughn.

It has to be Vaughn.

I lay on my horn and cut across traffic as best as I can. A cacophony of horns explodes in response, and if I had ten fucks to give I still wouldn't give any.

Five blocks away.

"She was in a meeting in the hotel. Dressed in the wig. I watched her for a bit and ran to use the head when she was wrapping up. *I need it now!*" he orders someone on the other end of the line and then sighs out a *Fuck* when all I hear is an *I'm sorry, sir.* "The manager. Get him."

"Stuart, what the fuck is going on?" Visions fill my head of some bastard manhandling her. She was dressed as Vee.

"I caught a glimpse of her getting on the elevator. Carter slid in right before the doors shut."

Dread drops through every part of me.

Four blocks.

"Where the hell are they, Stu?"

Thoughts. Visions. The worst. All fill my head, and I can't even venture to think that I'm the one responsible for this. That I'm the one who threw her to the wolves for a client who was playing games with me somehow from the get-go.

"I don't know. I'm trying to get a manager to let me know if either of them has rented a room. It's not exactly the easiest fucking thing to do here."

"Bribe them. I don't care how fucking much. Do your goddamn job and bribe them!" I shout the words even though I know it's not his fault.

There are muffled sounds on his end of the connection as he tries to bargain with the desk clerk.

Three blocks.

"They're looking through their database right now."

"Tell them to go fucking faster."

He has her.

My fucking God, he has her.

I swerve the car into the first valet podium I see and throw a hundred-dollar bill at them before taking off down the street in a full-on sprint.

CHAPTER FORTY-SEVEN
Vaughn

"The FBI knows I'm here," I lie as I try to move left and then right, but I know my back is against the wall, and that's the worst place it can be.

His eyes are dark, his body unimpressive but definitely more powerful than mine as he closes the distance.

A smile plays at the corners of his lips as his eyes devour every inch of me. My stomach churns.

And then he lunges.

I cry out as he grabs the front of my dress and yanks it down. My immediate reaction is to punch out, but he has my wrists in his hands, my attempt more than pathetic, my fear stronger and more potent than anything I've ever felt before.

"No wire here, sweet Vaughn." My breath hitches, and my head jerks from side to side as he leans in and licks a line up my cheek.

Bile revolts in my stomach and threatens to rise.

"They know I'm here. I'm supposed to meet with them afterward. I'm—"

"To discuss me?" He laughs. "You naive cunt. Do you really think they're going to let a whore like you off the hook after they get what they want from me? Do you really think they're not going to take credit for whatever it is you told them? Throw you into the fire to get all the glory?"

His words strike fear in me, much the same as how Noah and Abel made me feel, but so very different because of what he wants to do to me.

"I don't care who gets the credit so long as you get what you deserve."

I yelp when his hand smacks against my cheek. The sting on my cheekbone is real and painful, and it takes a minute for me to steady myself.

"Why couldn't you just play as perfectly into my plan as Ryker did, huh?"

"What do you mean?" I ask.

"Do you know how easy it was for Bianca to sell him on representing her? To pretend that she hates me and wanted a divorce? Us both vying for him to take us on as clients? He washed that money perfectly clean for us. What better place to hide the money we received than to give it as a retainer for a bogus case? And to top it all off, your little boyfriend helped to investigate me for her." His laugh sounds off.

"I don't . . ." My mind spins with the notion that they used Ryker. How we played perfectly into their hands without ever knowing it.

"His investigating me was our little measure to see if anyone else was noticing our scheme. Ryker has one of the best investigators out there, so if he couldn't sniff out the bribe, then no one could. Besides, it allowed him to gain a few billable hours for his trouble, so when he returned the remainder of our retainer, it didn't look like a perfect two mil."

I just stare at him, lips lax and thoughts racing as I try to fathom what they did. And I'm sure the haze of fear being here, in this situation, doesn't help to expedite my thought process.

He grins. "It's pretty brilliant, if I do say so myself."

"So that was the game?" I ask, dumfounded by their disposal of people. "Use him to hide your bribe?"

"Mmm. What we didn't plan on is you and the call log." He runs a hand up the side of my torso, and I fight to remain calm.

"You piss off enough people, betray them, someone's bound to return the favor," I say, finding my resolve.

"Exactly." His chuckle sends fear ricocheting through me. "I'm returning the favor to you right now."

With my hands still cuffed in one of his and his forearm pressed against my shoulders, pinning me to the wall, he slides a hand between my thighs.

My entire body tenses.

"Oh, this is going to be fun."

This is real.

So real.

The tears come. The random babbling as his fingers dig into me through the fabric of my clothes. I scream for help. For him to stop. But every movement, every show of fight, has him growing harder against my leg.

I can smell my own terror in the room almost as certainly as I can smell his arousal, and both make me dizzy and nauseous.

"Will Ryker still want you when I'm through with you?" His voice is a growl in my ear. "He's not really into *used* things—that's why Bianca and I had so much fun using him. Nothing like showing the best attorney in all of New York that he's far from fucking invincible. First with the representation and now with what I'm going to do to you."

I grit my teeth and fist my hands as I try with every ounce of my being to push him off me.

"Will you cry when I fuck you?" He lifts a brow. "I think you will. All tough on the outside but not an ounce of strength when shit gets real." He presses a kiss to my lips as I buck my head back and forth. "Will you fight me? Will you lock your legs around my waist and try to prevent me from ruining you?" He yanks my skirt off me, the expensive fabric giving way without an ounce of fight. "I love the sound of a hand hitting flesh . . . it turns me on. So go ahead and hurt. I'll get off on it."

This time he shoves his tongue inside my mouth, and I make a conscious decision to let him. It's the hardest thing I've ever had to do, but chomping down as hard as I can on it is probably the most satisfying.

He cries out and lets go of me as a reflex to the pain I've caused him.

I make my move. The door is too far away, and I'd have to go through him to get there, so I run to the nightstand, my sights set on the lamp.

He tackles me from behind with his entire body. My screams fill the room as I kick and claw and fight while his maniacal laughter echoes around us.

And then, as if I'm in a dream, Carter is off me.

There's a roar in my ears I can't comprehend from where I'm lying facedown against the carpet, one heel on, one heel off, the cool air of the room sliding over my bare skin.

Everything seems to go in snapshots of time.

Everything feels so very fuzzy. So very slow.

The textured carpet against my cheek.

The tenor of Ryker's voice. At least I think it's Ryker's voice, because it sounds like him, but with a rage I've never heard before.

My body being sore. So very sore. My fingernails broken. My knuckles raw.

The sight of my wig lying partially under the bed. The black hair so dark against the light carpet.

The heat on my cheeks from where my tears have streaked down them.

And then I know it's Ryker.

His voice saying my name.

His hands cradling me as he picks me up ever so gently and sets me on the bed.

His arms wrapping around me and holding on like he's so very afraid to let me go.

"I'm here. You're okay. He's never going to hurt you again." These words are on repeat on his lips. The repetition of them is almost as soothing to me as the feel of his arms.

There is more commotion in the room or hallway or somewhere close enough I don't see but can hear. The click of handcuffs. The groans of pain. The Miranda warning being recited.

"Please tell me you're okay?" The break in Ryker's voice all but snaps the hold I have on my own sanity. But he doesn't lean back, he doesn't look me over, almost as if he's wary of discovering truths he's afraid to acknowledge. That he didn't get here in time.

"I'm okay," I whisper, my voice hoarse from screaming. "I'm okay." I repeat it again, almost as much for my sake as it is for him. "I'm okay."

His fingers tense, and then there's a hitch in his breath as he pulls back his own emotions. As he fights the same fear I have. As he realizes this is all over now.

CHAPTER FORTY-EIGHT
Ryker

"Can I take her home now?"

The detective looks my way and holds up his finger for me to wait one more second.

I don't want to wait one more second. I want to get her the fuck out of this hotel room with its yanked-down curtains and knocked-over vase and broken lamp. All reminders of what that bastard tried to do to her. All reminders of how hard she fought.

And that has nothing on the rage I feel when I see the huge red welt on her cheek or the pieces of her clothing ripped apart on the floor.

I'm antsy and can't sit still and can't stand, and all I want is my arms around her so I can physically touch her and feel that she is here and whole and a little shaken but untouched in every other way.

With his digital camera in hand that documented every bump and bruise that mars her, he moves my way. "You guys can head out, but I have to stay while they process the scene. The FBI agents in charge are also headed in right now."

"FBI?" I startle at the word. "What does the FBI want with this?" I rack my brain and can only make assumptions.

"I had the same question when Ms. Sanders asked me to contact them." He shakes his head. "I got off the phone with them a few moments ago, and it seems the senator was under investigation for some things. Ms. Sanders here was the one who gave them the information to bring him down." His smile is tight, his expression stoic, as my mind races out of control. "You didn't hear that from me, but it might help to explain things a bit more."

I stare at him as if I'm really listening. As the past few weeks and Vaughn's sudden changes in demeanor run through my mind. Is this what was going on the whole time? Was she a pawn in this game of theirs?

Then it hits me: the call log.

Is that what this is all about?

So many questions but none that I can ask him, so I just nod as if what he said makes sense when it abso-fucking-lutely doesn't.

I look over to where the officer is finishing up with Vaughn. The white bathrobe swamping her frame and making her seem so innocent is in contrast to the red welt on her cheek.

"How's she doing?" I ask, hating that they want me away from her while they interview and question and document what that bastard did to her.

"She's a tough cookie, I'll give her that. He's got a good hundred pounds on her, and she held him off. If it weren't for you, though . . ." He shakes his head and glances back at her.

"I don't want to think about it."

"Neither do I. You're free to go now, Vaughn," he says and then moves over to the scene investigators.

I watch her move toward me. Her gait seems a little ginger, and her soft smile is one of reassurance that I'll tell her I don't need, but hell if it doesn't make me feel a little bit better seeing it.

"You okay?"

"I think I've been asked that a hundred times in the past hour." She smiles a bit wider. "I've been better."

"Well, at least you're honest." I wrap my arm around her shoulders and gently pull her against me. A million questions run through my mind, but I know now is not the time or place. "The detective said the FBI is on their way."

She tenses momentarily and nods. "Mmm-hmm. There's so much I need to tell you."

I bet there is.

And it kills me to know that whatever the hell was going on, she was going through it alone. That she couldn't tell me. That I couldn't help her. That I wasn't the one protecting her from it all.

But I shove it down.

"Let's get you home," I murmur, pressing a kiss to the side of her head.

"I need—I need a few minutes to myself, please."

There are people from the crime scene milling in the hallway, but I turn to look at her. My hands are on her face, my eyes level with hers. She still looks scared, still lost, still traumatized, and I hate that I don't know what the fuck to do to help her right now.

"Tell me what you need, and I'll give it to you. Do you want me to drive you home? Do you want my driver to take you home so you can have some time to yourself on the way there, and I'll follow alone? Do you want me to ride beside you and just hold on and not let go?"

The third has my vote, because her being out of touching range isn't an option for me . . . but this isn't about me right now. This is about giving her whatever she needs so she can manage her emotions.

This is about her having some kind of control in this situation when I'm sure she feels like she has none.

"Will you stay with me?" she asks, her voice trembling and my goddamn heart breaking.

"You're not going to get rid of me that easy," I murmur and press a kiss to her forehead.

"I still need to be alone. To process. To . . . to just—I don't know."

"Okay. Whatever you need, Vaughn."

"Can you have Al take me home while you grab your things? I just . . . I just need a shower and to be in my place . . . and I want to know you have what you need to stay a few days with me."

I fight back the tears that threaten when I don't fucking cry. Vaughn's vulnerability is such a foreign thing on her that I hate seeing it.

I hate that this fucker did that to her.

I hate that I let him.

"Of course," I finally say when I collect my cool enough to be able to speak. "Of course."

CHAPTER
FORTY-NINE
Vaughn

Al doesn't drive very far before everything hits me.

Six blocks maybe before the tears come.

All of them.

The scared-shitless ones.

The self-pity ones.

The I-was-almost-raped ones.

The ones for the concern on Ryker's face when he looks at me.

I'm lying across the rear seat of the town car, my palms on the leather, my face on the backs of my hands as my shoulders heave and my soul hurts.

And I cry for what almost happened and what could have happened.

I cry for things I never had and things I never knew I wanted but now have.

I don't know how long I sob, but I don't care.

Al closes the divider at some point to allow me my privacy. To allow me to grieve.

Both needed for me to realize that I have so very much to live for.

And when I'm done, when the tear tracks are stiff on my cheeks and my breath hitches every few seconds and my cheekbone aches like a bitch . . . Al pulls into my driveway with perfect timing.

CHAPTER FIFTY

Ryker

"Anything else, Mr. Lockhart?" Bella looks at me hesitantly as she sets the files I asked for on the edge of my desk.

My shirt's ripped, and there's blood on my knuckles. I'm sure I look like a fucking wreck.

"No. Thank you." I start to sort through the rest of the shit I need to bring, and when I look back up, she's still standing there with her notepad clutched to her chest and huge eyes like Dorothy facing down the wizard. "Yes?"

"Is she okay? *Is Ms. Sanders okay?*"

My hands still for the first time since I stormed in here barking orders. Her question is the same one I've asked myself on repeat. "She'll be okay, yes. It might take a while, but I'll do everything in my power to make sure she is."

"Good. I'm glad. I like her." Her smile is cautious, as she never opines on anything about my personal life. "Would you like me to order some flowers or food via Instacart or anything to be delivered to her house so she doesn't have to leave?"

My head spins with the suggestions. "Can you ask me that later, Bella? Right now I'm having a hard time focusing on anything other than getting to her."

"Of course."

"Thank you. They're good ideas . . . I just can't . . . thank you."

"Maybe you should—" She points to the box under the credenza. "Maybe you should bring her those things back. A reminder of good memories . . . or not."

"Thanks for your help, Bella. That's all." I don't look up. Can't. Too much shit in my head. Too much emotion on my face. Too much vulnerability for the guy who's always an asshole.

I move to the box once she leaves, but as I stare at it, all I keep seeing is Vaughn battered and bruised. All I remember is barging into that damn room and seeing him on top of her. All I hear is the desperation and fear in her screams for help.

The rage is so strong I have to refocus on my tasks every few seconds or I get lost in it.

I open the lid and laugh. Stupid mementos I sent her. Kitschy shit that reminds me of *before*, when from here on out I only want to think of *after*.

No more Carter. No more fuckups. No more thinking relationships don't work when I have her. No more wondering if I love her when I clearly fucking know.

The fury grows stronger.

A type of fury I can't describe and that punching drywall will nowhere near help. My body vibrates from it in such a way that my heart pounds and my pulse roars in my ears. Without thought and with a need to release the emotion, I kick the box as hard as I can.

Shit goes flying.

Stuffed animals and dried flowers and cards land fucking every-where. All the stuff I never took the time to unpack from the box and go through item by item.

What the hell? What is all this crap?

I look around at the contents strewn around my office like Valentine's Day threw up. I sent her a few of these items, but the rest? What the fuck is this stuff?

Lucy must have accidentally shoved stuff in here. That's the logical explanation. She saw my name on the box and figured she'd send me something to make me happy . . . just like the necklace she let me borrow.

She'll want this all back.

But it's when I look down at one of the cards at my feet that my heart drops for what feels like the second time in three hours.

We're good together. You'll see soon enough why I can't live without you.

What the fuck is this? I pick up as many cards as I can. A few are from me and were attached to flowers I sent . . . but the others? The others make my stomach churn.

These are not from me.

The dates on the top corners of the cards are from during the time frame we've been together, but not a single one of these is from me.

I rifle through them, each one alarming me more than the last.

These weren't sent by someone who was in love with Vaughn.

More like someone who was obsessed with her.

CHAPTER
FIFTY-ONE
Vaughn

It feels like ages since I've been home when it's only been hours. And what a difference those few hours have made in my life.

With a sigh, I drop my purse with its broken strap and my cell phone on the kitchen counter. I yelp when I see the figure move into the doorway of my office.

"Joey? What are you doing here?" My hand is over my thumping heart, my fingers holding closed the neckline of the hotel's robe.

"I have a key for emergencies. Remember?"

"Is something wrong? Is Lucy okay—"

"Fine. She's fine."

"Then what's the emergency?" I ask as I stare at him and fight the sudden unease tickling at the back of my neck.

"You know I don't care about your other job, right?" His words stop me cold in my tracks as he steps toward me.

Other job? *Does he mean Wicked Ways?* How in the hell does he know about my other job?

I take a deep breath, hating the feeling that slides up my spine. Fearing what he's doing here. Cautious how to play this.

"Joey? What's the emergency?" I say the words, dreading the answer.

"*You.* You're the emergency."

"I'm not—"

"Come on, Vaughn. It's me. The one who knows you. *All of you.*" He takes a step closer, and I freeze. "Sometimes when I know you're at the club, I'll come over here and just sit for a bit. I'll look at your stuff on your desk."

My stomach pitches. "The stuff on my desk?"

"Yeah. You don't have to be ashamed about Wicked Ways or that you're trying to get into college. You're flushed right now. There's no need to be embarrassed. It's okay that I know. I support you in every way possible. I love that about you."

It takes me a second to actually process what is happening. It takes more than that for me to comprehend that I'm not just being jumpy. The man is in my house.

"Joey, it's a bit creepy that you come and look at my things." It's the understatement of the year, but it's the gentlest way I can think of to say, *What the ever-loving fuck?*

"I just want to get to know you better is all." He smiles softly, but to me he looks like he's a man who has lost touch with reality.

"We know each other plenty." I make a move toward the kitchen island where the knives are.

"You're good right where you are," he says, the tone of his voice irritated and edgy all of a sudden, and then it's soft and coaxing when he speaks his next words. "When I sit at your desk, when I run my fingers over your penmanship, when I stare at all of your pictures on your shelves, I pretend like you've let me into your life. Like you love me how I love you. It lets me feel close to you."

My heart revolts, and my eyes flicker over to my knife block again.

This can't be happening.

Sweet Joey who takes care of Lucy and who has always been so kind can't be doing this.

"Don't you want to feel close to me too?" he asks, expression hopeful but eyes still dead.

I can't take much more today.

"I'm not sure how that's supposed to make me feel," I say, taking a step slowly.

My cell phone vibrates on the counter.

"Let's leave that there," he says with a chilling smile. "Did *he* do that to you?"

"What?" My hand flies to my cheek, and I realize what he's talking about. "No, it's nothing. Ryker didn't—"

"Don't lie to me!" He picks up a glass that's sitting in the dish rack beside him and throws it across the kitchen. It shatters into a million pieces when it slams into the wall beside my head. I shriek in reaction, my hands flying to cover my ears.

My pulse thunders. My hands tremble.

"Do you think you can learn to love me too?"

"Joey."

"Just think of what a perfect little family we could be. You and me and Lucy. We could live here or move out to the country and live off the land. We'd need no one and nothing but us. We could even have a child together." There's a sickening smile that spreads on his lips, and I just blink rapidly as I continue to try to process what is happening right now.

I'm shell-shocked. Trying to understand. Trying to fathom. I take a closer look at him. At the sweat on his brow when it's not hot in here. His jerky movements. "Is everything okay, Joey?"

"I wouldn't hurt you like he does, you know." But this time when he takes a step toward me, he pulls a gun from the back of his waistband and points it at me.

Fuck. *Fuck. Fuck!*

I have a hard time drawing in a breath as fear takes hold. One that is so very different and so much the same as the one I felt hours ago with Carter.

Was it really only hours ago?

This can't be happening. That's all I keep thinking to myself. *This can't be happening.*

"Ryker didn't hurt me. I—it's too much to get into. It was a man named Carter Preston."

"That's what happens in abusive relationships, Vaughn. You lie to protect the abuser."

"I'm not lying. It really was—"

"I love you more than he does. I love you, and yet I don't see any of the things I sent you here. You kept two cards on the desk, but both are from him. Did you throw mine out? Am I not good enough for you?" Each word resonates with more anger than the last.

"Joey—"

"No!"

Another glass from the dish rack slams against the wall.

When I duck, I see my phone and know I need to get to it to call for help.

"Don't tell me you don't want me too. I know you do. Do you know how it felt to come and pick up Lucy and see all of the things I bought you on display like you were proud of me? *Like you loved me?*"

Mayday.

It's the only word I can think of.

The one I have my girls text me when they're in trouble.

The one Lola texted me that started all of this. Me confronting Carter. Me meeting Ryker. Me being here right now.

Mayday.

CHAPTER FIFTY-TWO

Ryker

The shit I came to get from my office is forgotten as I run out of it—past a startled Bella and out the glass door—my cell ringing in my ear.

"Pick up the phone, Vaughn," I mutter as I wait for the fucking elevator to climb the floors. "Pick up the goddamn phone."

It goes to voice mail, and I slam my hand against the closed metal doors in frustration.

I try her house phone, but it doesn't ring. It just gives the busy signal.

I call her cell again. The voice mail picks up after two rings.

Within seconds my cell is ringing again. "Al!" I shout into it when he picks up. "Where are you? Did you drop Vaughn off?"

"Yeah, man. I walked her to the door. She went in. Why? What's wrong?"

I squeeze my eyes shut and fear I'm overreacting, but there is something that tells me I'm not. My gut instinct. A hunch. Something is telling me the universe is having a *Fuck with Vaughn Day* and she's in trouble.

"How far are you from her house?"

"I'm on the bridge headed back to the city."

"Fuck!" I shout and slam a palm against the wall. He can't turn around. He can't get back to her any faster than I can. *"Fuck!"*

I hang up and call her again.

If there wasn't something wrong, she'd answer.

She knows I'm worried. She knows to pick up so I don't freak the hell out.

Her voice fills the phone. "This is Vaughn. Please leave a message."

"Vaughn. Something is wrong. That box of stuff you sent back. I didn't give most of that shit to you. Someone is . . . if you get this, please just lock the doors and—"

My phone beeps in my ear, and I look down at the lone word that Vaughn just sent me.

Mayday.

And then the floor drops out from beneath me.

CHAPTER FIFTY-THREE

Vaughn

"I said don't touch the phone," he screams at me, his mental state unraveling more and more with each passing second.

"I was just turning it off," I lie, the text sent to Ryker in Joey's moment of panic over the unicorn he bought Lucy that he now can't find. "I can't stand the sound of it vibrating against the counter."

Please get my text, Ryker.

It's just as crazy as it sounds.

Almost so insane that I want to press my fingers to my eyes and cry and laugh all at the same time. I'm so exhausted, so burned out on crazy today that I'm almost in a state of total disbelief. Utter and total disbelief.

There's no way this can be happening.

But it is.

"What I can't figure out, Vaughny," he says, gesticulating with the gun in his hand, his feet moving constantly to abate losing his grip, "is how do I know if you really love me like I love you? I've tried everything to get you to notice me, and you still go for that asshole. You still want him instead of me."

"Joey." I'm breathless when I say his name, holding a hand to my head. "I think I'm going to throw up." I double over to sell the lie. "It's from today. I think it's all too much. Ohhhh," I moan out in pain. "The bathroom. I need the bathroom."

I run down the hall without his consent, more than aware that there is a gun aimed somewhere at my back, and slam the guest bathroom door shut.

And lock it.

"Vaughn? Don't do anything funny in there. I'll break down this door if I have to."

I moan louder and mimic vomiting sounds instead of responding.

There's a man with a gun on the other side of the door professing his love to me, and the only thing I can think of is that I'm all feared out right now.

I don't have another ounce of it to give someone.

I don't have anything left to feel.

Is this what it feels like to go crazy? To think the most rational thoughts at the most irrational times?

"One second." I moan the words. "I just need to lie on the tile for a moment. I'm sweating. And dizzy."

"Are you okay?" His concern—however misconstrued it is—is palpable through the closed door.

"I don't know." Another moan. Then another fake vomit followed by the flush of the toilet.

Joey is harmless. He won't hurt me.

Don't be stupid, Vaughn. He has a fucking gun in his hand.

But he won't.

You can't make crazy people sane, Vaughn.

But he's also not the smartest cookie in the jar. Anyone who watches television would know to never let the object of your obsessed affection be alone.

Bad things happen. Strategies are hatched. Escapes are planned.

"I'm not liking this. I need you to come out where I can see you." There's an urgency tingeing his voice.

"One more second."

I'm out of patience with being afraid.

I've been the victim too many times in my life.

Not now.

Not ever again.

I scan my own bathroom for anything that can be used as a weapon. Sadly, I can say that didn't turn out all too well for me earlier today with the lamp on the nightstand. Not many people get a second chance at it.

I laugh out loud at that. I can't help myself.

"What's going on in there? You're laughing." He pounds on the door, causing it to bow under his force. "Is someone else in there?"

Yep, he's definitely losing it.

But I feel like I am too.

"No." And then I moan loader.

Bang. Bang. Bang. "Open the door. I don't care how sick you are."

I grab hold of the top of the toilet tank cover and unlock the door seconds before hunching over with my back to Joey.

"Ooohhhhh," I continue on, each time louder than the last.

He jiggles the door for the first time, probably thinking it has been open the whole time.

"Vaughn, are you okay?" I try not to jerk in repulsion at the feel of his hand on my back. At the sudden compassion in his deranged voice.

And then with a roar and with every ounce of effort I have left in my aching arms, I swing the lid of the toilet tank at Joey's head.

There's a huge sickening thud when I connect.

Joey crumples to the ground instantly.

I kick the gun from his hand and run down the hallway just as the police break through the front door.

And then I collapse on the floor.

The adrenaline gone.

The fight all fought out.

CHAPTER
FIFTY-FOUR
Vaughn

"You're a goddamn warrior is what you are." Ryker's smile is soft, his eyes still guarded as he turns me around and pulls me between his thighs so that my back is against his front.

The city's lights are alive around us as we soak in his bathtub.

"A part of me is jealous that you got to take him out and I didn't. I was having a pretty shitty day until then and could have used him to get my aggression out."

"Mmm." I lean my head back on his shoulder and close my eyes. "This has to be the oddest conversation ever had between a couple."

"I told you we were far from the norm." I can hear the smile in his voice when he says it.

"Very far." I enjoy the feel of him and the total irony of how we are now versus how we spent our day. Almost as if it never happened. But I know. I'll remember. And by the way his arms are wrapped around me, he does too.

"It was the shittiest of shitty days. Don't you think?"

"Let's see. You selling your business. A crazy senator. The deranged counselor. A meeting with the FBI to clear you of everything." He shakes his head with a chuckle.

"Now we just need to find out what dirt Carter threatened me with, and we should be good."

"It doesn't matter what he had on you," Ryker says, his lips pressed against the back of my head. "Your immunity deal has you protected from him saying anything."

"I'd still like to know what he thought he—"

"It's all taken care of."

"What?" I startle and try to turn to look at him, but he just keeps me in place. "What do you—"

"There was some misfiled paperwork down at the Greenwich court-house that Stuart found. Warrants for theft, *I think*."

"It wasn't—Sam took—"

"No explanations needed, Vaughn." He presses a kiss to my bare shoulder. "None. It took a little finagling, but I was able to petition the prosecuting attorney to get the warrants dismissed. It's nothing you need to worry about now."

I close my eyes momentarily and wonder if this is what relief feels like. All my ghosts are gone. All my past protected against so I can have a future. And while a part of me wants to question Ryker on why he didn't tell me any of this in the first place, I almost don't care.

It's done.

It's over with.

It's time to have and live a life for me now.

"Oh." It's all I can manage to say as the day hits me.

"Definitely the shittiest of shitty days," he reiterates.

"But now we're here," I murmur.

"There's nowhere else I'd rather be."

"Lucy's going to be heartbroken when Joey's no longer at the facility," I murmur, my mind on her.

"At least she'll be with you soon. She won't need him anyway." He presses a kiss to the back of my head, his words a reminder that Lucy will officially be mine soon.

"The only non-shitty part of the day," I murmur as my heart swells.

"Yes. Besides this, right now, of course."

"Is it sad that a part of me was waiting for Brian to show up to profess his love for me too? I mean Carter, Joey . . . who else?"

"It'd be par for the course," he murmurs.

"Not funny *at all*." But there's a smile on my lips. Who goes through the day I had and has a smile on their lips?

It's because of Ryker.

"The only one allowed to profess their love for you, Vaughn Sanders, is me."

I slide my fingers through his and cross both of our arms over my chest.

"I can agree to that."

"You better." Another press of a kiss to my shoulder. "Thank you for letting me take care of you."

Those words are so softly spoken compared to the loud screams that filled the day. To Joey's accusations when he came to. To the abusive words that Carter spewed. But Ryker's words are the only ones I hear.

And a part of me thinks there is way more stuffed into those nine words than I'll ever know.

"I'm sorry I didn't get there sooner." The guilt that laces his voice despite my telling him this isn't on him eats at me.

"I'm glad you didn't get there later," I counter.

"Look at you, turning all glass-half-full on me."

"What can I say? I'm a work in progress."

"*We* are a work in progress."

And with those words, Ryker turns me some so his lips can find mine in a kiss as tender as it is packed with love.

The perfect way to end the shittiest of shitty days.

In his arms.
By my side.
Defending me.
Protecting me.
Loving me.
Giving me *the unexpected* I never knew I needed.

EPILOGUE
Vaughn

One Year Later

"What is all this?" I ask as I walk out to the patio. The warm breeze is coming off the ocean, the night clear, the fire bright.

"S'mores," Lucy says with a grin, lips smeared in gooey marshmallows.

"Mmm. Your favorite!" I press a kiss to the top of her head as I look over to Ryker across the fire.

His smile is warm, his eyes alive, his body completely and utterly relaxed.

"Why do you have that look, Lockhart?" I ask.

"Because I'm proud of you," he says.

"Proud of me?"

"Yep." He nods. "Your first semester toward your teaching credential is done, and you're at the top of your class." My cheeks flush from his praise. "I'd say that is more than enough reason to celebrate."

"We're celebrating, are we?" I tease.

"Yes! Yes! Yes!" Lucy all but jumps up and down in her seat.

"I have a surprise for you," Ryker says.

"You do?"

He nods and crooks his finger before pointing to the flat squares lining the retaining wall that faces the ocean.

"What are . . ." But my voice fades when I see the paper lanterns, the lighter, and the Sharpie sitting there. I look back at him, my grin widening.

He rises and presses a kiss to my shoulder. "You ready to give me your wish and your worry, Sanders?" he asks.

Tears well in my eyes, because I can't believe that he remembered. That he took the time to do this.

I nod, and we get Lucy with us over to the wall with chocolate smeared on her cheek and excitement bubbling up inside.

"You ready, Lucy Loo?" Ryker asks as he holds the lighter to fill up her first lantern. When it inflates, Lucy's wish can be seen written across the thin paper. *To become a unicorn.*

"Just like *Tangled!*" she squeals, her go-to princess movie as of late, when it takes flight into the darkened night. We watch it until it goes so high, a bright light in the black sky, until the flame extinguishes, throwing her wish into the atmosphere.

"You sure you don't have a worry?" Ryker asks Lucy, and she shakes her head emphatically.

"Nope."

"Okay then. Your turn, Vaughn."

I take my time, carefully writing on the delicate material, and then he lights my lanterns one at a time. My worry—*If this is all a dream, I don't want to wake up*—floats into the sky. Soon after my wish follows—*More days like today.*

When the light extinguishes, I look over at Ryker, and his eyes are on me. I've never felt this content in my life. Never felt this secure. Never felt this loved.

And I owe it all to him.

I smile and mouth the words *I love you.*

"I love you too," he whispers.

"Your turn, Lockhart."

"Mine?"

"Yep," I say.

"I'm going with the Lucy camp of having no worry to put up there," he explains as he begins to position the lantern.

"I can't see your wish," I say as I step closer, the writing on the opposite side of the lantern as it begins to inflate.

"Relax. It's getting there. I'll turn it around in a second."

I pull Lucy against my side as we watch the flame light up the night and its glow fill the inside of the balloon.

"You ready?" he asks, and we both nod. "Here goes."

Ryker lets the paper lantern begin to lift from his hand and turns it just before it takes flight so the writing is visible.

And then my heart stops when I see the words: *Will you marry me, Vaughn and Lucy?*

I stand frozen as I read them, as I try to believe that he really means them, but when I can tear my eyes from the words and over to the wonderful man who wrote them, I can't speak.

Tears are glistening in his eyes. His smile is wide. His invitation is written all over his expression.

I step toward him and press my lips against his for an answer. It's brief and tender, but it says everything I could ever want to say to him in that simple touch.

"Yes," I murmur against his lips.

He leans back. "Yes?"

"Yes."

And the look on his face will forever be burned in my mind.

Love swells within me.

I never wanted this. A man. A love. The promise of a future and happiness.

But then there was Ryker. The man who proved to me that you don't always have to find love in the sunrise because it can often be found in the sunset. The man who said he didn't believe in love, loving the woman who said she never could love.

And the rest is history.

We found our sunset.

Ryker

One Year Later

People are milling about on the green lawn down below. Decorations and flowers and lights strung across the terrace illuminate the space.

It's perfect, if a man can ever really think shit like this can be perfect.

But when her arms slide around my waist and the heat of her body presses against my back, I know I was wrong.

This is perfection. Her. Now. The ring on her finger. My last name attached to her first name. The life we're starting together from here on out.

"What are you doing up here all alone?" she asks.

"Just taking it all in." Just taking a breather to realize how much she changed my fucking life from a miserable existence of meaningless flings to actually wanting to share my life with someone.

"You know your friends down there are taking bets, right?"

"Bets?" I shift so that I can wrap my arm over her shoulders and pull her against me. When I look down at her, my breath catches again.

Who knew a woman could look so damn amazing in white?

"Yep." She smiles. "They're all taking bets on how long we're going to last."

My laugh rings out so loud it pulls the attention of our guests below to glance up at us. "Well, I guess I better go put my bid in too, then."

"Is that so?" She lifts a brow in mock protest, but her smile says she knows I'm joking.

"Yep," I say, repeating her word. "Everything we have to the winner that this till-death-do-us-part thing will be how long we'll last."

"Aw," she says and then leans up and brushes a kiss to my lips.

And every part of me—right here, right now—knows I've never done anything more right in my life than her.

No question.

I look down at her something borrowed—the key on the chain that was first Samantha's and is now Lucy's—and I can't help but smile and know it's the perfect time to do this.

It's the right moment to let her know.

"I have something for you," I say and reach into the front pocket of my tuxedo jacket where I've had it all night, waiting to give it to her.

"We promised we weren't going to give each other wedding gifts," she says in exasperation.

I don't respond. Rather, I hand her the folded piece of paper and watch as she opens it.

Confusion etches the lines in her beautiful face, and her eyes flash up to meet mine. "I don't understand."

"I bought something for you, Vaughn."

"I see that, but—oh. *Oh!*" Her voice breaks when I think she finally gets it.

"It's an empty lot now. When I bought it, there was an extravagant house on it that many said was gorgeous. They told me I was crazy to raze it to a level lot. That I'd lose a ton of money by doing that. But I didn't care about the money. I cared about demolishing the last thing that could ever physically remind you of *him* or the memories it held."

"Ryker . . ." Tears well in her eyes, and they are the last thing I want to see there today.

I point to the deed of her uncle James's property in Greenwich. The one that states her name as its sole owner.

"Take the lot. Sell it and use the money to start the charity you've wanted to establish for the Lucys of the world. Keep the lot and build something that's all yours. I don't care what you do with it, Vaughn— *it's yours*. All I care about is that you know it's no longer standing. Any chain you had holding you back from enjoying this incredible life we're going to make together is gone."

She opens her mouth to speak and then closes it in that way that tells me she has so much to say but can't put words to it right now. Instead, she frames both of my cheeks in her hands and presses a kiss to my lips. Our foreheads rest against each other's.

"Thank you, Ryker."

"Anything for you, Mrs. Lockhart."

ACKNOWLEDGMENTS

Just a quick thank-you for the continued support to all my readers. It's been six years now in this unexpected career of mine as an author, and you've been there with me every step of the way. Thank you for having faith in me, for trusting that I'll take you on an adventure in each book, and for being so passionate about my stories and characters. Sometimes the slightest *thing* can change the direction of someone's life . . . and *you* were that *thing* for me. Thank you.

ABOUT THE AUTHOR

Photo © 2017 Lauren Perry

New York Times bestselling author K. Bromberg writes contemporary romance novels that are sweet, emotional, a lot sexy, and a little bit real. She likes to write strong heroines and damaged heroes that readers love to hate but can't help loving.

Since publishing her first book on a whim in 2013, Bromberg has sold over 1.5 million copies of her books across eighteen different countries and has repeatedly landed on the bestseller lists for the *New York Times*, *USA Today*, and *Wall Street Journal*. Her Driven trilogy (*Driven*, *Fueled*, and *Crashed*) is currently being adapted for film by the streaming platform Passionflix, with *Driven* available now.

You can find out more about this mom of three on any of her social media accounts. The easiest way to stay up to date is to sign up for her newsletter (http://bit.ly/254MWtI) or text *KBromberg* to 77948 to receive text alerts when a new book is released.